# SKUL

Section of **K**nowledge and **U**nderstanding - **L**ycan

SKUL is a work of fiction. All characters and events portrayed in this book are fictional, and any resemblance to real people or incidents is purely coincidental.

Cover art by Marc Lee

Dedicated to the memory of Bruce Henry McGinnis.
Every day you are missed a little more.

# TABLE of CONTENTS

| Chapter | | Page |
|---|---|---|
| | Preamble | 1 |
| 1 | Old Mexico | 7 |
| 2 | Eldrich Wolves | 21 |
| 3 | Introductions | 39 |
| 4 | Family Ties | 51 |
| 5 | Pre-deployment Workup | 69 |
| 6 | Warrior Ethos | 89 |
| 7 | Pirates and Scallywags | 93 |
| 8 | A Whole Lotta Suck | 103 |
| 9 | Lessons | 125 |
| 10 | Beat Downs and Bloody Noses | 145 |
| 11 | Operation Uncle Drunkie | 159 |
| 12 | Black Socks, Blue Boxers and Wife Beaters | 169 |
| 13 | Uncle Drunkie's Hotwash | 185 |
| 14 | End Zone | 193 |

| | | |
|---|---|---|
| 15 | Mac's | 201 |
| 16 | Operation Nightshade | 213 |
| 17 | Side Job (part 1) | 227 |
| 18 | The Gunslinger | 231 |
| 19 | Side Job (part 2) | 249 |
| 20 | Nightshade's Hot Wash | 263 |
| 21 | Continuance | 269 |
| 22 | Side Job (part 3) | 281 |
| 23 | Would You Like Fries With That Foot? | 285 |
| 24 | Drinks With…Friends? | 293 |
| 25 | Outbreak | 299 |
| 26 | Operation Zookeeper | 313 |
| 27 | Into the Madness | 321 |
| 28 | Aftermath | 339 |
| 29 | The Fork in the Road | 355 |
| 30 | Killing the Thing You Love | 367 |
| 31 | Side Job (part 4) | 377 |
| 32 | Side Job (part 5) | 389 |
| 33 | Side Job (part 6) | 397 |

| 34 | Highway to Hell | 413 |
| 35 | Tortured Soul | 423 |
| 36 | Insubordination | 441 |
| 37 | Out of the Frying Pan… | 453 |
| 38 | …and, Into the Fire | 467 |
| 39 | Out of Body Experience | 477 |
|  | After Action | 487 |

# Acknowledgements

There's an old saying – *it takes a village* – in reference to raising children. There's been a lot of debate regarding the validity of said statement; but, I'm here to tell you, without the village, this book would not have been possible. I'd first like to thank my awesome, beautiful wife. You're a great mom and wife – two things I don't tell you enough. Thank you for giving me the time it takes to do this right. I love you. While I'm at it, Lila and Dean, you two give me more joy than I thought possible. I love you.

When you start naming people to thank, you inevitably forget someone; but, in this case, I'm willing to chance it. SKUL would not exist without James "Maddawg" Madaris, Leighton Tate, and Kim Clyde. James, I'll never be able to adequately thank you for all the work you put into this project. From editing every word in this book and on SKUL's blog, to the blog itself, and a quadra-billion things in between – from the deepest depths of my heart, THANK YOU.

Leighton, you and Kim are the reasons SKUL's story makes even the slightest bit of sense. THANK YOU for your ideas and direction. While I didn't always agree with them, the fact you guys were invested enough to read the book and offer your opinions means the world to me. You guys rock!

If you like the cover art and the SKUL shield over at the blog, then thank the artist, Marc Lee. Marc's a great dude who's easy to work with and produces some of the most righteous graphics known to man. Go give his *Coffee and Perspective* Facebook page a like and tell him SKUL sent you.

I'd also like to thank the gang at my old internet hunting hangout, MSDUCKS.COM. I still remember the first real story I wrote anywhere – *Grey Duck*. You guys were the initial *stokers of the fire* and for that, thank you.

Lastly, I'd like to thank YOU – the reader – for taking a chance on an unknown author and a crazy subject. I hope the ride is worth it.

**SKUL'S BLOG -** http://skulops.blogspot.com/

\*\*\*Do yourself a favor. If you have not read the biographies of the main characters or the three short stories, PLEASE hit those links and read. There is a ton of backstory for each character, and this is the one place to get it. The short stories are also very cool and actually lead up to the events portrayed in SKUL, book 1\*\*\*

**SKUL'S Facebook page -**
https://www.facebook.com/SKULops

**SKUL's Twitter feed -** https://twitter.com/skulops

Therefore put on the full armor of God, so that when the day of evil comes, you may be able to stand your ground, and after you have done everything, to stand. **Ephesians 6:13 NIV**

"Life, although it may only be an accumulation of anguish, is dear to me, and I will defend it." — **Mary Shelley, Frankenstein**

# PREAMBLE

**Millennia prior to the first recordings of human history...**

    He stared across the bitter, windswept plain with eyes of golden orbs falling across an unholy battlefield littered with the bodies of immortal beings made mortal. Thousands upon thousands of bodies, so many were there that the river cutting the plain in half ran an unholy green, tainted by the blood of demon-kind. His eyes told him what his mind could not fathom.

    It was over. All was lost.

    His most ancient of enemies had decimated his army, not by strength of will or fierceness in battle, but by sheer numbers.

    *Numbers,* he chuckled angrily as he glanced over his once white fur. It was stained dark green from ichor, the blood of gods and demons alike. His warriors, those left alive in any case – the finest and fiercest beasts to ever stalk this godforsaken land – had fallen back upon him; each fighting to the last. Werewolf and vampire alike pulsed and throbbed as they fought against one another. The noose was tightening now, his kind – surely less than a dozen still on their feet – had been flanked and subsequently encircled. The vampire legion was but a hand's-breadth away now. Suddenly, from the undulating amalgamation of immortal bodies, his finished warrior and ultimate protector emerged, cleaving heads from shoulders even as he leaped to his King's side.

"The battle is lost, my lord," panted his warrior, Red Moon. His wounds, dozens all told, healed instantly as he drained the writhing vampire in his paws of its life. Standing taller now he growled, "You must flee, my lord. Your survival is all that matters now." Red Moon thrust his hands before him and took the heart from a vampire that had broken through the last of their ranks. Another lunged at the two from seemingly nowhere only to be caught in midflight by Fenrir himself. With a lackadaisical pull, the great Wolf King tore spine and skull from the demon's body and tossed the useless body aside were it landed in its own offal.

"It is not meant for our kind to flee, my old friend. We're meant for this," he held his hands out gesturing to the battle now in its final stages. "For chaos." Fenrir, king of the werewolves, raised an ichor stained paw. Still gripping the base of the spine, he swung the skull still like a gory mace. He released an unearthly roar of defiance, and for an instant, the world and everything in it froze in fear.

As one, the sea of inhumanity parted to allow five cloaked figures enough room to walk through. Silently, they entered the circle of death created by the last of the Eldrich wolves. They held no fear for the werewolf king, only contempt. Time stood still, and the air thrummed with power, ancient power. As one, the five most powerful vampires – the Vampire Lords, death incarnate – raised their hoods to reveal gaunt yet beautiful features.

"Hello, brother." The Vampire Lord standing at the center spoke. His voice was quiet, and every word, blanketed in a deep sadness, felt heavy.

"Attila," Fenrir nodded, "finally you've come to face me upon the field of battle. Fitting, after all these years, you should now."

"No, dear brother," the vampire shook his head morosely. "I am afraid that's not the case. I'm simply here to…"

Fenrir, cutting his words off, pointed an angry, claw-tipped finger at the vampire lord and growled, "You always have managed to avoid facing me."

"He is here on my behalf," announced another voice. The voice was deep and resonant, like oiled mahogany, yet it rang across the blood drenched plain with the strength of a clarion bell. "He will stand witness to this sad day's conclusion, as will we all."

The Vampire Lords stepped aside to reveal another, one who was neither werewolf nor vampire. For the first time in many an age, Fenrir and the Eldrich wolves knew fear.

Real fear.

So primal and visceral was the fear that it shook Fenrir and his Eldrich to their cores. Involuntarily, they bowed low. They were cowed by a fear so pure, so raw, and yet so ancient, it could only come from one source.

The gods.

\*\*\*

**Present day…**

The hood shrouded his face in darkness as he moved quickly, yet with great intent, down the street. The task at hand had made him paranoid; so, he was careful to stay deep within the shadows. The area, several blocks away from New

3

Orleans' famed Bourbon Street, was quiet save for the random drunken revelers mindlessly trying to find their way home. The street, and more specifically, the alley, had been chosen as the location for the drop because it was far enough away from the madness that was late night in New Orleans to keep curious eyes away. It was also close enough so that no one walking the streets, even at this ungodly time of night, would draw any undue attention. The shadowy figure paused, letting a drunken couple locked arm-in-arm stagger past, before he ducked down a dark, narrow, grungy alley. The alleyway was nothing more than a dank corridor. It was littered with rotting refuse that created a miasma of molded detritus, human excrement and piss; God only knew what else was down there. Traveling the length of the alley, he stopped, reached high, and pulled at a brick lining the outer wall building. Proving harder to work loose than originally anticipated, he reached up with the other hand and began working the brick loose in earnest.

He wanted to get this job over with and get the hell out of this alley as quickly as possible. Unfortunately, the damned brick was hindering his progress.

Finally, he shimmied the brick loose and was showered in crumbling mortar and dust. Wiping the grit from his eyes, he cleared his lungs by spitting viscous, yellow phlegm, before laying the brick on a nearby dumpster. Gingerly, he pulled a clear, shatter-proof tube from his inside pocket. Even in the darkness of the alley the fluid within shimmered iridescently, its color a deep and striking green. He tilted the tube on its axis, and the liquid inside moved with the speed of mercury, like it was a living entity.

The hooded figure shivered in the liquid's unnatural glow. Ever since taking the job, his mind had been filled with dread, and his dreams had become violent and gory amalgamations of unknown horrors. He didn't know what the liquid was, and he didn't know where it had come from, or where it was going. Intuition and street smarts told him he knew all he needed to know. He knew he'd been paid an exorbitant amount of money for such a seemingly simple task. He also knew that the tube filled with the strange liquid was extremely important to someone, someone who could probably make life very, very uncomfortable for whoever chose to cross them. He sucked in a breath, took one last look at the tube he hoped he'd never see again, and then slid it into place. Quickly, he replaced the brick and mortar as best as possible. It wouldn't pass a close inspection, but maybe a brief once-over. But really, who in the world would be down this alley looking at the brickwork?

He left the alley at a brisk walk and without a backwards glance. His only stop was at the domed trashcan on the curb where he quickly scribbled an $X$ on its lid in chalk. This clandestine practice was called a *dead drop*. He imagined several more exchanges were in the tube's future before it made its way home. The job complete, finally, he took off down the street toward Bourbon, savoring the weighty feel of money in his pockets.

*Bout time for a drink,* he thought, now moving down the street nearly running. The faster he moved, and the further away from the tube he got, the better, more confident he felt. Again, he felt the comforting weight of the cash in his pockets. *No, piss on that shit,* he thought, refusing to settle on a simple drink, *tonight's a night to score some booger sugar and maybe a whore. Hell, maybe two whores.*

For the first time in his life, Elton Appleton, small time fence and dealer for the Della Rocca crime family, had a pocket full of cash and nobody to pay off.

Twelve hours later, Appleton's body was recovered from a nearby canal. His throat had been ripped out, and his bloated body was barely recognizable.

# 1)
# Old Mexico

The couple walked down the cobbled path of the small Mexican village arm in arm. The pair was striking and seemingly without a care in the world. The young woman's dark hair was pulled back in a loose ponytail that sashayed from side to side with each step. Her flawless, tan skin was highlighted by a beautiful smile that she flashed easily to the peddlers clogging the market. She wore designer black sunglasses and a yellow summer dress with black thong flip-flops. The muscles of her arms were taut, and her legs were incredibly shapely.

*A runner's body*, he thought.

The man holding her loosely by her slim waist was somewhere around six feet tall with wavy blond hair and glacial blue eyes. He had the body of an NFL linebacker. On his right forearm he could make out a strange tattoo depicting a fire breathing dragon with wings spread threateningly and a forked tail curved in a figure eight. The dragon was perched on top of a Templar's cross. Although he couldn't make out what the tattoo on the opposite arm said, he knew by the name and series of numbers that it was a Bible verse. The verse was a few sentences long and spiraled downward around his forearm. Other than the body ink, he wore a T-shirt highlighting some American band's summer tour and camo cargo shorts.

*A killer's body*, he thought knowing the woman was just as capable. The couple's descriptions matched the information he'd been given perfectly. Plus, he had worked with the woman before and would recognize her beauty anywhere. Quickly, he called his waiter over and paid for his coffee before moving into position.

***

"How much for the earrings?" asked the muscular man as he pulled either his new wife or his lover closer. He rubbed her lower back affectionately.

"Ah, that's pure silver. Very nice, very expensive, senŏr," replied the peddler almost apologetically. A subject of personal pride, he spoke English amazingly well considering how far into Mexico he lived.

The man pulled his wife further down the line of vendors growling over his shoulder, "I want to spend money not be told I can't afford something. C'mon, hun." He spoke with a Southern drawl as thick as molasses, and the poor, Mexican peddler had little trouble guessing what part of the U.S. the gringo was from. Quickly realizing he was in the process of losing a sale, the peddler blurted out his price.

"That's almost two hundred American!" snarled the gringo causing the merchant to flinch, "You think I'm an idiot?"

The woman purred seductively into the big American's ear and shifted her gaze across the street. "Oh, just pay the man, Dane. I want something to eat."

He smiled at her, lowered his hand a bit more, and patted, "Sure thing." He turned back to the peddler, "One fifty. Take it or leave it." The peddler's eyebrows knitted together as he mentally crunched the numbers. A moment later he handed the woman the earrings with a sigh, "I'm such a fool for true beauty. Enjoy, señorita."

8

"Right," said Dane flatly as he handed the salesman the money who snatched it greedily from his grasp. While walking away, Dane heard him mutter something under his breath about American snobs.

Moving with purpose across the street the Dane said lightly, "Almost broke the bank, but it was worth it for my beautiful wife."

Under her breath Sam Steele hissed, "If your hand gets any lower I'll show you *broke.*"

Her *husband's* self-confidence had been cute at first, she could admit that, but now it was beginning to grate on her last nerve. She particularly hated when his hands inched their way toward her ass as they had – several times – on their walk. "Wonderful bargaining job, by the way. Woowhoo," she gave a mocking, golf clap, "a whole fifty bucks off his price. Could you show me how you managed that again? I mean, wow, very impressive stuff."

Dane cleared his throat, growing slightly embarrassed, "Whatever. We're supposed to be newlyweds, hopelessly lost on the dark streets of old Mexico, Sam. Just playin' the part. You could stand to loosen up."

Before she could retort, he grabbed her hand and kissed it with a wink before approaching their contact, a fat man in a white, sweat-stained suit. He wore a matching white fedora with a black band.

***

Sam's insertion into Dane's squad had taken everyone by surprise, Dane included. As a rule, his unit did not work with newcomers, nor did they trust them, but Sam's approval as lead intelligence officer for the op had come from further up the flag pole than Dane could see. Further up the pole than even Dane's superiors could see, in fact. On any other operation, Sam would have been given such high priority missions as keeping the fridge full of beer or finding out if it was possible to find a decent slice of pizza this far into Mexico…real important stuff.

But, as implied, Samantha Steele and this operation were different. Sam had closed the net on the agents' whereabouts in a matter of hours; whereas, Dane and his crew had been rolling snake eyes for days. Dane found it curious, the ease at which she had pinpointed their location, but in the world of covert ops, results mattered.

*It could be worse*, he thought as they strolled along the cobbled street to their target. *Chic's hot as shit.*

***

*I'm going to punch him in the throat; I swear to God I am*, she thought as they approached Benicio "Benny" Perez. Benny claimed to be plugged in, somehow, to a previously unknown Mexican cartel that was known as *El Lobo*. *El Lobo* had appeared on the radar of several three letter government organizations earlier in the year. They ran drugs and guns across the border with equal fervor, were considered extremely violent, and had taken three undercover DEA agents hostage only days before.

Benny allegedly knew where they were headed, and Sam knew Benny. Reports were vague to nonexistent, but supposedly, on several occasions he'd supplied her and her colleagues valuable HUMINT – human intelligence – regarding ongoing South American operations. Dane had two issues he could not get past. The first concerned the beautiful yet unknown intelligence officer attached to his unit. His guys had attempted to find out about her and were blocked at every turn. He could only assume she was CIA or more likely, DEA, but that did not ease his misgivings. Secondly, he did not trust this Benny character. Discounting his appearance and smell – which left much to be desired – there was something very off-putting about the man and the way he carried himself. Something Dane could not place, but whatever it was, it kept scratching deep within the gray matter of his brain.

As the couple approached, Dane took out a city map adding to his cover as a stupid American trying to find his way. This was Benny's signal to move in. Just as scripted, he walked over, introduced himself, and began *helping* the couple. All this meant was that Benny helped himself to the envelope full of money within the folds of the map. Deftly, he switched it with another envelope.

"Are they alive?" Sam whispered.

"Sí, señorita, for now."

"Where?" Dane interjected, tensing with expectation.

"South...Mayan temple."

"Not where are they going, where *are* they?" Dane suddenly found himself having a hard time keeping his voice calm, his temper in check, and his outward demeanor pleasant.

Benny shrugged nonchalantly, as if American lives mattered little to him – which, in truth, they didn't – and Dane moved closer.

Dangerously close.

Close enough that the fat man could read the scripture inked into his arm:

*Revelation 22: 12-13 And,*
*behold, I come quickly; and my*
*reward is with me, to give every man*
*according as his work shall be. I*
*am Alpha and Omega, the*
*beginning and the end, the first and*
*the last.*

Benny gulped, nervously. He knew the tattoo'd scripture was the last thing many eyes had ever seen. Unconsciously, he recited a silent prayer meant to ward off demons. He fervently hoped this meeting would soon adjourn. Strangely, the big American stepped away. The fat, sweaty man was telling the truth. Sam could see in Benny's eyes what Dane failed to, and a gentle squeeze of his waist - one that no one else could see, not even Benny – was her signal for him to *calm down and let her do the talking.*

"When will they move them, Benny?" Sam purposefully laced her voice with extra sweetness to calm the sweaty Mexican. "It's very important we know."

"Tomorrow. They will arrive in the city at sunset." He jabbed a stubby little finger frantically at the envelope hidden within the folds of the map. "It's all there."

"It better be," Dane growled even as he smiled. It was a dangerous, threatening smile that said, *If you're lying, fat man, I will kill you.*

Benny shrugged nervously, then moved down the street and away from the couple. The whole thing had been a seamless exchange that took only a few minutes to reach its conclusion. Sam and Dane waved their thanks, completing the charade for anyone who may be watching, and began walking in the opposite direction. After a couple of blocks, they doubled back to the small villa Sam and Dane's unit were using as a TOC - tactical operations center.

As they approached the villa Dane commented under his breath, "I got a bad feeling about this."

"Benny's solid. Fat and worthless, sure, but his intel has always been spot on." Sam's words expressed a confidence in the sweaty toad she really didn't possess.

"Didn't count the money." He muttered so quietly that Sam wasn't sure if he was actually speaking to her.

She looked up to him, "I'm sorry?"

"He didn't count the money, Sam. Didn't even look at it to make sure he wasn't getting jobbed. People like Benny just don't *do* that." Seeing her sudden look of doubt, he continued, "El Lobo would slit his throat if they found out he was passing us this intelligence, and he didn't even look to make sure he was getting paid." After another step or two he added, "I don't trust him."

"Well, he's all we got."

At the TOC's front door Dane shook his head, "I got a bad feeling about this one."

***

Marcus Tolar slithered into position during the night and waited for dawn. A short black man originally from Meridian, Mississippi, he struggled mightily through BUD/S.

During that time, his hardships were so apparent the SEAL instructors mockingly joked they were training a toad not a frog, and the name stuck. From that day forward he was known as Toad. His struggles were due in no small part to the fact that he stood only five feet, five inches tall and weighed a meager one hundred fifty-five pounds soaking wet. Though a permanent fixture of the *Smurf Crew* during BUD/S – the boat crew historically filled with the shortest men in the class – Toad never put out anything but max effort. So focused was he on passing BUD/S, the thought of quitting never crossed his mind, not even after being rolled back to the next class due to injury. At one point, during a particularly exhaustive session of physical correction after a less-than-stellar timed four mile run, Toad looked to his tormenter and said, "You're going to have to kill me to get me out of here."

The pain and exhaustion did not stop, but the instructors silently developed a newfound respect for the smaller man.

Toad found his true calling in the SEALs elite sniper school where he excelled like never before. Eventually, he was deployed to Iraq and Afghanistan – several times – where his reputation as a *get it done* operator grew to near mythic proportions. His exploits eventually caught the eye of fellow Mississippian and former BUD/S classmate, Dane Stackwell, and his newly stood up unit.

Dane and Toad's careers where two sides of the same coin. Toad was an enlisted man; Dane an officer. BUD/S, certainly no cakewalk for Stackwell, was not the house of horrors that is was for Toad, either. When Toad would fall behind on the timed runs or swims, Dane would be there kicking his ass, forcing him to keep going, keep pushing. Toad never forgot that, and when Dane approached him about screening for the new unit, Toad jumped at the offer.

The unit, called *Section 8*, was classified *top secret* and drew from all branches of the U.S. special operations community and sister units from trusted other countries. Section 8's niche in the world of counterterrorism was its ability to identify, pinpoint, and take down terrorists cells *before* they had a chance to strike. Like all CT units, Section 8 operated in every third world shithole known to man. Unlike any other military unit on the planet, Section 8 also operated on American soil under the auspices an off-the-books exception to the prohibition of *posse comitatus*. This exception, approved by Congress under a cloak of extraordinary secrecy, granted Section 8 the ability to do whatever the unit deemed necessary, whenever, and wherever it deemed it necessary.

Legal precedent be damned.

Toad took a sip of water from his camel back and focused on the ancient, Mayan city. Up to this point, there had been no movement within its broken and crumbling walls, let alone the road feeding it. Other than periodically reporting to the TOC, there was nothing for company but boredom.

Toad knew from the pre-mission briefing that the old Mayan city had been discovered in the late 1800s, but due to the crumbling architecture that made it dangerous, it had never been listed on any tourism directory. In fact, very few other than area natives even knew of its existence. Given the assassinations and violence along its borders, the Mexican government, in an attempt to draw attention away from the violence, had begun renovations. It was hoped the opening of the city would bolster tourism in the area. The restoration project was years away from actually coming to fruition, and as such, the only sign of enhancements was a single road carved out of the jungle. Satellite photos yielded a basic understanding of the city's layout, and the photos Toad supplied filled in the gaps.

His orders where clear; insert, find a hide, and report any movement along the road. If no movement was noted, he would wait until midnight then make for an extraction point several klicks from his position. If El Lobo showed with the hostages, the rest of the unit would immediately move on the target. The op called for two fire teams to insert via MH-60 Blackhawks at each point of egress within the city. Their primary objective was the safe recovery of the hostages. Secondarily, they were to see that the members of El Lobo died a very quick, very violent death. Once the mission was initiated, Toad's task would be to maintain an overwatch position and take out any El Lobo tangos squirting from the buildings. When the hostages were secured, and the bad actors on scene were neutralized, the fire teams along with the hostages would rendezvous with Marcus. From there, they would move to the extraction site.

It had been a long, uneventful day, and just when Toad's confidence in the intel was beginning to wane, he noted a plume of dust to the north. His eyes snapped to his rifle scope, and instantly, he noted an old, battered utility truck with a covered bed moving quickly down the road toward the city. Perched on a hillside south of the city, nestled among the rocks and trees, he quietly clicked on his comms, "Red Leader, this is Darkside, over."

Seconds later the voice of Dane Stackwell – who was not-so-secretly a *Star Wars* junkie, hence the call signs – sounded in his ear piece, "Reading you lima-charlie, Darkside. What's going on?"

"I have truck movement along road to the city. Hold for ID."

All was silent as the truck pulled into the city proper before staggering to a stop. Seconds later, several rough looking, highly tattooed, and heavily armed Mexicans hopped out. They immediately began screaming into the back of the truck. The canvas sash was thrown back, and the El Lobo vultures jerked three bound and hooded figures roughly from the back. Unceremoniously, they dumped them onto the dusty road. One, unable to brace his fall, smacked the earth hard, face first. Marcus' blood sizzled in his veins as he watched several cartel pissants drag the agents through a darkened doorway of the central temple. He mentally, and not the least bit forcibly, stowed his anger, though he promised to use it on those El Lobo bastards later. His voice betrayed a calmness he did not truly feel, "ID positive. Repeat, ID positive." He knew the silence that followed was nothing more than Dane confirming with command Toad's findings. The order to execute the mission was a given, as were the ironclad rules of engagement. This was, after all, Mexico. Any mishap would place the already contentious relationship between the U.S. and its southern sister on extraordinarily shaky ground.

"Darkside, we're rolling. ETA sixty mikes." After another second, Dane's voice sounded in his earpiece once more, "Toad switch to OCN."

*OCN* was a predetermined secondary radio channel known only to Toad and his commanding officer, Dane. It simply meant *other channel now*.

Rudimentary? Yes.

Effective? Absolutely.

Toad hurriedly clicked his radio over to the appropriate channel, "Boss?"

"Toad, if the situation changes, handle it, understood?" Nothing more was said. Nothing more was needed.

"Solid copy, Boss," he replied and clicked his comm back to the standard channel. Marcus Tolar got as comfortable as possible, and pulled his sniper rifle tighter his shoulder.

He knew exactly what Dane meant.

***

All had been silent after the agents had been shoved through the doorway. The sun had set and the moon, so full and bright offering plenty of light for the naked eye, had risen. Off in the distance, he heard the first, faint *thump-thump-thump* of the incoming Blackhawks' rotors.

Suddenly, the wild and primal howls of some crazed animal rent the night air.

It was coming from the jungle and surrounded the city on all sides. The howls were so loud, so full, and so incessant that Marcus could not pinpoint their exact location. He didn't need to, for just then, just as something deep within his mind triggered a response to flee, run, and never look back, *they* poured out of the jungle howling wildly.

*They*...as in plural.

Shadows.

Big, voracious shadows moving with unnatural speed toward the temple.

Toad jerked NVG's into position, unable to comprehend what his eyes saw. He hoped the NVG's would add some clarity. Hoped they would prove it all a bad dream. He only got a glimpse before they disappeared into the bowels of the temple. What they were, he wasn't sure. He knew what he thought they were, but that couldn't be right. They didn't exist. Whatever it was, he knew they were big and bad.

And hungry.

His mind was still trying to make sense of everything when screams spilled from the bowels of the temple. Horrific, blood curdling screams that were filled with pure, unadulterated terror.

Frantically, he switched his comms on, shattering radio silence. Dane and the other guys only heard, "Abort...abort the mission!" before Toad's comm went silent.

"Darkside, say again."

Nothing.

"Red Leader to Darkside, repeat!"

Nothing.

Dane screamed to the pilots over the roar of the Blackhawk's engine, "Get us the fuck there, now!"

## 2)
## Eldrich Wolves

**Lafayette Square, Washington, D.C.**
**Two days later**

The two old men sat side by side on the bench and fed pigeons. Around them, protestors' chants rang out across the square, yet they sat contentedly in comfortable silence. Their long years on earth had afforded them the ability to tune out the mundane ruminations of the servile. At their feet, the pigeons pecked and thrummed with each new handful of seed, and they would tilt their heads sideways when the seeds didn't come soon enough for their liking. Finally, with the last of the seeds tossed to the group of hungry pigeons, the eldest of the two said quietly, "Explain."

The word was filled with anger and laced with threat. With it came a need, a force, an otherworldly desire to look away from the speaker. The other bared his teeth in a snarl and snapped, "Stop this childishness, Stefan! I did not come all this way to suffer your boorish petulance."

The feeling that attacked Guiseppi Della Rocca's senses dissipated on the wind as suddenly as it had enthralled him. Satisfied the challenge was well met, he shared what he knew concerning the attack on their Mayan city operation. "The agents had been delivered and were in the process of being tested for viability when the city came under attack. Americans, most likely some special operations unit, sent to retrieve their compatriots. Our allies tore the regiment apart, though. Unfortunately, there were survivors. How many and, more specifically, who they were we have yet to discern."

21

Stefan furrowed his brow in thought, "See it done."

Guiseppi snorted, "I hardly see the point. No one will believe their story. They are probably already in strait jackets. I see no reason to divert our resources chasing improbabilities, Stefan."

Stefan's eyes blazed at the challenge, and his voice was low. Dangerously low. "I said, *see it done.*"

As if in answer, one of Guiseppi's bodyguards – not that he needed any such servant but appearances must be kept – approached respectfully and spoke quietly into his ear. Guiseppi nodded then turned back with a sigh, "I presumed you would wish to know the identities of those involved; so, I made some inquiries. I have the names, though it may take a while to exact our revenge." Stefan crooked an eyebrow which caused Guiseppi to hold up an acquiescent hand, "I know, I know. *See it done.*" After a moment's worth of thought he added, "I'll put Billy and his Bastards on it unless you have objections?"

"They will do. If successful, we may have further use for them." There was a moment or two of silence before Stefan asked, "And, what of our experiment?"

Guiseppi shifted uncomfortably beside the other. "Better than previous attempts, but I'd hardly call it a success." He wiped a hand across his forehead, obviously both frustrated and perplexed, "The problem is that even those that survive the turn are driven mad. Our El Lobo agents had their hands full surviving their own creations, a difficulty obviously compounded exponentially once the Americans arrived. It's something with the blood; it just isn't a viable product, no matter the subject."

"Survival rates?" asked Stefan coolly.

Guiseppi shrugged, "Less than twenty-five percent. As stated, this is better than previous attempts but still less than desirable."

Stefan patted his friend patronizingly on the knee, "Keep trying. In the meantime, see that the survivors end up in New Orleans."

Guiseppi nodded, "Already taken care of."

"Good," Stefan replied quietly. "Whatever product you manage to produce should be made available to the public as well. Twenty-five percent is better than no percent by my math."

"Understood." Another moment of silence fell between the two before Guiseppi inquired, "What of other, more predictable means of drug production and subject retention?"

Stefan smiled, "Everything is falling into place. Costly though it may have been, it will prove its worth in short order."

Guiseppi's eyes cut toward his colleague, "And, I don't suppose you wish to share this newfound information with me?"

"Not at the moment, no," replied Stefan mysteriously, "We must be sure of the product before we enact the full scale of our plan, and we must be ready to act when the time comes, Guiseppi. Soon my old friend, if all goes accordingly, we'll turn this land into a feeding trough for our army."

They stood and looked over the protesting hippies whose body odor filled their noses.

Guiseppi sighed, "Yes, but I'm not certain which will be worse, to dine *on* them or *with* them."

With that, they parted, and the world was none the wiser that two of the most ancient beings walking the planet had just met on a park bench and fed pigeons.

***

**Many hours and a long private plane ride later...**

It was late afternoon when Guiseppi stepped from Rue Bourbon into the *Old Absinthe House*, an ancient establishment build of brick, wood, and of course, bourbon and absinthe. No one looked in his direction as he made his way to the back and into a chair opposite a small man clad in leather. Sometime over the last half century the short, wiry individual had turned in his horse for a customized Harley Davidson and his old guns for .45 caliber Desert Eagles.

Two of them.

He had no need for the pistols, had not fired them in years, but he too must maintain appearances.

Even now, they were concealed by the leather jacket with the Satan's Bastards patch. The patch was black and white and depicted a skeletal werewolf howling at the moon. Three drops of blood dripped from overlong fangs. The blood meant something to those who managed to *patch in* to the Bastards, but Guiseppi knew not what.

Honestly, he didn't want to know, either.

Billy Blackshanks, as he was known to the world, president of the viscous, outlaw biker gang known as Satan's Bastards, grinned with amusement. Guiseppi had always thought the man was a bit too diminutive in stature to carry on as arrogantly as he did. Still though, for all his faults, Billy

24

had lived an exciting, if not an overly long, life. In other, older times he had been known to some as William H. Boney, to others as Billy the Kid. True to form and verse, this violent, half-crazed gunslinger with a reputation the size of Texas, had stepped confidently into a Satan's Bastards' stronghold and sunk his teeth into the neck of the operation. From there, he left an unimaginable body count that even the most despicable of Satan's Bastards members feared. Over time - a relatively short amount of time - those that opposed his rule died in horrific fashion. Those that didn't were granted life everlasting...if they survived the initial bite.

"How ya doin', old man?" Billy tittered. The strange-sounding chuckle brought visions of hyenas wreaking havoc on the plains of Africa to Guiseppi's ancient mind.

"Good, Bill." The older wolf replied evenly. Not caring for pleasantries, he cut to the chase, "You and your Bastards ready to work?"

"Pshh, of course we are. Was there ever a doubt?"

He was ever confident, ever arrogant; yet, despite those shortcomings, Guiseppi liked him. He couldn't help himself. In the past, he had used Billy's crew as the heavy muscle for many of his less-than-legal dealings over the last several decades, and the Bastards never let him down. Guiseppi bypassed the obviously rhetorical question and responded simply, "Outstanding." He slid a thick envelope across the table and sat back with his chin resting on steepled fingers and smiled.

Billy arched an eyebrow as he stuffed the envelope in an inside pocket, "What's this?"

"Names, addresses, family, close friends...that kind of thing, Bill. Right down to the blood type and girlfriends of those involved with our little, shall we say, *problem* down South."

Billy whistled low, "You're going to start a war. You know that, right?"

Guiseppie said nothing, only stared into the insanity locked within Billy's eyes until the silence became uncomfortable – Billy hated long silences, "It'll take time."

"Take as long as you'd like, just do it right. No loose ends...no survivors."

Billy thrummed his knuckles on the table in thought, "The others approve this?"

Guiseppie, recognizing the slight, fought to remain outwardly calm, "Of course."

He nodded, "Good enough for me."

It was Billy's turn to fall into silence.

Guiseppie, sensing his unease, prodded him, "Ask, Billy." Guiseppie leaned forward, setting his elbows on the table in a non-threatening manner, and with his hands outstretched, smiled greasily, "Let there be no secrets among friends."

Billy was wise enough to know there was no true friendship between them, just a working relationship that had been profitable for both parties. "I'm just curious about the other issue." Guiseppie remained silent as the old gun hand continued, "I understand, or think I do, what we're after with this drug, but they ain't us. They ain't our kind. I've watched the ones we've turned. They can't control their blood lust. Their minds are broken, and all they can think about is the next meal. They are more unpredictable and uncontrollable than the Lesser Wolves running in my crew. If they are unleashed upon this city they'll be no stopping them. *We* won't be able to stop them, Guiseppie."

Guiseppie was silent for a moment longer, suddenly uncomfortable with how much the underling knew of their plans, and then stood, "You speak of worries that are not your own, Billy. Just do as you're told."

The old man vanished before his voice died in the room. The *Eldrich,* like Guiseppi, had powers they called *gifts.* These powers enabled them to perform incredible feats when compared to others of their kind, and they guarded them as they would life itself. Whether Guiseppie had just moved with blinding speed or had simply disappeared was anyone's guess, but whichever it was, it was awesome to witness.

Terrifying, absolutely, but awesome none-the-less.

The fact Billy, himself capable of extraordinary acts, could be startled by anyone or anything spoke volumes of the Eldrich wolves power. He rose, his arrogance tempered somewhat by Guiseppie's departure, and walked silently from the Absinthe House.

***

Dane slid the boat onto the shore of Chotard Lake and secured it before he walked up the bank to his favorite watering hole, *Chotard Landing.* The locals knew only his face and nothing of the last few months of hell he'd been through; therefore, no one bothered him. Haunted by demons locked within his mind, the brief respite of Chotard Landing was one he welcomed daily. He had been duck hunting up Tennessee Chute all morning, alone as was the norm, and breakfast was calling. He sauntered through the door and ambled up to the bar. It was nearly empty with only a few other hunters along with a pair of game wardens sat eating quietly, barely cutting their eyes in his direction. He had not gotten comfortable in his stool before an old, wrinkled lady with blue hair and a cigarette choked voice sidled up to the bar. Ashes fell over the countertop from the fresh cigarette hanging from her lips. She held an order pad into the light filtering through the window, feigning to study it intently, before asking, "What can I do for you, hun?"

He grunted, shifting on the stool, "Usual, please."

Doris, proprietor of the establishment, took a healthy puff of her cigarette, allowed the smoke to creep out of her mouth sideways, and lowered the pad, "You know, one day you're gonna actually ask me to go make you something hot from the kitchen." She reached into a cooler under the bar, brought out an ice cold Budweiser, and slid it across the table.

"Maybe so," he smiled warmly, "but not today."

The exchange had become their daily routine, and despite her complaints, she rather enjoyed the company.

Dane Stackwell, former Navy SEAL and commander of another, far more obscure unit, had recently moved into an old shotgun house on the Prescue Farm, a large tract of land his old high school buddy Mike managed. There, shrouded in anonymity, he waited for his life to normalize. With thousands of acres to roam, Dane lost himself on the Prescue Farm in an attempt to find his way back to his family and out of the hellish nightmares and self-doubt that lurked in every shadow.

Knowing Dane's background, Mike had only asked that he helped out with the farm equipment when it broke down – which it did almost daily – and, in Mike's own words, "Shoot ever' fuckin' hawg you see." Dane was good at fixing broken machinery and even better at killing hogs; so, the situation, thus far, had been mutually agreeable.

Mike's generous offer was something he'd hold dear to his heart – what was left of it, anyway – for the rest of his life. The fact of the matter was the last several months had been the roughest stretch Dane had ever been forced to go through, and it had all started that night down in Mexico.

He never really left that ancient, crumbling Mayan city; not totally intact, in any case. How could he considering the carnage he witnessed? Every minute of every day he relived the mission…over and over and over again.

*** 

He lost two of his men before reaching the main chamber of the temple. They were shooters to the bone and brothers to the blood. Something huge, moving faster than his eyes could follow in the green glow of his NV, fell upon them from the shadows and tore them apart.

*Literally.*

Dane remembered a nauseating feeling of terror overtaking him as he took point and led the remaining member of his element, Chief Petty Officer Ansil Lattimore, through the warren of dark corridors. At six feet, four inches tall and two hundred thirty pounds of solid, unadulterated muscle, Lattimore was a veritable mountain of a man. Sarcastically, he had been called Tweeker, due in part to his nasally upper Midwest accent and partly to...well, nights during BUD/S are cold, and everything shrinks in the cold.

Despite the horrors they faced, the two moved further into the temple. In silence they rounded a corner, hunched over their guns, and entered the central chamber of the temple. The scene that met them was straight out of a Wes Craven horror flick; and, for the rest of the two men's lives, the terror and utter carnage of that night would haunt them. Even now, thousands of miles and several months removed from that night, Dane could not stand the sound of a howling dog. As a result of that night, he rarely slept. The nightmares of whatever demon they had awakened haunted him even in his dreams. Eviscerated bodies and half chewed appendages littered the stone floor which had become slick with blood. On one side were several rows of stainless steel tables and tubes holding a fluid that shimmered a wild green in the glow of their NV goggles.

"What the hell, Boss?" gasped Tweek.

"Survivors?" Dane hissed over the sound of his own heartbeat pounding in his ears.

"Shit, *sir*, are you looking at the same room I am? Hell no there isn't any survivors. I can't even tell if these…" He searched for the right word to describe the macabre scene, "…*pieces* are our guys or not."

Dane ripped a canvas bag from his kit and hissed, "ID any of our guys you can, I'll cover you."

He thrust the bag to Lattimore who looked to the bag then back to Dane, genuinely confused, "Sir?"

"Faces, familiar looking body parts, tats. Goddammit Tweeker, anything that looks like it belongs to our guys, bag it."

Tweeker nodded grimly and set about the gruesome chore while Dane trained his weapon into the depths of darkness the room held. Several skylights, high above and central to the temple, allowed the light of the full moon into the room. The light threw long, fingerlike shadows across the floor that looked like a demon's hand.

Nothing moved; nothing made a sound until Tweeker reported the job done.

"Bout fuckin' time," Dane whispered. "Don't fuck around, Tweeker. Get us out of here, but maintain noise discipline."

"Roger that," Tweeker muttered and hefted the now heavy sack over a shoulder.

Dane had to step over several mutilated heads that were missing their faces to make his way down the corridor. Fear threatened to cripple them as the two moved quickly, yet silently, through the unnatural silence that perverted the night. Finally, Dane stopped at a hard turn in the corridor, opened his comms, and requested a sitrep from the other assault elements.

His request was met by only silence.

"Fuck," Dane mumbled in uncharacteristic fashion before slamming his fist into the closest wall.

The pair of assaulters were debating their next move when finally, as if in answer to a silent prayer, Dane's comm unit squawked.

"Red Leader, this is Darkside, over!"

Dane's relief was short-lived as Marcus reported the inevitable, "Assaulters are down, Boss. Besides you and Tweeker, there's no one left. I've maintained my position, T-dubs and Yugo are here with me. Advise you move to exfil, Boss. We'll provide overwatch and rally with you at the extraction point once you guys are clear."

"Marcus..."

"Jesus H, Boss, do you hear me? They're gone!"

"Marcus, shut the fuck up and listen! Tweeker's here with me. We're going to search the temple and round up the rest of the guys, give us a few..."

"Fuckin' Christ, Boss! THEY! ARE! GONE! All of 'em! Get out of there, now!" Tolar was all but screaming into his comm unit by this time.

This wasn't like Toad; he didn't come apart like this. Something had definitely spooked him, something other than the normal, run-of-the-mill butchering at the hands of terrorists. Whatever had befallen his comrades in the temple, and whatever Toad had seen from overwatch, had been enough to nearly unhinge the war-hardened warrior. A soldier intimately acquainted with the less-than-stellar circumstances life had to offer.

Dane acquiesced and quickly looking to Tweeker, said, "Dude, we gotta move to extract like yesterday. This ain't right, none of it."

Ansil leveled his weapon and took point, "No shit, Boss."

Dane talked while he moved. "Toad, listen to me. We're moving to extract now. Forget covering our exfil. You move now, understand?"

32

"Boss, you guys need someone covering you."
Toad's voice was instantly calmer, instantly cold and hard,
grasping the weight of leaving his teammates behind. "Not
leaving you."

"Goddammit, do as you're ordered!"

A pregnant moment of silence ensued before Toad's
begrudging reply, "Copy that."

Dane and Tweeker moved quickly but quietly through
the winding corridors of the temple's inner sanctum and
eventually spilled from the temple and into the moonlight.
Behind them, the howling started again and served to only
spur them on faster.

Neither man looked back.

They were too terrified to see what was chasing them,
too petrified to make the nightmare more real than it already
was. Their sole focus was on staying upright and making
their extraction point alive. As if in a dream, Dane could feel
something rushing up from behind. Still, he refused to look
back and focused only on putting one foot in front of the
other as quickly as humanly possible. The howls, louder now,
were angry and made his mind quiver with panic. All he
could think about was getting away from whatever was
behind him. He could tell Tweeker was wrestling with similar
fears. Dane's eyes told him the big man's mind was being
raped and pillaged by whatever unholy terror was rapidly
overtaking them from behind. The howling was on top of
them now. As they crashed through the jungle and into the
opening where the waiting choppers waited, Dane could feel
its power, whatever *it* was, breathing down his neck.

He looked up in time to see Marcus shoulder his rifle, eyes to the scope. The helo pilots – SOAR (160th Special Operations Aviation Regiment) trained and Section 8 approved, ergo the best in the business – began slowly lifting off the deck. There was no turning back. They would either make the leap into the helicopter, or the *things* – whatever they were – would take them out. Either way, the pilots had given them all the time they could.

Dane could see – and hear – the emphatic arm waving and screaming, "Come on! Hurry your asses up!"

Suddenly, Tolar fired over his shoulder.

Dane and Ansil looked over their shoulder in time to see a beast that couldn't possibly be of this world shrug off the bullet wound to its chest. It affected the animal no more than a gentle breeze, and the spawn from hell barely took a misstep.

*Goddamn,* Dane thought, *that thing is big!*

Big and bad.

Big and bad and mad.

The simple phrase *Fuck me!* entered Dane's mind as he lunged for the Blackhawk.

T-dubs and Yugo pulled the two ad lib marathoners into the helicopter at the last second while Toad covered their ascent. Below, the shadows swirled with unnatural speed, and, over the whine of the rotor blades, Dane could hear the angry howls of...

***

The old waitress had the news on.

A personal mantra, Dane never willingly watched the news, not anymore. He had long ago lost the ability to understand a world that glorified the wretched and decrepit - and that description just covered Congress - yet a name shook his thoughts from deep within old Mexico.

Doris grabbed the remote from behind the counter, "So tired of the news. It's always bad. Let's see who won the game last night."

"No! Wait!" demanded Dane. He held her wrist in a viselike grip.

"Okay, hun," she said, wrenching her hand from his grasp. "No need to get excited." She placed the remote on the table and backed away. Doris was more than a little unnerved by the instantaneous change in his demeanor.

*Theodore Walker Williams*, announced the pretty blond on the screen. Dane always thought that was a long-winded name, even for a black man from Jersey. A quiet man above reproach, he was known simply as T-dubs, both in his MARSOC unit and Section 8.

*How many other men could possibly have the same name?* Dane wondered silently, having no real clue, but it couldn't be many.

The picture being flashed upon the screen shocked Dane to his core. It was a photo of his old friend T-dubs, who wore a face of stoic concentration while toting his SCAR on patrol through the streets of Sadr, Iraq. Dane began to visibly shake and his mouth went slack. Shortly thereafter, his mental faculties fled for greener pastures. The beer bottle he held shattered on the floor which caused the other patrons to turn a wary eye his way.

Dane knew the pic well.

He had taken it.

He sat in stunned silence, taking agonal breaths like a fish out of water, while the pretty news anchor continued:

*...known as T-dubs to his friends. We understand he and his family where the first to be murdered. Petty Officer Breck James, a.k.a Yugo, was found later today after failing to show up for morning PT. His body, along with his girlfriend's - we will not release her name as the authorities have been unable to reach her family - had been mutilated in much the same fashion as Staff Sergeant Williams'.*

Dane's body started to shake even more violently as the reporter announced the names of more of his former Section 8 teammates, men he'd recruited. They were more than just teammates, though. They were his friends – his brothers.

All were dead.

Every one of them.

Moms, dads, brothers, sisters, aunts, uncles, children, girlfriends...no one was spared. Behind him a door slammed, yet barely registered it. His mind was locked in a battle for its sanity.

And, it was losing.

His friends, the guys under his charge while in Section 8 were gone. They had been assassinated. The only thing left to him now was *his* family, and thank God Abbey had finally agreed to visit.

*Oh Christ,* an awful thought hit him like a semi-truck transporting a load of bricks, *Abbey and Henry are here!*

She and their son had only just arrived this morning and were more than likely getting settled in to the cabin he had rented for the weekend. They needed this weekend, if for nothing more than to try to get their marriage back on track, but now this? They could be in danger, real danger, and it was all his fault. His choices in life had led them down this road, a road his wife never failed to remind him about.

"Doris, I gotta go," Dane said hastily, "I'll pay the bill later!"

A low, gravelly voice called from the direction of the screened front door, "Have a seat, Commander Stackwell. We need to talk."

# 3)
## Introductions

In one motion, Dane spun off the stool and landed. He stood in a fighter's stance, bouncing on the balls of his feet, knees bent. The man who spoke was older, about average height with closely cropped white hair and a matching, well-groomed goatee. He wore a patch over his right eye under which a scar emerged and traveled the length of his face, accentuating craggy, weatherworn features coupled with a stern, grim countenance.

Dane looked to the men flanking him, and his heart dropped into the pit of his stomach.

He would have gulped, but his mouth had turned to cotton.

His day had officially gone from bad to worse.

Each man wore some sort of black, formfitting suit in which the knees, shoulders, flanks, chest, and thigh areas had obviously been strengthened. Even so, the articulated construction looked to allow for a free range of motion. Their boots were state-of-the-art tactical jobs made of similar material – whatever it was – with thickened soles. They wore full-faced helmets with dark green lenses that were set at diagonal slashes. The angle of the lenses gave the helmets an evil look. Dane was struck with the odd notion that the headgear strangely resembled a mishmash of a Storm trooper's helmet and the alien's face in the *Predator* movies. A bulge above the temporal region of the helmet – on either side – caught his eye. Several thoughts concerning what they may be came to mind – flashlight, infrared, or video. It could be any one of them, and for that matter, it might be all of them.

Dane had no doubt what he was looking at.

He'd never seen it before – which was troubling considering his career – but, it was definitely some new kind of body armor.

All in all, they looked a lot like the soldiers in many of the futuristic first-person shooter video games.

Did it look bad?

*Sure.*

Did Dane's heartbeat sound in his ears?

*Absolutely.*

Did he think he was making it out of the bar alive?

*No. Fucking. Way.*

Clipped to the suit were oddly shaped and constructed grenades, along with various other items. Each compartment was similar albeit slightly different, making the suit and *kit* appear highly customizable.

The shooter on the right held a suppressed HK 416 assault rifle with an EOTech holographic sight mounted to its top rail. A .45 USP from the same manufacturer was secured in a right drop-leg holster, and a tomahawk that appeared to be made out of...*solid silver?*...lashed to his left.

Dane's eyes took a second look.

*Yeah,* he thought, *that's definitely silver.*

He took a breath.

*Shit.*

The other carried a suppressed SOPMOD M4A1 with the same sights on the top rail plus a M203A1 grenade launcher running the bottom rail. His pistol, another .45 but this one a Sig Sauer, was holstered on his chest rigging just left of center over the heart. Along each thigh was a sheathed hatchet, again made of silver. Even without being able to see their eyes, the ease of motion and the quickness to carry out orders, told Dane all he needed to know.

They were killers.

Each man stood motionless but with a hand around the grip and a finger resting gently on the trigger guard. Dane took a deep breath to calm his nerves causing the old man between the soldiers to flash a knowing smile.

*Dear God,* was the immediate thought that slammed into his gray matter.

*I'm screwed,* the next.

"Boys, clear the room," the leader commanded in a quiet, gravelly, yet powerful voice.

Each man responded by moving toward the other patrons, one to the table with the hunters – who had stopped eating to gawk at the scene – and the other to the table with the game wardens. The two LEOs were standing, barely. One was desperately trying to draw his sidearm while the other was even more desperately fanning his crotch. In his haste to stand, he spilled hot coffee into his lap.

His partner, pulling security detail on Operation Hot Crotch, trained his weapon on the futuristic-looking soldiers.

Doris, blue hair standing on end like an angry cat, laid a sawed-off, double barreled shotgun – the ends of which looked big enough to be subway tunnels – over the bar.

"Ain' nobody clearin' this bar 'cept me...and it ain' closin' time." She aimed the hand-canon at the older man, finger on the trigger lightly, and she never took her eyes from his. The message was crystal clear.

*Hurt my people and your leader's head gets turned into a canoe.*

The men, soldiers, aliens from another universe – whatever they were – faltered. Each looked to the old man. Their body language screamed uncertainty, and Dane couldn't help but admire the old barkeep's ferocity. This definitely wasn't part of any script they had read. The white haired leader took a noticeably deep breath and gave a low shake of the head before turning to Doris. Dane hadn't moved and, still poised for a fight, was beginning to feel rather ridiculous as no one seemed to be paying much attention to him at all.

"My dear lady," the old man's accent was southern but not from the part of the world Dane knew as *the* South. The rest of society could not discern the nuances, but Dane could. To his ear the leader was obviously from Texas. Dallas area if he had to guess. "I truly regret the intrusion upon your fine establishment, but this is a matter of national security..."

Doris cut him off, which the man was clearly not used to, and poked the short gun with the ridiculously large barrel into his chest.

"You a soldier?" she asked in her trademark, gnarled, cigarette-choked voice.

The old man smiled. It was warm, genuine, and full of hope...

Hope that the lady would put the damned gun down.

"Sailor, actually, but I trust you won't hold that against me."

Doris's gun wavered, "Well, why didn't you say so? My old man – God rest his soul – spent a few tours over in that shithole in Southeast Asia. He was a Marine. I know I'm not supposed to say *was*, but he's gone now, so to me, he was."

She twisted her waist and trained her gun – more a hand canon, really – on Dane. He flinched and became very aware of just how completely ridiculous he looked.

"He one of them terrorists?"

The old man laughed raucously enough to fill the bar with a sound akin to a prisoner hammering big rocks into smaller ones. Comfortable the threat of violence had passed, he lit a humongous cigar and, between puffs, answered the old bat, "No ma'am. Our boy Dane here is a warrior to the bone, a patriot, who has seen more than most. Before becoming a staple upon your bar stool, he was involved in more than one firefight in the name of God and country. That is, until he was unceremoniously discharged for doing nothing more than his job..." the old man rolled his shoulders and leaned gingerly into the next part, "...and, telling the truth about that job to the wrong people. Isn't that right, Dane?"

Dane didn't know what to do. He felt like a deer in headlights, felt like a bad comedy act on stage, and the spotlight shone directly on him. With nowhere to hide, he attempted to do the only thing he knew to do.

Check on his family.

"Doris, if you'll lower your gun and you..." he pointed to the old man, "...whoever you are, will call off your men, I'll go check on..."

"Dane, we need to talk, and time is truly of..."

"Piss on you..." Dane said over his shoulder.

"Trust me when I tell you your life, and those you love depend on the next few minutes."

Dane froze at the door, turned, and fought against every fiber in his body screaming to rip the man's throat out.

Instead, he growled low and dangerously, "I'm listening."

As if there was no threat hanging in the air, the man smiled again, "Dane, I'm Rear Admiral Bartavious Briggs, and these are my men." He held out his hand which Dane shook. Dane's firm handshake was met by the same from Briggs. It wasn't an arrogant handshake meant overmatch the other. Rather, it was full of life and warmth...and, *strength*. Briggs then turned back to Doris laying ten one hundred dollar bills upon the bar, "Ma'am, this should cover the gentlemen's' meals as well as an empty bar for the next hour or so. Correct?"

The old lady looked at the money, nodded, and called out to the patrons, "Gotta cut this'un short, boys. S'on me to'mar." As the last one walked out, more relieved than anything, she flipped the sign from *Open* to *Closed* and locked the door. "Ya'll take the back office, and I'll start on a proper breakfast." She tapped the shotgun with her trigger finger meaningfully, "To go."

Briggs nodded, understanding exactly what she meant.

Mollified, Doris showed them to the back office. Before leaving, she gave Dane a look that said *good luck and holler if you need me* before saying to the group, "Despite the looks of this heap, we have internet access if you need it."

"Boys," the Admiral looked to the armored-up soldiers, "the door."

Without a word, the soldiers slid outside and flanked the doorway. Briggs then punched some numbers on a small yet rugged looking cell phone. Seconds later he said, "Send in Stratham."

***

What had to be the high priest of computer *nerd-dom* appeared at Briggs' side before the period had been put on the Admiral's command. A slight man with dark brown hair, Stratham had the pasty complexion of someone who'd rather be looking at a computer screen than actually tasting a bit of sunlight here and there. He wore tennis shoes, khaki pants, and a long sleeve button up shirt. He held a ruggedized laptop in each hand. Elbert, Dane came to know as his first name, placed the two computers on the table, sat in one of the surrounding folding chairs, and started booting them up silently.

While he was doing that, Briggs said, "Dane, I know everything about your life, your career, and your missions." He lowered his voice and emphasized each word of the following so Dane knew exactly how much clearance he had. "I know about Section 8, about its mission statement, and how you were the driving force behind the unit's creation. I have read through your file, poured through it, but there's one particular mission that is still a bit of a mystery."

Dane's mind lurched and reeled, yet again, with the anguish of those memories.

"I need to know what happened in Mexico," Briggs leaned back in his chair nonchalantly. "And, I need to hear it from you."

Dane's jaws clenched as he ground his teeth together. It was a habit, a bad one, he had developed as a child when he was under intense pressure. He poured the anger and frustration into his teeth, and only when his jaws began to ache did he speak. Invariably, he told the Admiral everything just as he had done during the mission's after action report and subsequent interrogations. At that time, the looks on the senior officers' faces and in their eyes had all been the same.

*Incredulous.*

From the moment he opened his mouth and from the second he saw the looks plastered on the faces of those higher up the flagpole than he, Dane had known, without a shadow of a doubt, one thing.

*He was fucked.*

But, here with Briggs, instead of the incredulous looks the CIA spooks, DoD psychiatrists, and those higher up the pole had given him, the Admiral looked on with rapt interest. Briggs listened – truly listened – and periodically nodded his head in a sympathetic yet knowing fashion.

*Oh my God*, Dane thought, *He knows. He knows.*

The feeling of relief and liberation coursing through his veins was fleeting, and eventually, it disappeared altogether. In its place was only dread; dread strengthened with the knowledge that what he had seen that night could not be explained away as a simple, nightmarish hallucination. Quite the opposite Dane now realized. The numbing brutality and unnatural deaths of his men was as real as rain,

46

there could be no doubt, now. Without preamble, the cold, black fear of understanding settled in the pit of his stomach like it was finally home.

"Werewolves," Dane whispered while rubbing his temples, "Jesus Christ."

"Indeed," Briggs nodded in agreement. "Elbert, pull it up."

"How much, sir?" The computer geek's voice was low but strong, confident even, and his fingers flew over the keyboard of both laptops simultaneously.

"The beginning, son," the Admiral laced his fingers together, resting his chin between his thumbs and forefingers, before looking fiercely into Dane's eyes. "He deserves to see it all."

***

Elbert's fingers tap-danced across the keyboards, and within seconds, he turned the screens so Dane could see. One screen showed the ancient tome of Norse mythology known as the *Prose Edda*, while the other depicted a Paleolithic cave drawing of a monstrous man with long, braided, snow white hair. He wore doeskin, calf-high boots, and a cape that matched his hair so closely it was hard to tell were one ended and the other began. At his feet knelt a myriad of other men, shoulder to shoulder, with creatures caught somewhere between man and beast. All were in an obvious fervent state of servitude.

"Fenrir," Briggs said gravely. "He is the first, the Wolf King to whom all others bow."

Dane commented by way of a question, but considering he already knew the answer, he framed it as more of a statement of fact, "I'm assuming the cave was found somewhere in Scandinavia, and the drawing was some caveman's way of paying homage to one of his gods?"

"Actually, this cave was discovered in the Ozarks of northern Arkansas within eyesight of Fayetteville. Carbon dating estimates its age at approximately fifty thousand years old, give or take a few thousand years," replied the Admiral matter-of-factly. Not allowing Dane's look of bewilderment to impede the progress of their conversation, the Admiral pushed on with raw facts, "We don't know much about Fenrir, other than a few obscure texts on the subject, but what we do know that the rest of the world doesn't was paid for in blood." Briggs paused for effect and then continued, "At some point just prior to known history, Fenrir amassed an army of werewolves bent on destroying what he presumed as a growing problem for his kind."

"Humans," Dane said in a matter of fact tone to which Briggs nodded.

"Correct, and he was almost successful in his efforts."

"Almost?" queried Dane.

"Almost," Briggs said contemplatively. "The fact we are having this conversation is proof enough of his failure. We have reason to believe he was stopped cold. We're relatively certain his army was nearly destroyed - *nearly*, yet by whom is up for debate."

"Debate, sir?" interrupted Dane as if in question.

In response, Briggs gave only a noncommittal shrug of the shoulders forcing Stackwell to change tact, "I have always been under the impression that Fenrir was bound in

48

mythical chains created by dwarves working in concert with the gods?"

Briggs cut his eyes to Elbert and smiled, "An educated man I see." Elbert shrugged, though remained quiet, as the Admiral continued, "While we believe this was the case, and one of the driving forces behind the cessation of the war, one must remember that Fenrir's sire was none other than Lokki, Oden's bastard son. Lokki, as much a deceiver as anything else, was both friend and foe to his pantheon of gods in equal measure."

"So you're saying Lokki…" Dane rubbed his temples again, "…I can't believe I'm having this conversation, but Lokki helped Fenrir escape?"

"I'm saying it's possible. This is all really just conjecture and hypothesis, unfortunately." Briggs sighed, "At any rate, that brings us to present day concerns. The time between is a mystery I'm not sure we'll ever fully understand…"

The bar suddenly shook with the reverberations of motorcycles speeding down the levee. Seconds later, one of Briggs' commandos tore open the door, "Savages riding the levee, sir." His voice was flat and metallic, almost otherworldly.

"How many?" came Briggs' taut voice.

"Half a dozen, sir."

"Oh my God!" Dane leaped up from the table, realizing his worst fears were coming to bear, and screamed, "Abbey and Henry! I had almost forgotten about them!"

"Don't worry, son. I've had a unit dispatched to your house to secure their safety."

"You don't understand. It's what I was trying to tell you earlier. They're here! They drove over early this morning!"

Briggs looked as if he'd been punched in the gut – Dane worse than that. Immediately, the Admiral began speaking into his comm unit, "Renegade-actual, this is Blackbeard-one. The package is here. Repeat, the package is here. Redirect your chopper for pickup on my position ASAP."

He looked to Dane with fire in his eyes, "Where?"

"Sir?"

"Your wife and son, Dane. Where are they?"

"Cabin 13."

"Meadows, status?"

"Apache has the perimeter. Titan has fallen onto your position and are ready to move, Skipper."

Briggs reached within the folds of his Navy issued peacoat and brought out twin HK MP7 submachine guns. "I'm hoping you still know which end to point with?" Dane nodded, and Briggs handed him one with an order, "Only use this for protection. You're not ready to face a savage yet. Let my boys do their work."

Even though Dane nodded agreement he was thinking, *Screw you, sir. I'm fixing to take the last few months out on some werewolf ass.*

# 4)
## Family Ties

Before leaving the bar, Briggs ordered Doris to stay hidden; imploring upon her that under no circumstances was she to come outside. Not until his men gave the *all clear* at least. He also slid a piece of silver shaped like a shield across the counter. "Thanks for your hospitality, ma'am," Briggs said with a wink of his good eye causing Doris to blush.

The old, blue haired woman turned the silver shield over in her hand before shoving deep into a pocket, "Twirnt nothing." To Dane she added, "You take care of yourself, you hear."

"Yes ma'am."

Once outside, Dane immediately knew the world had gone to hell. Two bodies lay crumpled alongside solid black, chopper-style motorcycles, each with tall, ape-hanger handlebars. They wore matching black leather vest with a skeletal beast that had a human body and wolf's head standing in a cemetery. The skeletal man-wolf howled at an eerie, low-hanging full moon, and in the background stood a lonely gravestone with *R.I.P* engraved in big letters on its face. There was no name below the letters. It was an undefined place of death and welcomed all. The only color on the patch came from three red drops of blood that dripped from the miasmic skeleton's fangs. Above the emblem, following its circular contour was big, block lettering that read *Satan's Bastards,* and below it – following the lower curve – *Motorcycle Club.*

"Status and ID?" asked Briggs in an authoritative tone.

"Heat signatures are roughly two hundred fifty degrees and dissipating quickly, sir. Two thirty...two twenty five. Savage is dead, sir." The soldier rolled the closest biker over with his boot, his weapon system – a SCAR H-CQC rifle – was still trained on its head, "This one's known as Joker." He rolled the other over, "Here's Acidboy. Both are low level ass-hats in the Bastards' New Orleans chapter." Dane looked at the holes in their chests and faces and became aghast upon realizing they didn't bleed red. Rather, they oozed viscous fluid that shimmered green in the morning light. It looked just like the fluid he remembered seeing in the test tubes and beakers down in Mexico. The memory – while not being buried, he thought he had at least managed to kick a little dirt over it – caused a cold chill to grip his spine and a black void in his heart.

All those teammates – friends – were all dead now.

Suddenly, three more commandos appeared as if out of thin air, and reported to Briggs in the same, flat metallic voice of the other operators, "There were six savages, sir. These two we took down initially. The others broke ranks and escaped through there." He pointed to an area choked with house trailers and cabins that sat on stilts high above the ground. They were built off the ground to keep them above the floodwaters of the Mississippi River. "I don't think they were expecting us, sir."

A shot rang out from somewhere south of their position in the direction the soldier had pointed.

"Pretty sure they know we're here now," Briggs observed. His hard look commanded without uttering a word.

Immediately, the soldier spoke into his comm unit, "Mike, need a sitrep."

Dane could not hear the reply, but after a moment, the soldier reported to Briggs, "Savage down, sir, fifty meters south of our position. The other two split, and we have no visual at this time."

"Thank you, Tim." Briggs turned and handed Dane a small, hands free comm unit that would allow him to communicate with the team, "Son, you better guide us to your cabin."

"Straight ahead between those two cabins," he pointed in the direction of the last shot as he adjusted his headset.

After a quick headcount, the unit began a slow, deliberate patrol through the warren of rental cabins. About halfway through their stalk, another shot rang out. Over comms, Dane heard the apparent team leader – Tim – demand a sitrep.

"Status?"

"Another savage down; he's spilled out the window directly ahead of you. Heat sig is already dissipating...he's dead."

Now able to hear the actual accent and inflection in the operator's voices, Dane was struck with each one's steely yet calm professionalism. He had worked with men just like this. Quickly, they moved to the savage's position. As expected, it was another Satan's Bastards member. More of that strange green fluid dripped from the window seal.

The point man reported a name calmly, "Yaeger," and kept moving.

The air was tainted with a nauseating scent that assaulted his nostrils and delivered blunt force trauma to his olfactory system. It was an amalgamation of the metallic odor of blood and the fetid stench of feces. Whoever was inside had been torn apart, and yet again, the memories of what happened in the bowels of that old Mayan temple came flooding back in horrifying detail.

Finally, after what seemed like hours, they made it to the cabin numbered *13*. A security perimeter was quickly formed. This left Dane, the Admiral, and Tim – the team leader – to climb the stairs to the cabin's front door.

"Look, you guys may want to stand back. We're not exactly on the best of terms, and seeing you in these suits may set her off."

Neither moved.

Dane shrugged and mumbled, "Don't say I didn't warn you," before quietly knocking. After a few seconds, they heard the lock being turned and the chain taken off the latch. A pretty blond stepped into the light of the doorway, her eyes flaring wide at the faceless commando armed to the teeth and the one eyed, authoritative looking man. Her initial shock evaporated instantly, replaced by molten anger. Incensed, she jabbed a finger into Dane's chest, "I told you, Dane Stackwell! I told you this day would come. All these years fighting *the enemy* has finally come back to haunt this family. You're worse than worthless; you're dangerous. You wanna get yourself killed?  Fine, whatever, see if I care!"  She stomped her foot, "You promised me you were done.  You *promised* Dane!  I don't know why I ever believed you; I must be as stupid as my parents have said I am...repeatedly!  It's not like you've ever worried about what all this is doing to your family; so, why start now?  You want to walk away from me?  Fine!  But for chrissakes, Dane, think about your son!  Dammit Dane, he barely even knows you!"

They had always made a concerted effort to never lose their tempers when Henry was around, and, for the most part, they had stuck to the rule.  Now, though, in the face of the futuristic soldiers and the one-eyed man, the frustration Abbey Stackwell held deep inside had finally torn its way loose from the better thinking part of her soul.

Dane looked sheepishly around her shoulder to their son standing deeper within the elevated cabin, "You okay, Big Hank?"

The fourteen-year-old boy, Henry Michael Stackwell, so-called *Big Hank* from birth, smiled uncertainly.  His eyes were wide, but Dane didn't see fright there.  No, as his son's eyes darted from the soldier to the eye-patched old man, Dane recognized the look of someone who was prepared to fight anyone at any time in order to protect his family.

Specifically, his mom.

"What's wrong, Dad?"

Dane pushed past Abbey, otherwise known as his highly agitated and overly remonstrative better half, and knelt before his son.  Taking his son by the shoulders, he said, "People have died, son, and we've got to get you and your mom to safety. These people are here to make sure that happens; so, I need you do exactly as I say, understand?"

The boy's blue eyes became shimmering pools of determination as he nodded his blond head, "Yes sir." The strength in his voice was unmistakeable. At this, Dane's hands slid past his shoulders, and he drew his son into a great bear hug.

Abbey rolled her eyes, "Oh sure, be a dad, *now*. Where have you been his entire life?" Dane tried to speak, tried to defend himself, tried to tell her he was out fighting battles so Henry wouldn't have to; but, she was having none of it. She cut his words off at the quick, "Let me answer that for you. *On a mission!*"

The tiny droplets of spittle that had collected and formed in the corners of her mouth finally tore loose, coating Dane's face in what could only be described as spite. Her chest heaved like she'd just run a marathon.

"Mom, stop!" begged her son.

She froze; so powerful was her anger – and maybe her hatred – for Dane she only just now remembered Henry's presence.

"Abbey, please, not now. We have to get out of here," Dane pleaded even as he wiped his face clean.

She had every intention of responding with yet more venom; but, thankfully, Briggs intervened, "Mrs. Stackwell, we have two savages prowling the grounds hunting you, your husband, and your son; not to mention, I have men on the ground willing to sacrifice their lives for your safety. That fact alone takes precedent over your inability to reconcile the situation you signed up for when you married a SEAL. We're

56

moving out, *now*. If you so much as look crossways at your husband, I'll have you bound, gagged and carried out of here. Am I understood?"

Abbey Stackwell was aghast.

No one had ever talked to her like that, certainly not her husband, no matter how often she tried to trigger that kind of response. Anger bled into her eyes and face, but she remained silent, too stunned to speak. Dane turned away, unable to hide the smirk brightening his face. When he swiveled back around, he noticed the look on Briggs' face which said *wipe that freakin' smile off your face, now!*

Dane did. Sort of.

"We need to move, sir."

Seconds later, Dane heard communication between what he could only guess was the primary team surrounding him and his family and another team, "Titan-lead to Apache-two-nine."

"Reading you lima-charlie, Titan-lead."

"All packages secured. We are moving to primary extract, approaching south-southeast of your position. Hold your fire, over."

"Copy that, Titan-lead," came the voice of Apache's team leader, "Titan moving to primary extract via the south-southeast. Will hold fire in that direction. Be advised; two savages are unaccounted for."

"Roger. Moving now, Titan out."

They began moving silently through the warren of elevated cabins, and Dane was suddenly struck with a strange feeling that took a moment to recognize. When he finally pinpointed what was bothering him, a cold fear ran down his spine.  He had been here for several days and knew every cabin was full of duck hunters.  The diversity of the hunters' background was extreme, ranging from oil rig roughnecks in from a two week stint to doctors and lawyers.  Despite different backgrounds, one thing remained the same.  Once the hunt was over, they wasted no time in cracking open the first beer; yet now, no one was milling about.  No one was checking out who shot what or hanging out drinking post-hunt brews.

In fact, the only noise other than their footsteps was coming from the area dogs.

Every dog for miles around was howling its head off.

Dane was just about to mention this to Briggs when the side of the nearest cabin exploded.  A gigantic *something or other* leaped through the wood and sheet rock of the wall like it was a piece of wet paper.  The beast speared the point man and raked its massive paw across the man's chest.  In reaction to the trauma, the suit erupted in a shower of sparks, and the beast recoiled as if burned.  The werewolf then leaped and landed some thirty feet away while simultaneously dodging the barrage of bullets the unit unloaded.  Two dozen rounds, minimum, and not one touched the savage.  The beast was so fast and graceful it seemed inconceivable to Dane that the soldiers stood any real chance of killing it.  The obvious and primal power possessed by the werewolf sent fresh shockwaves of terror coursing through his body.  Dane knew, beyond a shadow of a doubt, he was staring at a breathing nightmare, the ultimate predator, an unparalleled killing machine completely at home at the top of the food chain.

The thing standing before them was quite literally a horror story come to life.

The beast howled and shook its burned paw. Filled with rage, it sprung to the opposite cabin then leaped to the opposite cabin's wall. With each pounce, whole sections of the cabins' walls were ripped away by its claws.

Dane could barely follow the movement and found getting a bead on it with his MP7 impossible. He doubted the underpowered weapon would do anything more than piss the werewolf off anyway. In a blink, the savage landed before them and snarled. Drool dripped from tremendously overlong, canine teeth. *Huge* was too small a word to describe the size of the savage. Covered in course, brown fur, not a square inch of its body held anything but throbbing, pulsating muscle. The werewolf had nasty looking, blood stained paws tipped with razor sharp claws. As terrifying as the beast's appearance was, it was the werewolf's eyes which caught the whole of Dane's attention and wonderment. They were yellow, feral eyes that held irrepressible hate, unfathomable malice, and a whole lot of crazy.

Its eyes quiet literally burned with hunger.

*So, this is what death looks like,* he thought just before another wall exploded.

This time, everyone dove for cover. Reacting too slowly, two soldiers went down from a clothesline delivered by the newest savage. More sparks poured from the various points of impact, which elicited more howls of fury. Suppressed gunfire smacked through the air.

Instinctively, Dane fell over his wife and child and covered them with the only tangible thing he had to protect them.

His body.

As the melee between the werewolves and soldiers continued, Dane drug Abbey and Henry under a four by four parked nearby. He looked to his wife with pleading eyes, "Abbey, stay here, and take care of Henry." Dane only called Henry by his first name when things were serious, and that should have been enough. But, it wasn't. She began another tirade, but Dane cut her off, "Dammit Abbey, keep your mouth shut and your ass right here. Make sure Henry does the same, understand?"

She nodded through the palpable fear that finally managed to temper her anger. She had lost a lot of faith in Dane over the years, but in this she would trust him explicitly. Satisfied she would do exactly as he said, Dane ran back into the fray.

Suppressed, automatic gunfire raged, filling the air with dull snaps. He dove, just in time, as two bodies – one a savage, the other a commando – flew overhead. The beast straddled the soldier and worked him over with lightning quick blows from massive paws. Its monstrous, teeth-filled jaws snapped and tore at the apparent body armor. More sparks erupted from the suit that now looked to be fraying. The commando, his weapon lost in the fight, fought furiously for his life with only his hands until a paw got past his defenses and knocked him cold. The blow shattered the lenses of his helmet, and ripped half of it from his face.

Dane scrambled to a knee and fired reflexively just as the werewolf turned its head skyward in a triumphant howl.

The bullet entered the temporal region of the werewolf's head causing an entrance hole the size of a dime. The exit hole, however, you could have driven a truck through. Bone, brain and that same greenish blood splattered on the wall of one of the cabins. The wolf fell to its knees; and, for a brief second, its wolfish face was painted with shock, whole and complete. It swayed, and then completed its fall, landing face first on the gravel. Dust billowed from its snout as it took it last breath. Suddenly, it began contorting wildly, and its body folded back over itself – several times – as bones snapped, shattered, and reformed.

Dane stepped away in disgust and nearly retched.

No longer a wolf, the man beyond the demon had a long brown beard that was matted with the blood and viscera of its latest victims.

Dane rolled the savage off the prone soldier, held out a hand, and helped the commando to his feet.

"Thanks," said the soldier shakily. Because his helmet had been destroyed, his voice sounded human. Tough as hell, but human. The unknown soldier held his hand out, "Tim Meadows."

"Dane Stackwell," he replied in kind after giving a single, firm pump of his hand.

They were quickly joined by the rest of the unit. The men reported there had been no serious injuries, and the other savage was dead.

While this was going on, Dane quickly ran over to the vehicle where he had hidden his family, only able to breath after seeing both where he had left them.

"Strengthen the perimeter until we're ready to move out." Briggs seemed to speak to no one yet every member of their unit moved to carry out the order. To Dane's trained eyes, it looked like two teams of operators working in tandem to establish a perimeter around a large clearing of flat ground butting up to the river's levee.

Dane, Henry in his arms and Abbey at his side, walked up as the last of the men dispersed to their tasks.

"Mrs. Stackwell," Briggs motioned to a park bench with an open hand, "May I have a word?"

Abbey was shaken and confused but managed to walk the short distance in silence.

Dane, who had an idea of what was coming next, knelt beside his son, and gave him another bear hug. Tears began falling before the first words came out of his mouth; his voice choked with emotions that were deep and sorrowful, "Henry, you and your mom have to go away for a while."

The boy bristled, straightened his back, and stood tall even as his own tears began to collect in the corners of his eyes, "Why dad? You promised we'd never be apart again. Can't you come?"

Dane shook his head. His eyes were blurry and swollen with tears. He wiped them away before explaining, "No son, I'm not. I'd only put you and your mom in danger. She's right, I caused this. I didn't mean to, but it's still my fault. I can't explain all of this right now. Honestly, I'm not even sure what's going on, but when I can, I will." He held his son at arms' length, holding his gaze in his own, "Do you understand how much I don't want this?"

Henry wiped away the tears that were now falling, "Yeah, I understand, Dad. I do. I don't have to like it, though." Within the boy's eyes burned a determination that made Dane so very proud. In that singular moment, he knew he and Abbey had done at least a few things right over the years.

Dane pulled the boy close and held him again. Softly into his ear he said, "You have to be the man of the house now, and protect your mom. She'll need you now more than ever. She's mad at me and confused about all this. She'll need you, understand?"

His son only managed a silent nod.

"No one has the right to ask this of you, let alone me. I know it's not fair, none of this is, but you have to be a man, now."

"Yes, sir."

Both of them – long having lost the battle with their emotions – sobbed together for a long while. It was Dane who willed himself through the hardest part of their conversation, "I may not be able to call you for a while, but it's the only way I can be sure you're safe. Bad people, bad *things,* are after me and can get to me through you and your mom. I have to know I can count on you, son."

The boy wiped his nose on his sleeve leaving a trail of snot and nodded. In the sky above, a *thump thump thump* filled the air, drawing closer with each second. Shortly, a nondescript helicopter with absolutely no identifying markings landed in a clearing.

"Who's that dad?"

"I think that's your ride, bud." He looked to Briggs who nodded solemnly. Dane gave his son one last hug, taking in the moment and burning it into his mind, before finally saying, "You should go, Henry, but don't ever forget how much I love you, son." He felt as if he was about to break down, to rip apart at the cellular level.

"Love you too, Dad."

Henry pulled against his dad, and though it was quite possibly the hardest thing he'd ever had to do, Dane let him go. Alone, he watched as Abbey and the Admiral finished whatever it was they had been discussing. She put her arms around Henry; and, as if the weight was too much to bear, his head bowed, and his shoulders shook. Abbey looked back to Dane who nodded briskly through tear-filled eyes.

She shook her head, turned, and led Henry to the waiting chopper.

Briggs approached as the cadence of the chopper's rotors increased to a whiney pitch, and the helo rose up and over the distant tree line.

"I don't want to know where they are, okay?" Dane's voice was husky with hurt. "It'd only cause them trouble, and I don't want that. Someday I will, but not right now."

"They'll have the best protection on the planet; you have my word on that." To Dane's ears, the Admiral's voice seemed thicker than normal.

He nodded but said nothing. His eyes were still trained on the part of the horizon the helicopter had disappeared over.

With nothing to add that could possibly make it any better, Briggs began barking orders. With the exception of a heavy heart, Dane felt numb and empty. He could hear the steady *thump thump thump* of more helicopters – his trained ears told him two – and before long, both landed in the spot left empty by Abbey and Henry's chopper.

After a moment, Dane asked the admiral, "What am I supposed to do now? Go into hiding?"

Briggs turned, his smile returning, only now it was as devious as it was sincere, "How does a new mission sound to you, Lieutenant Stackwell?" Briggs's smile broadened, "It's not like you have a lot going for you at present, and we could certainly use someone with the experience your career has afforded."

Dane chuckled softly then his face became stone still, "Just who are you?"

"Officially, we don't exist. Unofficially, we were born out of a small think tank of scientists within a little known and even less cared about Department of Defense contract known as *Advanced Research Group 223*. That think tank, so-called the Section of Knowledge and Understanding – Lycan or, as those initial scientists, intelligence officers, and shooters simply called it – *SKUL*, has been buried under a mountainous minutia of Congressional bullshit for a long, *long* time. Buried so deeply, in fact, that not even the most conscientious of D.C. bean counters would waste the time it takes to wipe his or her ass looking into where the money's coming from or going to. Even then it wouldn't matter, because we're an entirely self-sustaining organization with only the thinnest of ties connecting us back to any government entity. There's more to it than that, obviously, but the rest you'll just have to see for yourself." He motioned to the nearest helicopter, "You need only board the bird there to see just how far down the rabbit hole goes."

Dane looked silently between the helicopters and Briggs. He felt like a man standing at a fork in the road who was unsure which direction he should go. Or maybe, the feeling was more like a starving man who just had a perfectly prepared steak laid before him.

"Red pill or blue?" he mumbled.

"I'm sorry, son?" The Admiral heard the comment, but had no clue what he might have meant.

"Nothing, sir. Just a line from a movie."

Without another word, Dane headed for the nearest chopper. The other men were doing the same, splitting into groups before boarding. The door to Dane's chopper slammed closed as it began lifting off the ground, and the men began taking off their helmets and strapping in.

A hand appeared before him, "Name's Kris Metcalf, but everyone calls me *Twitch*." The two shook as the new face continued, "Dude, we've been looking all over for you."

"Dane Stackwell," he replied, "sorry for the trouble."

Kris – Twitch – had a firm handshake which Dane appreciated, though his eyes darted here and there. The man was obviously the excitable type, and was unable to focus on any one thing. Twitch plopped down in the seat beside Dane with an audible grunt and strapped himself in. Two hours later, Dane knew exactly why Metcalf had been given the name Twitch. The guy absolutely could not sit still nor did he ever shut up.

A living, breathing *Energizer Bunny*.

As the helicopter banked hard to port, the pilot announced they were two minutes out from the Silver Moon – whatever that was. The last few months had been the strangest of his life; though, none more so than the last twenty-four hours. The uncertainty of it all, quite frankly, weighed heavily on his mind. But, other than the safety of his family, there was one overriding question that troubled him more than everything else combined.

*Just what the hell had he gotten himself into?*

# 5)
## Pre-deployment Workup

### Flight Deck of the Silver Moon
### 1530

Dane stood alone, digesting the events over the last several days, as two helicopters banked hard to port out over the blue waters of the Gulf of Mexico. He felt overwhelmed and more than a little insignificant with all he'd learned about SKUL, those that operated within its ranks, and the enemy they fought against. But, SKUL was not the only thing weighing heavily on his mind. There was, of course, Abbey and Henry's safety he had to worry about. With that came the knowledge that the only way he guarantee their safety was to stay as far away from them as possible. Oh, and there was the little factoid that his wife pretty much hated him. He denied the obvious for years, but he could do so no longer. The truth was found in her eyes. They forced his brain to recognize what his heart refused to accept. And, that was just his domestic life – or, whatever was left of it.

There was more…*obviously.*

Dane forced further negativity from his thoughts and focused on the frenetic activity occurring on the flight deck. The support crews were prepping the landing pads to receive the incoming birds in a manner that could only be described as *controlled chaos.* Moments later, the birds touched down lightly on the deck, the first a few seconds ahead of the second. Dane stood in the shadows of an overhang watching the operators disembark the helos. Immediately, his eyes focused on the gigantic form of his old friend and Section 8 teammate, Ansil Lattimore.  Lattimore was known as *Tweeker* within the small, SpecOps community.  Chief Petty Officer Ansil Lattimore had been the first operator Dane had recruited when Section 8 was being formed...a decision he never regretted.

*Never.*

"About freakin' time, man!" Dane screamed as he stepped from the shadows.  He felt both excited that he finally had a familiar face around and relieved his old friend, teammate, and former instructor was still alive.

It had been dicey there for a minute.

Tweeker turned toward the familiar voice.

Dane noted his hair was longer, and he now sported a full beard.  The big man smiled wickedly, dropped his gear on the deck, sprinted Dane's way, and...

"No, Tweeker!" Dane yelled while backpedalling, "No!"

...he form-tackled his old boss.

Most of the air was forced from Dane's lungs on impact.  What little was left was squeezed out – forcibly – by the viselike grip Tweeker applied.  Dane attempted to box his ears and failed.  Just as blackness began to creep in from the corners of his vision, he managed to muster enough air to grunt, "Dude, you're killin' me."

He tried to suck in more air, but that only allowed Tweeker to cut more of it off.

Now, Dane was begging, "Let...go!  Please!"

"Better do what the boss says, Tweeks.  Sounds like he's still gonna have us by the balls, *again*, soon enough," said yet another recognizable albeit overly dramatic voice.

Tweeker momentarily loosened his grip, stunned upon hearing a voice he thought to be dead. The grip slackened for only a split second which was more than enough time for Dane to shift his weight, break Tweeker's hold, reverse the grip, and toss the hulk.

"Toad!" the two yelled in unison, though Tweeker was now on his back.

Dane jumped to his feet and gave his old friend a bear hug. Not to be outdone, Tweeker engulfed both in his massive arms. The big Nordic – what Dane described him to others as – nearly squeezed the air out of both of them this time.

"Tweeker," Dane grunted, struggling for air, "let go, man."

Toad, his nose forcefully buried in Dane's shoulder, was barely able to breathe himself. Choking on clothing, he mumbled somewhat incoherently, "Dude, you're breaking my damned ribs," only it came out as "Wud, wur brucking my wamned wubs."

The pressure subsided, and the three separated quickly. They looked around, hoping no one saw the way they had just been acting.

"Get a room, Nancies!" someone screamed loud enough to catch the attention of seemingly everyone aboard the ship.

They winced. *Too late.* The newcomer, a lean yet muscular fellow with dark, wavy hair and pools of green for eyes ran across the flight deck. He was agile as a cat but there was an inner *unquiet* about him that overrode all the rest.

"Thanks, ass," growled Tweeker. He punched the newcomer – or, town crier – in the gut, with absolutely no warning, hard enough to send him to a knee.

"Twitch…Tweeker, Tweeker…Twitch." Dane dropped to one knee, "Don't worry, man, if he doesn't break a bone or two, he doesn't like you."

Twitch looked up, held out a hand, and grunted, "Pleasure."

Dane and Tweeker pulled him back to his feet whereupon Twitch looked his assaulter over, starting at his feet and moving up to his face, "Damn, bro, where'd you park your beanstalk?"

"Ask your mom," sneered Tweeker.

Twitch's face clouded over, and he became very still, "My mom's dead."

That caught Tweeker off guard. Thankfully, Dane broke in, "Moving right along, this is Marcus Tolar, my ebony brotha-froma-nutha-mutha. Call him *Toad*. He ain't ever gonna win a race, but he won't ever lose one either."

Toad nodded toward Twitch, "What Dane calls slow, I call patience. Makes me a better sniper."

Dane chuckled, "Guys, this is Kris Metcalf, goes by Twitch." Dane dramatized a huge eye roll, "MARSOC."

Groans, obnoxiously loud, belched from each man.

"Toad," Tweeker quipped with a bright smile, eager to put his mouthy faux pas behind them, "you ever notice how the damned Marines like pretending to be SEALs?"

"Yeah, dude, but they always wind up being our bitch, instead." Both guys laughed again, louder still when they saw Twitch's cheeks redden.

"I know, I know, MARSOC...stepchildren." Dane said through raised hands. "Look you two, Twitch's wired pretty tight, but he's a pretty cool cat otherwise."

Twitch looked ready to kick a puppy. "Pretty cool? Seriously?" questioned Twitch who seemed genuinely put off by the comment. "I'm the coolest cat you know, Dane."

"Yeah, yeah. Whatever. You guys just keep the explosives out of his reach," Dane quipped as he slapped Twitch's shoulder. "I've heard that's a bad combo. Sucks knowing he's the explosives dude, but when it's all you've got..."

"IT'S ALL YOU'VE GOT," the others added in raucous unison.

"Uncool. So very uncool," said Twitch shrugging off Dane's hand. "You guys need to get cleaned up and changed. Briefing's at 1700 in the Ops Center. You'll meet the other member of the team then." Twitch tossed both a cell phone, "Be on time. Dane knows the way. See you then."

***

**1645**

Dane led Tweeker and Toad past the bustling swimming pool with its bar full of boisterous patrons and rock climbing wall teaming with lean, muscular men scaling its face. From there, he led them through a set of sliding glass doors. On the other side of the doors were countless cubicles housing men and woman working at computer terminals. They walked through the buzzing viper pit of activity with purpose, down one hall, up a flight of stairs, down another hall, and through a large oak door. They were greeted by *Millie*, the Admiral's personal assistant, who showed them into a large amphitheater. They entered from the top and took the stairs that spilled down onto a stage and podium. There were three groups of men, maybe thirty or forty in each, scattered over the seating area chatting and carrying on. The seating area, capable of holding several hundred people, was flanked on either side by kiosks holding more computer terminals with technicians that intently monitored their screens.

The fact that the shipboard mission center and SKUL network at large had maintained such an unprecedented level of secrecy seemed unfathomable to Dane; yet, after several decades of operating within the borders of the United States, not even a whisper reached his ears, let alone the general public and the media machine they mindlessly followed. They slid down an aisle to Twitch's seat just as he was logging into a computer terminal built into his seat.

"S'up guys." Twitch looked up from the screen beaming with a broad smile, "This section of seats is our team's home in the Ops Center. You can log in the computers using the first letter of your first name and complete last name as the log in, four nines for the initial password. You can change it after that."

Looking over his shoulder, Dane recognized the page he had pulled up.

"Dude, *Wookiepedia?*"

"Hell yeah, bro. There's some good shit on here." He typed a name in the website's search engine and tapped the screen. Dane looked at the character it pulled up, Darth Bane, a personal favorite Sith lord, but not one just an ordinary fan would recognize. "You pick a character from

74

the books or movies, and you can be damned sure there's a bio on here." He looked up to Dane unsure if anything he was saying was making sense, "You a *Star Wars* fan?"

Dane plopped down in a seat, unsure if he should actually answer the question but certain he was warming to the younger operator. Instead, he changed tact, "You mentioned another team member?"

Twitch shrugged, obviously a bit disappointed with the change in subject matter, and only pointed toward the stage. He returned his attention to the webpage in and said off-handedly, "Yeah, Jed Blackmoor. He's up there talking with Commander Taggert."

Dane eyes darted to the stage.

*Taggert,* he thought, *oh crap.*

The Conroy Taggert he knew was a by-the-book Navy SEAL platoon leader. He had an exemplary record and had managed to rise up the chain of command easily yet with relatively little real combat experience when compared to that of his contemporaries. Taggert was, by Dane's estimation at least, an arrogant ass that pompously looked down upon the enlisted men. He continually bludgeoned with a hammer constructed of micromanagement and lorded over them with a Napoleonic flair. The man had a reputation for leading from the rear and, in private, was known as *Bobby Fischer.* This was due to the fact his men felt they were nothing more than pawns on his great chess board of personal gain. It was Conroy Taggert who Dane was chosen over to stand up the ultra-secret unit known as Section 8. This was a fact many in the community made known at every opportunity. The decision and subsequent fallout were career-killers; and, in only a few short months, Taggert had fallen off the radar.

Now, much to Dane's chagrin, here he stood, staring daggers through Dane...*his* subordinate.

*Oh hell,* he couldn't help but think. *This is going to be awkward.*

Jed Blackmoor, however, was just the opposite, or so Dane had heard.

Jed had been taken off the grid long before Section 8 became operational, but the name Blackmoor carried a lot of weight within the special operations community.

A lot of weight.

Jed had been an operator of nearly unmatched skill for over a decade, yet one day he was just gone. No one in the Unit was talking, either.

A moment later, their conversation obviously over, Blackmoor made his way over to where Dane and the others were sitting. Before taking his own seat, he held out his hand to Dane, "Jed Blackmoor, your assistant team leader, or *ATL* as we're referred to here at SKUL."

Dane shook his hand, "*My* assistant team leader? I'm still not sure what I'm doing here to be honest."

Blackmoor smiled in an easy manner, "We're going to kill savages, Commander Stackwell; as many of them as possible, as often as we can." He looked down to Twitch's screen and shook his head, "Dude, turn that crap off and try to focus."

Twitch looked up, his eyes deeply contemplative, and in his best *Yoda* voice said, "Try? There is no try..."

Dane finished the famous movie line, cutting him off with his own impression, "Do or do not."

"Hell yeah, dude. I knew there was something about you!" The two fist-bumped excitedly as Jed, Tweeker and Toad groaned in unison.

"Another nerd," said Jed through a face palm.

"Dude," Tweeker added, "you have no idea." Tweeker held out his hand to Jed, "Ansil Lattimore. Everyone just calls me Tweeker, though."

Toad followed, "Marcus Tolar. They call me Toad." Seeing the strange look on Jed's face, he followed with, "Long story." The two shook, "You'll get used to the Star Wars quotes, maybe."

"Don't bet on it."

Dane started to say more about the virtues of the *Force* which would have completely ruined any reputation that may have followed him to SKUL. Thankfully Commander Conroy Taggert took the podium. Hearing his voice for the first time in what seemed like a lifetime was enough to give him pause, "Gentlemen, take your seats."

The rumble of butts in seats slowly died across the large room just before Taggert addressed the audience.

"I'm not much for long-winded speeches, but as the assistant commanding officer or *ACO* of SKUL, it's my job to brief you on your upcoming training evolution and subsequent deployment. A lot's changed since your – Whiskey platoon's – last active deployment rotation. Take this as fair warning – you've got a lot work to do before you'll be considered operationally ready; and, there's going to be a lot of sleepless nights between now and then."

Though he addressed the entire audience, his eyes never left Dane's. Refusing to grant Taggert any satisfaction, Dane held his gaze for a long while. His eyes began to cloud over from dryness; and, not willing to lose the childish, schoolyard battle of wills, Dane's face broke into a broad grin.

Taggert diverted his eyes to the other side of the room. Dane's smile turned internal, and his face was again unreadable as he thought, *Same ol' Taggert.*

"Some of you are new to the program while others were operating in harm's way when I was still in high school. For you veterans, you've heard it all before. So, I ask only that you keep the new guy crap to a minimum and focus on mentoring these guys. It's important they hit the ground running."

He paused for effect before continuing, "The expectations I have can be summed up with four simple words: honor, integrity, honesty, and courage. Upholding and living by those four words, while maintaining a consistent level of professionalism, is this organization's imperative. These are non-negotiable expectations that I know I'll never have to worry about but need to say anyway."

He looked the room over, "As in all things, it goes deeper than that. It's about commitment, gentlemen. Commitment to stay the course, to stand before the most powerful and evil force on the planet, and do so fearlessly. As a SKUL operator, you carry the burden of knowing that we are the only thing standing between the werewolves and humanity. In saying that, be mindful that SKUL has actively carried the fight to the savages for nearly five decades without a single hint of its existence, and I expect that to carry on long after I've left this organization."

Taggert looked evenly over the audience, betraying no sense of anything other than the stated and absolute path each of the warriors must walk. After several seconds, he began anew, "Now, let's get down to brass tacks, shall we? On a rotating schedule, one or more teams from Foxtrot platoon have been on the island for three weeks preparing for your pre-deployment training cycle. These men will be your cadre of instructors while on the island. Per the norm, the platoon is finishing up their twelve month deployment and should bring a fresh approach to your training. Veterans, expect new twists and wrinkles to what you experienced on your previous training cycles. New guys, understand this is serious business. At all times, we conduct ourselves not only with SKUL in mind, but our teammates, as well. I understand you've all come from battle-hardened units, but the enemy you will face is unlike anything you've ever confronted. They make the most violent jihadist cell seem no more threatening than a turd in the punchbowl. Werewolves are a stronger, faster, and more powerful force than any single thing on this planet. As such, the training you are about to receive will reflect an intensity you simply cannot imagine. It will be long days and longer nights, but unlike many in the armed forces, you have the knowledge and wisdom of your previous assessment and selection programs to fall back on. This, hopefully, will be the edge you need to see the mission to completion. Gentlemen, make no bones about it, you are being trained to do a single task – kill werewolves. When we go out, we go out to kill savages and save human lives, period. Hostage rescue is for the FBI, negotiations for State, and we are neither. We are hunters and killers in the purest sense. It's us or them, gentlemen, and there is no room for anything but a cold beer after a hot barrel." Taggert looked over the room one last time, "Get some rest, men. You're wheels-up at 0800 for the trip to the island. Good luck."

The room rumbled to life as operators stood at attention while Taggert strode off the stage. Dane had a hard time focusing on anything but what he'd just heard. The succinct yet thoughtful speech Taggert had just delivered was in direct contrast to his memories of the SEAL officer. Frankly, he was having a hard time squaring with it.

Twitch broke him from those thoughts with a slap to his shoulder, "C'mon dude, let's go get a beer and some chow at Mac's."

***

Twitch, flanked by Tweeker and Toad, led the way toward Mactavish's pub. According to Twitch, the pub's namesake and proprietor was the only surviving member of the original SKUL team, a *plank owner* of this ultra-secret organization.

Twitch related this in his distinct *boarder-speak,* "Shamus is a gnarly dude, bro."

Dane and Jed walked a few steps behind and listened as Tweeker and Toad continually lobbed questions that Twitch was more than happy to answer. For all the misgivings Dane had initially felt concerning the young operator, he could tell Twitch took life aboard the ship, as well as his job as an operator within this small community, very seriously. He could not help but smile. Despite himself, Dane was beginning to enjoy his company. He could tell his friends were starting to feel the same, especially Tweeker, who had tried to apologize for his earlier comment. To his credit, Twitch accepted the apology graciously and carried on like it never happened.

"Just how big is the Silver Moon, Twitch?" asked Tweeker. "Damn thing seems like a floating city."

"Pretty much. She's nearly four football fields long." He paused, apparently cataloguing his thoughts before continuing, "The ship's capable of a top speed of thirty knots when at full capacity which is three thousand souls. We'll never have that many in-house, or at least we never have since I've been a part of SKUL."

He looked over his shoulder to Jed who'd obviously been around longer. The older operator thought for a second then replied simply, "Never seen it either."

"Right," Twitch replied with a nod. "Don't worry, you guys will get used to Jed's longwinded commentary." Everyone laughed at that, even Jed, and Twitch continued with his lesson, "The Silver Moon is basically a customized cruise liner retrofitted for war-fighting. You've seen the helo pads, but she's also fully capable of engaging an air assault along with flooding certain bulkheads to allow for the rapid deployment of a fleet of Mk V SOC's – special operations craft, RHIBs, and SOC-R's among others. You guys were SEALs, right?"

They nodded.

"Well, you should be familiar with the boats then. They are pretty much the same except they've been up-armored with plated silver."

"I'm sorry, Twitch, did you say plated *silver*?"

It was Dane who asked the question. Quite frankly, it was hard to believe anyone could afford to up-armor a boat with silver, much less a fleet of them.

"Yeah, silver." Twitch looked back to Dane, "I know. Expensive as hell."

The group rounded a corner and spilled out into a massive open area. Sunlight filtered through skylights high above. Five solid marble statues ringed the landing. Each man depicted rocked a full, tactical load and brandished weapons as if heading off to battle.

"This is known as the Point. Think of it like a mall. Anything you need you can find here; and, if it's not here, you don't need it. The cafeteria's open twenty-four hours a day, seven days a week. It's buffet style, but the cooks will fix you up with anything you want, even if they aren't serving it that day."

Toad walked in a circle looking up. His voice was one of fascination, "What's up with the statues?"

"Those were the first five, bro. The plank owners I told you about." Twitch pointed up to the nearest statue, "That one there is Shamus. He led the first mission – Operation Full Eclipse – and hundreds more just like it over what amounted to nearly two decades of service. During that time, he was the *de facto* commander of SKUL until he finally formalized the process. At that time, he handed the reigns over to another but maintained his status as an active operator long enough to reorganize and refine SKUL's selection and training process. Some say it was his idea to buy the first of our silver mines which, if you don't know, spring boarded SKUL to what it is today."

"You talk about him like he's a god," quirked Tweeker and for the first time, Dane could tell Twitch was having trouble putting his thoughts into words.

Jed stepped in and articulated what he guessed Twitch's thoughts were, "Oh, I doubt that he's immortal, though I think we can all agree it took a Herculean effort to pull off all you've seen. Shamus isn't just a former operator and commander of SKUL; he *is* SKUL. Heart, mind, and spirit, Shamus is the core of all you see and everything you will experience here."

"And," interrupted someone at the door to the pub in a clipped yet heavy Irish accent, "he's also wondering why you're standing around babbling like a bunch of idiots." The accent undoubtedly came straight out of the boroughs of Boston, "Jed, you and Twitch bring the new boys in for a beer and something to eat. Let me handle the storytellin', got it?" Shamus held out his hand to Tweeker and Toad calling them by their given names before coming to Dane, "And, you must be Commander Stackwell."

Shamus was baldheaded with a gaudy, handlebar mustache and a chest shaped like an old whiskey barrel. He held Dane's hand in an iron grip and smiled broadly at Dane and the other newcomers, "Always good to have more frogmen as part of SKUL. I was UDT, myself." Looking to Jed with a crooked smile, he added, "Keeps the Army trash beat down and inline." He led the guys into his pub and showed them to a table. "Take a seat, gents, and I'll grab the brews. Menus are there on the table. If you see anything you like, lemme know."

While Shamus went behind the bar, the others fell into jovial conversation. Dane scanned his surroundings. The pub was adorned with a wide mahogany bar that held a deep patina from years of pints of ale being slid across its surface. The booths and tables were constructed of highly figured and polished teakwood. Plush, leather seats were full of fellow operators, many Dane recognized from the earlier briefing. Four pool tables were positioned in a back room along with several dart boards. A sign hung from the ceiling that announced hand-carved chess boards and pieces were available upon request. Hundreds of photos hung from the walls of the main room. These photos showed the afterimages of operations, operators in action. More than anything else, the photos were a visual history of SKUL. Thirstily, he allowed his eyes to fall on a photo from the first operation – codenamed *Full Eclipse*. Easily, Dane recognized the endearing and boisterous image of Shamus leading the AAR. He inhaled heavily, noting the heady scents of beer, cigar smoke, old leather and polished wood as he allowed his mind to catalogue everything his eyes had seen.

*This is home now,* Dane thought with a smile. *This is exactly where I'm supposed to be, and I'm going to be doing exactly what I'm supposed to be doing.* Then, an image of Abbey and Henry slammed into the gray matter of his brain, and the smile faded.

While he knew he did not fully understand nor appreciate the enemy they faced, he knew the men on his team and the others fighting under SKUL's banner would do everything they could in order to prepare him for what lay ahead...or die trying. He also knew they would lay down their lives for his family – for any family – and that meant everything to him.

*Abbey, you and Henry will be safe if you just do what Admiral Briggs told you to.*

Shortly thereafter, Shamus dropped off their beers then made his way around the room. There was not an operator in the bar he did not know, nor one he would not take a second to swap tales with. The man truly loved talking to the guys.

Dane smiled, finally relaxed, and leaned into Jed's ear, "Jed, you mentioned you were my ATL?"

"Correct," replied the operator while taking a pull of his beer.

"How? What I mean is, how can I be expected to lead men when I don't even understand who – or rather, *what* – we're fighting."

Jed nodded, understanding his concerns, "It's pretty standard for SKUL to draw the new guys from the military's special operations community, and – once up to speed – place them in corresponding positions here. Officers, such as yourself, already have the skills necessary for planning ops, coordinating with intelligence and logistics, and giving strong briefings and AAR's; we just have to train you to fight savages. Same goes for the enlisted ranks we draw from. They are already SME's - subject matter experts – in various battlefield specialties which allows everyone to focus on the equipment and training necessary to eliminate the threat. Make sense?"

Dane swallowed a sip of beer nodding, "Does now."

By listening to the conversation Toad, Tweeker and Twitch were having and the ensuing laughter, Dane could tell the guys were already becoming a tight group. After a few minutes, he asked Jed to clear up a subject that still caused a certain degree of trepidation, "What do you think about the ACO?"

"Who? Taggert?" Dane nodded but kept quiet allowing the older operator to collect his thoughts. Finally Jed shrugged, "Solid enough operator. Never worked with him when he was active, but I've got no complaints regarding his ability as an ACO." Seeing Dane's furrowed brow, Jed commented, "You seem surprised."

"Just not an opinion I've heard shared by many, myself included."

Jed downed his beer then added, "I can only comment on my experience with the ACO. Most officers I've dealt with over the years had as many detractors as they had proponents to their leadership." He winked, "I'd bet a wooden nickel the same can be said for you."

Dane snorted into his glass, "Yeah, you could say that. Point taken."

Jed grinned then looked to the others, "C'mon guys. We gotta get loaded out and hit the sack. Got a long flight tomorrow."

As ATL, it was Jed's job – and his alone – to ensure that everyone was where they needed to be, when they needed to be there. He expected every man on the team to be prepared for every eventuality, both during training and when the team was activated. This was a job Jed took very, very seriously.

"Flight?" Tweeker asked. Apparently, he had forgotten the Silver Moon was only a brief stopping-off point before their formal SKUL training began.

Jed and Twitch exchanged knowing glances before the younger of the two exclaimed, "Yeah, dude, a long flight. How else you think we're getting to Tortuga Island?"

The two experienced SKUL operators walked out of the pub with Tweeker and Toad in tow. Dane followed a little further behind. Even at a distance, he distinctly heard Toad ask Tweeker, "Did he say *Tortuga Island? Like Pirates of the Caribbean,* Tortuga?"

Tweeker looked over his shoulder to his old boss. Dane returned the look with a confident, award-winning smile; but the truth of the matter was, he didn't have a fucking clue what was about to happen, either.

# 6)
## The Warrior Ethos

After packing up some of the gear he would need during training – the rest would be issued on the island itself – Dane had a few more beers with the guys. They lounged in Whiskey's private team room and discussed with the veterans what they could expect during the months to come. Sometime shortly before midnight, Dane quietly excused himself and slumped into a chair in his stateroom. Thoughts swirled through his head like whitewater rapids on a swollen river, and his mind ached over Henry and Abbey. Those thoughts, coupled with the visions of werewolves and the uncertainty of what lay ahead, made focusing on anything all but impossible. He took a pull from his beer and began writing what he knew he should have said so many times before. Now, more than ever, Henry needed to know he was there for him even across time, space, and the unknown.

*Dear Henry,*

*Last week I had to do the hardest thing I have ever had to do. I had to say goodbye to you and your mom, even after I had promised you both I would never to do it again. I know your life has been full of one goodbye from me after the other, but I need you to understand that I would not have done it if I was not convinced it was absolutely necessary for you and your mom's safety. I hope you are able to choose a career that keeps you home at night with your family. Honestly, the reason I fight is so you do not have to. I know that is hard to understand; and, truth be known, I do not understand it fully myself. Just know, the wish I have for you keeps me warm on the coldest nights in the worst places imaginable. Regardless, though, of the path you choose, it is my sincerest hope that when your time comes to turn around and look back upon the long road that was your life, you can stand tall with your head held high, knowing the world is a better place for you having called it home.*

*You need to understand that life is hard, son; harder, more unforgiving and unfair than you can imagine. Just like the characters depicted in those superhero comics you like to read, you will find yourself on the ground - haggard and sore - more often than you like. It is what you do in those times that define you as a man. Do you pick yourself up, dust off, and with a smile on your face, trod onward? Or, do you fold your cards?*

*The man - the warrior enshrined in his self-made ethos - slaps his hat to his thigh, checks his shooting iron, and grins before moving down the road toward sunset.*

*The warrior ethos. Find it, live it.*

*Loyalty, friendship, honor and tenacity. That, above all, is the life I hope you choose, Henry.*

*Lastly, I want you to know I have never been as proud of anyone or anything in my life as I am of you. You are growing up on me, and I am sad that I have missed so much of it, but what I saw in your eyes tells me your mom and I — mostly your mom — are doing things right. And, while I am thinking about it, take care of your mom, Henry. She is the only mom you will ever have, and she is going to need you over the coming months. Never disrespect her and never make her life harder than it already is. If nothing else I have written sinks in, I pray that last sentence does. She is one of the strongest women I have ever met and deserves more than I have been able to give her. I hope and pray you guys are okay, and I promise I am doing everything on my end to make sure of that.*

*I love you, son,*
*Daddy*

The next morning, Dane handed his letter to the Admiral, "Will you see that Henry gets this?"

The Admiral nodded, "It'll be my pleasure." The Admiral held out his hand. The two shook as old friends though they had only known each other for a few days with limited contact even then. "Enjoy the island, son. It'll be the most intense training you've ever experienced, and I expect you to lead your men as you always have, from the front."

"You can count on that, sir."

The Admiral smiled, this time it looked to be tinged with an ounce of sadness, "I am, son, as is all of SKUL."

***

Whiskey platoon's Chinook lifted off from landing platform three whereas Kilo platoon's left from platform five. Five minutes after takeoff the Chinook ferrying Kilo platoon banked hard to the North and, seconds later, disappeared from view.

Dane leaned to Jed and, over the roar of the helos' engine, asked, "Where are they going?"

Jed tilted his head relaxingly toward Dane, "Kilo will be our support and security. They're going into New Orleans with three teams from Foxtrot to spend some time with intel. They'll get brushed up on defensive and offensive driving, communications, trade craft, that sort of thing, then hook back up with us about half way through the training cycle. They'll mesh what they learn with what we're doing."

Dane nodded then looked over to Twitch who was flanked by Tweeker and Toad. Over their shoulders leaned other men, many of whom Dane had not met, and they were all glued to the screen of Twitch's tablet.

"What are you guys watching?" Dane asked, genuinely curious.

Twitch looked up in confusion, then to Tweeker and Toad, obviously perplexed. They both shrugged noncommittally.

"The guys tell me they used to call you *Boss?*"

Dane nodded but kept quiet, unsure what the unpredictable operator was driving at.

"Well, Boss, it's getting pretty close to the holidays; so, we're kicking off the season by watching the best Christmas movie of all time, *Christmas Vacation.*"

Dane leaned back, relaxing, and gave a thumb's up, "Shitter's full!"

Twitch laughed and quickly returned his attention to the screen. With nothing to do for the next few hours, Dane shut his eyes for a nap.

# 7)
## Pirates and Scallywags

### SKUL Black Site
### Codename – Tortuga

The Chinook delivered Whiskey platoon to a SKUL black site huddled deep within the swamps of southwest Mississippi. There, the platoon hopped aboard a C-130 for the journey to Tortuga, which would take several hours. They would fly over the Gulf of Mexico and skirt the southernmost section of the Florida Everglades. From there, they would take a south by southeast heading.

To Jed, Dane said, "So, I did an internet search last night and found out the real Tortuga Island is a part of Haiti."

"Yep."

"I'm assuming that's not our Tortuga."

"Correct again."

The man's simplistic and direct nature was borderline infuriating, and Dane began to realize it would take some getting used to.

"Okay, so where is Tortuga anyway?" he asked Jed over the roar of the aircraft's engines.

His ATL smiled, "Smack dab in the center of the most feared waters in the world, the Bermuda Triangle. The island is completely off the grid and away from any major shipping lanes. Fighter jets out of Eglin enforce a strict *no fly zone* over a one hundred square mile perimeter." The plane banked then began a slow decent that prompted Jed to add,

"We're about forty five mikes out now. Hope you got some rest, because it'll be in short supply for the next few months."

The seasoned warrior pulled the brim of his hat low. This was his unceremonious signal the conversation was over.

True to Blackmoor's words, the pilot announced they had begun their final approach. They had a tailwind, and just under forty minutes later, the plane's wheels touched down on the runway gently. After a short taxi to the hangar area, the platoon disembarked the aircraft and stepped into the gentle, salt-tinged, oceanic breeze. The humid air was sticky and heavy, and it took Dane only seconds to figure out the next few months would be tough sledding. As he walked down the ramp, a large, hand-painted sign caught his attention. It was the flag of the pirate, Calico Jack, except the skull had slanted eyes and very, very long teeth. He guessed – rightly so – that it was meant to be a werewolf skull. The words painted under the skull and crossed sabers read:

*Welcome to TORTUGA ISLAND*
*Ancestral Home of SEE-S and the SKUL Warrior*
*Here, the Soldier's Heart and the Pirate's Spirit are*
*Forged as One*
*Per Tenebras Venimus Tamquam Lux*
*Ye be warned*

The corner of Dane's mouth curled, and his lips puckered, "Saying's a bit dated."

"Anything like *the only easy day was yesterday?*" Jed asked mockingly.

Dane chuckled at the barb pointed at his Naval Special Warfare roots, "Something like that." A second later, he asked thoughtfully, "Per tenebras venimus tamquam lux?" Dane looked to Jed and Twitch for explanation.

"Latin," Jed replied simply.

"Yeah, I figured that part out on my own, Jed." Mild irritation leaked through on his tone. "What does it mean?"

"Why didn't you say so?" Jed returned before he added, "One translation reads *through the darkness we come as light*. It's SKUL's motto."

"C'mon dude," Twitch slapped him on the back as he shouldered past, "we've got a meeting with Colonel Gholar and the guys from Foxtrot in five minutes."

Twitch and Jed led the others under the sign, and into a large, cinder block building filled with dozens of metal folding chairs. A group of men and women in street clothes, presumably intelligence support staffers, were clumped in a group of chairs talking quietly, while others sat empty. Along the walls stood a few dozen sweaty yet hard-looking men.

At the front of the room stood an older black man – fifty, maybe sixty years old – who was well over six feet tall and close to two hundred fifty pounds, conservatively.

All of it muscle.

The two men he spoke quietly with, while not small men by any measure, looked almost diminutive next to the much larger man.

Jed and several of the older guys from Whiskey busied themselves catching up with the operators from Foxtrot platoon. The others quickly found seats and talked amongst themselves. Dane, Tweeker, and Toad grabbed seats and waited for the briefing to begin.

Twitch, unable to remain quiet for any length of time, took it upon himself to identify the men talking at the front of the room. "The big guy is Colonel Alvin Gholar, Commander of SEE-S or Savage Education and Eradication – SKUL. Everyone just calls it *C-school*, though. Gholar's old school Delta Force. He's not a plank owner in the Unit, but close enough to have felt the ripple effects of the disaster at Desert One. Legend has it he saved both Shamus and the Admiral's life back in the day. Supposedly, the two were on a mission that went sideways, and the Colonel stepped up in a big way. Nobody knows what exactly went down, and nobody's talking, but the Colonel earned his place at the table that very night. Anyway, he signs off on everything Foxtrot does here. He's a helluva officer and knows the score; so, he tends to hold the reigns loosely and let the boots on the ground handle the training during a pre-deployment workup. Gholar and the crew of old SKUL guys that live here year round tend to focus more on training the new guys that haven't been assigned a platoon yet. They make up a small part of an off-the-books platoon called *Wraith*. The guys in Wraith are older and, though they have lost a step, still have a lot to offer SKUL. My dad's involved in it, though I'm not sure where. Last I heard was Alaska, but he was one of Gholar's boys when I went through C-school."

Dane nodded but remained quiet. He knew enough about Twitch's backstory to know it was a wonder he was just motor-mouthed and fidgety. He had every right to be locked up in an asylum. To think he still did not know exactly where his dad was and what he was doing...well, damn. Still though, because of Twitch's ramblings, he was beginning to form faces with the names and positions he had come across over the last few days.

Twitch continued while pointing to the stage which was mildly embarrassing. "The redheaded guy on the Colonel's right is Stan Woods. Everyone calls him Woodrow." Twitch's face twisted in concentration as he said almost to himself, "For the life of me, I can't remember his home unit before SKUL, maybe ISA?" He was quiet for a long moment trying to place Woodrow's former unit but, drawing a complete blank, he continued, "Anyway, he's Foxtrot's platoon leader or *PL*."

Dane nodded. He remembered him from the briefing he'd been allowed to sit in on a few days ago.

Twitch fidgeted with his SICS device. The guy could not sit still, and he talked without looking up. "The guy with the white hair cut high and tight…that's Wild Bill Kipling, our PL. Wild Bill's a former Army colonel from the 75th Ranger Regiment, 3rd Battalion. Dude, trust me when I tell you the man is a badass, and you do not want him down on you. I think he and Jed served together at some point, but I'm not sure when. Either way, once this thing shakes out, you'll be dealing with both of them – particularly, Wild Bill – a lot more than any of us. Chain of command is pretty succinct around here. Orders flow from the Admiral and his staff down to the PL's then to the team leaders – you being one of them, obviously – and then to us. After actions and debriefs flow in the opposite direction."

"Seats people." Gholar's voice boomed across the room and ended Twitch's dissertation. His deep, resonant voice lent perfectly to his commanding presence. Everyone quickly took a seat, and the Colonel began, "Gentlemen, welcome to C-school. As most of you know, we hit the ground running around here. We're already working under a serious time crunch, and we don't have time to dick around. Our goal here at C-school is simple. We want to get you guys up to speed and operationally ready as quickly as possible. Woodrow and his guys have worked tirelessly over these last few months to make sure you people get everything you need to be *mission successful*. Understand, C-school is *not* a selection process. That job was accomplished by your parent units and by the way you conducted yourselves after facing the hard reality of the existence of werewolves. SEE-S is about training, period. Training that is high speed and low drag; so, get your shit squared away PDQ. As commander of C-school, I expect you guys to be professional at all times and give the guys from Foxtrot everything you've got. I won't tolerate a lack of attention nor will any safety violations fly. Get your mind right – right now – or I'll see that it's scrambled somewhere along the beach. Am I clear?"

"Yes, sir!" the men in the room affirmed enthusiastically.

Gholar smiled, "I thought as much and have no doubt you guys will uphold your end of the bargain. Good luck." He looked to the redhead on his right, "Woodrow, they're all yours."

"Thank you, sir," began Foxtrot's PL in a decidedly northeastern accent. Turning his attention back to Whiskey platoon, he began, "Guys, as Colonel Gholar alluded to, we've got a lot to do and little time to do it. You are here because you've proven to be solid operators in other special

98

operations units. This can be both a good thing and a bad thing. It's good because your cadre – us – can cut through the bullshit, and focus on honing the skills you already possess to a level you never thought possible." Woodrow paused and looked directly at Dane and those sitting nearest him, "I see you new guys rolling your eyes. Well, all I will say is look to the vets in this room, guys with multiple pre-deployment workups. Guys who've survived deployments that found them in harm's way day after day after day. Missions where they battled immensely powerful savages and survived when others didn't. Look them in the eyes and see if there's not a next level."

Unconsciously, Dane looked around the room until his eyes fell on Jed. The man exuded quiet confidence and oozed professionalism. Dane half-grinned then turned his attention back to Foxtrot's leader.

"There's a flip side to the coin, though," Kipling admitted, "and, as stated, it can be bad deal. No, check that, it can be deadly. It's called overconfidence; and, in my experience, overconfidence gets people killed. LIGHTS!"

The room suddenly became dark, and a previously unnoticed big screen TV behind Woods sparked to life.

"In ninety-two, between late July and early November, approximately thirty-two souls were lost along with Mississippi River corridor. Many were boatmen hauling raw materials down the river. Their deaths were conveniently pawned off as accidental. This was understandable, to a point, because the job is fairly dangerous. It was only when the death toll started to mount within the river's port cities that SKUL's interest was piqued. Eventually, during the deep winter months, the death toll became centered in the area of Memphis, Tennessee – specifically, the farmlands north of there. Realizing the probability of the involvement of werewolves was high, we immediately sent out a QRF – quick reaction force – to meet the threat."

Woodrow clicked the *play* button. The op – from start to finish – lasted approximately twenty minutes, only about two of which were SKUL operatives in contact with savages. Those two minutes, however, had to have been torn from the ninth circle of hell. The men in the room watched what could only be described as overt carnage. It was gory and sickening and unlike anything they had seen in even the bloodiest of Hollywood horror flicks. In short order, the entire team had been annihilated by things that just simply should not have *been*.

As the last SKUL operative was torn in half and used as a feeding trough, the footage on the screen snowed. The silence that hung over the room was oppressive and heavy, like it had manifested into the tangible.

"Jesus," Tweeker muttered louder than intended.

"We'd like to think Jesus escorted those boys to the Pearly Gates, Lattimore," Woods responded quietly.

He gave the audience a moment before he began anew, "You just witnessed an operation that nearly devastated SKUL. To this day, no single mission has resulted in a death toll even close to what SKUL experienced that day. The mission, as well-intended as it may have been, was brutally flawed. Intel was spotty, at best, without so much as an educated guess concerning the number of savages on target. In retrospect, we should have inserted a recce squad to gather more intel, but that's hindsight. And, hindsight's a luxury we don't have. We were overconfident in our ability, we rushed in without proper intelligence, and we paid for it with the blood of good men."

Woods paused and took in every operator's eyes with his own, "While on the island and under my charge, you will focus, you will learn, you will remain professional, and above all, you will develop into a savage killing sonavabitch, understood?"

Again the room erupted resoundingly, "Yes, sir!"

Woods smiled, satisfied with the attitude that dominated the room, "You've all been issued a phone and tablet. So you new guys know, these function using a proprietary technology we call the SKUL Integrated Communications System or SICS – pronounced *six*. These are your communication lifelines. Each evening at 1900, the next day's schedule will be posted and uploaded to these units. Any changes deemed necessary will be made by 2300. At the start of the last month – your third here on the island – each team will be introduced to their respective support staff. These include the intelligence officers and computer analysis directly attached to your fire team. At that time, your training focus will shift entirely to mission preparation and execution. Your support staff is your life blood and will be with you for the duration of your deployment. Trust me when I say *treat them well* as they can be the difference between a mission ending up as filet mignon or you ending up as ground beef. Any questions so far?"

There were none.

"Outstanding," he said with a smile. "Take tonight to get squared away. After evening chow, you new guys are to report back here – the Bixby Room. You'll receive a technical briefing regarding the Kinetic Tactical Defense System v. 9, officially designated *KtacS* by the developing company. Platoon PT is set for 0500, but this isn't always the case. Schedules depend on the day ahead, the night before, or where the cadre feels you are in training. So, keep your SICS and tablets on you and refer to them often. Understood?"

Again the room erupted, "Yes, sir!"

"Thought so," said the PL of Foxtrot and cadre leader of Whiskey's training cycle over a wide grin. "Tighten your jockstraps men, because tomorrow the shit gets real.

# 8)
## A Whole Lotta Suck

### The Bixby Classroom
### 1900

The four new guys sat together in the main classroom. Dane, Tweeker, and Toad were joined by Tom Wilcox. Wilcox – call sign *Hammer* – was a thirty year old Air Force Joint Terminal Attack Controller or *JTAC*. Hammer had enough deployments to Afghanistan under his belt to match the other three story for story regarding courage under fire. He was tall and built like an NFL wide receiver. He had a mop of thick, dark hair, a full beard, and sleeve tattoos covering both arms. He also had a soft spoken yet confident disposition and a quick smile. Just like Dane and the others, Hammer was both completely at ease with the world and rapturously enthralled with this new unit and the enemy they'd be facing. They all drank from both cups in equal measure.

Unlike Dane, Toad, and Tweeker, who would be on the same team together, Hammer was assigned to Copperhead. Copperhead was a notoriously tight run team with a good reputation within SKUL.

The banter continued until the door to the classroom opened. Three of their cadre pulled two huge strongboxes on dollies across the stage. A bookishly attractive woman in her mid-thirties followed in their wake. The cadre consisted of two heavily muscled black operators with shaved heads, and a shorter, muscled-up operator with distinct Vietnamese features. The Vietnamese operator took to the lectern while the other guys cracked open one of the strongboxes. Silently, they began to lay out the contents on several tables.

Dane sat rigid in his seat. He immediately recognized who was about to speak. He'd only seen him once, in Mactavish's the day after an op gone wrong, but he had no doubts.

*Dax Nguyen*, he thought though he gave no outward appearance of recognition. *He's the TL that blew his best friend's head off after he'd been bitten and turned by the werewolf, Virginia Dare.*

Nguyen looked not to Dane, but through him.

*Potter and Hootch*, he said to himself. *Jesus, these guys should be in a rubber room somewhere after their last mission.* Dane had heard the rumors that followed in the wake of Operation Grindstone. He'd also seen the aftermath in Mactavish's shortly thereafter. By all accounts, it was a death trap, and it did, in fact, claim one of Cobra team's – the team Dax led – members.

"Guys, I'm Dax Nguyen, TL of Foxtrot's Cobra team," the solidly built operator began in a decidedly Californian accent. It was the kind of accent that told anyone within earshot the man was entirely at home on a surf board. "We're here to get you up to speed on the Kinetic Tactical Defense System version 9. Dr. Monica Taylor will begin with an overview of technical aspects of the system. She'll also educate you on a bit of SKUL's history as it relates to the evolution of the suit. Be warned, this is some heavy shit, so you'll need to devote your full attention to her over the next few days."

Though Dax smiled, there was a sadness to it.

"Don't worry. I don't understand a lot of it, and I've been with SKUL for eight years now. In any case, after Dr. Taylor finishes we'll suit up, and spend some time getting familiar with the system. Dr. Taylor, the floor is yours."

"Thanks Dax," the woman began warmly. "As stated, I'm Monica Taylor, chief of research and design here at SKUL. At the risk of boring you with my credentials, I have doctorates in both applied physics and polymer science. These skill sets afford me insight into the unique requirements of the modern day SKUL operator. It is my job not only to oversee in-house tech advances but to liaise with outside companies when their technology advances supersedes our own. The system we are about to discuss started with the basic premise that not only will silver kill a werewolf, it can and will repel a werewolf attack. Initial suits were constructed much the same as typical ballistic plating. They were big, bulky, and heavy. While they certainly protected the critical areas of the human anatomy, they offered little-to-no protection to non-vital areas such as the extremities." Dr. Taylor turned to the guys from Foxtrot, "Lights, please."

The room fell into darkness; and, with a click of a remote, the big screen TV came on. The screen showed a grainy video feed from a helmet camera. The video revealed an operation being conducted in the tight confines of a hotel hallway. Taylor gave a running commentary while Dane and the others watched, "What you are seeing is an operation conducted in the late seventies. As you can tell, everything from the technology of the weapons, to the camera and quality of the video, to the soldier's protection would be

105

considered archaic even by conventional military standards a decade ago."

As Dane watched, the soldiers knelt outside one of the doors and checked the handle.

*Locked,* he heard the lead soldier say over the squad comm-link.

He then inserted a hooligan tool between the door and jam, and with a violent tug, the door flew open. Before the team could initiate its room cleaning sequence, the first soldier through fell, and the room reverberated with gunshots. Even then, the video picked up the anguished screams of the downed soldier.

The screen snowed, but the lights remained off.

The four men were silent in their attempt to digest what they had just seen. After a moment, Taylor put words to the carnage, "What you just witnessed was the death of Tim Bixby, a Major in the British SAS on loan to SKUL. His duty was to hone skills that our military, quite frankly, wasn't proficient in at the time. These skills, a big portion of which dealt with counter-terrorism tactics, were thought to be useful to SKUL's needs. The operation was to be Bixby's last order of business with SKUL before he reported back to SAS. Sadly, in all respects, and more than a little ironically, it was very much his last mission. Cause of death was due to massive blood loss suffered from a mortal wound to the femoral artery – the direct result of a heavy strike from a savage's claw. The death of Major Bixby brought about a fundamental change within SKUL. The organization had been heavily involved in understanding its adversary, but only inasmuch as developing the fighting techniques necessary to defeat the werewolves.

That changed with the Major's death.

Collectively, SKUL stepped back and recognized the need to place as much emphasis on protecting its operators as it did in hunting the enemy. Advancements in body armor, optics, and weaponry were introduced, slowly at first, but each small step allowed the operator a little more peace of mind. With increasingly renewed confidence in their equipment came the ability for the men in harm's way to focus a bit more on the mission at hand. We still suffered losses, but at a much more manageable pace – if there is such a thing. This slow crawl in technological advancement continued for an additional twenty years until New Year's Eve 1999 and *Operation Scorpion*. Scorpion involved a task force of three SKUL teams from Lima platoon. They were sent in to take down one of the most fearsome savages SKUL has ever confronted. A savage that initial intel hinted to, and later confirmed, was the werewolf that historical scholars had long known about."

Dr. Taylor paused and took a drink from her water bottle.

"They just didn't know they knew about him," said the doctor with a smile. "Operation Scorpion yielded one of our most incredible victories; unfortunately, SKUL also suffered heavy losses. The target – as it happens – was Mictlantecuhtli, the Aztec god of the dead."

She turned, clicked her remote again, and the screen revealed another operation underway. Dane noticed the gear looked more modern yet was still nowhere near what he associated with a SKUL shooter. Again, Dr. Taylor gave a play by play. The operation was successful only in the sense that the savage was dead. Dane and the others were horrified, yet again, by what they saw on the screen.

Only three survived.

Three out of fifteen soldiers, all at the hands of a single savage.

A chill rode bi-directionally along Dane's spine as the lights clicked on.

Taylor continued, "Even though the werewolf was eliminated, I think I'd be hard pressed to find anyone in this room that thought of the mission as a success, correct?" She introduced her comment in the form of a question, and everyone shook their heads. "Still though, the sacrifices of those twelve men paved the way for a new day within SKUL, and with it, the playing field was brought closer to level, if only slightly."

Taylor turned to the three men from Foxtrot, "Gentlemen, if you would please reveal our special guest."

The three soldiers began unstrapping the second strongbox. Moments later, they unbuckled a series of clasps and revealed a set of huge bones within a glass case. The bones looked almost human – almost – if not for the elongated face and long, serrated teeth. Also, the leg and arm bones were too long and thick to be human and gave birth to hands and feet caught somewhere between humanity and the nether world. Each appendage was much longer and more formidable looking than they had any right to be. The fingers and toes – if you could really call them that – were tipped with massive, razor sharp claws.

"Gentlemen, meet Mictlantecuhtli, or as we call him, *The Dude.*" She flashed her brilliant smile again, "Yes, before you ask, the person who named him is a huge *The Big Lebowski* fan." She winked to everyone at once, "He'll be the one drinking white Russians in his bath robe up at the bar."

On an ordinary day, the comment would have elicited a movie quote or three from the group; but, on this day, silence prevailed. The men in the room were simply too stunned at the enormity of the werewolf skeleton. The silence held on for quite a while. Too long, in fact, for Dax's taste.

"Well, don't just sit there like a two dollar whore in a Baptist church!" he yelled at the top of his lungs. "Men died so you could see this thing!"

The four new guys, startled back to reality, jumped to the lectern and began their examinations of the bones. They examined the remains, first in contemplative silence, before commenting to one another. They marveled in awe at the sheer size of the beast. Dane could not help but notice Dax donning a KtacS suit even as Taylor began her latest lecture, "Not long after Operation Scorpion and the retrieval of The Dude, I was recruited by SKUL. Someone in intelligence stumbled upon a research paper I had authored the year before. It was titled *Resolution to the Liquid Metal Question.* The idea came to me when I was a kid watching the movie *Terminator 2.*" The doctor's voice became wispy as she continued, "I thought the applications of the liquid metal that formed the *T1000* where unlimited – if reproducible...and, I was going to do it. It's why I went to school really. I spent a lot of my life chasing after that dream. Unfortunately, I never found what I was after." The doctor's eyes became distant for a second until she shook her head and waved her hand dismissively, "You guys don't care about that. What you guys need to know about is the suit and what it can and can't do."

The doctor reached inside the glass casing and grabbed one of the beast's humongous claws. She gripped it with both hands and took a batter's stance, "Dax?"

The operator stepped forward, "Ready, Dr. Taylor."

The doctor swung the dead werewolf's paw with surprising speed and power. The claw slammed into the operator's chest so hard he staggered backwards. Instantly, a shower of sparks erupted from the area of contact. The operator stepped forward and showed his chest to the small audience. The area where the claw hit him was misshapen and torn but only superficially. Despite the blow only seconds prior, Dax stood tall and was relatively unfazed; a rather remarkable feat considering just how hard the doctor had swung the clawed paw.

Dr. Taylor looked to the men, "I know you all have questions you want answered. That's what I'm here for, so if you'll take your seats..."

She motioned to the seats behind them, and the guys followed her direction.

"First, understand the specific science behind the suits, while truly remarkable, is well beyond the scope of this lecture. Understanding it on a molecular level would require a year's worth of you sitting here listening to more of my boring lectures. Since we don't have a year, it's best you understand the basic concepts behind the technology and how to use it to your advantage. The makeup of the suit is that of a micro-fine, electro-conducive polymer that is set in a chain-of-pearls configuration. At the basic polymer level, its matrix has been injected and filled with silver nitrate globules. These globules are electrically charged, and when they burst by, say, a powerful blow, they react violently."

Taylor paused long enough to note the blank looks of incomprehension. Realizing her folly, she backed up and made her presentation a little more relevant to their experience, "I'm sure you've all heard of *Liquid Kevlar?*"

The men nodded sheepishly. Liquid Kevlar was a concept straight out of a 1950s sci-fi novel. The thing is, not only had the government experimented with the technology, they had employed it...with *varying* degrees of success.

Plainly speaking, nobody trusted it.

"I can tell by your looks that some of you are more familiar with it than others."

Hammer remained still. He'd never used the armor while Dane and Toad nodded again. Tweeker rubbed his left pectoral area out of habit. During an op-gone-wrong while he was with DEVGRU, he'd had an errant round slip through the liquid armor.

The KtacS suit was now slipping on his scale of *badass new toys.*

"Yeah, I know," Taylor admitted, "but, hang with me, okay?"

The men shifted nervously in their chairs. *What in the fuck had they gotten into* was the primary thought in everyone's mind.

"The KtacS suit uses similar, albeit, upgraded and refined principles."

Eye rolls all around.

"Anyway, think of it like a thin layer of bubble wrap. When struck, the bubbles burst and send a flood of silver nitrate instantly to the pressure point. This creates a momentary shell of pure silver. As you know, werewolves can't tolerate silver – in fact, penetration into the skin will kill them – hence the effectiveness of the suit. This layer is sandwiched between two lightweight yet ultra, high-density layers of rubberized polymers. The structure of these layers is articulated and octagonal with a slight overlay between each. If you've seen snakeskin, you've seen the basic design of the system's outer and inner layers. The tensile strength of these combined layers is such that you will be all but immune to stab wounds and blunt force trauma. Furthermore, state-of-the-art ballistic plating – also coated in a thin layer of pure silver – has been molded into vital areas of the chest, thighs, and upper and lower arms. The resultant product, while extraordinarily protective, was so heavy and stiff that its protective attributes were nullified. Realizing we had solved nothing if our operators couldn't effectively operate, we had the guys in biomechanical engineering sit down and develop a solution. What they came up with – in extremely short order, I'm proud to say – is what we call *Reverb*. Reverb is a reinforcement of the structurally pertinent and load-bearing joints of the body such as the ankles, knees, and elbows. These reinforcements take the kinetic force of an operator's movements and respond in kind, thus doubling his output. Before anyone asks, no, you're not going to be able to leap over tall buildings in a single bound. Reverb just gives you that little edge while wearing the KtacS. Like an echo in a cave, as long as you guys are moving the system responds in kind."

Dr. Taylor paused for a breath and looked the men over, "Clear as mud so far?"

She flashed that award winning smile of hers again. While Dane certainly thought she was attractive, he could tell someone else had marked her for his own.

Tweeker. It was written all over his face.

Dane sighed. He doubted anyone else had noticed, but he should have freaking known better.

The doctor was still talking, "Pretty much anything you want – pouches, pockets, holsters – is already molded into the suit's outer shell. What's not there, or not there to your liking and preference, can be fully integrated per your specs, granted you give my guys twenty-four hours' notice."

She leaned forward into the lectern, and her heels lifted off the ground slightly to reveal a pair of very shapely legs.

*Dear Lord,* Dane thought. He looked to Tweeker.

Tweeker winked back at him.

*Oh hell,* Dane thought again.

Taylor continued, unaware that two of the supposed *super-task-oriented* shooters in the room had just mentally undressed her; and, worse yet, one had raised his leg and marked his territory.

Figuratively speaking, of course.

"While I'm thinking about it, on whichever forearm you prefer, a docking bay for your SICS device will be incorporated. Once integrated, your phone, tablet, and helmet will communicate seamlessly. This will allow you to change settings either on your forearm or within the helmet itself."

She could see eyes being raised among the new guys. After a moment of hushed whispers, she held up her hands in placation, "Sorry guys, I don't do computer programs. Rest assured, though, when these few months are over you are all going to be sick of hearing about the KtacS. Questions?"

"Ma'am," Toad jumped at the chance to speak, "you've mentioned on several occasions an electrical current. What's its importance?"

"Glad you asked, Petty Officer Tolar," she began with a smile. "Silver is one of the highest conductors of energy on the planet. The small amount of electricity running between the protective layers of polymers allows – no – it forces the surrounding areas of silver nitrate to the area of insult."

Toad nodded.

*Did he understand?*

No, not really. Not in full in any case, but the way he had it figured, it was all going to come out in the wash anyway.

"Ma'am," this from Hammer Wilcox, "several times now you've mention *high velocity attacks*. What exactly does that mean, and how does it affect me?"

"Great question, Tom," Dr. Taylor said now beaming at the attentiveness of her audience. "It means exactly what it implies. The KtacS can be described very succinctly as a *smart* system. This basically means I could punch you, kick you, even hit you over the head with a baseball bat and the system would remain whole. But, the power and velocity delivered from, say, a werewolf strike or gunshot will break

114

the bubble wrap. Repeated insults to a given area will render the suit useless."

"Ah, Mrs. Taylor?"

If Dane's eyes had been laser beams, Tweeker would have been sliced in two.

Instead, his big, Nordic friend and teammate sat with his legs stretched out and his feet propped up in the chair before him. He adjusted what lay between his legs, winked, then spit a mouthful of Levi Garrett spit into a Styrofoam cup.

*Here we go,* Dane thought.

"*Doctor,* Mister Lattimore."

"Huh?" asked Tweeker, nonplussed by the bite in her tone.

As if the previous second had not been clue enough — which they had to anyone with half a brain and thinking with only one head — the next few made it clear. Taylor was not here to put up with some hot-shit operator with a hard-on for intellectuals. "My title starts with a *D* and ends with an *R*. It's the abbreviation for *doctor* which is exactly how you will address me, *Mister* Lattimore."

For a brief moment, Tweeker looked like a deer in the headlights of an oncoming eighteen wheeler. Only they were not headlights, but Taylor's slitted eyes that burned white hot with anger, "Is that that easy enough to follow, sailor?"

"It's *chief*, ma'am," Ansil replied.

"I'm sorry?"

"Well," Tweeker began with a hard look that softened over time, "I figure since we're all thumping our chest over accomplishments and initials, you should get mine right. So it's *Chief Lattimore;* as in twelve plus years of putting my ass on the line for the good of people I didn't know, who'd never appreciate any of it, anyway."

Now it was Taylor's turn to stand around stumbling over her words. In fact, she looked like someone had just run over her in a school bus, stopped, backed up, and hit the gas again. "Well, I..." she stammered, "...certainly I can..." she fumbled her words, knocked completely off kilter.

Dane leaned over and spit into the spittoon they shared before hissing, "Are you shittin' me dude? Knock this shit off, man."

Tweeker did not even look his way, his eyes never wavering from Dr. Taylor's, "It's no biggie, ma'am, and I meant no disrespect. Apologies for overstepping my bounds," Tweeker said rather emphatically. "I guess what I really want to know is what's the suit's viability?"

He smiled warmly to the doctor, and Dane saw this was the point he'd been pushing the conversation to all along.

*Game, set, and match* Dane thought. *She might as well give him a key to her suite.*

"I'm sorry?" responded Taylor. Her face was noticeably flushed. She was struggling to recover from the verbal contest of *whose dick was bigger* she had unwittingly participated in.

Tweeker sat upright and cleared his throat before clarifying, "Well, ma'am, you have mentioned the storing of energy and the use of energy. You've also mentioned the breaking of microscopic strings of bubble wrap and subsequent releasing of silver...but what you haven't mentioned is how long a single suit remains protective. It'll be my duty to patch 'em up and keep 'em moving during an op, so this is something I need to know."

Tweeker, as he had previously been in the Teams and Section 8, was the team's medic.

The depth of his question, along with its intelligence and forward thinking, caused Taylor to pause. She wanted to hate his ass, she really did, but she was having trouble doing so.

*Hell,* she thought quickly, *he's really cute.*

*I suck,* she thought just as quickly.

Tweeker smiled a confidence-filled smile.

*Oh god, I hate myself.*

She found she had to literally force herself to answer matter-of-factly and with no emotion, "Data is conflicting. As you can imagine, each strike we've recorded is different. Best practice has always been to plan for the worst and hope for the best. What I mean is, hope you get two strikes out of a given area but pray you never find out." Despite every fiber in her body screaming *No!,* she looked deeply into Tweeker's eyes, "Understood?"

Tweeker nodded then asked a second question, "The energy and kinetics you've mentioned the suits use, where does it come from?"

Taylor, appreciative of the intellectual discourse she hadn't thought the heavily-muscled soldier was capable of, responded with a smile, "From you."

Noting the incredulous looks she confided, "There are sensors in high friction areas such as the soles of your boots, between the thighs, and your armpits. These sensors function much like the Hoover Dam. They collect the energy and convert it to a usable form before it's allocated to fit the KtacS needs."

After a moment of silence, in which everyone attempted to digest all they had been told, Taylor looked to Dane, "You've been quiet, Commander. Surely there's something you'd like to know?"

Dane thought of his son and wife and prayed they were somewhere safe. He also prayed for the strength to help ensure their safety, and wondered if he'd ever see them again. Silently, he looked to the men sitting around him and the expectant eyes peering down from the stage, before asking, "Yeah, when can we get started?"

***

**2100**

After Dr. Taylor wrapped up her class, Dax and his men helped the new guys into their suits for the first time. It only took a second for Dane to realize the suit would definitely take some getting used to. Just as quickly, and after only a few steps, he began to feel a subtle spring with each footfall.

*Reverb.*

"Alright, guys, here's the deal," began Nguyen from the passenger seat of a 4x4 pickup. He took a pull of his beer, "There's only one way to become familiar enough with the KtacS to become a competent operator in a hazardous environment. That's through testing yourself and this new piece of equipment, simultaneously. It's a time honored tradition that you slug it out on SKUL's obstacle course as your first experience with the KtacS." Dax pointed down the dark beach currently being pounded by waves from an

118

offshore storm, "The O-course is four miles away. You've got thirty-two minutes. We'll see you there."

Dane, Tweeker, Toad and Hammer all shared looks that said, *Dude, you've gotta be kidding.*

"Is there a problem, gentlemen?" asked Cobra's TL in a perturbed tone.

"Negative, sir!" shouted the four guys in unison.

"Well, get moving!" Nguyen bellowed as the truck launched down the beach and spewed sand back in their direction.

They took off at a run in the wake of the speeding truck. The first few minutes were difficult for each man. They had to focus on finishing in the allotted time while wearing what amounted to an exoskeleton. Dane set the pace with Tweeker and Hammer close behind. Toad, who had never been a strong runner, was further back.

After the first mile, however, all four settled in and began to eat away at the distance.

In between breaths, Tweeker asked, "You guys feel any spring back?"

"Yeah...maybe," Hammer puffed.

From behind, Toad spoke between huffs, "Ain't nothing cool about this shit.
I...Ain't...Built...For...Running."

Dane called over his shoulder, "Well then, shut up, and keep putting one foot in front of the other."

"Roger..." big breath "...Boss."

Seeing his old friend struggling more than the others, Dane gave a nod to Tweeker and fell back. The nod from Dane was the only thing that kept Tweeker from falling back as well. Both men knew Toad had no quit in him, knew he would go until he died, but they also knew he was about half their size. The added weight of the KtacS would eat at anyone - it was getting to them, in fact - and neither man wanted to leave anyone alone with their thoughts tonight. As such, Tweeker and Hammer took the lead. They smoked the run while Dane and Toad managed to make it in time.

*Barely.*

But, they finished…together.

"We sure appreciate you gentlemen deciding to join us," said Dax to the two late-comers. "How about you both drop and knock out fifty pushups before we continue?" He reached into the bed of the truck and pulled two rucksacks filled with bricks. He tossed them on the sand at their feet. They had to weigh a hundred pounds each. "Do the fifty with those on your back."

Dane and Toad hit the deck, and Dax introduced the others to the O-course. "Gentlemen, welcome to SKUL's obstacle course, your hell away from home. The course runs in a rough straight line and is composed of twenty stations. Each station is set in between the sand dunes stretched out before you. You'll find the usual suspects here. We have dips, tires, wall climbs, cargo net climbs, ropes swings, and tons of other shit that culminates in a five story climb to a rappelling station. Beyond that, you simply gotta sprint, balls out, to the finish. Be forewarned, the dunes themselves are a bitch and do nothing but add to what's already a whole lotta suck. A whole lotta suck you must complete within thirty minutes."

Dane and Toad finished pounding out the fifty pushups. Though they were smoked, they stood tall. Tall being relative in Toad's case.

Dax smiled and said rather evilly, "Starting now."

The truck sped off into the night with Dax yelling over his shoulder, "See you at the finish line…don't be late!"

*** 

Later that night in the barracks, Dane, Tweeker, and Toad talked quietly, trying not to wake up Jed and Twitch.

"Dude, Dax wasn't kidding about the amount of suck built into that O-course," observed an exhausted Toad.

"No shit, Sherlock. Figured that all by yourself, did you?" quipped Tweeker before he turned to Dane. "What's your take on the suits, Boss?"

Before he could answer, Twitch rolled over. Seeing his comrades covered in sand and sweat, he said simply, "O-course."

It wasn't a question.

Toad grunted and to Tweeker said, "And, you call me Sherlock?"

This brought a smile from the big Nordic.

Twitch just shook his head and, in his stoned voice, said, "Gets worse, bro. But, we'll all be there with you next time."

Tweeker half-growled, "Yeah well, bring that shit on, bro."

Dane grinned. The comment by and large defined Tweeker on a cellular level.

"Boss?" The big Nordic turned to his team leader. "Yeah?"

"The suits. What did you think?"

"Shit man, I dunno. I definitely felt a little extra spring in my step on the outset. By the end, though, it was pretty much suck city as usual. You?"

Tweeker shrugged, "Not enough sugar for the dime, man."

"Your ass won't be saying that when you're up against some savage," commented Jed harshly. He was more than a little irritated at being woken up. He rolled over, using his elbow as a prop on his cot, "You chuckleheads don't know jack yet. These suits are your lifeline, the only leg-up on a savage you'll have in a fight, and you *know nothings* are sitting around analyzing the shit.

Don't.

Suit up, hunt, and kill. Bottom line.

These things are damned near unstoppable and only care about inflicting pain and causing chaos. You've just scratched the surface on this deal, and you've already formed an opinion. Well, here's mine: You're wasting time talking about shit you don't even know about, and I'm missing out on sleep having to listen to your incoherent babbling. Now shut the hell up and get some damned sleep!"

From the darkness came a poorly executed John Wayne imitation, "I think that we owe a big round of applause to our newest, bestest buddy, and big toe... Sergeant Hulka."

It was Dane poking fun at Jed's little hard-lined speech.

"Stripes," called out Twitch. "Too damned easy, bro."

"Ward..." sounded Toad in an overly whiny rendition of June Cleaver.

"...don't you think you were a little hard on the Beaver?"

Childish giggling began to crescendo from all parts of the dark sleeping quarters.

"Leave it to..."

"Dammit, Twitch, who doesn't know that?" yelled Jed across the pitch black room.   He rolled over and put his back to the others while mumbling *Assholes* just loud enough for all to hear.  But, even Jed was laughing now.  The snickering had become barely controlled by this time, and all that was needed for the room to become nothing more than a bunch of twelve year old boys at a sleepover was a gentle nudge.

That's when Tweeker ripped off a monstrous fart.

"Idiots," Jed, still smiling, said past a yawn.

The guys told stories and shared laughs until late in the night.

# 9)
## Lessons

### The Bixby Classroom
### 0800, Day 2

The new guys had been warned the platoon's PT would be as demanding as any they'd been a part of in their career. Those men had certainly not been lying. In fact, they may have been downplaying just how demanding the smoke sessions would be. The platoon-wide PT had been led by none other than Colonel Gholar along with the other full time C-school staffers, all former SKUL operators in their own right. Those men, older than the oldest active Whiskey operator – Jed, cruised through the workout with ease. Sweaty and gritty though they may have been, they wore wide smiles through every second of torment they dished out.

They were inhuman...demented.

Minute by sadistic minute, the men veritably chewed up every member of Whiskey platoon and spit them out slowly, man by man, along the beach. It didn't take long for the cadre to turn the operators' arms and legs to jelly, smoking them beyond measure, and still the SKUL instructors demanded more. They demanded more of their charges. They demanded more of themselves, as well.

This was a pride thing as much as it was a PT session. The men had to know who was in charge.

As bad as it seemed, if the operators enduring the torment were honest with themselves, the cadre demanded just what they all craved.

*More.*

Dane had spent his entire military career around men who took the worst that life had to offer and supped upon each bitter spoonful, only to smile before asking for seconds.

The men operating within SKUL's ranks were no different.

*Why would they be? They were all cut from the same cloth.*

After morning PT, Whiskey enjoyed a hearty breakfast in the SEE-S cafeteria. These few minutes of unmolested leisure allowed Dane to review the days schedule and make sure everyone on his team understood where they needed to be and when. They were grown men, but at the end of the day, any screwup reflected on Dane as their team leader.

Came with the territory.

According to the schedule uploaded to his SICS, the new guys were in for more classroom studies in the Bixby room early. There, they would receive an introduction regarding the helmet – an integral and integrated part of their KtacS – and its various nuances. Dane knew this would be his last, best chance to ensure everyone was playing from the same sheet of music.

Once breakfast was over, they'd simply be too busy.

That afternoon, after the classroom work and lunch, the men of the platoon would separate into their various specialties. There, among others with similar educational backgrounds, they would discuss specific subject matters and later, conduct exercises. Other than the morning PT, this would be the first time the new guys would work with SKUL's more seasoned shooters. This would be the first time they would be able to show the experienced guys in

SKUL what they knew, what they could do. Toad would hit the sniper course. Tweeker would head out with the combat medics. Twitch, the team point man, breacher, and explosives expert – although the latter had been a highly debated and contested issue for some time – would hook up with the men from the other teams to review breaching techniques. They'd also experiment with new ideas.

Twitch always had new ideas for the use of explosives.

Everyone was nervous about this part of the training evolution.

They would also review and perfect every lock-picking technique known to man and invent a few as of yet, unknown to man.

Jed, as the assistant team leader, had arguably the most demanding and stressful job of anyone – including the team leader. He had to know every other man's role, and be prepared to take up their slack should any teammate be taken out during an operation. Simply speaking, Jed was the team's jack-of-all-trades, a position he thrived in. He also served as the team's jump-master, a position he'd held even before SKUL. As a senior NCO, Blackmoor had logged more jumps than any other active shooter in the Unit, though it was probably more like any other person on the planet.

The man loved to jump out of planes.

He was at peace in the air, alone, with only the roar of the wind for company.

Conversely, Tweeker would serve as the team's dive-master. The right man for the right job, Ansil's initial SEAL billet was with SDVT-1 where he logged more dive time than any three other SEALs. He held a similar position within DEVGRU so he was a natural fit this team.

There was a difference though.

For Jed, this was *old hat* stuff, but Tweeker did not yet understand the equipment nor its capabilities. He would need even more classroom work regarding the alternate KtacS suit used for dive operations.

*More.*

Rounding out the team was Dane. He and the other TL's would bone up on intel gathering, mission planning, and tactical execution. A lot of weight was placed on the proper delivery of succinct yet complete pre-op briefings. The same could be said for the subsequent after-action reports. It sounded like a simple matter, but as anyone with experience could attest to, that could not be further from the truth.

But, that was later in the day, and worrying about that any more than necessary would do no one any good. Right now, it was just the new guys staring down the barrel of the proverbial loaded gun. They had to learn everything there was to learn about the helmets and become comfortable operating in the enclosed environment they created.

And, they had to do it *quickly*.

The savages were not waiting on them to get it right, nor was SKUL's leadership.

*Do it once. Do it right*...that was their mantra. It was a mindset of expectations Dane and every member of SKUL – along with the special operations community at large – took very, very seriously.

Those that didn't were shown the door.

The Bixby Room's door blasted open, and another operator walked purposefully across the stage to the podium. He looked across the room at the sweaty, grimy operators and grinned.

"I see Colonel Gholar led this morning's PT session?"

The room erupted with a rousing round of *fuck you's*.

The man at the podium laughed deeply, "Been there. It gets better but not for a while." The operator paused and looked to the syllabus he'd created for the class before continuing, "Anyway guys, I'm Rod Baker, but everyone calls me Doughboy which I hope is because of my last name, and not because I'm fat."

It had to have been the name, considering the dude looked like he had been chiseled out of granite.

Doughboy smiled again, yet the room remained silent, the irony missed by the men he spoke to.

"Right," slightly off-put by his icebreaker missing its mark, Doughboy cleared his throat. "So anyway, it's my job to get you guys up to speed on how to use your helmets as quickly as possible. I believe in a hands-on approach; so, get up here, and let's dive in."

The guys stepped up to the stage and each grabbed the piece of headgear with their last name taped to it.

Doughboy unsnapped two levers on his personal helmet. "The buckles here and here," he pointed to two levers embedded within the shell of the helmet, "open the helmet enough for most to slide it over their head. We've had a few guys with gigantic noggins who have to have their gear custom fitted, but I don't see anyone here with a mutant melon. So, we should be cool. Once on, these smaller dials here..."

He pointed to two very small dials on either side of the helmet near where the ear would be.

"...are for fine-tuning the fit."

Dane ran his hands over the helmet, "I'm assuming there's an oxygen feed of some sort?"

Doughboy's head made a comical circling motion. It wasn't a *yes* nod or a *no* shake.

"Yes and no. Under normal conditions, you'll breathe through the filtered respirators there." The senior man pointed to the front face of the helmet. "If a mission requires HALO or HAHO insertion, you'll be equipped with a bailout kit with two hours plus of oxygen carrying capacity. The kit attaches directly to the respirator on the front face. Once you're on the ground, you simply ditch the kit and rock on to the target."

He pointed to the front of the helmet's face mask again, "You can speak through those as well, but the helmet digitizes your voice. Sounds like shit, but you can't trace it. When we go in, we go in quiet, and communications are handled internally. As a rule, there's typically not a hostage situation; so, we've spent more research dollars in areas other than external communications. The long and short of it is you're gonna sound like a robot, but you'll get used to it. Big thing is, there's no biometrics system in the world that can accurately thread your voice out of the KtacS digitized maelstrom."

Dane remembered the voices he heard the day he was picked up and nodded.

"Other than that, we have specialized suits and helmets for missions requiring underwater."

Dane looked to Tweeker who nodded, "I'm already on it, Boss. A PowerPoint is sitting on my SICS, and I already have some dive time on the books. Once I'm ready, me and Rabelo will bring you guys up to speed.

Rabelo was Foxtrot platoon's senior dive master.

"There won't be any trouble with competencies." The big Nordic may have a hard dick with no internal monologue, but he was a consummate warrior, and Dane trusted him explicitly. Ansil turned to Hammer, "I've already got it squared away with *higher*. You're with us during dive training, bro."

Hammer nodded by way of reply, happy to be getting his dive training from former SEALs.

Doughboy then took up the conversation again, "Having said all that, the real cool stuff is on the inside. Get your helmets on and check out what we call Retinal Recognition Technology or *RRT* for short."

The guys slid the helmets on and, after a moment of clumsiness, got them buckled and dialed in. The telltale whining noise, indicating the helmets were booting up, began as Doughboy explained, "Helmet turns on and off automatically with the buckles. Crank 'em down; helmet engages and vice versa. Right now, your goggles should be blacked out with only two small green dots in the center. I need you guys to stare into those spots without blinking for a few seconds."

"Why?" asked Dane in an uncertain voice.

Doughboy explained, "At its base level, the helmet is a biometric chamber. Right now, it is mapping facial landmarks, gathering cardiac dynamics, and scanning your retinas. When this is finished…" He visually checked that each man's helmet was secure then added with a chuckle, "…well, you'll see."

After about ten seconds of silence, Toad exclaimed in a nondescript, metallic voice that lurched from the respirators, "Holy shit!"

Doughboy laughed, "Damn right, bro. That's some high speed shit sitting on your heads. You're looking at a souped up version of a *head-up display*. You can control everything you see on your displays with just your eyes. It's decades ahead of anything in the military or private sector. To illustrate my point, you see the little blinking cursor in the center of your goggles? Grab it and click the *daylight* tab on the top right of the screen."

"Grab it?" Hammer asked incredulously, "How?"

"With your eyes. Just look at it and move it to where you want then hover."

Seconds later, Hammer mumbled in shock, "Damn."

A sentiment obviously shared by them all.

"Yeah," Doughboy agreed, "Damn." He allowed them to look around the room for a minute or two before beginning again. "Okay, so you've experienced the basic function of the system, but there's a lot more to it than that. You guys see those tabs on the right? *Daylight, Night, Thermal, Infrared,* and *Fusion?* The first four you should be familiar with. Fused visual, however, is a specialized optics system developed by one of our contract companies. FVS, as it's called, blends – or fuses if you will – daylight, night, thermal, and IR vision seamlessly. The result is a reproducible image that can be utilized in the worst situation possible when battling savages – the dark. Again, this only swings the pendulum back to our favor slightly as werewolves have visual capabilities that allow them to see in the dark as well as our body heat."

Offhandedly, and nearly to himself though he certainly didn't mean it to seem that way, he added, "Thankfully, the KtacS negates most of that...most of it."

After a moment of reflection, he continued, "Anyway, forget thermal *blobs* with no real shape. Definition and clarity is the name of the game here, daytime or night, and you will not find a more advanced visual system on the planet."

Perfunctorily, Doughboy added, "On top of that, you'll receive the subject's vitals – heart rate, body temp and the like – in real time. This may be the most important aspect of the helmet. Anyone know why?"

Dane thought back to the savages he saw gunned down outside the bar, Chotard Landing. He remembered the information the Admiral wanted to know just after the soldiers had dusted the savages. Like puzzle pieces, the conversation fell into place, finally making sense, "Somehow, this tells you whether or not the person in your sights is a savage or not. I'm not sure of exact numbers, but I know dogs in general have a higher body temp and heart rate when compared to humans. I'd imagine werewolves aren't any different."

"Damn dude," admired Doughboy, "so, you're the one that smoked the savage that was going to end Meadows?"

Dane nodded but remained quiet.

"Strong work," said Doughboy before returning to the lesson. "Commander Stackwell is correct on all accounts. The average body temp of a savage is around two hundred fifty degrees with a resting heart rate of two hundred plus beats per minute. It's thought the drastic change in body function coupled with a metabolism locked in hyperdrive lends to their insanity, but who really knows? I just kill 'em."

For the next few minutes, the guys worked on controlling the cursor with their eyes which was more difficult than it seemed. Here and there, Doughboy would offer advice when an operator became frustrated until, eventually, everyone began to get a little more comfortable with the system. "Guys, it's important to remember that your SICS device can control the RRT system. That's what the docking port is for. Some guys never really get the hang of the helmet's functionality and choose to use the SICS on their forearm instead. Hey, I'll admit, when things are going to shit, sometimes it's just easier to punch a button than get your eyes in the right spot, but it's there guys. RRT can and will save your ass if you let it, understand?"

Everyone nodded as they continued to work with the RRT system.

"Another thing to know, and no one likes it, but everyone understands its importance, is this. Everything your goggles see, they record – every missed shot, poor judgment, loss of composure, or torn apart teammate and civilian."

This brought raised eyebrows from the guys and more than one grumble of discontent that sounded a lot like *Dude, what the fuck.* Doughboy raised his hand in placation, "Hey guys, I get it. I do; but, every piece of data we can get on these savages is worth the minor discomfort of having *Big Brother* looking over our shoulder, savvy?"

The guys nodded, but it wasn't exactly enthusiastically.

"Okay," the operator from Foxtrot said. Changing tact, he flipped the lights off plunging the room into darkness, "Switch to FVS mode, and let's check the cool shit out..."

\*\*\*

## The Range
## 1430, Day 2

"Cease fire! Cease fire!" exclaimed Darren Trucks, call sign *Smooth*, over the heavy *clap clap clap* of automatic gunfire. For the next several minutes, he fervently glassed the targets down range before lowering his binoculars, "Weapons safe!"

It was a command, not a request.

Down the shooting line came confirmation from the operators that their weapons were, in fact, safe.

"Outstanding job, guys. Okay, you old fucks are dismissed to IST." Smooth was referring to *Individual Specialty Training.* "FNGs, you're with me for the rest of the day. Take a minute to get hydrated, and I'll see you guys back at the shed."

Smooth, a native Californian and former West coast SEAL, looked the part of both SEAL and surfer to a dictionary definition. Tall and lean with a copper tan, he

135

sported a wavy mop of sun-bleached, blond hair, and used *bro* and *dude* enough in his vernacular to cement the preconceived stereotype he'd been branded with. Dane knew Smooth from his time with the Teams as a straight shooter, an eager mentor to the younger guys, a solid operator, and an absolute lady killer. Before Dane could stand up Section 8, Smooth disappeared off the grid. Everyone naturally assumed he had been billeted for DEVGRU's selection and assessment program known as Green Team, but even those guys were still around...still *visible*. SKUL and the soldiers operating under its shield were different. They didn't maintain former military ties; they severed them. They became ghosts, memories.

They were simply *gone*.

The *shed*, as Smooth called it, was nothing more than a small, one room classroom of cinderblocks cooled by a window unit AC. Once their break was over, they began learning about the more exotic weapons at SKUL's disposal.

"Good job out there today, guys," Smooth began. "The ballistics can get a little funky with these silver rounds, but by the time you rotate out of C-school, you'll have them dialed in."

Smooth reached into one of the many weapons lockers lining the room and started pulling out some weaponry.

These *killing irons* had long ago lost all form of compliance and adopted a far more apt dress.

That of the felonious.

"We're about to talk about some of the most righteous pieces of savage-killing artillery available to you

136

guys. We'll flesh out their effective ranges and the environments they are best suited; so, get out your pencils and wheel books. It's note taking time."

Tweeker ran a finger along the barrel of what appeared to be a shotgun – if the shotgun had been working out for months and pumped full of steroids, that is.

"Damn, this thing's a bad looking mofo."

"Damn right it is, bro, and its capabilities more than fit your description," expounded Smooth. "It's called the *Capone*. The first prototype was a drum fed apparatus that resembled an old Tommy gun, hence the name. While absolutely deadly in a fight, the fucker was too heavy and bulky to be much use. Still though, seeing how that thing could effectively neutralize an entire pack of savages in the blink of an eye, the good folks in R and D put their heads together and came up with a solution. That solution is what you see here, the modern day Capone. Doesn't look anything like its ancestor, but that doesn't make it any less badass. It's a semi-auto weapon bored out to fire a wide array of eight gauge rounds. The Capone can sling pretty much anything from flechette to Puffer rounds downrange with sickening consequences for the savages in its line of sight. With a five round tube, the Capone can unload a round a second, raining maximum firepower in a minimum of time. In short, this sonavabitch will make a savage tuck its tail, grab its dick, and get the fuck out of dodge."

Toad, always fussing with ballistics, brought back a little levity to the conversation by asking, "What kinda range are we talking here, Smooth?"

"Good question," replied the Foxtrot instructor. He laid out several big eight gauge rounds that, to the untrained eye, would have more closely resembled a Cuban cigar. "You want them inside of a hundred meters, but each flechette round holds over forty silver projectiles. Trust me when I say you can completely decimate a target...*instantly*."

"Sounds too good to be true, Smooth," Dane observed pointedly. "Downsides?"

Smooth nodded, "Limited environments of use. Nine times in ten you guys are going to be hitting targets in urban environments, and you can't very well be firing off these things with nothing between you and a family of innocents but a wall of sheetrock and wood paneling. Considering what I just said, let's talk *Puffers*. As far as they go, you're basically lobbing them out of the Capone; so, you can lay down an effective silver mist out to roughly three hundred meters."

Smooth laid three familiar-looking, yet not quite right, hand grenades out on the table.

"They're called Puffers for a reason," he began. "No explosion, and no human-killing shrapnel. You just pull the pin and toss, or shuck and shoot if you're flinging them out of the Capone. Things act like a smoke bomb, effectively coating – and killing – any savage within a circumference of approximately twenty meters. You want to see a savage sizzle, then the Puffer is for you. Down side is wind. A decent wind can shift your killing field away from your target. Make sense so far?"

Everyone nodded.

"Any more questions?"

138

There were none.

"Right, well, let's hit the range again. This time with the Capone." Smooth flashed a toothy smile, "You guys are going to freakin' love this thing."

*** 

**Bixby Classroom**
**Day 3**

Dr. Monica Taylor was back to present a lecture on SKUL's history and past operations – considered capstone events within SKUL's ranks – along with everything they knew regarding their enemy. The Dude was present to give the guys a visual but, by and large, it was another belligerent beating provided by PowerPoint presentation.

Finally, after several hours of monotony, they were given a break in the lecture. Everyone took a few minutes to hit the head, refill water bottles, or just turn their brains off for a moment.

"Ya'll want to head on back in and get this thing started early?" asked Dane to the others after a several minutes.

"Better yet," Hammer handed Dane his sidearm, an HK45 Tactical, "just shoot me in the head, bro."

"Yeah, I know, this shit's a real dick-dragger, but we ain't gotta like it..."

"Yeah, yeah, we just gotta do it." He took the pistol back from Dane and smiled, "You SEALs and your fucking sayings."

Dane shrugged as if to say *I have no idea what you're talking about.* To the others he turned, "Ya'll ready to get this junk behind us or what?"

139

"Lead the way, Boss," begged Tweeker. Toad was already pushing the door to the classroom open.

Taylor, as she was prone to do, began by asking if anyone had any questions.

"Dr. Taylor, is any of the accepted information correct?" asked Hammer. "What I'm specifically asking about is the moon. Does a full moon play any role in the lives of these things like it does in the stories?"

"That is a very good question, Sergeant Wilcox," began Taylor. "Unfortunately, yet again, we really don't have any hard facts, only theories; but, several decades' worth of experience tends to say we have the subject pinned down pretty well. We have a pretty good idea that it takes a full moon to complete the change in young werewolves. Also, as the nights move closer to the turning of a full moon, the more powerful, insane, and out of control younger werewolves tend to be. All werewolves react to the moon this way, though older werewolves are able to control their cravings far better. This is pretty much the source of the perceived weirdness on the nights of full moons. Young werewolves typically become consumed by the madness around full moons and draw our attention. For that reason, most werewolves, luckily, never make it more than a year or two before they are exterminated. Older werewolves, those who have managed some sense of control over their cravings, are far more dangerous. They have mastered the moon's call, can change at any time – day or night, and tend to be far more calculating when on the hunt for food. They don't stand out nor draw attention to themselves even during nights of a full moon; and, they are infinitely more powerful.

If the power a young werewolf possesses equates to a drop of water, the power of an older werewolf is that of Niagara Falls."

Dane cleared his throat to grab Taylor's attention, "Dr. Taylor, the day I was picked up we made contact with and killed several savages."

Dane's brows knitted together as he thought back to that day and what he had seen.

"Yes, Commander Stackwell?" asked Dr. Taylor, curious to know what was troubling the operator and keen to urge him to voice his thoughts.

"Well, ma'am, they *changed*...back to their human form. And, they bled green. I guess what I'm getting at is, one, why is The Dude still in wolf form, and the others changed back to their human form. Secondly, what's up with the green blood?"

Taylor thrummed her knuckles on the podium and collected her thoughts. A moment later, she began, "Excellent questions, Commander, but let me answer in reverse. All werewolves bleed green. Theories abound as to why, but the strongest of these – and the one I personally place stock in – is that it's not blood, but *ichor*, the lifeblood of the immortals. Many books on Greek, Roman and Norse mythology mention ichor. In some places it's gold in color and in others, green. As far as why the werewolves you came in contact with changed back to human form versus what you see here, I can't offer much more than theories. The strongest and most accepted being that the werewolves you mention were most likely what we've come to know as *Lesser Wolves*. In modern terms, they are, quite literally, the runts of the litter. A more accurate description is that they are newly turned werewolves – relatively speaking – and they've developed none of the *gifts* a more mature werewolf possesses. Whether or not werewolves in general, and specifically Lesser Wolves, are what we would call immortal is unknown at this point, but it's highly probable. Either way, they certainly age at a much slower rate than we do. What all that means is those werewolves are still much closer to being human than truly demonic, hence they change back to their natural form. *True Wolves* are just the opposite. Each has mastered at least one gift given to them by the one that turned them and can change into what is accepted as a *werewolfian* form. It's also theorized that the older, more accomplished savages can take other forms as well. A lot of theory, I know, but understand this. Regardless of True Wolf or Lesser, these things are unquestionably powerful, and their hunger is sated only by feeding off pain."

Silent...the room was silent...for a long while.

Finally...

"Dr. Taylor, you mentioned *gifts,*" the question was from Tweeker.

He and Dane had had their talk, and Dane had made it clear he was to get his dick out of the way of his focus. Still though, Dane was nervous.

*Please keep it in your pants, bro,* he found himself thinking.

Ignorant to his TL's thoughts though lost in his own, Tweeker studied the elongated canines of the Dude. He stood abruptly and was surprised to find himself face to face with Monica Taylor. Honestly, it was more like face to

142

pectorals. Quickly, realizing she had moved like a ninja into his personal space, she stepped back blushing.

Tweeker cleared his throat, suddenly uncomfortable under the stares of his colleagues, "What exactly do you mean by gifts?"

Taylor, now in control of her faculties, spoke with a flat voice that carried all the inflection of a judge delivering a death sentence; which in some ways, maybe that's what she was doing. It was a worried voice, a concerned voice, "Werewolves, on the whole, are indelibly linked to the Earth, none more so than a True Wolf. They're basically elemental beings. As such, they are capable of controlling the very building blocks of nature – earth, fire, air, water – to varying degrees, depending on age and mastery. Unfortunately, they do so with a strong bend toward destruction and chaos. The Dude definitely controlled fire, and we believe he may have been able to control other forces as well."

Tweeker gave Taylor a strange look.

That of fear.

He was seriously hoping she was kidding. Seeing no humor on her face, he gulped and looked to the others in the room. The same thought went through each operator's mind at nearly the same time. That singular thought was simple, succinct...and primal.

*Oh fuck.*

## 10)
## Beat Downs and Bloody Noses

**Hand-to-hand combat training**
**1300, Day 21**

"Gentlemen, name's Rusty Burgess, call sign, Buster. Let me be the first to welcome you to your third week of C-school," said the boulder of a man standing akimbo – hands at the hips – before the platoon. Buster, a black man standing about six feet tall and weighing around one hundred and eighty pounds, looked as hard as stone with ropey knots of muscle covering his entire body. Spread along his visible skin was a mix of tattoos ranging from skulls and crosses of various types to a cigar-smoking bulldog complete with a drill instructor's campaign cover. Buster wore combat boots, olive drab shorts and T-shirt, and his eyes were shadowed by a pressed and peaked utility cover pulled low over his heavy brow. One side of his face bulged from a wad of tobacco the size of a grape fruit. To complete the look, he spoke overly loud and clear, using the choppy speak of a drill sergeant.

It was easy for everyone to imagine him screaming at the top of his lungs, *You. Will. Get. Over. That...insert any obstacle, anywhere on the planet, that no sane human would ever attempt to climb, crawl under or run through here*...mere inches from your nose, flinging tobacco laced spittle all over your face.

*Marine,* Dane thought. *Only a knuckle-dragging jarhead can make every single word its own command.*

"You're here to hone your hand-to-hand skills, but let's be honest. If you're down to grappling with a savage, you're hard-fucked like an inmate at shower time." He

145

looked over the platoon and allowed those words to sink. After a moment's pause, "Still, it cannot be overlooked that the first mission in SKUL's history ended only after one of the operators skull drug the savage with a solid silver hatchet. Those padded sticks over there," he thumbed over his shoulder in the direction of a wooden box that contained hundreds of padded sticks, "that's what we'll train with. We can't very well have you turning each other's heads into a canoe with your issued scalp taker."

Briefly, Dane thought about those silver tomahawks to which Buster referred, issued to every SKUL operator upon graduation of C-school. Most active operators carried at least one as a tertiary weapon system, a practice which indeed dated back to that first mission.

Buster's voice brought him out of his revelry, "I need two volunteers for a demonstration."

Jed was on his feet and moving to the box of sticks before Buster had put the period on his sentence. Tweeker was rummaging through the box just as quickly. This training block was a platoon-wide evolution, and there wasn't an operator in the room who didn't cut their eyes to the man on either side of them.

Twitch just shook his head while mumbling something unintelligibly about *needing a medic.*

Satisfied with their choice of training weapons, each gave ground to their respective edges of the training mat. While Tweeker held a single, padded stick in his left hand, thus leaving his right free for punching, Jed chose to wield a stick in each hand. The seasoned operator bounced lightly on the balls of his feet, knees bent, eager to get started. Other

146

than skydiving, this was Jed's stress reliever...*fighting*. He was a master practitioner of multiple martial arts forms, including Krav Maga and Brazilian Jiu-Jitsu, and knew dozens of incapacitating pressure points. He was, quite literally, death's beating heart.

Buster handed a set of padded headgear to Tweeker who looked at it with disdain. He had at least six inches and close to fifty pounds on the older man plus he was a Navy Seal *by God*...protective equipment be *damned*.

He waved Buster away growling, "Get that crap out of my face."

Buster shrugged as if to say *your funeral, dude* before he turned and walked to Jed's side. He did not offer Blackmoor the headgear but mumbled where Tweeker could not hear, "Don't do anything permanent."

Jed, bouncing lightly like he was jumping rope without the rope, grinned evilly, "No promises."

Buster walked back to the center of the mat, clapped his hands, and yelled, "Go!"

Tweeker slid quickly to the right in an attempt to flank his opponent. Jed countered quickly by stabbing his left foot firmly, and closed his body off to attack. With little-to-no effort, he was in front of Tweeker's assault.

Tweeker bounced safely away.

The move was meant to judge the older operator's quickness, and now he knew he would have to be on his game.

"You sure you want some of this, old man?" Ansil taunted as he shifted left.

147

Sure they were about to witness an epic battle, the seated operators held their breath collectively.

Jed shrugged his shoulders at the question, "Sure. Why not? I guess I just always wanted a question answered."

"Oh?" Tweeker nearly came to a stop, thrown off balance by his opponent's blasé attitude, "Oh yeah…what's that?"

Jed smiled. It was a wicked smile, mirthless and full of chill, that did nothing but egg his opponent on, "Well, I know a shit stain stinks to high heaven, but does it bleed? Guess I'll finally find out."

Tweeker, incensed, snarled like a wounded animal as he lunged at Jed.

*** 

The fight was over nearly as quickly as it began. Two minutes, on the outside, which truthfully was a very liberal time estimation. Tweeker rolled off the mat with a groan and looked for all the world like he had just been run through a meat grinder. Blood poured through the fingers of the hand he held over his nose.

"I think that old fucker broke my nose," he complained. It came out sounding more like *Ah fink fat oldh phluker bwoke mah noe* though.

Toad sputtered, "Yeah, that looked like a total dick-dragger, dude."

Twitch added to Tweeker's ire by observing nonchalantly, "Next time, maybe you should try to do something different than breaking Jed's hands with your face."

Tweeker snorted a laugh but was stopped short by pain, "Asshole may have broken a rib." Again it sounded distorted through the blood and snot.

"Or, using your body to cushion his blows," Twitch added absentmindedly.

"Fuck you, you damned hippy." Tweeker groaned, "Least I had the balls to get in there with that sadistic bastard."

"May have been ballsy...*maybe*," observed Dane, "but it was definitely stupid."

"Piss on you...ow." Tweeker, in a matter of seconds, had been reduced to the dictionary definition of a pulp of meat.

Buster was smiling brightly. Apparently, he walked a bit on the sadistic side as well.

*Marines*, Dane thought again, *God bless them.*

"Okay, the rest of you guys pair up, and let's get started." He looked back toward Tweeker as everyone stood, "Lattimore, you need some time to get yourself unfucked?"

Tweeker groaned with one hand on his side and the other cupping his nose, "How's a week sound?"

"Like a Navy puke's excuse." Buster bellowed at the top of his lungs, "You have exactly one second to un-ass yourself from the floor and partner up. I'd suggest the headgear on the next go-round."

Tweeker jumped to his feet flinging blood in all directions, "Aye aye, sir!"

"Judas titty-twisting Priest!" Buster bawled. "Belay that order, Lattimore, and get your ass to the med wing."

\*\*\*

149

## The Resort
## Day 27

The Resort, as it was known to those within SKUL's ranks, was a collection of eight peripheral kill rooms spread out from a central, five story weapons training facility like the spokes of a wagon wheel. The entire twenty acres was set inside double fences. Each fence was ten feet tall and topped with razor wire. Guard towers, positioned at every corner and every one hundred yards in between, were manned twenty-four hours a day, seven days a week. Additionally, roving patrols of SKUL's ultra-secretive Wraith platoon walked the Resort's fences on a schedule known only to one person on the planet – Colonel Alvin Gholor, Commander of SEE-S.

It was, quite literally, the most elaborate, most technologically advanced, and most sadistic series of kill rooms on planet Earth.

It was also the least known and most secure.

Bottom line…no one on the planet outside of SKUL, the Joint Chiefs, and the President knew the first thing about the island codenamed Tortuga. Even less knew of the Resort.

The kill rooms – called KR-alpha through KR-theta, respectively – contained moveable walls that enabled the operators thousands of different scenarios to train on. These KR's were equipped with unique, silhouetted targets integrated with sound sensitive, stop-motion projectors. These rooms were where SKUL's live fire CQB training occurred.

As completely mind blowing as the peripheral kill rooms were, it was the central building, colloquially known as the *Den*, that amped up the training a thousand fold and made it stand alone in the world of close quarter combat training. Every recorded mission – thousands of operations dating all the way back to SKUL's inception in 1975 – had been turned over to a private company specializing in computer imaging and animation. With a budget augmented by silver bullion complements of mines owned by SKUL, the company invented, tested, and reinvented CGI technology dozens of times over. The developing engineers and bill-paying bean counters called it *COMSEP* or Computerized Sensory Perception. Decades from now, when the science finally filtered into the gaming world, it would be called *revolutionary*.

Today, however, SKUL shooters just called it *bad ass*.

COMSEP was an interactive, three-dimensional hologram pumped into every operator's head-up display that produced the next best thing to real world combat ops against werewolves. The speed, strength, and agility of werewolves in downloadable form and with very, very real consequences.

The Den was five stories of suck, five stories of discomfort, confusion and pain.

When training within the Den, the operators wore a series of electrodes capable of delivering three hundred joules of electricity, enough to effectively start a heart.

Or, stop it.

The Den was like a game of Laser Tag – if the weapons and equipment already had a foul attitude and subsequently been pumped full of steroids. The operators working within its walls of sadism had a very finite amount of time – mere seconds – to enter a room or hallway, identify the targets, and make the decision to engage or not. Any mistake – too long to engage, missed shot, the shooting of a hostage versus a savage – any mistake at all, resulted in the entire team receiving an incapacitating shock compliments of those damnable electrodes. It didn't matter who made the mistake, everyone on the team paid the penalty. There wasn't a SKUL operator alive who did not remember his first shock – or any of the others, for that matter – giving reason enough for everyone to concentrate on the task at hand.

And now, Dane's team was at the door ready to make entry into the Den. They had three *targets* to take down that were holding anywhere from five to seven humans as hostages. As assistant team leader, it was Jed's job – among a thousand others – to keep a head count and assess team readiness prior to the executing the mission. He looked the guys over and noted they were in position before giving Dane a quick nod of confirmation. Dane, who knelt with a hand on Twitch's shoulder, gave a slight squeeze. The team's internal comm unit sounded with their TL's voice, "Execute!"

A split second later the door lock picked by Twitch in the bat of an eye, fell open on silent hinges, and the team flowed into the first floor of the Den.

*Three minutes.*

They had three minutes to climb four flights of stairs and take the floor down, or they would pay dearly. Despite their growing comfort and bravado, no one on the team had any delusions of grandeur; all fully aware the difference between mission success and failure was going to be tight.

*Real tight.*

***

## Day 61

The seven teams making up Whiskey platoon had been separated into their individual units to begin the month of intense mission oriented training. Each team was now in isolation, calling a different section of the island home, and would remain so until they had been secured from their pre-deployment workup. The missions would be conducted both on Tortuga as well as the outlying islands dotting the surrounding waters. Sometimes they would be required to insert by land, others by helo or boat. Other missions would require them to insert by parachute or underwater dive.

The month was collectively known as *Task Force Silversmith*, though the operators simply called it the *Forge.* This was likely because they were bent to the point of breaking and molded into something more than themselves while wallowing in the heat of combat. The Forge was SKUL's litmus test. Every scenario conceivable, every trained concept, every bit of knowledge they had been granted; it all came down to these last few weeks.

Life for Whiskey platoon at this time would be distilled down to a very, very basic level with only one concern – hunt down and kill savages.

As the saying goes, the basics always work.

For the next month, the teams would dine on MRE's, PT would be on their own schedule, and their only interaction with anyone not a part of their direct fire team would be with Wild Bill Kipling, their PL, and their support staff.

153

By 0700, Dane's team had finished morning PT, choked down a cold breakfast, and was now waiting Kipling's orders. They were sequestered in a small, cinder block hooch that doubled as their command and control or *C2*. The hooch's decor was cold and Spartan with only a flat screen TV on the wall, a couple of video cameras and computers, a table constructed of plywood and two by fours, and a row of folding steel chairs.

Nothing more.

The guys, eager to get started, were carrying on excitedly among themselves as Bill entered. He was followed by the group of men and women in charge of the team's intelligence and logistics support. Dane recognized Elbert Stratham, the computer genius and hacker extraordinaire, that only months prior had been with the Admiral when he had been recruited to SKUL. Elbert had also been the driving force behind the success of Operation Slingshot – the mission to save Ansil and Marcus.

It only took Dane seconds to recognize the man's savant-like keyboard skills, and he quickly sought out Stratham's help to locate Tweeker and Toad. Both of the former Section 8 shooters had gone dark and fallen off the grid following their discharge in the wake of incident down in Mexico. Elbert had hunted them down, his genius alone allowed SKUL shooters to pick them up just in the nick of time. Elbert Stratham, king computer nerd, more than anyone else, saved Dane's friends.

And for that, he would be eternally grateful.

The wiz kid gave him a nod and a thumbs-up that Dane was in the process of returning when...

154

Dane shook his head, hoping to clear a vision from his eyes, before taking a second look.

...he noticed another walk in.

His mind turned to mush.

Tweeker leaned over and whispered none-too-quietly, "Dude, is that..."

"Hell yeah," Dane growled, surprised by the anger his voice held. The individual in question had a beautiful set of almond eyes that busily scanned the gathered operators until...they met Dane's intense eyes.

"You gotta be shittin' me, man!" exclaimed Toad, not even attempting to whisper.

In his periphery, Dane saw both Jed and Twitch looking between him and the others then to those standing with Bill at the front of the room. Jed leaned into Dane's ears and asked, "Is there a problem?"

Dane shook his head.

"No," he said quietly at first then cleared his throat and added more forcibly, "No."

"Well then, tighten your shit up and pay attention," Jed growled before spitting a mouthful of tobacco spit in his coffee cup. "We do it once. We do it right."

Dane nodded his head quickly, "Okay...okay. It's cool, really."

Before he could add anything further, much less cool his jets, Bill began, "Gentlemen, as of today, you'll do nothing but plan and execute missions. This month of training most closely resembles what you'll face while on deployment, and we aim to get it right. Each morning at 0800 there'll be a mission briefing. After this, you'll plan the mission, and hit a

155

target at the designated time. Sometimes you'll run both day and night missions during a single twenty-four hour evolution, but regardless, from the time the intel is uploaded to your SICS devices and tablets, you're on the clock. Failure to meet the time restrictions of a mission will result in mission failure. For three weeks, the missions will be one or two day ops, mostly less than that. The tempo is high for a reason. We want to run you through as many possibilities as we can. Anything short of that, and we haven't done our job."

Kipling spit into one cup and took a sip of coffee from another. "The last mission you'll run will be in tandem with another team, possibly even a third, and you will be given a week to complete. Trust me when I say you'll need it. I'll be present via live feed for all briefings and after actions each day, but if you guys need something, just pick up the satellite phone, and I'll try to make it happen." He looked around the room to each of the operators, "Questions?"

No one had any at the time.

"Good."

He spit again.

"As stated, you've got an 0800 briefing which gives you a few minutes to hit the head, grab some coffee – whatever – but first I'd like to introduce your support. This is the group that's going to make sure you stay safe out there..."

Wild Bill rattled off each and every name along with what they would contribute to the team. Having heard the only name that mattered, Dane had already fallen back into his memories of Mexico. After what seemed like an eternity,

Bill cut the group loose, and Dane flew out the door intent on speaking to the lead intelligence officer for his team. He caught her by the elbow and spun her much more forcibly than had been intended.

His anger was in control now, guiding his every word and action, and there was not a damned thing he could do about it.

Her almond eyes flashed white hot when Dane hissed, "Did you know?"

He all but spit the words onto her face, but he didn't care, not anymore.

"Did you know you were sending men to die that night? Good men! My men!"

Dane was not sure then and could never be entirely sure whether his questions were truly questions or if he was indicting her of what he already knew – had known for months, actually.

The woman he held pinned against the doorway knew nothing she said would matter, so Samantha Steele – *Sam* to her friends – returned his glare with one of her own. She then did the one thing he had not expected.

She told him the truth.

"No, Commander Stackwell, I didn't. But, I knew the likelihood was highly probable. SKUL sent me in under CIA cover to gather intelligence on the werewolves' movements and strength south of the border, and that's what I did. They killed your men, not me."

She wrenched her arm free, eyes blazing furiously, and stormed off down the hall, obviously flustered.

In her wake, Dane's voice grumbled just loud enough for his teammates to hear, "The only thing you didn't do was rip their throats out."

# 11)
## Operation Uncle Drunkie

### Silver Moon Ops Center
### 1700, Day 87

Tim Meadows stood behind the podium of the Ops Center, clicker and laser pointer in hand, and a broad smile on his face. Dane stood behind and off his right shoulder. His smile was downright infectious. Contrasting the teams' comical yet otherwise calm demeanor were the support personnel who were buzzing away at their computers like a hive of angry, overworked bees. Seated at the front of the room was Admiral Briggs flanked by Commander Taggert – SKUL's 2IC, Whiskey's platoon leader – Bill Kipling, and Foxtrot's PL – Stan Woods. Seated behind them were several of their pre-deployment cadre who would grade out the two during the mission briefing. The operators from both teams were seated in their respective areas, each with the same wicked smile on their faces as Tim and Dane. Even Jed, who rarely – if ever – showed any outward emotion sat grinning like a puppy with two peters.

"Well," the Admiral began, "I'd like to hear what's got Metcalf grinning like a mule eating saw briars." Per the norm, the Skipper kept the briefing as casual as possible with his light manner buried under a deep, Texas drawl. Of course, he was referring to Twitch and the shit-eating grin etched across his face.

"Sir, I realize the request to run the final operation from the Silver Moon is highly unusual, but I think after hearing our briefing, you'll agree this operation will prove that

159

both teams are operationally battle ready." Titan's TL had intended to say, "We hope to exploit the areas on the island where security may be lax" but at the last moment, thought better of it, and abstained. Instead, Meadows turned and clicked the remote. The center screen revealed their target.

The silence within the room was palpable. That is, until a snicker of laughter shattered said silence and brought with it more of the same. Initially, the laughter was low and choked as the offending operator tried to maintain some semblance of professionalism, but like a series of dominos, that initial laugh set off a chain reaction that lasted far too long and became way too obvious.

The photo was a profile pic of Colonel Alvin Gholar. He was sweaty from a workout and wore only tennis shoes and Ranger panties. The room erupted, and many – Twitch included – nearly fell out of their chairs laughing. In an attempt to gain control Tim said, "Target's codename is Uncle Drunkie. Uncle Drunkie's a high level member of Satan's Bastards MC and is responsible for the recent string of murders on the island, possibly as many as a dozen all told."

Of course, this was false, but it gave the mission some teeth and helped make it real for the assaulters.

The Skipper, himself caught completely off guard, choked off a laugh then pulled a cigar the size of a sausage link from the inside breast pocket of his coat, "Well, you've got my attention, but this is definitely gonna put you boys on Alvin's shit list. Incidentally, this is a list no sane person even thinks about getting on. So, I hope you boys know what you're doing." The Admiral sucked and drew the flame from his zippo into the end of the cigar, lighting it. He took a long, deep puff – breaking nearly a dozen ship board policies in the process – before speaking around the fat cigar, "Let's hear it."

Tim nodded and clicked the remote.

The photo of the target disappeared and another, this one of the Colonel's island home, popped up. "A two man sniper team, one from each squad – Watchdog-blue and Watchdog-gold, respectively - will make a nighttime jump approximately thirty miles off the southern tip of the island were they'll boat in and perform an over-the-beach insertion here." Tim used his laser pointed to identify the area he was speaking of, "The beach here is fairly well protected, and the location is away from most of the island traffic. By inserting here, the biggest concern will obviously be the island's roving security patrols. From there, they'll move to their AO – area of operation, establish an overwatch position, and set up comms."

Tim clicked the remote again and called up a wide view of the Colonel's residence along with the surrounding area, "Watchdog-gold will observe the Colonel's quarters." Watchdog-gold was Toad. Tim clicked the remote again and pulled up a photo of a small airport with a double runway. "Watchdog-blue will observe the airport, and once the mission is initiated and the opportunity arises, secure it." Mike Ragland, Titan's sniper was more than up to the challenge.

"You are aware these patrols aren't made up of private military personnel, but former SKUL operatives, correct?" This from Taggert, whose voice was dry and damned near robotically inflectionless, "Because I can

161

guarantee you it won't be a simple matter of just sneaking into position, particularly when one of the men is an unproven SKUL operative."

SKUL's 2IC had been the only man in the room that had not at least chuckled, had not so much as given a sideways grin, when the target for the mission was unveiled. It was like his face had been frozen at the precise moment he got the first scent of a particularly odoriferous fart. Maybe it started when Taggert was passed over for Section 8 leadership, but Dane had his doubts. More than likely, Taggert was the kind of person that was pissed that he had been born at all.

The Admiral eyed SKUL's second-in-command, tilting his head in obvious thought and interest. The disdain in Taggert's voice was undeniable and turned what had been a fairly lighthearted and innocuous briefing – given the circumstances – instantly tense.

"I got this," growled Toad, who shared many of Dane's thoughts regarding SKUL's ACO and had done so since his time in the teams. His time in Section 8 and the stories he'd heard had done nothing but fortify those misgivings. Dane gave his friend a slight tilt of the head and a stiff look. Together, they spoke to Toad's subconscious the words Dane could never say, *Dude, he's not worth it.*

Instead, Dane stepped forward and met the challenge, "With all due respect, Commander Taggert," Dane began calmly but firmly. "I thought the point of the exercise was to assess our training and operational readiness. Further, I can assure you I have complete confidence in the recon team's ability to insert unseen and report the needed intel." Dane

162

shrugged, "And hey, if they don't, nothing's lost except our dignity."

It was a brilliant play by Dane, and everyone saw it.

Well, almost everyone.

Taggert got caught up in the part about Dane losing his dignity and failed to hear the true meaning behind his words. In one simple sentence, Dane laid out the reasons for approving the mission to the Admiral – which was he and Meadows' responsibility in the first place – and let Taggert know that when his team passed, he would look like the asshole and not the two fire teams or their leaders.

And, he said as much without having to actually say as much.

Better still, he did it without Taggert knowing he'd done it which was more than a little gratifying.

Meadows, like Jed, was a former Delta Force operator – a Major, in fact – glanced his way. Dane caught the look and the meaning. He'd just gained a couple of cool points with the senior SKUL team leader.

"Okay guys, can we hear the primary assault scenario?" The question came from Kipling, eager to get the briefing back on track.

Dane took the laser pointer and remote from Tim before stepping forward, "The primary objective is the neutralization of Uncle Drunkie and any savages getting in our way. Secondary mission objective is intel gathering. The assault force will conduct a nighttime HALO – high altitude, low opening – insertion to the island from a C-17 platform. The lead element – call sign Titan – led by Tim will land here," Dane pointed the laser to an open field on the screen.

163

It was separated from the Colonel's house by a wide expanse of trees, thickets and brush. "From there, they'll patrol to the objective from the northeast and assault the main dwelling. My guys will be the secondary element. We will assault the smaller dwelling, a guest house, from the west and neutralize any targets there. Once done, a security perimeter will be established and transportation to rally point alpha secured. Once the perimeter is secure, the recon element will fall back to the rally point, located here, for pickup. From there, we'll travel to the airfield. Initial intelligence has shown that the airfield is guarded only by a small three man unit. We will secure the airfield and radio confirmation that the mission is completed. Questions?"

"I'm sorry; did I miss the secondary unit's call sign?" The question was asked by Stan Woods, Foxtrot's PL, but Dane couldn't help but see the smug look of satisfaction on Conroy Taggert's face.

Dane grimaced, as did most of the other assaulters, and he silently cursed himself for failing to note such an obvious and valuable piece of information. Unfortunately, that was Foxtrot's job — to judge mission planning and performance and not let *half ass* pass — and Dane had just made his own shit sandwich.

*Might as well eat the sumbitch,* he thought. It was not a death sentence, but he would get reamed for the slip-up in the after action. "Team call sign is Saber, Woodrow."

The name was meant to pay homage to *Star Wars;* and, appreciative of the fact, Twitch gave him a hearty thumbs up.

"Enemy concentration expected?" Smooth, the former SEAL and Foxtrot's range master, asked. Dane, knowing the man was attempting to take the spotlight off his mistake, immediately felt a swell of gratitude toward his brother SEAL.

Tim stepped forward, taking over the briefing again, "Intel's spotty at this point, but not counting the savages already accounted for, we suspect squad-sized units spread out over the island with an additional number of a dozen or less at the objective. We'll know more once the recon team is in place."

"Weather?" asked Rusty "Buster" Burgess.

Tim nodded as it was a very good question, one he'd asked many times before when he was part of the training cadre. "Clear skies and calm seas, but our insertion will be covered by this week's new moon."

Buster nodded and jotted a quick note.

"Time on target?" asked Dax Nguyen, the operator from Foxtrot who had introduced all the new guys to the KtacS suit. The same team leader Dane had watched get another's numbers inked into his skin. For whatever reason, Dane's skin crawled.

"From insertion to extraction, time on the island is estimated at ninety minutes," replied Dane coolly, "with the recon element being onsite an additional twenty-four to forty-eight hours."

The room fell quiet for a few moments as everyone put their heads together to speak in low tones. Tim gave everyone the time they needed before he finally asked, "Okay, any more questions?"

There must not have been any as the room remained quiet.

"Good, now let's do a time hack." Everyone in the room pulled at their sleeves to get to their wristwatches. "It's seventeen forty-eight in ten seconds... five seconds, three, two, one, mark...seventeen forty-eight.

Dane returned the remote and laser to Tim, primary the assault leader. He clicked the remote again, "This savage has killed a lot of good people, guys, so pay attention to what we're about to discuss. Here's the list of assignments and gear." He allowed the assaulters to jot down info in their notebooks and tablets before asking, "Questions?"

Again, there was none so he continued on to the next subject. It went on like that for another hour. Tim and Dane fielded questions regarding everything from what happens if the teams get separated, to *no-earlier-thans* and *no-later-thans*, to every other possible visit by Murphy and his *Law* along with contingencies for each. After the mission workup had been exhausted, the Admiral rose in his seat and addressed the two teams and their leaders, "This is as audacious a final pre-deployment mission as I've ever seen, and I'd be a lunatic to not approve it. If for nothing else, we'll see what our guys on the island are doing right and wrong. Mission success will prove beyound a doubt that our newest team is fit for battle." The Skipper cast a warning eye over the room, "Just remember this is a mission *scenario* you're executing and that's one of *us* you're assaulting. With few exceptions, myself included, most in this unit would kill for Alvin's reputation. He knows what's coming, and you damned well treat him with the respect he's owed. Keep the egos in check when

166

you're in the man's house, or I'll see to it you disappear off this planet with nothing to show of your being here but a shit stain in an old pair of briefs. Am I understood?"

The operators of the two teams, Titan and Saber, a-firmed full understanding of the Admiral's order and were dismissed to prep for the mission.

# 12)

## Black Socks, Blue Boxers, and a Wife Beater

The crewman flashed two open palms with splayed fingers. Over the unit's internal comm link, the team leaders heard, "Ten mikes!"

Dane and Tim gave a thumbs-up and repeated the process to their teams eliciting an instantaneous response. Suddenly, what had been a scene bordering on tranquility with the men lost in their thoughts or listening to iPods, exploded to life. The men were quick to unfasten their seat belts and begin the process of gearing up under the glow of the red cargo lights. No one talked as there was no need, yet the interior of the cargo hold was the picture of efficiency. Once their helmets where on and engaged, each member of Saber team turned to their partner and began a systematic, last-minute equipment check. One by one, each operator confirmed with a thumbs-up and a *good-to-go* over the comms then turned and allowed their partner to do the same. Once everyone was secured and confirmed by each team's ATL – Jed in Saber's case, Rex Carston, who everyone called *T-rex*, in Titan's – Dane and Tim followed suit and double checked each other's gear.

Tim, a meticulous former Delta operator, scrutinized every piece of his junior colleague's gear before he slapped Dane's shoulder, gave a thumbs-up, and confirmed over comms, "Good-to-go."

The crewman moved into position and announced, "Five mikes…going dark!"

169

The red glow of the interior lights went dark as the men switched their helmets to its FVS setting. Slowly, the bay door of the lumbering C-17 began to lower causing a sudden influx of humid yet fresh air. Outside the bay door, only the deep black of a moonless night lay beyond. Dane loved jumping out of perfectly good planes, always had, since becoming qualified at Fort Benning, home of the U.S Army's famed jump school. Still though, diving out of a plane with nothing but one's own thoughts and the inky, seemingly endless night for company was a surreal leap of faith for anyone. Suddenly, the crewman slapped Dane on the shoulder and held up two fingers.

Dane snapped a nod and announced over the comms, "Two mikes, guys!" Dane would exit first, followed by Twitch, Tweeker and Toad, respectively. Jed would be the last member of Saber to jump.

Moments later the crewman held up a single finger. "One mike!"

Both teams crept slowly into position at the edge of the open bay. Dane could sense the building tension as the men of Saber and Titan teams steeled themselves for the jump.

"Strobes!"

The men flicked on the infrared beacon built into their helmet. The strobes allowed everyone to keep track of the members of the assault force without giving away their presence to the outside world, particularly any savages that might be looking up.

"Ten seconds...five seconds, four, three, two!" The crewman then held up a closed fist then grabbed it around the wrist and pulled downward, the signal to jump.

"Go go go!" yelled Dane.

Saber filed out uniformly; and, seconds after Jed leaped into the great beyond, Tim and his guys followed. The roar from the C-17's engines, nearly deafening just milliseconds earlier, began to fade into the night. The operators regrouped into their fire teams at roughly thirty thousand feet, drew their arms in tight to their sides, and *flew* through the night. Using the RRT system integrated into their helmets' head-up display, the operators of both teams called up their altimeter. They free fell to five thousand feet before separating. At one thousand feet they deployed their chutes, gliding the rest of the way to their targeted drop zone, landing staggered in a field of high sage. Silently, Saber waited with weapons at the ready for the island's natural sounds – insects, birds and animals – to return.

The helmet's clock display read 2300...right on time.

"Titan-lead to Saber-one-one," said Meadows quietly into his comm unit.

"Reading you lima-charlie, Titan-lead. Saber intact at LZ," came Dane's reply.

"Roger that. Wait five."

"Copy, Saber out."

***

Tim switched his comm link to an external frequency and hailed the Silver Moon, "Titan-lead to Nest for radio check. How copy?"

No reply.

Several seconds later, Tim repeated, "Repeat, Titan-lead to Nest for radio check. How copy?" There was no panic in his voice as he knew higher command was both watching and listening via a satellite feed linked to their helmets' video camera and mics.

Another wait and then, "Titan-lead this is Nest. We have you lima-charlie, over."

"All boots on the ground, preparing to move to target," whispered Titan's team leader into the comms.

"Roger that Titan-lead. Be advised, you are now T-minus one-eight-zero mikes to mission failure."

"Copy. Teams Titan and Saber are one-eight-zero mikes to mission failure. Titan-lead, out." Tim, clicking back to intra-squad comms, repeated the same to both teams, "We are T-minus one eight zero mikes to mission failure. Move to target. Titan-lead, out."

Dane gave a slow twirling motion of his hand, and Saber began to move quietly through the tall sage brush. Running point was Twitch, with Dane five meters behind followed by Tweeker. Jed took tail gunner duties. Given the late hour and remote location of their drop zone, it was doubtful many, if any, SEE-S personnel would be out and about. Silently, Twitch led the others out of the clearing and entered a wide grove of live oaks and palmettos and the darkness they held. Their patrol would take them dangerously close to the Resort, an unavoidable consequence of the size of the island and the direction they were to hit the target from. The risk of security patrols grew as they closed the gap between them and the high double fence of the Resort. Given their close proximity to the ultra-restricted area, it came as no real surprise to anyone when Twitch suddenly raised a closed, right fist.

The team froze, knelt silently, and trained their weapons outward.

"What's up, Twitch?" Dane asked while trying to make himself small within the shadows.

"Two man foot patrol, Boss. Fifty meters and closing fast." Silently and smoothly, so as to betray no movement, the team slunk deeper into the shadows of the live oak grove. Their black KtacS suits made them all but invisible. The patrol was made up of former SKUL operators who had chosen to stay on with the unit even after age or injury had taken their toll. SKUL veterans, unlike other branches of the military, always had a place to find work and be of use. There were operators in their sixties still performing vital tasks to the unit, still active in the brotherhood they had help build, still a contributing to the effort. They stayed active within the community, and they stayed happy. In short, SKUL took care of its own, which is probably why there had never been a blog post on the net, a book written, or a movie filmed about its existence.

These aged and grizzled SKUL warriors were members of Wraith platoon. They had seen it all and done it all... *twice*.

As the security patrol approached Dane hailed Titan, "Titan-lead, this is Saber-one-one, over." Although there was no worry that the enemy could hear his voice through the helmet, he still found it more comforting to whisper.

The patrol stopped at this point, mere paces from Twitch who knelt within the chasm of shadows provided by an ancient live oak with low-hanging limbs. One of the men lit a cigarette then passed the lighter to his partner.

"Go ahead Saber-one-one," came Tim's reply.

"Be advised, we have a stalled roving patrol near our position."

"Will this be a problem?"

"Possible. They're practically in our lap. Should we eliminate the threat?"

Tim's response was terse and authoritative, "Negative, do not engage unless mission compromise is unavoidable. Those patrols check in every thirty minutes. If they miss check-in, we'll have the whole island on top of us before we can blink."

"Roger that."

The patrol was so close Dane could hear their hushed voices, and he shook his head.

*These guys should be tighter than this*, he thought. *Night vision's gone...damned near criminally negligent.*

Finally, after what seemed an eternity, the patrol moved off to the south. Twitch waited several minutes before he rose, a safeguard against an organized feint where another patrol rolled up on them without warning. When he did, he led the team at a quicker albeit still perfectly silent pace.

"Titan-lead, be advised, we are again moving to target."

"Copy Saber-one-one. Get a move on."

After several minutes, the denseness of the grove began to abate until it became what could only be described as sparse. Again, tall sage brush dominated the area.

Seventy-five meters later they were staring at a two story Victorian style home with tall, white columns and a circular drive that cut through a finely manicured yard. Rows of azaleas whose buds were just beginning to bulge lined a wraparound porch. A large pool and outdoor fire pit separated the main dwelling from the guest house, and a wooden walkway led from the pool in the direction of the beach. Tracing south, the boardwalk disappeared behind a wall of sand dunes.

"Saber-one-one to Watchdog-gold. Need a sitrep."

The recon team of Toad and Ragland had given a steady stream of updates since establishing their overwatch positions nearly thirty-six hours earlier. Their last update had been just before the teams had made their jump. At that time there had been seven savages on site.

"Saber-one this is Watchdog-gold. Be advised, there are six savages on site," came Toad's voice. "Three guards total, one on the east side of house, another on the north, with the last standing watch in front of the guest house. There are two more in the guest house, but I haven't seen them in a while. Uncle Drunkie's by his lonesome in the main house."

"We got the north and east guards," Tim said. "Saber you take the guesthouse guard and the savages inside, copy?"

"Roger that, moving."

Minutes bled into hours as both teams slowly crawled into position. Once at the objective, Titan split its force so they could take out both savages simultaneously. Finally, Saber team slipped around the back of the house. Twitch was on point with Dane over his right shoulder, a subjective hand's-breadth from the guesthouse guard.

Quietly and calmly Dane hissed, "Titan-lead, Saber is in position."

"Roger that, Saber-one-one. Wait one." Dane could only guess what was taking Tim so long to get into position; but finally, his voice sounded again. "Execute on my count...three."

Dane laid his hand on Twitch's right shoulder.

"Two."

Dane felt Twitch tense.

"One."

Twitch's breathing came to rest.

"Execute."

Twitch pulled the trigger, twice, and caught the savage guarding the guest house with two to his center mass. It happened so fast it took a few heartbeats for the guard to realize what had occurred but, as the green paint from the sim round dripped down his ballistic vest, he could only lament, "*Oh fuck,*" before he sat down.

He was officially out of the game...*dead.*

There was no time to think, just move. Twitch slid to the door, testing the knob, before confirming over comms, "Locked but the mechanism's ancient. I can pick it."

Dane nodded with his HK 416 at his shoulder, "Do it."

Two seconds later Twitched turned the knob and swung the door open. Dane flowed in and took the *heavy,* right side of the room, Tweeker to the left, with Jed taking the center. Twitch took up rear gunner a.k.a hall monitor duties. The assault caught the two savages – who were really just older SKUL operators on Colonel Gholar's staff – completely unaware. Each of the former SKUL operators wore tactical gear and sat sipping coffee with their face shields on the ground at their feet. They had been alerted of the pending training operation, but they had not been told when it would occur. Apparently, the teams hit their targets at break time.

In heartless fashion, Dane caught one of the faux savages in the chest with a controlled pair of sim rounds. Likewise, Tweeker squeezed off two methodically deliberate rounds with the same result. The two operators called out, "Clear!" and Jed answered in kind.

The older, inactive operators looked stunned, stricken as the green paint slid down their chest rigs.

*Their problem,* Dane thought.

No time for anything but movement, Tweeker slapped flex-cuffs on the two *dead savages,* careful to not cause any undue discomfort to the old operators. Once done he updated all hands, "Savages secure, ready to move."

Dane, now on point, called out, "Moving," to which the others answered with the same before following him into the only other room of the house, a bedroom. It was empty.

"Clear," called Dane.

"Clear," answered the others.

"Moving," Dane called again, and the three made their way out of the guesthouse. Twitch was kneeling, his weapon trained across the yard, when Dane and the others made their way back to the front of the guesthouse. Now that the guesthouse was secured, Saber's responsibility was twofold. They would serve as security for those still within the main house, falling in on Titan's position, and covering their *six*. They also needed to commandeer a vehicle or two for exfil.

"No movement, Boss."

"Good deal, man," Dane said then switched frequencies to call up Titan. "Titan-lead, guest house is secure. Securing perimeter now."

"Copy that, Saber-one-one," came Tim's voice, "Primary objective secure, conducting SSE now. Ready to move in five mikes."

SSE was *sensitive site exploitation* which, in most cases, meant taking photos of the dead, grabbing hard drives from computers, thumb drives, notes in offices, anything. In the case of Operation Unkle Drunkie, it just meant Titan was taking a bunch of photos of the faux savage, Colonel Alvin Gholar, who had been gracious enough to go along with this little exercise. Dane was positive Gholar never imagined the teams would be successful.

Not here.

Not on his island, surrounded by seasoned SKUL operators.

Jed tapped Dane on the shoulder then tapped his watch, saying nothing. Dane nodded then into the comm unit, "Roger that, ready to move in five." After a moment of thought, he felt the same thing he knew Jed was.

This had been too easy.

"Tim, you guys need to be rolling sooner than that. We're cutting this thing too close as it is."

"Roger," came Tim's voice again. He then added, "Watchdog-blue has secured the airport."

Dane shook his head is mild disbelief though, honestly, he didn't know why. Ragland was one of the best in the business – as good as Toad, which was saying an awful lot – so he really shouldn't be surprised that one lone sniper could neutralize a seasoned crew of guards and secure an airport.

But, he was.

He had to constantly remind himself that those he worked with weren't gods...they were just men.

"I'm sending Deebow out to help you guys out with security," Titan's TL announced.

Twitch took point and led the team across the patio whereupon they met Titan's medic, a former member of Force Recon. Deebow was a big, bald-headed black guy from North Carolina. He liked to hunt and, in his off time watch *rasslin'* – his words. He was also an ordained minister and dead serious about his job.

How serious?

He always referred to Dane as *sir*, a highly unusual practice among SKUL shooters. Most of the time, the guys referred to each other by their call sign, and rarely used their given names. At one point during their pre-deployment workup, Dane had asked Deebow – very nicely – to cut out all the *sir* bullshit.

Deebow's response?

"Sir, regardless of the window dressing, this is *still* the military, and you outrank me. So, you're name's *sir*, sir."

That was weeks ago, and this was now, and time was getting scarce.

"We'll be ready to move soon, sir," said the shooter from Titan.

Dane smiled.

"We might need to rustle us up some wheels." Deebow's voice was methodically slow and deep – like Michael Clarke Duncan deep – and he was big, like...well, Michael Clarke Duncan big. The man was also a pillar of calm. Maybe it was his faith; maybe it was just him; but, the simple fact was, that he was the rock that the members of Titan unfailingly lashed themselves to.

Dane nodded agreeably then looked to the driveway. No sooner had his eyes fallen on the two four wheel drive suburbans than the islands alarm system begin to wail. The system, nothing more than a common tornado warning alarm, began to peel open the night at a volume that made ear drums quiver.

And it did so, one brain numbing wail at a time.

*Fuck me,* was Dane's immediate thought.

His second, and more appropriate thought, was to look to Twitch and Jed, "Get 'em open and cranked!" Both men went to work without a word, each working on a separate vehicle. His eyes, enhanced by the FVS, picked up halogen lights weaving across the island's open expanse. They were moving in the direction of Gholar's house.

*Quickly.*

And, they were coming from the barracks.

"Tim!" he all but screamed. "We're out of time, dude!"

As if in answer, Tim and the rest of his team spilled out of the house with a blacks socks, baby blue boxers, and a wife beater wearing Colonel Alvin Gholar. No way the Colonel expected them to get this far if he was dressed like that.

Worse yet...he was flex-cuffed.

*Same clothes...*

No one on Titan spoke, nor did the Commander of SEE-S. Abject murder, however, currently resided in the man's eyes. Tim, his guys, and Colonel Gholar piled into the nearest Suburban driven by Twitch. Dane and Tweeker dove into the rig Jed was driving. Both vehicles barked their tires and burned an inch of rubber as they forced the SUVs away from the house.

The car lights – still distant – loomed closer, and there was no doubt as to their intent.

Dane acted reflexively, "Saber-one-one to Watchdog-gold, over."

A moment later Toad's steady voice came over comms, "Watchdog-gold reading you lima-charlie, Saber-one-one."

At that second, a previously unseen vehicle sprung out from the dunes and blocked the most direct path shooting simunition. Paint splatter, red this time, dotted the windows and side of the vehicles as Jed smoothly turned down another road with Twitch on his heels.

"We're taking fire, primary extract's burned."

Exactly at that time, the back windshield and part of the long, side window became dotted with green paint from the sim rounds.

"Roger that, Boss. Have already repositioned to secondary."

"You've already moved? How long ago?"

Pissed, Tweeker kicked out the back glass and coated the chaser's windshield with an entire magazine of the same. With their vision down to zero, the trailing SUV had no alternative but to pull to the side of the road.

Others followed while Toad continued his sitrep, "Long enough to get it done."

Dane and the others could almost hear Toad's smile on his voice and, in turn, he smiled behind his own face mask. Toad – hell, all of them – where the best hope this country had, and they'd just proved it.

"You heard him, right?" Saber's TL turned to Jed.

Jed grinned, despite his natural, salty disposition, and struggled to negotiate the turns of the road. An expert of both offensive and defensive driving, Jed took each change of direction coolly even as the vehicle teetered precariously between the world where it remained on all fours and the one in which it was flipping end over end.

"I did."

No excitement and no worry anywhere to be found in the operator's voice.

*That's Jed Blackmoor for you,* Dane thought admiringly.

"Well, fuckin' drive, dude!" Dane allowed himself a minute of excitement, "What the hell are you waitin' on?"

"Yessa, Mista Stackwell," Jed said almost jovially, which was strange because as a rule he wasn't a jovial person, "I be drivin'."

182

Tweeker piped in from the back, "Dude, seriously, you finally loosen up enough to have a little fun, and all you got is a tired-ass *Driving Miss Daisy* quote?"

"Well, it fits, don't it?" Jed grunted as he worked the wheel through a hairpin turn at nearly sixty miles per hour.

Tweeker chewed on it a moment then admitted, "Yeah...yeah, it fits...whatever, man."

Dane smiled through the exchange even as another vehicle shot out from behind a live oak grove by way of a road he hadn't noticed. This time, luckily, their timing was off, and Jed just managed to skirt past the vehicle before it boxed them in.

While Jed and Tweeker discussed more acceptable movie quotes – on an unknown gravel and sand backroad...at night...while running dark...at nearly seventy miles per hour – it hit Dane.

He *still* had to figure out how to pick Toad up, and get behind the wire of the airport...without his team being caught.

# 13)
## Uncle Drunkie's Hotwash

**Bixby Room**
**0400, Day 89**

Tim and Dane had just delivered their after action reports to their pre-deployment cadre and the island security staff – all highly trained, semi-retired, yet inactive SKUL operators. Colonel Gholar was there in his workout clothes, along with Commander Taggert and Admiral Briggs who were participating via satellite link. The video of the entire operation – taken from KtacS helmet cams – had been played in its entirety. There were also certain photos presented that were taken during the SSE; photos no one – particularly, the Colonel – were thrilled about seeing. The worst photo in the bunch, one sure to continually make its presence felt for years to come, had been the photograph of Colonel Gholar dressed in baby blue boxers, black dress socks, and a tactical vest over a wife beater. He was standing in a pool of milk with a goofy, surprised look on his face. The milk carton had been dropped when Titan took the house and its occupants down. It was only the white hot glare from Gholar's eyes that kept the quiet chuckling from turning into overt laughter.

But, Gholar's presence managed to stymy the operator's mirth...*somewhat.*

The man was seething, and there was little doubt why.

SEE-S had security issues – plural – which meant, in Alvin Gholar's mind at least, *he* had security issues. To the Colonel, Tortuga was *his* island, *his* place at the table, *his* way of giving back to the organization that had saved him from a life of boredom and had given him a renewed since of purpose.

Of belonging.

*I've let everyone down.* He spit those words in his mind so forcefully they physically hurt.

Regardless of the accuracy of Gholar's feelings – and, there was some truth to them, no doubt – the larger, more sobering revelation was that SKUL had security issues.

Again, plural.

If the island codenamed Tortuga, one of the most secure facilities on the planet, the beating heart of the blackest, most top secret military unit the world has ever known, could come under threat – internal and fictitious, be damned – then SKUL's leadership must ask itself one overly simple and utterly terrifying question…

*What else could be threatened?*

The room now sat in tomblike silence as the expression on Gholar's face called up visions of the *Grim Reaper* trying to decide which soul to take first. On the big, flat screen, Briggs sat chewing the inside of his cheek in contemplative silence while Taggert looked like he had just swallowed a particularly malodourous fart. Dane could not help but imagine it was not because the island had proven vulnerable but rather, because Saber and Titan had succeeded in completing an audacious training mission. He also imagined that most of SKUL's second-in-command's ire was focused directly on him.

Dane smiled and said to himself, *Fuck you, Taggert.*

After what seemed like an eternity, but in truth was only a minute or so, the Admiral spoke. The cadence of his speech was formal and regimented. He was obviously paying particular attention to the choice of each word, "This operation, for those that don't know, was conducted with two goals in mind. The first and most obvious goal was to test the mettle and operational readiness of the two teams involved under the most arduous circumstances available. It was an audacious mission conducted to exacting standards, and to that end, gentlemen, job well done."

The room erupted with fists pounding on tables, an ancient sign of welcome, brotherhood, and general well-being that dated back to the time of the Vikings.

It was a warrior's welcome.

The Admiral waited for the room to become quiet again before continuing, "The second objective was to assess the island's security. Again, I believe it's safe to say the objective was a success if for nothing more than to bring to light our failings and shortcomings. As we all know, the AAP was started some years ago in order to fill both the need of the organization as well as that of the warriors who call SKUL home."

*AAP,* as the Admiral called it, was SKUL's After Action Program. The program was aimed at veteran SKUL shooters whose age, along with the rigors of the job, had finally caught up with them. It allowed them to be taken off the active duty roster and placed them in other, still valued, positions. Some men – such as those Titan and Saber had thwarted – were slotted for security details within SKUL's fabled Wraith platoon. Wraith was charged with the security of SKUL black sites, silver mines, Tortuga, and even the Silver Moon. Others went on to training at SEE-S and other

SKUL specialty installations like M-WOD – the mountain warfare training center.

The idea was as simple as it was ingenious.

It kept men busy, kept them feeling useful, kept them moderately in the game, and in theory, kept them from exposing SKUL by writing books or appearing in the news.

The program had been a resounding success...thus far.

"Further, I do not feel this to be an indictment on the program," the Admiral continued, "but rather, an eye-opener for us all. We have improvements to make on the island, and I have no doubt the Colonel and his men will see them through in as exacting and professional a manner as humanly possible, correct?"

"Yes, sir!" confirmed the Colonel firmly. It was apparent the Colonel was more than a bit chafed.

In fact, he was overtly pissed off.

"We will dissect our procedures and make the necessary changes, starting the second this meeting is adjourned."

"I know you will, Alvin." The Admiral paused to effectively change the mood of the debriefing. "Now that that's behind us, we have four new members that are ready to graduate C-school. Commander Stackwell, Chief Lattimore, and Petty Officer Tolar, you may consider yourselves secured from SEE-S. Graduation for you three plus Tom Wilcox is set for sunrise which gives you a couple of hours to get cleaned up. We'll see you back on the Moon in forty-eight hours. Enjoy the downtime, gentlemen, because you're about to jump from the skillet smack dab into the frying pan." The Skipper smiled brightly, "Dismissed!"

***

**Silver Moon**
**Admiral Briggs' Stateroom**
**0430**

"Con." The Admiral's voice stopped his second-in-command at the door leading from his quarters.

"Sir?"

"Stackwell's one of us now. It's time to forget the past."

"Haven't said a thing, sir."

The Admiral chuckled, yet Taggert's ears twisted the sound into something that was mirthless and bitter, "You haven't had to, Con." The Skipper's craggy, scar-riddled face involuntarily twitched as it so often did when he was stressed. "I'm going to tell you something that is going to make you angry, but you need to hear it. General Pattridge made the right choice when he chose Dane. He was the right man for that particular piece of work. You had already crossed paths with the savages; so, there was no way for you to effectively lead Section 8. Hell, son, there was no way for you to continue operating outside of our protection. Stackwell had the operational experience and the unquestionable loyalty of his men. I think even you can admit that compared to the Commander, you came up short."

Taggert shifted uncomfortably before the Skipper. Briggs was opening up wounds he thought he had long ago buried.

The Admiral continued, "But, I'd be hard-pressed to find anyone here who would say you've done anything but acquit yourself in fine fashion." The Skipper's body language softened, "Con, what I'm trying to say is that I hope you're not letting your past eat away at your present...at all the good you've done here. Do you understand my meaning?"

The pointedness in which the Skipper spoke took him by surprise. Had he really been that transparent in front of Briggs?

He didn't think he had, but now he was not so sure.

"Yes, sir," was all he managed and those words came out flat and cold.

"There's a storm brewing, Con." The Admiral's facial features now looked more exhausted than ever. A shadow passed over his eyes, and his mood darkened in response. "I've never seen this much activity among the savages before; and, as each day passes, the world gets a little spookier. I need every man's eyes to the front and ears open wide."

"Always, sir," replied SKUL's second most powerful officer softly before stepping from the Admirals quarters.

This time the Skipper let him go. Something in Taggert's countenance worried him.

Something was *off*.

It was apparent this thing between he and Stackwell was toxic, at least as far as Taggert was concerned. Just as apparent was the fact the better part of valor may dictate he would need to reassign one of the men. Stackwell was out. He needed him here, leading Saber team, and reassigning Taggert would mean...well; he didn't even want to *think* about what that would do.

"Unless," making his thoughts verbal, "that reassignment would maintain Taggert in the eyes of the men and protect that legendarily brittle ego of his." He poured a glass of bourbon, took a sip, and again, verbalized his thoughts to an empty stateroom, "Ah, the joys of leadership."

# 14)
## End Zone

**Outskirts of New Orleans**
**1200**

Billy held the clear, shatterproof tube at arm's length. The viscous liquid flowing within seemed to move of its own accord. The substance held a deep green hue and seemed to shimmer and glow from a nonexistent source of light.

It felt like a living thing.

It felt *angry*.

Billy knew both were closer to the truth than he was comfortable admitting. The substance assaulted his senses with a force so palpable he felt it in his marrow.

It was visceral. It was...*wild*.

Strange visions came to his mind, the shades of some distant past's nightmarish horrors.

He found the simple act of breathing all but impossible as he placed the tube within the lead lined box and closed the lid. He was immediately and self-consciously aware he had become lost within the contents of the tube. He had been staring into the otherworldly shimmering green substance like a stargazer might look into the depths of the universe.

It felt like the power of Creation itself was housed within the tube.

He took a deep breath to collect his thoughts that had been unwittingly scattered over the ages. Fear crept up his spine; and, looking to the man standing before him, he suspected he felt the same. "There and back, that's the job. Protect this like your life depends on it...which, incidentally, it does. Do that and we may just have a place for you in the pack."

Looking at the box greedily, the courier – a man named Andre Brussieux – nearly jerked it out of Blackshanks' hands. This was the moment he'd waited his whole life for, and the excitement was taking him to places he rarely visited.

Or, was he feeling cold, stark fear?

He couldn't be sure. "Ye, ye, yea, yeees sir," he stuttered, an anomaly that occurred when he was excited...or, scared out of his mind. He fought his entire life to control his speech impediment, but today's job, the most important he'd been given since becoming a *prospect* of the Satan's Bastards MC, pushed him over the edge.

"You're still standing here."

All around, the horrific screams of agony called out as men and women visited hell on earth only to find immortal pain in the end. Involuntary images of destruction surged into both their minds.

*It's that shit in the tube.* Billy had to physically pull himself away from an unseen yet crippling fear. *It's got to get out of here, now!*

"Su, su, sir?"

"I said," Billy growled, his voice becoming dangerous, "you're still standing here, and I'd like to know why?"

Again, more of the screaming, more of the pain, more of the bloodletting assaulted their ears from all sides. It was like the depths of Hell were being pumped into their ears, all in high definition surround sound.

Andre looked around helpless, visibly shaken, then darted from the porch, kicked off his bike, and sped away without a backward glance.

Billy smiled as the feelings of dread began to slowly dissolve. He pulled a phone from his pocket. Again, the screams of agony crescendoed. The very air and earth had become saturated in misery, and Billy, as happy-go-lucky as you could be, made a call.

***

The beer had just hit his lips when his phone vibrated. Irritated, he took a sip then looked at its face so see who was calling. He couldn't say the name associated with the number made him fell all warm and fuzzy. Looking to his sergeant-in-arms, he pointed to his phone, jerked his thumb toward a side door and followed its direction. The door didn't slam shut so much as it was granted a spot beside Mac, the MC's sergeant-in-arms.

"Yeah," was all he said, and it wasn't in the friendliest of tones either. Had he known who – or, better yet, *what* – he was dealing with, he may have spoken with a little more care. As it was, he knew the piece of shit on the other end – or thought he did – and didn't like him…not one little bit.

"Three-Nip, how does life find you?" Billy asked – way too casually for Nip's taste – as he took a swig of his own beer.

Three-Nip, so-called due to the fact the round, brown protrusion just below his right nipple looked exactly like a nipple, answered gruffly, "Fine. I suppose you got something on your mind, or you wouldn't be calling. So, why not cut through the bullshit and lay it out there?"

195

"Need a favor," said Billy, his voice neutral, flat, controlled.

"Never a doubt," stated an unamused Three-Nip. "So, what is it? Or, I guess I should ask you what do you need?" Three-Nip wasn't stupid nor was he naive. Billy never, ever, sought outside help unless he was in a bind.

Or, when he didn't want the blood on his hands.

Billy laughed into the phone, and Three-Nips heard that strange, hyena-like laugh Billy had been cursed with, "Storage space."

Three-Nip, president of the South Mississippi chapter of the Satan's Bastards MC, looked at the phone dubiously, "Need more info than that, brother."

"Does it really matter?" Billy asked, now impatient.

"To my guys, yes, it does." Nip took a swig of beer. "More importantly, it matters to me; so, start talking. What am I baby-sitting?"

Billy sighed. This wasn't going as well as he'd hoped.

"I'm sending one of my guys up to deliver something to you for safe keeping. I need you to keep – and protect – the package for a few days, and that's all I can say. Trust me; you really don't want to know any more than that. My guy will also pass along a phone. When it rings, answer it. The voice on the other end will provide you with follow-on instructions. Phone's encrypted, and it's yours. Think of it as my gift for being such a good sport."

Billy said the last bit in an overly patronizing fashion.

Three-Nip scoffed, "Jesus, Billy, I still need more than that."

"No," Billy said flatly, but the word carried with it a warning buried just under the surface. "No you don't, especially since my guy will also hand over a rather large sum of cash."

"Define *large sum*."

"How's a down payment of two hundred and fifty large sound? Second half will be delivered upon satisfactory completion of the secondary instructions."

Three-Nips' eyes flared wide, not with surprise but with greed. Like a nomad finding water after a month of wandering through the desert, he downed his beer, hoping to steady his nerves, "Okay, dude. When's your guy heading my way?"

"He left fifteen minutes ago, should be there about dark."

Billy could hear Three-Nips speaking to someone off the phone. After a quick second, he was back on the line, "Fair enough. Just make sure you trust the guy you send. I'd hate to find the payment light."

Billy's angered flared briefly, but he managed to hold it in check which wasn't really his style. His style was to rip out the throats of people who pissed him off; but right now, he needed to remain calm and keep his eyes on the prize.

For the time being, in any case.

He needed Three-Nips at the present; so, instead of feeding off his anger he simply ended the call. He did not have time for Three-Nips; he had another call to make.

A very important one at that.

*\*\*\**

Stefan picked up the call on the first ring, "Is it done?"

He listened to Billy's report and smiled.

"Outstanding," Stefan answered. He was genuinely pleased by Billy's professionalism thus far. This was not the impression he had been given by the young werewolf's contemporaries.

Red Moon had called him a *wild card* that needed a short leash. The old, Eldrich wolf should know. He turned Billy after all.

Others had not been so kind in their assessment. They had called him a crazed, murdering psychopath which, Stefan had to admit, was not necessarily a bad thing.

Either one would suit Stefan's needs.

Billy had questions. He always had questions, an annoying habit. Still though, Stefan heard his concerns then replied, "Do not worry of reprisals from Mr. Della Rocca, Billy. I will talk to my old friend and explain the situation. It's time for him to have full disclosure, anyway."

Another question came, and sent a wave of white hot anger coursing through one of the most ancient beings on the planet. He nodded into the phone even as he fought against the nature, the very essence and fabric that made him immortal. "You needn't worry, my young friend. By the end of business tomorrow, your South Mississippi brethren will be no more, and you will effectively control..."

\*\*\*

Billy's face split into a wide grin at Stefan's words, "...no more, and you will effectively control the South's drug, weapon, and human-trafficking interests."

That said, the line went dead; and, again, the air was rent asunder by screams of pure terror. He flipped the phone in the air and stepped back into the house.

"Might as well have something to eat."

The meaning was clear though no one was standing around to hear it.

# 15)
## Mac's

**1600**

Dane stood at the well-worn bar stretching across Mactavish's drinking a cup of strong, dark coffee. Shamus' pub excelled at three things: great food, strong coffee, and cold beer. Several of the guys on his team and those of Titan and Rhino – the alert teams for the next forty-eight hours – were there as well. They were all drinking coffee. There would be time for beer, there always was, but now was not that time. Kipling, during his most recent address to the platoon, made clear his expectations regarding alcohol consumption while on active deployment and combatting savages. His words – *I'll accept no less than twelve hours from jigger to trigger.* This, he emphatically stated, was part of being a professional, part of being a SKUL shooter, and – again, his words – *part of the motherfucking gig.* There had been no need to say all that; but, given he was leading men who routinely walked on the wild side of life, Wild Bill felt the need to be assertive in all areas of his command.

Dane took another sip, savoring both the coffee and the weighty feel of the SKUL shield around his neck. The *Shield,* worn by SKUL operators like the dog tags of old, was a solid silver shield with two crossed tomahawks. The SKUL motto – Per Tenebras Venimus Tamquam Lux – ran along the emblem's edge. Each operator's unique serial number was stamped into the back of the Shield.

Dane, along with Ansil, Marcus, and the other new guy, Tom Wilcox, had also received one other piece of hardware during their SEE-S graduation ceremony.

Solid silver tomahawks.

But, these were no simple mantle pieces meant to denote the passing of some great milestone. No, they were as functional as they were prized, as deadly as they were elegant. They harkened one back to SKUL's beginnings and would see the elite unit into the future. Stamped into the face of the tomahawk's business end was the name of a fallen SKUL shooter. The practice had been borrowed from the SEALs, who had been doing the same with their infamous K-BAR knives since the early days of the global war on terror.

Dane took another sip of coffee and thought of the name engraved on his *hawk* – Rodney Jefferson, a.k.a Rocket.

As expected, Dane learned everything about Rodney's life, both within the military and outside of it. He had initially been delighted to learn that Rocket was a member of DEVGRU – formerly SEAL team 6 – prior to being recruited to SKUL. That feeling was short-lived, however. While learning of Rocket's life, realizing he had climbed to the top of the special operations world – *twice* – only to die at the hands of some savage in brutal fashion, Dane's delight was stomped into a proverbial mud hole. Heart-sickening somberness filled that hole. Rocket's story initially stopped him cold, and now was no different.

Fortunately, he finally had work, real work that he was born to do, with a team of the best warriors on the planet to help push those misgivings aside. The men on his team along with the men operating under SKUL's banner, served to plug in the gaps of nothingness that had become his life.

Abby could not – would not – understand that he never wanted to break his promise to her…he simply *had* to. Then there was Henry; the son he barely knew. He didn't even know where they were, what they were doing, and he could only assume they were safe. None of that mattered, though. He would lay down his life for Abby, no matter how much she hated him. But, for Henry…

…for Henry, he would freely give his soul.

Absently, Dane looked to the table where his team sat talking.

Closest to him was his assistant team leader – Jed Blackmoor. Jed was as stoic as a monk and as mean as a pit viper. His ATL was capable of dishing out mercy and death in equal measure. Blackmoor, a former Delta operative, had been raised on a ten thousand acre cattle ranch just west of Wichita Falls, Texas. There, his parents had been both fair and strict, expecting young Jed to fulfill an assortment of chores that saw him up before dawn and in bed well after sunset. His only reprieve in those years had been high school athletics, particularly baseball. He excelled on the diamond and received all-state honors his senior year. One known for a tenacious work ethic, young Blackmoor was rewarded with a baseball scholarship to Baylor University, but he never stepped foot on the campus. In early October with the scholarship on his family's dining room table, the metaphorical world at his fingertips, Jed pushed it away from him.

With determination in his mind and steel in his eyes, Jed said, "Mom...Dad, you remember watching what those people did to our soldiers over in Somalia?"

He was speaking about the Battle of Mogadishu. His parents nodded but remained quiet, afraid of the look in his eyes.

"Those were Rangers, the Army's BEST...I'm going to be one."

His mom's body started to quiver. His dad could only clear his throat. Frank Blackmoor was a veteran, serving in the Marine Corps during the Vietnam War, and he knew the hard row his son wanted to plow. "Jed, son, that's a very noble and honorable sentiment, and your mom and I surely won't stand in your way, but you must be sure. Those books you've read make things look easy – maybe even fun – but the reality of it is that it's hard, dangerous work and a lonely life with little pay and even less appreciation. You've got a chance your mom and I never had. You've got chance to go to college; and, if you continue to work at it, a chance to be something great on the ball field.

Jed bristled, and his voice flat-lined, "Being a Ranger is being something great, Daddy."

For several long minutes, Frank and Maureen studied their son. Eventually, with tears streaming down her high cheek bones, his mom acquiesced with the faintest of nods. Seeing his wife's answer, Frank reached out and shook his son's hand. His words were short and simple, "Go be the best damned soldier you can be."

Jed became a Ranger, sure enough, and after several years of strong work backed with a *can-do* attitude, he became something else…something not even Jed could have imagined. He became a legend within the small community of soldiers operating with the Special Forces Operational Detachment – Delta, a.k.a the *Unit,* a.k.a *Delta Force, CAG,* and a dozen other names. Delta gave him everything the Regiment did…a hundred times over.

He lived his life with a full heart and only one regret – not getting to say goodbye to his dad. Frank Blackmoor had been diagnosed, failed treatment, and died within a matter of months. The whole time his son was deployed and working a deep cover op in one of the most decrepit, earthian shitholes on the planet – Mogadishu, Somalia…where it all began.

He did not count his contact with the savage deep inside the mountains towering above Glacier National Park as regret. In fact, he felt like God had leveled the scales of judgment in his favor.

And then, there was Kris Metcalf. Everyone called him Twitch – for painfully obvious reasons to anyone who spent just five minutes with him. Twitch had been born in San Diego, California, to Kyle and Kourtney Metcalf. Kris' mom was killed during the family's first vacation up the California coast when he was only five. A werewolf who was hunting his father attacked them as they traveled north on Highway 1. That was his first experience with death, let alone the undying. To his knowledge, the senior Metcalf was dedicated Force Reconnaissance Marine; but, in reality, he had moved to a different stage in his military career. Kyle Metcalf was a SKUL operator. The fact that the werewolves had managed to parse out Kyle's identity forced him to send his son away to his wife's sister, Whitney Belcher, who lived in Breckenridge, Colorado.

Sometime later, Kyle Metcalf was killed in under mysterious circumstances. The official report stated he died in a training accident. Unofficially, however, Kyle was still very much alive, though it would be years later before Twitch learned the truth about his dad's official employer. When the *Twin Towers* were turned to rubble, Metcalf was a bright mechanical engineer student just eight hours shy of his degree. That day changed Kris Metcalf and lit a fire in the pit of his gut. Instead of finishing his degree and living a life of relative comfort, Twitch followed in his old man's footsteps and enlisted in the Marines. After years of hard, loyal surface, Kris was selected to help shore up a burgeoning special operation unit's formation, MARSOC. Twitch flourished within the freedom of the unit's autonomous structure. It was after a particularly brutal deployment that Twitch discovered the truth of his father's *death*. He also learned of the existence of SKUL.

Over the years, the only complaint leveed against him was the fact that, from time to time, he suffered from a bit of bad luck.

Well, a lot of bad luck, actually.

Jed and Twitch, while new to Dane, had been operating within SKUL's ranks for quite a while. They had seen the worst inhumanity had to serve up and had the outer strength and intestinal fortitude to smile and ask for seconds. The others on his team – Toad and Tweeker – were men he knew well and loved like brothers.

Marcus Tolar, at five foot five inches tall, was one hundred and fifty-five pounds of badass black man from Meridian, Mississippi. His diminutive stature made him – pound for pound – the meanest, toughest sonavabitch that Dane had ever come across. Toad had never had any other goal in life than to be a Navy SEAL, to beat the odds, and show the world that the size of the man did not mean a damned thing. It was only the size of a man's heart and the conviction locked within his mind that equated to success or failure. He desperately wanted a seat at the table, wanted to make a difference in this hell-stricken world. Tolar was convinced the only way to truly judge heart was to grit it out through impossible circumstances and rise above it all; to succeed where countless others had failed. And succeed Marcus Tolar did. His refusal to give in, to quit, had inspired the same from Dane during some of the darkest times imaginable.

Together, Dane and Toad – enduring off each other's encouragement and probably only thus – survived the ugliest and most wretched circumstances one human could inflict upon another.

Ansil Lattimore, aka Tweeker, was born and raised by his parents, Lukas and Jill, in the prairie potholes of North Dakota. Ansil loved his mom with all his heart but, in contrast, could not have given two squirts of Bedouin piss for his overbearing, often belligerent, beer-swilling father. *Daddy* Lattimore pushed Tweeker to the brink, making all these plans for him, living his dreams through Ansil's life; a life forced upon the near giant of a man. Like polar opposites on a heavy duty magnet, Ansil and his dad pushed each other apart forcibly, as they argued incessantly about what Ansil *needed to be doing with his life.*

Eventually, Ansil began pushing the boundaries that had been placed – often forcibly – upon his life.

Late one night, after Ansil's last high school football game, there was a fight. At some point his mom tried to get between the father and son to prevent the irreparable family damage she knew would occur. Blind with rage, Lukas struck his wife causing her to fall and bump her head on a coffee table. The blow knocked her momentarily unconscious. For his efforts, the elder Lattimore found himself in a North Dakota hospital emergency room a broken man. Later, after all the details had shaken out, Ansil enlisted in the Navy and got the hell out of town. Eventually, he volunteered for and passed BUD/S – the SEALs brutal rite of passage – and, years later, screen for and was accepted into DEVGRU, the Navy SEALs elite counter-terrorists unit. Four long years after that, Chief Petty Officer Ansil Lattimore reported to the selection course of a newly minted and freshly formed, completely black, CT unit. That unit's name was Section 8.

This was the life he wanted. A life worth living.

Dane knew both his parents were gone now, and he knew Tweeker still missed his mom. He also knew he wouldn't piss on his dad's tombstone if it was on fire.

*Hard men with a hard job,* Dane was thinking when a coffee mug and a tattooed forearm slid across the bar top, dragging Dane from his reverie. The tat was the simple, triangular Greek sign for Delta...for *change.* He knew the tattoo and who it belonged to.

"You've got that look, boss," said Jed with a knowing smile, "lose it."

"Dude," Dane said, knitting his fingers behind his head and resting in the basket made, "what look?"

Jed spit a wad of tobacco juice into his cup, "The look that dickheads get when they're getting all introspective. Like I said, lose it."

"I'm just sitting here thinking about what a great group of guys I work with, that's all." Dane said it with a sarcastic smile and more of the same in his voice; but hell, he meant it. He just did not really want Jed to know he meant it.

Jed took a drink of coffee before spitting another wad of tobacco in the cup, "Whatever. Lemme tell you something, Boss." He stabbed a finger at Dane's heart, "At the end of the day, these things are better than us. They're faster and stronger; hell, they're *wilder* than we could ever hope to be. On every mission, during every action, every time your SICS buzzes with a message to head to the Ops Center, the Reaper walks with you. He walks with me and with every other sorry fleck of scrotum lint on our team and beyond, and he does it every second of every day. And, you wanna know a secret they don't tell you at C-school, a secret they allow you to figure out on your own?"

Dane nodded, now sipping his coffee.

"Eventually, that cold-hearted bastard's gonna turn his head your way and smile his nasty smile. We may walk a nut hairs' width this side of death, but eventually, we all overstep our bounds. Understand?"

Dane took another sip of coffee, seething on the words, "That's some darkness, hombre, man. What are you, some combat-hardened Gandalf?"

"I prefer Yoda, actually," Jed said in what almost sounded like a cheery voice.

"Jed, you a *Star Wars* fan? How'd I miss that?"

"Like the old trilogy. New stuff sucks," he offered with blatant conviction, one not to be argued with. "You never knew because you never asked. Please don't tell Metcalf, though. It's hard enough to get him to shut up as it is." Jed smiled then changed the subject. "Anything spin up yet?"

Dane looked into his coffee still trying to put Jed's morbid words into perspective, "Lots of scuttlebutt coming down the pole, but who fuckin' knows man? Whatever it is, it's got weight."

Jed's eyebrows knitted together, "Like what?"

"Fuck if I know, man," Dane took another sip of coffee, savoring the flavor. A few seconds of silence later, he added almost flippantly, "But, we're primary along with Titan. Rhino's putting fingers in whatever hole the dam may spring."

Jed spit, took a sip of coffee then asked, "The guys know?"

"Figured I'd let you handle that," Dane said, reaching in a pocket and pulling out a bag of chew. He placed heavy wad in his mouth before adding, "Round 'em up. I want 'em in the team room in thirty minutes. The next forty-eight is ours. So, let's be ready to rock when the time comes."

"Roger," Jed slid the last dregs of his coffee to the edge of the bar then moved to the table Saber team was calling home. A few quick, crisp words from Jed, and his guys filed out of Mac's without a second look. He was watching the last, Twitch, saunter through the door when Shamus slid another cup of strong coffee across the bar. The look in his eyes was all business as he thumbed toward a booth in the corner, "A word?"

"Good seein' you too, Mac." Dane grunted but moved to the booth the legendary operator indicated.

The old warrior snorted and leaned over the top of the bar, plucking a pint of beer from the cooler for himself. His old joints creaked as he slid into the seat opposite Dane. Dane grimaced, literally hearing the snap and pop of the old codger's knee joints. Seeing the look on his face, Mac snapped gruffly, "Keep smilin' punk. Before long you'll be wishin' you were as spry as I am at this age." Shamus took a pull of his beer and smacked his lips with satisfaction, "Gotta give it to the crew at Abita. Those folks sure do brew a fine beer."

Dane smiled into his coffee, silently swirling the contents in the bottom of the mug.

Mac watched him curiously for a moment or two before he asked, "Anything on deck?"

Dane shrugged, "Something's spinning up. We're on alert for the next forty-eight hours." He slid his mug, now empty, toward the edge of the table. Less than a second later it was filled by a pretty waitress that was a part of SKUL's support staff, "Any advice?"

Mac chuckled, "Don't get bit."

Dane rolled his eyes, "Thanks, Mac. You're all heart."

"Hell son, whatcha want me to say? Want me to hold your hand? Give you a parting gift? This shit's simple, and don't let anyone tell you otherwise. Go in there and kill every fuckin' savage you see. Period."

Dane smiled with him at that. The dude was a warrior to the bone and never, ever pulled a punch with anyone. "Anything else?"

Mac took another swallow of his beer, "Yeah, don't do anything stupid like getting bit. Seriously."

Dane stood and Mac offered his hand, "Good luck, Boss."

"Thanks, Mac," Dane said before turning for the door.

The old man nodded and watched him go. A single thought overrode all others in his head. He wished he was the one about to kit up and ride out into the night to kick down some doors.

# 16)
## Operation Nightshade

Dane's SICS buzzed, and he immediately read the message. The tension among the men had been building with each passing hour as the rumor mill churned out whispers of an upcoming mission. The words on the face of his SICS confirmed the rumors simply enough:

*Nightshade*

*Whiskey, 1/3/7 active*

*AR-1*

*30 mikes*

*Game time,* he thought with a thin, grim smile, *finally.*

*Nightshade* was the name of the operation. Teams one, three, and seven equating to Titan, Rhino, and Saber, respectively, were active. The mission briefing was in Action Room-one in thirty minutes. The action rooms were smaller, dedicated briefing rooms set off to the side of the gargantuan Ops Center.

After reading the message, he sent a follow-on to his guys. Twenty-five minutes later they cruised past Millie Studameyer, the Admiral's older but attractive administrative assistant. She was speaking into her desk phone but managed to give the men her trademark smile and a quick wave as they strolled through the door to AR-one. They had a few minutes to kill, and per the norm, Tweeker and Toad began their nearly decade's long discussion that generally devolved into an argument rather quickly. Twitch laid his SICS on the table and pulled a Leatherman utility tool from where it was

213

clipped to his belt. Dane had a bad feeling Twitch was fixing to destroy his SICS device...*again.*

"Seriously, dude. *Christmas Vacation?*" This was directed to Tweeker. Toad's question was only slightly different from the million other *best movie, best actor, best Mafia character, etc.* the two had attempted to answer over the years.

Tweeker nodded as if he couldn't believe there was even a question in his choice, "Yes, you cock-breathed hick, Va...ca...tion. It's the quintessential Chevy Chase movie, and you damned well know it's true. It's not even close."

"Ah, hello, *Caddyshack.*" Toad countered decisively.

A rough *snap* caught Dane's attention.

He cut his eyes over to Twitch's position just as he pulled the SICS apart. Instantly, the device's innermost workings spilled out on the table...and chair...and floor. Dane shook his head. He was certain this had no chance of ending well.

The argument escalated.

"Dude, he wasn't even the main character."

"Which is exactly why it's the obvious choice. Tell me you don't laugh your ass off at every scene that dude's in. Tell me that scene with Bill Murray in the tool shed isn't epic material."

Tweeker switched his chew from one side of his mouth to the other, obviously evaluating Toad's stance. After several seconds he gave in, "You may have a point here."

"See?" Toad looked to the others, "That's why I love this dude. He's all about compromise." At that, the others in the room, now including both Titan and Rhino teams, laughed.

Tweeker glared around the room before spitting into his spittoon, "Great. Glad that's out of the way. Now, will you leave me the fuck alone?"

"Done," Toad smiled before grabbing a wad of chew from Tweeker's pouch. "Next question's mine."

"I can hardly wait," grumbled Tweeker.

A small mumbling noise, not unlike the disgruntled employee in the movie *Office Space,* forced Dane's eyes back to Twitch. Twitch had recovered most of the parts from his completely dismantled SICS and was now picking through the pieces with a pair of tweezers. The quiet mumbling was Twitch talking to himself.

His focus bounced from part to part like he was following the flight of a tennis ball during a match.

"Dude, what the hell?" Dane asked purely out of disbelief and through a face palm.

Twitch's face scrunched, unable to comprehend most the fact that most people truly did not care about *how* things worked, just that they do. "Like, haven't you ever wondered how these things work? Seriously?"

"No," he said quickly, "I haven't..."

Before Dane could answer further, the door flew open and caused everyone to *snap to.* In his haste to stand, Twitch knocked the demolished SICS and all of its parts off the table. Briggs' glare was white hot, "That's the third SICS you've destroyed this month, Metcalf! I'm fed up with you wasting your time and my budget on crap like this!"

"Sir, I'd hardly call understanding the inner wor..."

"Stow it!" snapped the Skipper. "And, if I have to replace one more SICS device due to your stupidity, I'll personally boot you off this ship while she's underway! Am I understood?"

"Perfectly, Skipper!"

"And Tolar?"

Toad's face became a flaccid mass of confusion. He had no clue what he could have done to draw the Skipper's ire, "Lattimore's right. There is no way you can possibly call *Caddyshack* Chevy Chase's best movie. It's *Christmas Vacation*, hands down."

Toad looked first to Dane with eyes that asked *how did he know?*

Dane shrugged, cutting his eyes to the ceiling where the speakers and video cameras were hung.

Toad refused to look at Tweeker, who was no doubt smiling brightly, as he responded meekly, "Yes sir."

"Good," the Admiral looked around the room taking in every individual at once, "now if you don't mind, we've got an operation to plan."

Tweeker leaned into Toad's ear and whispered loud enough for everyone to hear, "Guess that makes next question mine, huh?"

Toad nodded though he still refused to look at Tweeker. Several of the operators seated chuckled. He refused to look at them, too.

Behind him, intelligence personnel, including Sam Steele, much to Dane's unease, flowed into the room and took seats along the walls. The large, flat screen on the opposite wall came online, and Sam began calling up overhead images of a large antebellum mansion surrounded by miles of flat, featureless field. Another intel tech began pulling photos out of a vanilla folder and placing them on the large table the SKUL operators sat around. Other men that Dane recognized as part of the air wing – specifically, the helo crews – pulled up chairs around the table and began looking over the images.

Satisfied everyone who should be at the briefing was at the briefing, the Admiral began, "Gentlemen, I want you to understand that anytime I give the order for SKUL operators to be put in harm's way, I do so with the utmost of care and give it the highest level of importance. Any mission, any circumstance, no exceptions." He gained every person's gaze with his eye simultaneously, a trait most good leaders had. "As many of you know, we've been working several angles for the actionable intel you're about to receive. Unfortunately, two of our SKUL second tier intelligence agents, or *SI-2s*, were murdered by savages in the line of this duty."

A palsy silence fell over the room as the operators adjusted themselves in their seats. The shit just got real. Their own were gone, and it was up to the men in the room to make it right.

"We've locked down their whereabouts to the plantation you see before you. Sam, you want to take over?"

No matter how much he thought he hated her over the Mexico mission, Dane could feel his pulse race. Sam weaved her way through the operators and stood at the head of the table. She was dressed smartly in a navy blue skirt and white blouse; lean yet with all the right curves, in all the right places. After their initial, heated meeting, the two had settled into a cordial, albeit, stiffly professional relationship.

"Thank you, Admiral." Sam changed the image on the screen to a photo. It was a very old, very well-known photo. "I'm sure you've seen this photo before, it's rather famous."

Every man from the three teams nodded. Everyone knew that photo. It was of the young outlaw known as Billy the Kid. Dane, along with every other shooter in the room, looked up to Briggs, confused. The Skipper returned their gawks with a look of stone. His face read, *This is your job, and you will do it.*

Sam clicked the remote and another – far more recent – photo popped onto the screen, "This was taken sometime in the early eighties. Anyone recognize the man wearing the vest on the bike?"

Dane nodded, "A Bastard." The morning the MC tried to kill him and his family was still a fresh memory.

She looked to him with dark, intelligent eyes. Her eyes pierced his self-imposed aura of protection and seemed to look straight into his soul. "Look closer," she urged.

He shrugged studying the photo for several moments before exclaiming, "Holy shit! You can't be serious!"

He looked up and saw Briggs staring fiercely, judging his reaction. Dane locked his eyes on the Admiral as Sam continued, "That was the last known photo of one, William H. Boney, until today. Based off recent intel reports, we were able to deploy one of our Pegasus drones to provide overhead coverage of the area in question. It managed to capture this image."

She clicked the remote again.

The still photo was grainy, pixelated, and heavily cropped; but, there was no mistaking who it was. "His current alias is Billy Blackshanks, president of Satan's Bastards Motorcycle Club." She let that sink in for a long moment before adding, "His codename for the mission is *Gunslinger*. Questions?"

Jed, his voice soft spoken yet one that commanded respect, asked, "Any updates regarding the number of savages on the ground?"

"Negative," Briggs replied, "we estimate six to ten, maybe more."

Jed nodded and started to say something else when Sam added, "That's minus the Bastard that left today."

"I'm sorry," Dane blurted, "but are you saying you *allowed* a savage to leave the site? He's just going to skate?"

Sam's jaws clenched incessantly, and her glare would have melted a glacier. "Commander Stackwell, I did *not* say we allowed a *savage* to get away. I said we *allowed* a *Bastard* to leave the premises. As anyone who's taken the time to research the outfit knows, there are as many – no, there are more – perfectly shitty humans running around wearing a Bastards' cut as there are savages."

Dane's facial features softened, "Unders..."

"No, I'm not done, Commander," said Sam, the bitterness leaking into her tone. "Since we couldn't retask another drone quickly enough, we hedged our bets and decided to focus on the one constant...our need to take the Gunslinger out. We did, however, activate a Kilo team and an intelligence support element to pick up the *unsub*. I've also

219

tasked a group of analysts to put the drone's footage under the microscope for anything we missed initially. We hope to have the unsub in custody for interrogation by the time this operation is over. Other than supporting your operations, non-savage intervention is Kilo's primary mission responsibility on this deployment." She paused and forced all emotion from her tone. "This isn't Mexico, Commander Stackwell, and I suggest you remember that the next time you question my motives or that of my intelligence staff."

*And there it is,* he thought but dared not speak.

Sam looked around the room not coolly but coldly, "Anyone else?"

The room as a collective was silent, many shaking their heads, none wanting her venom directed their way.

Finally, Tim Meadows – Titan team leader – broke the silence by clearing his throat before asking, "How many doors open to the outside?"

"Seven," stated Sam evenly. "One door on each side of the lower level of the house plus another three on the second level balcony, one to north, one east, one west. They all swing inward. The lower level porch wraps around the entire dwelling, upper balcony around three sides."

"Lots of potential for squirters," noted Toad, referring to savages escaping the battle. Those in the room agreed.

"What type of material are we dealing with concerning the house and is it on a slab or conventional foundation?" asked Tommy Granderson, Rhino's team leader. He had been drafted to SKUL out of the ISA or the Intelligence Support Activity or just the Activity, depending on who you asked.  Rumor had it that he and Jed had worked together in Iraq during the outset of the second Iraqi war.

"Johnny, pull up the blueprints, please," said Sam to one of her subordinates.  At a side computer, a man presumed to be *Johnny* began hammering away at a keyboard.  Seconds later, the blueprints to the plantation's construction showed on the screen.  "The main house is over half a century old; so, you can bet it's made mostly from heart pine."

"Basically, kindling," commented Rex Carston, Titan's ATL.  He shook his head frostily.  One errant spark and the whole thing might go up in flames.  The work environment was going to suck.

"Basically," acknowledge Sam.  "So, keep the explosives in check around this thing."

All eyes instantly turned to Twitch.

"What?" asked Saber's point man.  For a quick second, he was truly flummoxed by the wall of incredulity he faced from his brother warriors.  But, it lasted only a second before he realized what they were thinking about.  "Oh, good Lord, guys, I'm not an idiot."

"Yes, you are," quipped Jed, "but that's neither here nor there."

"It was just *one time,*" Twitch mumbled in countering.

"Cooooontinuing," Sam said impatiently, drawing out the word and bringing the focus back on the briefing.  The camaraderie these men shared felt impenetrable, making her feel as though she was always on the outside of things and always would be.  "The house sits on a conventional frame with about two feet of crawlspace underneath. This may allow one or more of you guys to insert there."

"Just as likely to alert however many savages are on site," Deebow, Titan's medic added. "We need to hit the target hard, fast, and with maximum violence."

Sam shrugged while nodding at the same time, conceding the point. "As you can see from the blueprints, there are two stairwells. One is here," she pointed a laser light to the area on the screen indicating the location of the stairwells, "and the other is here. The upper level is made up four separate rooms. The largest, we assume, is the master bedroom."

Tweeker leaned into Dane's ear and whispered, though not nearly soft enough, "Hey Boss, maybe after all this is over, you can show her around that room, huh? You know, maybe a little *makeup* session."

He really had meant the comment to just be shared between he and his team leader, but it was nearly impossible given the number of people crammed into the room. The sounds of choked laughter muffled by hands, coughs, and the crooks of elbows rumbled across the room, and Sam's face was aghast. Her skin was no longer olive but flaming red...a dangerously hot, flaming red.

Dane turned slowly to Tweeker, his eyes livid, "Dude, seriously? Shut the fuck up and concentrate. Everyone's ass is on the line here."

Tweeker nodded sheepishly, "Sorry, Boss. Overstepped myself."

"Damn right you did," Dane agreed icily with his old friend before turning back around. Interestingly enough, Sam was staring a hole in his head but her eyes didn't show anger. Rather, they were darks orbs welling with deep-set appreciation.

She took a second to collect herself then continued, "There's also a second dwelling, a guest house, on site. It's newer, built a little over a year ago, and made of brick and mortar. It sits on a slab foundation. It's a large guest house, almost twenty-five hundred square feet, that has its own air conditioning unit and phone lines. Overhead aerials have shown a lot of traffic between the two structures; so, you expect opposition from both targets."

Everyone nodded while continuing to aggressively take notes.

"What about the owners of the house?" asked Tweeker. "Anyway to bring them in and get some answers before we start blindly kicking doors in?"

"I'd love to, Chief Lattimore," answered Sam. "Unfortunately, our intelligence shows that at about the time the ground was broken on the guest house construction, Mr. and Mrs. Thomas Latresse received a large deposit into their bank account. Shortly thereafter, they purchased plane tickets to Prague and have subsequently disappeared. Why they left the country and who deposited the money is, at present, anyone's guess; though, we're looking into several avenues."

Joel Lightsey – call sign *Fuse,* Titan's point man – asked, "What kind of weather and moon phase are we looking at, ma'am?"

While Sam spoke, Fuse and the others continued to scribble notes into their wheel books.

"Full moon but initial meteorological reports indicate heavy yet intermittent cloud cover. Not the best situation, but not the worst either." The beautiful intel analyst shuffled through some papers and added without looking up, "I'll download any updates to your SICS devices and tablets as I get them. Changes will be highlighted in yellow."

Again, the men buried their faces in their notebooks and jotted the info down.

The Admiral stepped forward and took over the briefing. All eyes, every one full of anticipation, were locked on the Skipper. "Okay, gentlemen, *Operation Nightshade* is a *go* at midnight. Call signs per protocol. Titan and Saber, you guys are the primary fire teams. Rhino, you are tonight's QRF. I want you stationed off site but within a stone's throw, understood?"

"Roger that, sir," replied Granderson. He looked to the rest of his guys – who were already laying out maps of the surrounding countryside – and nodded, "Shouldn't be too difficult to locate a proper staging area. Nothing but farmland for miles around."

"Okay, guys, you've been briefed and have the intel. I need a workable operation, and I needed it yesterday." The men *A-firmed* their understanding and began looking closer at the satellite imagery available. The Skipper turned back to Sam and her intel agents, "Sam, I want you in these guys pockets so you can answer any questions the guys may have."

"Yes, sir."

"We'll kick the tires on what you guys come up with at 1900 in the Ops Center," said the Admiral before stalking stiffly from the room without another word.

He had another team to brief and another operation to get off the ground; an operation that was just as important as *Nightshade* with just as many possible ramifications.

*Tired*, the Skipper thought, *I'm getting too old for this.*

# 17)
## Side Job (part 1)

The Admiral pulled his SICS from his pants pocket and confirmed the men were assembled in the designated action room. Jason Whitherton, Kilo's PL, had sent a message A-firming all hands were present as of five minutes ago. Briggs then checked in with Millie, his assistant.

"Mills," said the Admiral, calling her by his pet name, "I need the next several hours free."

"Already taken care of, Bart." The two had long ago ditched formalities when in each other's company or speaking directly to one another over phones or SICS devices. "Short of the President or another Head of State, you're not to be bothered."

"Thanks, Mills." He severed the comm link and stepped into AR-5, the action room where Kilo's Iroquois team would hear their briefing.

***

"Gentlemen," began *English*, Whitherton's call sign, "at approximately 1300 today, the unidentified individual you just witnessed leaving the target area was spotted by a two man element of SI-2s working the area under the cover of NOPD patrol officers. They pulled the individual over and managed to tag the unsub's bike with a small, GPS transponder."

"Ballsy work," commented one of the guys from the direct fire team. *Diggs,* as he was called, was a former Air Force JTAC. These days, he was Iroquois' ATL. He was also a hard man who was even harder to impress.

He was impressed.

"Very," admitted English. "They also managed to obtain this series of close-up photos of the unsub as well as lifting some fingerprints. A quick run through NOPD arrest records and the FBI's NCIC ID'd our unsub as Andre Brussieux, a low-life prospect with the NO chapter of Satan's Bastards MC." English called up a highway map with a blinking red dot, "As you can see, the transponder is moving north along Interstate 59 and is closing on the Hattiesburg, Mississippi area. Mr. Brussieux is transporting a box with a tube inside that's been deemed a national security threat. That box is your primary target. Questions? I know you've got 'em so let's hear 'em."

"Sir, are we certain the unsub is human?" The question was asked by Ed Jackson – call sign, *ChiTown* – a former Force Reconnaissance Marine. ChiTown was the blackest, black man this side of the Sahara. Interestingly enough, he was one of the smartest, most loyal officers the Corps had ever produced...he was also one of its most lethal. These attributes made him the perfect Team Leader which was exactly the position he held within Iroquois.

"Thermals from overhead drone footage at *Nightshade*'s target site indicate he is. The SI-2s were able to scan Brussieux as well. Their findings confirm...*human.*" English let his men jot down their notes for a quick second then asked, "Next?"

"Any overhead support?" again from ChiTown.

"At the moment, negative." answered English honestly. "However, a Pegasus drone has been re-tasked and will be on station within the hour. The voice manning the

228

drone carries the call sign *Snake Charmer-two-five*. Also, satellite support will be online before sunset as well."

The men on the fire team made further notes.

"English, I understand our target is the contents of the box," began Dimetric Cortez, another Recon Marine that everyone called *Poncho* – the team's point man, "but what about the *runner*?"

He was referring to Brussieux.

"Understanding Mr. Brussieux's human nature, your ROE – *rules of engagement* – are to offer Mr. Brussieux every opportunity to surrender, and if he refuses…" English's voice trailed for a slight second before he finished firmly, "you terminate his existence."

This was the slippery slope SKUL faced. They were tasked, time and again, with operations to snuff werewolves from the earth and, likewise, time and again, humans got in the way. Humans that were their countrymen; hell, they were their freaking neighbors. Many times – as seemed to be the case here – they were the unwitting combatants in a much bigger game, one in which the loser faced extinction. After a brief bit that saw the eyes in the room flicking to one another, the team set back to the job at hand. Questions came and went, notes were taken, and final orders of chain of command given by the Admiral. His words were ominous to all, like he knew this was not going to be the simple *snatch and grab* that most in the room felt it would.

"*Operation Side Job* is a go. You're wheels-up at 1900 and will base out of *Black Site Shelby* on the grounds of Camp Shelby, a National Guard base. You'll be on the grounds by

2100. Supply drop at 0400 and follow-on orders by 0600. Updates to your mission profile per protocol."

Again, the men exchanged raised eyebrows and confused glances. *Follow-on orders?* they were all thinking. *We'll be back by sunup.*

"A SEAL team and a squad of Delta shooters have been positioned at the base for a joint training evolution. This is routine; your existence is not. Lay low and let *intel* do their work. If you slip up and the weekenders start asking questions, use the training cycle as cover, and for God's own sake, stick to it. I'm placing ACO Taggert in command of this side of the operation. Any questions you may have or anything you need take it to English for Commander Taggert's approval. Men, do not doubt the importance of your mission." The Skipper took the room in with a single gaze, "You have your target and your orders. Get it done. Good luck, and I'll see you when you get back."

The Admiral stalked from the room as the team began putting together a rudimentary profile. Eventually, the Skipper knew, this profile would evolve into a workable mission plan for execution.

# 18)
## The Gunslinger

"Titan-lead, this is Saber-one-one. We are in position. We have one savage in human form guarding the front door, another on the eastern side of the house." The stress in Dane's voice was apparent, as was Meadows' upon reply.

"Roger that, Saber-one-one," replied Tim from somewhere in the field west of the property. "Guest house is free of security, will assault on your mark."

He could feel Toad next to him and could almost sense the elite sniper calming himself and getting into rhythm with his breathing. The rest of the world no longer existed to Toad. His vision was tunneled, and the guard at the front door was the star of the show.

Presently, Dane's voice sounded over comms, "Execute on three...two...one, execute!"

The savage was only able to savor the first drag of his freshly lit cigarette when a round of silver slammed into its chest. The savage was pinned against the wall of the antebellum home in a splatter of green. He took one last gasp and slid to the ground, dead. Suddenly, the other savage, the one on the east side of the house, appeared seemingly out of thin air. The heavy *thump* had caught his attention enough to leave his post to investigate.

"Titan-lead, hold one!"

"Copy," came Tim's terse reply.

"On it, Boss," replied Toad coolly, fully in his element now, before pulling the trigger a second time. The latecomer only had enough time to register his dead comrade, and his splattered green, ichorous blood on the walls, and the ever-widening pool of the same on the porch before a second silver bullet shattered his temple. Brain and bone blew out of the back of his head and began grotesquely mingling with the bone and fluids of its comrade.

"Moving to target," Dane said as he rose. They were close, just inside the edge of a cotton field that formed all four boundaries of the house's expansive yard. The teams had crawled across the huge field under the cover of darkness, using the thick, leafy row crop as concealment. Between the leafy boughs of row cropped cotton and the thermal dampening properties of their KtacS, the shooters were all but invisible to the savages they were hunting. Swiftly, the team patrolled across the yard's wide expanse and took the porch stairs.

"Savages neutralized," reported Dane as he stepped over first one then the other.

While Jed worked to secure the dead werewolves in silver bindings, Dane and the others positioned themselves to either side of the door. Once the savages were secure and Jed in place, Twitch tested the door.

"Locked," Twitch noted over intra-squad comms. Twitch let his favored rifle, the FN SCAR-H he had come to love during his time with MARSOC, drop to his side and palmed two *Werewolf Incapacitating Percussion Projectiles,* called WIPPs. These small grenades were SKUL's answer to the flash bangs used by conventional and special operations forces worldwide. Once activated and following a five second delay, the device emitted an ultra-high-pitched sound

232

hovering within the ultrasonic range and many decibels above the range of the auditory range of humans…but, not werewolves

There was no explosion, no rendering of flesh and material into oblivion, just a complete mind crunch. During SEE-S, WIPPs were described as dog whistles…if those dog whistles had been on a religious workout program fed by a strict paleo diet and anabolic steroids. Werewolves within the little percussive grenade's range would be momentarily incapacitated, giving the entry team a tactical advantage for a few seconds.

Dane was just about to order Twitch to breach the door when the muffled rattle of suppressed gunfire, controlled and precise, creased the night air. These shots were answered by the wild and sporadic sounds of untrained small arms fire. The angry bark of gunfire was overwhelmed by voracious howls of hunger emanating from somewhere deep within the assault targets.

The werewolves now knew they were there.

Tim's voice immediately sounded over the intra-squad comms, "Contact front. Contact front. Three non-savage combatants." Behind those words came more gunfire. Some were the suppressed weapons from Titan operators; others were not.

Titan operators were constantly calling out battle actions now.

"Moving right, moving right!" called T-Rex Carston, Titan's ATL.

"Cover fire left!" added Fuse, the team's point.

They were in for a fight, a real fight. The amount of resistance they were met with left little doubt.

Twitch, instantly recognizing the element of surprise had evaporated, reacted by simply slamming his boot against the door. The door was ripped off its hinges and fell to the floor in pieces. The two small WIPPs were tossed into the darkness first with the operators flowing through the gap only seconds later. In reaction to the devastation the WIPP grenades rendered on their eardrums, the werewolves in the house howled in agony. Every piece of glass – every windowpane, every vase, every piece of fine crystal – shattered, turned to sand in answer to the both the ultra-sonic and the savage's hell-bound howls.

The first thing that met their FV-enhanced eyes was the nearly nuclear plume of a savage struggling to maintain its senses. The beast was on one knee, its claw-tipped paws were slapped to its ears, and its head – snout full of elongated teeth – was turned to the heaves in anguish. The thing sat at ground zero as far as the WIPP grenades were concerned, and its ears had taken a beating for it. A silver slug from Twitch's SCAR caught the savage in the throat, and another two from Dane's HK 416 slammed into its chest, thus ending its pain and suffering. In an eye's blink, they had dominated the entrance to the target, but they were not done...nor were the savages.

Twitch kept moving, not bothering to see if he was alone. There was no need. He knew without a doubt the others were following on his heels. Inside, the house was beyond dark, and the only sounds came from their own breathing and the unnatural howls that were already beginning to fade as the strength of the WIPPs waned. It was a blight that seemed to laugh at them, to have its own breath, its own way.

Dane felt a sublime, yet fear-inspiring, sense of claustrophobia as the walls seemed to push in on them from all sides. Making things worse was the knowledge that somewhere within the far recesses of that deep fortitude of inky black lurked the very heart of destructive evil. Somewhere close, one of the most dangerous beings known to walk the earth, and one of SKUL's highest priority targets, waited.

And, he waited for them.

Dane's heart could have wavered; he and the rest could have given up and likely survived the night. The problem with that was elementary. Quitting meant failure, and men like Dane and the rest of SKUL did not do failure.

They endured; they pressed forward; they traveled on.

This was their mission; this was the hand they were dealt; and, they *would* succeed.

Or, they would die trying.

*** 

**100 miles off the coast of Mississippi**
**Ops Center, Silver Moon**
**0010**

Briggs and those in the Ops Center fell silent. Their tension and anxiety grew with each tick of the clock. The battle to take down the Gunslinger raged on the plantation grounds both in the physical and electronically by way of the flat screens decorating the walls of the Ops Center.

235

The Skipper white-knuckled the chair he stood behind. Humans could be just as dangerous and cunning as their savage counterparts...if not more so.

His own men were proof enough of that.

He looked over to where Samantha Steele sat following the action and made an addendum to that last train of thought. His own men and *women* were proof enough of that.

Having the two species intermingled here turned the screws tighter on an operation that was already a pressure cooker. Mollified to the fact there was absolutely nothing he could do to change the situation for those on the ground, he simply watched.

He felt worse than worthless; he felt impotent.

Involuntarily, the hairs on the back of his neck stood on end as Twitch's screen went wide to reveal his boot kicking the door open. Collectively, the three other screens representing Saber's assault element moved into the darkness of the house. A split second later, they saw the plume of nuclear white from the team's video feeds. Three holes of green ichor suddenly formed on the savage's throat and chest in rapid succession. From hundreds of miles away, it was all they could do to keep up with the battle. So, they nearly missed the guys from Titan, who had finally eliminated the three men guarding the guest house, enter the secondary target.

The Skipper's scar twitched underneath his right eye patch. This was a holdover from old injuries that appeared when he was nervous or tired...or scared shitless.

He was all three at the present.

"Clear," said the four operators in near unison, each acknowledging the foyer landing and sitting areas to each side were empty of threats.

Instantly, Twitch was moving further into the house with the others falling in behind him. They moved silently, deeper into the darkness, like wraiths intent on soul-taking. Their training dictated they were always pressing, always on the offensive when clearing a target. The wooden floors creaked underfoot and thumped with each booted step. In the silence that had spookily overtaken the house, those thumps sounded loud enough to wake the dead. Within seconds, Twitch came to a side door and halted to allow the others to stack up.

Dane signaled his friend to move with a simple squeeze of his shoulder.

Twitch tested the knob then pushed the door open. Dane entered from the left of the door crossing to clear the right corner and side of room, Tweeker the opposite with Jed taking the center line of site. Twitch, now rear guard, monitored the hallway for movement.

"Clear right," called Dane over the inter-squad comm-link.

"Clear left," repeated Tweeker.

"Clear," called Jed before adding, "Moving."

The other two operators repeated the same and moved from the room. Back into the tight confines of the hallway, they again stacked behind Twitch. Down the hall they continued, room after room, and the story was always the same. The house seemed empty with nothing stirring, not even a mouse. Even so, there was a certain malice, an evil that permeated the air. After what seemed like hours but, in reality was only seconds, the team came to a stairwell.

"Tweek, Jed. Upper level. Twitch, you're with me."

"Roger," said the two men in unison. They broke off with Jed in the lead and moved ever deeper into the darkness above.

Dane and Twitch pressed forward and eventually reached the back of the lower level of the house. They moved across an area that married the kitchen to a breakfast area to a swinging double door on the far side. The doors rocked gently back and forth on silent hinges, obviously in the final stages of momentum. The two noticed this at the same instant and moved to stack up on either side of the doorway. Twitch to the right side of the door, Dane the left. After a millisecond, Twitch looked to Dane who nodded stiffly. The former MARSOC operator flowed into the room and took the heavy, left side. Dane mimicked his movements, taking the right side of the room.

It was then that they made contact.

At the head of a pool table, chalking up a cue stick, stood a savage. It was in human – male, rather large – form yet looked radioactive, freakishly so, in the thermals of the FVS. They had just time enough to register the smiling savage before the thing lunged at Twitch. It moved so fast it blurred in Dane's head-up display, and before he struck the shooter, the savage changed. It was no longer wholly human nor entirely a wolf, but something in between.

That *something* in between was all claws and teeth.

That *something* in between was very, very dangerous.

238

Even under the ultra-violent and intense duress provided by the charging savage, Twitch managed to fire three controlled rounds. Ordinarily, they would have struck the assailant center mass, yet all three fell wide of their mark. Dane allowed a single shot before the beast was just too close to Twitch to shoot safely. Within a millisecond, the savage slammed into Twitch. What followed was a shower of sparks caused by the werewolf as it tore into the operator's KtacS suit with clawed paws and snapping fangs. Dane let his weapon fall, jumping into the fray while simultaneously drawing his silver tomahawk. So hungry and lustful for human flesh was the beast, he forgot about the other operator in the room. That single-mindedness was his doom as Dane split his skull in half with a single blow of the hatchet. Dane helped roll the dead savage – now in human, nearly naked form – off his friend who was groaning in apparent pain. Twitch rubbed a hand across three long gashes in his KtacS and brought away a fistful of blood.

"Damn," he groaned, "that hurts."

Dane didn't know what to say, had no movie quote to bring levity to the situation at the ready – not yet anyway. So, he simply grabbed Twitch, helped him into a sitting position, and began checking for other wounds. Seeing no other issues, he began working on the wounds he knew about, saying only, "Fuck man."

Twitch, in obvious discomfort, groaned, "Dude. I heroically use myself as bait, obviously with only your safety in mind, take a beating in the process, and all you can say is *fuck man?*"

Dane grabbed Twitch's blowout kit – the emergency med kit located in the right thigh pocket – and began ripping into a foil packet. "Always two there are, a master and an apprentice," Dane said quoting *Episode 1* of the *Star Wars* series. "Better?"

Twitch groaned louder, feigning more pain than he was really in, "Dude, why? Why quote from that one?"

Dane, now frustrated, growled, "How 'bout *shut the fuck up*, and let me get this sealed?"

Twitch tensed as Dane slathered the thrombin gel thickly over the wounds, "Sounds better, anyway. You were starting to sound like a pansy." The thrombin gel Dane was using was a wound sealant developed by SKUL's medical research and development staff. When it came into contact with blood, the gel hardened, effectively sealing off most surface wounds.

Once done Dane activated the intra-squad comms, "Saber-two-wolf, this is Saber-one-one. We have one savage down, but it is not the Gunslinger. Repeat not the Gunslinger."

"Roger that Saber-one-one. We have one down upstairs as well," said Jed in businesslike fashion.

"Be advised," Dane continued, "Twitch got nicked. No teeth, just claws, suit is compromised, though. I hit the wound with thrombin, and he's on his feet. Needs to be sealed properly, ASAP, though."

"Copy," Jed's voice again sounded, this time mottled with concern. A second later, his voice came over the comms in strained fashion, "Shit." Another heartbeat or two passed and then Saber's ATL said, "Hold one." Moments past until both Jed's voice and Tweeker's sounded in time, saying simply, "Clear."

"Upper level is clear. Boss, you need to take a look up…"

Jed's voice was cut off by the muted staccato of suppressed gunfire, and to Dane and Twitch, the world around them seemed to explode.

\*\*\*

Three savages exploded through the walls of the upper floor. Two slammed into the far wall, pressing huge claws into the sheetrock – howling – while the third just hung there.

In the *air*.

Like he was *flying*.

Jed and Tweeker opened fire but were blown off the upper level landing by a gust of wind so fierce it ripped apart walls. A strange amalgamation of soldiers and furniture slammed into the far wall of the great room. Shaken but unharmed, they quickly scrambled to their feet. Dane and Twitch, laying down covering fire, gave them just enough time to slam fresh mags into their wells and dive for cover.

Dane directed them while firing on the move, "Right! Move right!"

There was an inch of water on the pine floor stemming from a burst water line. Jed used the reduced friction and his momentum to slide behind an overturned *La-Z-Boy* recliner. He turned, fired two shots, and forced the nearest savage back and behind a wall. A second later a large body slid beside him.

Dane.

He worked his trigger and the comms with equal passion, "Saber-one-one to Titan-lead. We are in contact with multiple savages…" He sprung up, intent on laying down some fire, but stopped short of the action. His eyes had fallen on the hovering savage. A savage that was in human form wearing well-worn jeans, heavy boots, a Satan's Bastards cut…and a smile.

Dane gulped, fired, then announced over comms, "…be advised, Gunslinger is live. Repeat, Gunslinger is live!"

"Roger that," was Tim's stoic reply. "Secondary is secure, moving to your position now."

Dust from the shattered walls and broken infrastructure mixed with the speed of the savages made it impossible to acquire a target in their sites. As one, all three dropped to the bottom floor. The two savages in front were in full wolf form while the gunslinger – Billy the Kid – was not.

Instead, he simply laughed.

The laughter, high pitched and tittering, sounded more like a hyena's bark and caused the hairs on Dane's neck to rise. Billy – for there was no doubt who the savage was, or used to be – drew two semi-auto pistols that looked to be big enough to serve as anchors for an aircraft carrier. He fired as the wolves before him – obviously his guards – lunged, mid-howl, at the team of SKUL operators. Between the wolves and the guns, the team dove and took cover where they could. Some slid behind chairs, others behind overturned tables and around corners. Really, any-damned-where they could find cover. Jed and Twitch managed to get a few rounds off to keep them from being overrun in the tight quarters. Beside Dane, Tweeker was knocked backwards and came up grasping at his sternum. He'd been shot but the suit and plating had held.

"I'm okay," he gasped, painfully, before sending two precisely aimed rounds over the table. One savage fell dead, shot in the face, while the other kept coming. He swatted a huge paw that Dane ducked like he knew it was coming. The savage landed in a heap beyond, dead, taken down by the combined fire of Twitch and Jed. Dane whirled, training his gun on the last place the Gunslinger had been standing. Billy was nowhere to be seen, but Dane had zero time to worry about that. Two more savages – one, a woman, who changed instantly into a lithe killing machine – leaped into the fray and monopolized every ounce of his worry.

Anticipating their blood lust, Jed yelled, "Puffer out!" before tossing the silver nitrate grenade into the room.

The others covered him while he made the tosses.

As expansive as the living area was with regards to square footage, it was still an overtly confined room riddled with nooks and crannies. Precisely the type of environment the Puffers were made for. Instantly, the little grenade unleashed a fog of silver throughout the lower level of the house. In the truest since, Puffers were dispersal agents rather than explosive ordinance. As such, its destructive capabilities followed hallways and seeped under doorways, limited only by the overall size of the internal structure and wind. Not knowing the weapon's capability, or maybe it was just the overzealous nature of savages at large – most likely, a little of both – the two werewolves charged into the silver nitrate fog and were killed instantly. Their skin blistered like they had been dipped in hot oil until only white bone and unrecognizably desecrated tissue remained.

Dane's team quickly reformed at the foot of the stairs.

"Where the fuck did all of them come from?" demanded Dane of Tweeker and Jed.

"Panic room, Boss," reported Tweeker in obvious disgust. "I missed it on the first pass. Wasn't until they blew the door apart, and tossed Jed and I down here that I saw it. It's on me."

"We can debate this bullshit later," scolded Jed, obviously pissed more with himself than anything. "We need to take that target down. *Now*."

Immediately, Twitch began moving with the others on his heels, when that strange *fingernail-to-chalkboard*, hyena-like laughter began again. It was as if the savage was enjoying the fight he was in, as if he was ill-concerned about his safety, as if he felt he could not be killed.

He was playing with them. The men knew this fact like they knew their names.

The team made the upper landing and rounded a corner silently, entering a large room. Before them, illuminated in pearly-white moonlight, stood Billy the Kid in front of a tall window.

He looked highly amused.

Each member fired and the savage before them blurred, moving with such speed that their eyes couldn't fully grasp what they were seeing.

Not one bullet found their mark.

"You can't stop it. No one can. We're coming, legions of werewolves all bent on your destruction."

He laughed again.

Dane and the others answered Billy's ominous declaration the only way they knew how…with violence.

They fired.

All of them.

Again, nothing touched Billy and as he moved, he literally disappeared from their enhanced, fused visual system. Simply put, he moved faster than their goggles could comprehend.

"Not even gonna ask me?" Strangely, he made no move to take down the team, which he undoubtedly could. He just moved inside and around the fray. Honestly, he seemed genuinely interested in conversation.

Dane momentarily obliged.

"Ask you what?"

The old gunslinger laughed crazily, and then his face stilled.

"Oooh oh oh, I get it. You don't know we have it yet, do you?" He clapped his hands together excitedly, "Hot damned, this is gonna be better than I thought!"

Suddenly, he turned, becoming the wolf in full.

The transformation was terrifying and disjointed the commandos just long enough for Billy to make his escape. He dove through the gaping, glassless window created by the earlier WIPP blast faster than the eye could hope to comprehend. Dane ran to the window and looked out across the expanse of flat farmland surrounding the home.

Billy was nowhere to be seen.

Worse yet, the window faced away from Toad's position, as well as that of the target Titan had taken down.

Dane cursed. He knew where the men were.

"Toad?"

"Here, Boss."

"Better get to the house and help lock it down," Dane said, his voice a curious mix of bile and wonderment.

"Roger. Moving now."

"Boss, you better come look at this," called Jed, confusion and concern heavy on his voice. He led the way inside the well concealed doorway of panic room. It was easy to see why his men had missed it. The edges of the door slid perfectly into place, leaving not a millimeter's gap in the wall's surface. It was like the doorway to a hidden passage in an old *Scooby Doo* cartoons. If you did not know it was there, you would never know it was there. The team's feet squelched on the blood saturated carpet as they walked within the room. Mangled bodies ripped part by great claws and powerful teeth littered the floor.

"What the hell?" asked Dane, aghast at the carnage.

"No clue," Jed reported, "but Tim and his guys are reporting similar shit in the other building. Lots of drug paraphernalia and test tubes filled with that green shit werewolves call blood. But, Boss. Look at that face."

Jed pointed to a severed head over in the corner. It was puffy with bloat but recognizable and a moment later, Dane gasped. He knew the face. Jed turned his finger to another area, "And, that one over there."

"Christ," Dane spat, stopping him before he saw – or, had to see – more. He looked to Jed, his eyes begging for answers he knew would not come, "What the fuck is going on here, Jed?"

246

The old warrior was still, silent for a long moment, before finally lamenting, "I truly don't know, Boss."

He offered nothing further.

Dane shook his head, *this is bigger than we thought, worse than we imagined.* Over the intra-squad net he called, "Titan-lead, we need to scramble forensics. I want them going over this place with a fine-toothed comb before we turn it over to the cleaning crew."

"Already on it. ETA thirty mikes. I've got a Kilo element securing a perimeter as we speak."

"Copy that," replied Dane before turning to his guys. He ripped his helmet off his head and let it dangle at his side. Knowing what he knew, he could puke at any second had he kept the claustrophobic helmet on. "I want photos of everything...every room, every savage. Hard drives, documents, anything you can find..."

At that very instant, the faint sound of a ringing phone could be heard. It sounded like a horn bugle signaling a fox hunt, both anticipatory and forlorn in equal measure.

"Find that phone!" Dane ordered. "Find that phone, goddammit!"

A second later Twitch tossed it to him. How he found it so quickly was anyone's guess. It was impressive though. Dane put it on speaker before answering, "Hello."

In the background they could hear raucous laughter, loud music, and glasses clinking together.

The unsub was in bar.

"Billy, it's Andre."

The person on the other end of the line was having to scream over the noise of the bar. On a hunch and hoping the

247

noise in the background would make it impossible to know who was speaking, Dane answered, "Yeah, what's up?"

"De...dee...deeeelivered the pa...pa...package," stuttered whoever was on the other end.

*He's nervous, even on the phone,* thought Dane quickly as he began cataloguing the conversation in his mind.

The other party – Andre – continued, "Look, I kna...kna...knoooow you said here and ba...back, but I was wondering if I cu...cu...cu...could wait 'til morning? I've got something cookin', ya know?"

A giggle, obviously female, obviously right in the other man's ear, could be heard.

"Rog..." Dane shook his head with irritation. This pissant would not know *Roger* from his asshole, but you could damned well be it would give Dane away, "Where are you?"

"Da...Da...*Donanelle's*, su...su...south of Ha...Ha...Haaaaattiesburg."

Dane grinned and Jed began relaying the info to those back on the Silver Moon.

"Man, you just stay right where you are," Saber's ATL said before ending the call.

He looked to Jed. The older operator was still in his helmet, so the fright-inducing green eyes were what turned back to Dane. With a digitized voice, Jed said flatly, "Iroquois' on alert. SI-2s moving to target now."

As impossible as it was, Dane swore the respirators on the front of Jed's helmet turned upwards into an evil grin.

# 19)
## Side Job (part 2)

### Donanelle's Bar and Grill
### 0130

"Sorry folks, kitchen's closed," said the bartender without looking up from the glass he was wiping dry. He was a young, college student earning a paycheck at nights by working the bar. Without a word, two of the men moved toward the door that led to the back yard where a party was apparently being held. This caught the barkeep's attention. "That's a private party, fraternity..." he looked up and saw the suits, then noticed the big men wrapped in those suits. He sputtered, "...they payed good money!"

The men never stopped, though a third, older gentleman stood silent. After a few, uncomfortable minutes of silence, the men returned from the back. Neither said a word, they just shook their heads.

*They're looking for somebody*, thought the young man behind the bar. His unease was steadily on the rise. It was the silence in which they performed their tasks.

It was *unnatural*.

Finally, the older man moved unevenly to the bar.

*He's got a limp*, thought the bartender. *Looks like he used to be a fighter. Probably deserves whatever he got.*

The man placed a photo on the counter and spoke for the first time, "I'm looking for this person." He tapped the photo, beckoning the bartender to look. "I know he was here tonight...where is he?"

The kid looked at the photo and then, realizing it was a mug shot, leaned down for a closer look. "Yeah, he was here. Hard to miss him, harder to miss the babe he was spending all that money on if you know what I mean."

The kid chuckled. It sounded palsy and unconfident on their ears.

The older man looked up expectantly but did not say anything. His hard gaze made the kid even more uncomfortable until he finally realized the man had asked for the person's whereabouts.

"He left about half an hour ago. You guys just missed him," said the bartender, happy to oblige and hopeful to be rid of these patrons.

The man in the suit spat a curse and turned to the others, "Call it in. Tell them to start canvasing the area. He couldn't have gotten too far…"

"Ah, sir, I can show you where he is…" the men looked up from what appeared to be squat and chunky cell phones, "…if you'd like."

"Where?" demanded the older man.

"The owners built some small bungalows out back – six of them actually. Keeps the drunks off of the roads and brings in some extra change. Pretty good idea, actually, especially during football season. Biggest problem is keepin' the sheets clean. Man, there is a *lot* of fu…"

"Which one is he in?" interrupted the leader, obviously uninterested in any savvy business decisions or stories of promiscuous activity they kid may have seen.

"Number 3."

"Need a key."

The kid tossed a ring to him, "It's the one with the red tape on the head."

"Thanks," said the older man, turning for the door.

"Didn't get your name, man," called the kid after him.

"That's because I didn't give it to you."

"Need a name to mark down so we know who has the keys," pleading the young bartender who was now regretting his decision to be so helpful.

"No," stated the unidentified man firmly, "you don't."

Outside, the three SI-2s huddled together around the blacked out Tahoe they were using, "How you wanna play this, Armand?"

Armand Sarasse had learned a lot since that ill-fated night outside of a Magazine Street nursing home. He'd seen more in those few short minutes than his mind could comprehend, a mind that was nearly driven to insanity by the whole damned thing. That night, Mike Fornet – then his understudy, now his boss – saved his life by making a similar call that he was about to make.

Months later, Mike Fornet saved his life again by simply offering him a job.

*This* job.

"I'm sending an update to the Moon; then, I'm calling Black Site Shelby to get the boys there moving…after that, we're making a house call."

***

**Somewhere South of Hattiesburg, Mississippi**
**Satan's Bastards clubhouse**
**South MS Chapter**

## 0145

The black Range Rover slid through the junkyard's open gate and made its way, slowly, through the warren of crushed cars. Suddenly, a cell phone on the dash buzzed. The passenger read the simple message:

*They have Brussieux*

The passenger then said into the darkness of the vehicle, "Our source indicates they have Brussieux in custody. It's only a matter of time before they back track his movements back to here. We have to make this quick."

The flattened cars, stacked over ten feet high on both sides, bracketed a drive full of twists and turns. Eventually, the narrow, manmade road spilled out onto a gravel parking lot which was the open expanse in the junkyard. It was filled with motorcycles of varying shapes and builds along with revelers pissing and puking in dark corners. Others were engaged in far more explicit and carnal activities. Wild music spilled out from the large, cinder block building in the middle and joined with laughter, screams, and sporadic, undisciplined gunfire.

And, absolutely no one was having anything less than the time of their lives.

This was the *church*, the clubhouse of one of the largest chapters of the Satan's Bastards Motorcycle Club in the continental U.S.

The Range Rover moved through the lot and rocked to a stop mere feet away from the front door and, subsequently, the muscle guarding the entrance. Surrounded by women in varying degrees of dress – undress, really – the door guard did not initially react to the unknown vehicle that

252

just made his territory its own. In fact, it was not until the engine began to rev that he even bothered to take notice. By the time he fought himself through the small crowd, the Range Rover had belched out its occupants.

The men were small and nondescript though their olive complexion and slicked back, black hair spoke of Mediterranean descent. Dressed in similar business suits and dark sunglasses, they stood several feet apart surveying the situation. They were relaxed, nonplused by the ruckus and carousing that bordered on the obscene. And, this was just the doorway. There was no telling what lay beyond in the Satan's Bastards den of debauchery.

The big, pot-bellied guard wearing a Bastards' cut broke through the gaggle of giggling girls – many of whom looked well underage for the outfits they wore, let alone the activities they were participating in – and strode to their position. The guard put his hand to his waist in such a manner as to the expose the .45 pistol slung under his armpit.

This was meant as a warning.

He had been told to expect outsiders.

The two standing to either side of the center man looked inward. Obviously, the one in the center was in charge.

"You girls must be lost," the big Bastard said, grinning and winking over his shoulder to the girls behind. These men did not have business with him. They were here to see Three-Nips. This was just a show of dominance, the *hook* he needed to pull two or three into his bed. Panties would be dropping tonight. Chicks looking for a snort of booger sugar and some dick were always easy…and, these would be easier than the rest.

"And, you are?" asked the man in the center coolly.

"Mac," he looked back over his shoulder, still smiling on the outside, but something began scratching at his mind. Instinctively, he became nervous. Something about these guys was *off.*

"Well, Mr. Mac, we are here to take possession of something of value, something very precious to our Master."

The word *master* was spoken with such conviction it startled Mac who turned back to the girls for any amount of courage their presence may offer him. Unable to dampen their curiosity, they had crept close…too close. Mac mouth silently the word *Master,* much to their delight, and then turned back.

"Dude, Master? This is Amer…"

He did not get to finish his sentence. It's hard to speak when your head has been cleaved away from your body. The young girls' screams were lost on the heavy metal screaming out of the Satan's Bastards clubhouse.

***

**Donanelle's Bar and Grill**
**Bungalow #3**
**0145**

"Where is it?" Sarasse asked forcefully.

They had hit the room at just the right time…right at the apex of the couple's copulation. Both Brussieux and the girl – underage and putting everyone in a precarious situation – were taken without a fight. It's hard to put up any kind of fight when you're naked, harder still when on the threshold of sexual ecstasy.

Now the two were blindfolded, bounded, gagged, and separated, one on each of the small beds in the room.

"I...I...I duuuuuon't know whu...whu...what the fu...fuuu...fuck you're talking about," Brussieux stuttered, sputtered, and spat.

For a second, Armand Sarasse shook his head, not out of any irrepressible sign of respect but out of sheer disbelief someone could be so fucking stupid.

They *would* get their answers.

Sarasse nodded to the men on either side of Brussieux's bed. One man tilted the bed – feet first – while the other laid a towel from the bathroom over his face and pulled down. Brussieux was naked and tethered to the bed – his doing...his request from what they understood from the girl's ramblings. Sarasse laid the flat of a large knife across his *wedding tackle* – for effect, he'd never cut a man there – and began slowly pouring water. Brussieux's scream turned to spitting, gasping, and gurgling. Fifteen seconds later the water stopped, and the sheet was lifted.

Sarasse got in his face and again demanded. "We know you delivered a package to someone. Who did you deliver it to, and where are they?"

Brussieux spit a mixture of tears, saliva, and piss-pot motel water in his face. That little bit of defiance only resulted in a slap that was more patronizing than vicious. Because of that, it probably hurt worse. The man at Brussieux's head slammed the sheet back down on his face in anticipation of the next round. Brussieux's world went dark so he did not see Sarasse stand back and hiss, "Shoot her."

Cold fear gripped his marrow. Water boarding was one thing...but *murder?*

"Sir?" questioned one of the men.

The girl screamed for a split second, then she gagged and Brussieux could tell she was struggling against her captor. A second later she became quiet, the gag obviously seated properly once again.

"I said, *shoot her.*" He seethed. "She's nothing but a whore, and she's in my way. She should've listened to her dear old daddy and kept away from shitstains like she is with tonight. Either way, this sack of shit will probably talk once the chance for some more ass is out of the way...So, *shoot her.*"

"Fuck," the man hissed, obviously in both disagreement and disgust. A second later, suppressed gunfire that sounded like a large phone book being dropped on a table, five rounds total, bounced off the room's walls.

"Jesus," said the leader. His voice was laced with obvious revulsion, "Watch the fuckin' blood spatter. These are new shoes."

More water came then. It was poured for nearly thirty seconds this time, all the while, Brussieux screamed, spat, and slobbered. He was given a five count then the barrel of a gun was placed to his head.

"The cunt died...you don't have to. I'll repeat again, for the *last time,* where is the package, and who did you deliver it do?"

More water, he did not even have a chance to respond this time. Thirty second count, five second break, and again, more water.

Sarasse stood back and thought, *Jesus…I'm going to hell for this.*

By this time, Brussieux was begging through the sheet, and he was whimpering through the water.

"I'll tell you anything." He was crying also. "I swear, I'll tell you anything, just stop."

"I don't give a fuck about *anything;* I want to know where that package is."

Before Sarasse could finish, Brussieux was telling them the name of the junkyard and how to get there. He could hear one of his unidentified assailants was speaking to someone else on a phone.

The way he spoke sounded almost…*military?*

That could not be right…could it?

Before he could process anything, the gun barrel was back against his head, and the gag was stuffed deeper than ever into his mouth. "Make one sound, one fuckin' sound, and I swear to all that's good and holy, I'll end you like I had that whore ended a few minutes ago, understand?"

Andre Brussieux could not speak, and since he had already pissed down both legs, he chose to nod and hope for the best. He wanted to scream for help, but believed what the man said.

They would kill him.

A subjective eternity passed until the door of the bungalow flew open with a slam. The men entering the room identified themselves officers of the Forest County Sheriff's

Department. Shortly thereafter, his blindfold was ripped from his face, but he kept his eyes shut. He really, really did not want to see his dead hookup…

*What was her name? Goddammit, what was her name?*

Involuntarily, his eyes came open. But, there was no blood and brain matter splattered over hell's half acre. Nope, the girl was alive.

*Kim…fuck yeah, her name was Kim.*

She was bound and gagged and looking at him through eyes wide with fright. He tried to roll over, only he couldn't. He was chained to the bed and so was she. He had an eight ball of heroin in his right pants pocket – which he could not get to if he wanted to – enough cocaine lined out on the room's table to get half of China high, and if that was not enough, the Kim chick was only seventeen.

*Seven-fucking-teen,* that fact was like getting a kick to the nuts followed closely by the realization that there was not a person on the planet that would believe their story about the men from earlier.

*I'm fucked,* was his third thought, the last one Andre Brussieux had as a free man for over thirty years.

***

Armand and the other guys wanted to puke after the torture and maniacal orchestration of human emotions they had just been a part of. It was not natural to fuck with another human like that, and at their core, they knew it was wrong. Equally though, they knew they had to push through it and do their job, or all of humanity would pay.

Their souls or mankind's…for them, the choice was easy.

"Call it in," commanded Sarasse. Call it old, crusty cop-sense, but deep in his marrow, he knew this was bigger than anything they were prepared for. And, frankly, that scared the living shit out of him. "Get them moving to the target, *now*. And, for chrissakes, confirm Snake Charmer is on station.

***

The three werewolves were done, and so was the South MS Chapter of the Satan's Bastards. The inches deep river of blood and stench of feces and piss confirmed that much. All three savages stalked from the back of the clubhouse to the front, sloshing through the blood and gore, sated for the moment. The leader bent at the waist and wrenched the box from Three-Nips' hands. He was still alive, but only just, bleeding from several mortal wounds.

It would not be long.

At a table nearest the front entrance a cell phone vibrated. The icon on the front of the phone showed the message being nearly fifteen minutes old. Seeing this, realizing they had been careless, the werewolf cursed. In their blood lust they had neglected the phone, their lifeline that aided in keeping doom and destruction from making a visit. The message was quickly read:

*They are coming*

For the first time in a long, long time, the three savages felt fear and bounded from the clubhouse. As their clawed paws hit gravel, the walls of the flattened vehicles spat out a blacked out SUV.

A growl escaped one of the savages, a quick tempered True Wolf just under a century old. He was spoiling for a fight, he lusted for a fight, but his brother - older and more mature by a subjective power of ten, turned to him, "No brother. This is not our fight." Rounds of silver stitched the ground causing the three to dive for cover. One of the rounds creased the elder wolf's shoulder. It was nowhere near a mortal would, but it hurt like hell. The silver burned like nothing he had ever felt or ever wanted to again. Through gritted teeth he said, "Not now at least. Run, brothers! We have to get the package away."

The three turned and in a single, monstrous bound, leaped over the wall of flattened cars and disappeared into the night.

***

The SUV slid sideways to a stop and five KtacS clad operators spilled out instantly. They knew they were just seconds too late, and in this game of mortals versus humans, seconds counted. They also knew they had failed to successfully complete their mission, for the moment, in any case. That bit of knowledge cut the group of men – so unused to anything other than outright success – deep. Moreover, though none would ever admit to such vanity, it stung their egos.

"Poncho...Nightmare, check the building," ordered ChiTown. "I doubt there's anyone left alive, but we can't have a bunch of bikers turning on us."

"What the hell do you want us to do to anyone that's bit?" snapped Poncho.

"End the threat," said ChiTown flatly. The men disappeared into the clubhouse and ChiTown turned, "Diggs, you and Shakes secure the area and make sure those things are outta here."

"Roger that," a-firmed both men as they stalked off into the night.

ChiTown switched frequencies to the one owned by the all-seeing eye. "Iroquois-six to Snake Charmer-two-five, over."

"I have them in my scopes, Iroquois-six," said a voice, female and not unattractive sounding. "Savages are three klicks out, moving north-northwest…damn these things are fast."

*Rookie,* he thought, *they're always in awe the first few encounters.*

"Sir, my baby sports two, one hundred pound hellfire missiles. More than enough to end this situation, and the area is rural enough to support the action. Request permission to terminate with extreme prejudice."

*She's got balls, I'll give her that. Taggert's liable to have her ass for even suggesting the use of hellfire missiles on the homeland.*

"Negative, Snake Charmer. It's the package that's the priority."

"Roger that, sir." The disappointment in her voice was undeniable.

"Cheer up, soldier," said ChiTown through a smile. "You'll have more than enough opportunity to blow shit up. Right now though, I need you to scope those savages. How long are you on station?"

"As long as you can dance, sir," the woman UAV pilot said. Her enthusiasm was infectious.

"Solid, Snake Charmer.  Gives us five, and we're following your lead."

"Negative, Iroquois-six…"

*Fuckin' Taggert,* ChiTown thought though managing to suppress his anger.

"…you and your team are to stay on target until forensics gets there.  They need to know what you've seen and need some support until we can get the area locked down.  After that, I want your guys ponied up and on the hunt.  How copy?"

"Solid, sir," ChiTown Jackson said through gritted teeth.  "Commencing SSE now.  Iroquois-six, out."  In his mind he thought, *you spineless sack…they'll be gone by the time we can get cut loose.*

# 20)
## Nightshade's Hot Wash

**Action Room 1**
**Silver Moon**
**0500**

Tim, assault force lead, had just finished walking the audience through the stages of *Operation Nightshade*. His voice was punctuated by the split screen video feed as seen through the operator's eyes. This was the *after action review* which every team and, subsequently, every individual involved in the operation would give their own report, from their own perspective. What the team felt worked was highlighted along with where they felt they fell short, in equal portions. Just to sit in on these reviews and continue to work without holding any animosity demanded thick skin or you would not be long for any special operations force, much less SKUL. Strictly speaking, there was not a shooter walking SKUL's ranks that had not had their performance broken down to a cellular level during these hot washes.

Today would be no different.

"Metcalf," Taggert called from the shadows of the back wall, "was this not to be a silent breach? Who ordered your entry?"

Twitch was as cool and calm as the breeze, "No one, sir. We lost the element of surprise when the shooting started. We needed to get out of the open as quickly as possible, and our only option was a hard entry."

"I see," Taggert said as he thumbed through his notes. "And, what about Titan? Is it habit to leave men in battle stranded?"

Twitch leaned forward in his seat, his shoulder muscles rigid and his biceps and jaws clenched in time, "No sir." His coolness waned now, slightly unnerved by this line of questioning, "My habit is to get my team to the objective, *sir.*"

Seeing the raw, exposed nerve that was beginning to drive his friend's thoughts, Dane stepped forward, "It was the right move, sir."

Tim added, "Our mission was Gunslinger. Twitch did what needed to be done. I would have done the same."

"I didn't ask either of you a damned thing," Taggert snapped, driving the room to silence. "What about the savages that showed up *after* the target was secured?"

"Sir," Tweeker said standing, "that was my responsibility. It's on me."

"I missed it too, Con," Jed said, coming to Tweeker's defense. Dane's heart swelled with pride as he watched his team gel into a single, solid unit. This was not about SKUL; hell, it was not even about the savages. This was about one brother's love for another. Jed continued, "It was a panic room, built to be hidden. There ain't an operator under our shield that would have seen it under the operational strain we were in."

For a long, metaphorical moment the room was again silent. Finally, the Admiral, flanked by Shamus – whose appearance at an operational debrief was unusual – and Wild Bill Kipling, spoke, "Taggert, mistakes are made on every

264

operation. The important thing, as you know, is to figure it out and fix it."

"Sir," Taggert said, quietly ending his line of questioning.

"You and you," the Skipper pointed to Dane and Jed, "you mentioned knowing these savages? How so?"

"Some of them, sir. Two to be exact," acknowledged Dane while skipping through the PowerPoint for the slides he wanted. They were photos of men in the throes of death taken on-site at the plantation the Gunslinger had used as a base of operations. "Chief Petty Officer Chip Tredwell, former DEVGRU operator." Dane looked to the Admiral, his eyes heavy, his voice husky and so sad even Briggs cringed.

He clicked the remote and Jed announced, "Master Sergeant Tate Sax who served in the 82nd Airborne, Special Forces, and finally, the Unit. He spent time in Serbia, Iraq, Malaysia, Afghanistan, and dozens of other shitholes in between, sir."

The Skipper looked from one man to the next slowly and completely slack-jawed. He was only just beginning to comprehend the weight of what had just been said. The terrifying enormity began falling into place.

Dane added to the silent room, "Eventually, General Pattridge recruited both to Section 8 where they served in the squadron I commanded until their deaths."

The nods from Tweeker and Toad confirmed what Dane was saying.

Tim took up the narrative from there. He clicked his remote and brought up a series of photos of a man and woman. "Mr. and Mrs. Thomas Latresse. Obviously, they never made it to Prague. We believe they were taken hostage, and the paper trail was nothing more than a false lead meant to confound anyone that came looking for them. We also believe they are newly changed savages...like in the last few days newly changed. Their mental state alone at the time of our operation speaks to that fact."

Tim's synopsis sunk to the marrow.

"Meadows, you're saying these..." Wild Bill, Whiskey's platoon leader, searched for the proper word, "...*things* were turned just a matter of days ago, some of whom were special operations' personnel?"

"Possibly today, Bill," Titan's team leader confirmed flatly. "Moon's full, so it stands to reason we're correct."

Dane looked to the Skipper.

His face was slack as he wrestled with each and every possible implication. Each one was more horrifying than the previous. Coupled with the intelligence gathered from Kilo's failed recovery of whatever was in that box...well, the possibilities were too horrifying to imagine. His voice was but a hoarse whisper, "I've never seen activity like this, never even heard of it. You just don't survive a bite from a werewolf, the trauma caused is catastrophic for most. It's the one thing that's kept werewolf kind in check all these years. Those that happen to survive the bite are generally driven mad or killed by their own kind, and you're saying these savages have been newly turned?"

Dane nodded and said, though no one was looking his way, "Like to-fuckin-night newly turned....*sir*. But there were no signs of them being bitten."

The Admiral nodded, taking in every eye with his own instantly, "Then we have to assume they have finally figured out a way around their evolutionary quandary that has been mankind's saving grace for eons."

Upon hearing this, a deep and foreboding silence as complete and unyielding as the front gates of hell slammed shut on those in the room.

# 21)
## Continuance

**0600**
**Action Room 1**
**Silver Moon**

    "At approximately 0130 this morning, an element of intel agents and Kilo shooters began an operation codenamed *Side Job*. The goal of the mission was the capture and apprehension of Andre Brussieux, prospect of the New Orleans chapter of the Satan's Bastards MC. He was the same individual you witnessed leaving your target site via the Pegasus feed. He was also the person you spoke to on the phone during your operation. It was also hoped we could obtain whatever it was Brussieux was transporting. To that end, we failed.

    Briggs clicked a remote, and a large flat screen came to life.

    The view was from the helmet cam of one of the operators, the team leader – ChiTown. From the video, Dane could tell the team was speeding down an airport runway in pursuit of a small, private airplane. The plane was rolling sterile meaning it had no identifying serial number or any other markings. Suddenly, three savages appeared in the operator's FVS as plumes of heat carrying all of the intensity of a super nova. The three positioned themselves between the on-coming SUV and the outgoing plane. The team – Iroquois – was pressed into a fight, and fight they did. While they managed to take out the savages in relatively short order, precious minutes were lost. As the silhouette of the plane disappeared into the night, the audio feed from ChiTown to the drone operator painted a grim picture.

"Snake Charmer-two-five, tell me you have a fix on that airplane!"

"Roger that, Iroquois. Be advised, we are *bingo* fuel." The crowd listening shook their collective heads. Bingo fuel meant just enough to make it back to base.

"Fuck!" cursed ChiTown. "Where is the other drone?"

"Five mikes out," replied Snake Charmer flatly.

"Dammit. Gimme a few more minutes on station Snake Charmer?" requested ChiTown desperately.

"Negative, Iroquois," broke in another voice. "Snake Charmer is RTB – *return to base.*"

*Taggert,* Dane thought as he sat grinding his teeth. He felt the frustration ChiTown much have felt on the ground. *Some things never change.*

The screen went black as the Skipper took up the narrative. "The package – whatever it is – is in the wind. Iroquois is on the hunt...let's pray they run it down."

Tweeker raised his hand to which the Admiral tipped his chin, "Sir, any idea what was in the tube, and why it's so important?"

The Skipper looked to Samantha Steele who answered with all the emotion of a rattlesnake eyeballing a wounded mouse, "Conjecture at this point, but given the description related by Mr. Brussieux to an SI-two on the scene, we believe it may be blood...werewolf blood."

"And, that's important why?" asked Jed while thoughtfully stroking his handlebar mustache.

270

"Again, we're working with too many unknowns to be certain," Sam stated rather emphatically, "but the initial tox screens show the residue in those test tubes you found at the plantation to be a mixture of werewolf blood and cocaine." This set the room to motion as men put their heads together to speak in hushed tones. The talk was troubled, and Sam suspected they had already guessed what she was about to say…but, she said it anyway. "We've suspected for years they were searching for a way to improve *turning* rates with an end goal of creating some means of mass dispersal. It's a safe bet they are at least in the right ball park, and may very well be stealing the other team's signs."

Her words were black and ominous, causing the men to devolve into unrest as the mad grumble of discourse rolled through the room. The implications of Sam's concerns not lost on any of them.

Finally, Tommy Granderson – Rhino's TL – managed to quieten the crowd by bellowing a simple command, "Shut the fuck up!" Granderson was an enigma even within SKUL, an organization filled with enigmatic characters with *sketchy* backgrounds. What could not be argued about Rhino's TL was that he was a well-liked and extremely competent leader. He was also very, very deadly…like a black mamba strike to the jugular type of deadly. And now, his dark eyes were turned on the room which had fallen still and quiet. "You're all acting like a bunch of pussies! Our mission hasn't changed one iota – find, fix, and finish." His face then broke into a wide grin, "Just gonna have a larger workload, that's all."

With that, the attitude picked back up, and the discontent waned. The Admiral was no fool, though. He knew it was likely to return.

*Hell Bart, who can blame them? You just dumped the world's largest shit sandwich in their lap, and it's just the beginning.*

With that morbid thought still a fresh gash in his mind, he dismissed all present, "Alright, people, this is doing us no good. We should have follow-on information later today so keep your SICS and tablets within arm's reach."

***

Billy leaned against the wrought iron fence and watched a new day being born in all its pink and orange glory. He was in the Garden District, and the mansion spreading out before him was the home of the New Orleans crime boss, Guiseppi Della Rocca. Billy knew enough to know *Della Rocca* was only the latest in a long line of surnames. Surnames that spanned the course of millennia and dated back to the first recordings of human history. It's a safe bet the werewolf was older than that. Unlike most werewolves he'd dealt with over the course of his long life, he knew Della Rocca to be level headed and thoughtful. He also knew this was just a fancy way of saying the old wolf was calculating and, above all, very, very dangerous.

Instinctively, he felt eyes on him from somewhere in the shadows, felt them boring subjective holes through him, even before Della Rocca's men appeared from the shadows of the wooded yard. These men were not of his kind and could not so much as make eye contact with him. They were subservient beings who moved very slowly, very deliberately around him. Had they been capable, they would have pinned

272

their ears to their heads in submission, a fact that long since ceased to amuse him.

"He's waiting in his study," was all the man in the dark blue suit said as he opened the gate.

Nonchalantly, Billy walked across the finely manicured yard whistling a long forgotten wagon train tune. When he topped the stairs, the door slid open on its own accord. *This* caused Billy pause. There were a lot of uncertainties with this meeting, but it was only now that he truly felt the ripple of fear that rode his spine.

From deep within the house came a simple command, "Enter."

Della Rocca's voice was soft, dangerously so, and suddenly, Billy was struck with horrors that bubbled up from unfathomable depths. Every ounce of his being began to scream *Run, run you idiot.*

But, he couldn't.

In fact, for a moment he was paralyzed with fear until the voice said again, "Come in, Billy." Behind those words came more, these with the greasy smile of malevolence attached, "I've spoken to Stefan. There's nothing to fear here."

Unnerved yet forcing himself to calm down, he stepped through the door.

Once through, the heavy door slammed shut behind him, ominously. The old wolf sat lounging in human form, resting his hands on the head of a cane, before a blazing fire. To add to Billy's anxiety was the fact Della Rocca was smiling yet there was no warmth in it, no comfort, no *anything* save for death. His yellow eyes burned hotter than the fire in the hearth, the heat therein worming its way into his mind. Billy gasped from the pain of it and begged, subconsciously, to be released from its grasp. Finally, and through great effort, he managed to say, "It's done."

His voice sounded ragged, like old, yellowed paper crumpled and left to decompose.

The old man casually motioned to the chair before him, "Sit." The motion and tone were so patronizing it felt like a psychic slap to the face with an empty glove. Old school chivalry at its finest. The type of thing that beings as old as Billy and Della Rocca understood.

Even so, Billy did as he was commanded, still wanting desperately to run…still unable to. The man's dominance dripped so strongly it stung and forced the younger wolf to look away. Della Rocca's mere presence made Billy feel weak and insignificant, like comparing a single raindrop to a wild, rushing river. These were completely foreign feelings that Billy was not at all familiar nor comfortable with. Billy was used to being the most feared creature in the room, but Della Rocca was on another level of fearsome. Della Rocca was one of the last of the Great Wolves, the Eldrich, and that bit of knowledge struck Billy with mind numbing terror. He could feel the man's eyes on him, searching, probing until he could not take it anymore. Finally and with no warning, the pressure subsided. It was like an outgoing tide, and Billy's chest heaved from the sheer relief of it.

Billy, crazed and psychotic as he was, easily regained control of his faculties. Enough, in any case, to fake a minor bit of joviality, "Well, here I am, as requested."

"Well, well…if it isn't Stefan's dog?"

Billy's smile faded, and its place was reclaimed only by fear. The old Eldrich wolf Della Rocca was referring to had promised he would explain everything. "I was told you were aware." Unlike the werewolf he stood before, he held no desire to rule the world. He had always use his immortality as a sort of pleasure seeking Ponzi scheme and the only things he cared about was the next adventure and the next *go-round* with Kayla, which were pretty much one and the same. But, these wolves were different and played by a different set of rules. Rules that could find even Billy the Kid waking up on the wrong side of the dirt. As it was, he was glad he had good news to share for a change, "Thought you were bat shit crazy until I actually used the blood on those test subjects."

Della Rocca chuckled. It sounded deep and throaty but lacked the warmth of a human's basso laugh. "I take it you were successful?"

Billy's cheeks puffed in mocking scorn, "Sheeeeit yeah. Damnations, I ain't never seen anything like that. I don't know what wolf you pulled that out of, but it's a keeper. Every last subject was turned."

Della Rocca's face clouded, and there was an edge to his voice, "It's best you not think too hard about where or more specifically *who* the blood could have come from." There was no mistaking the growing, feral growl that accompanied those words.

Billy held up his hands, palms forward, in placation, "Hey man, that's cool by me. You're the boss."

Della Rocca smiled and realized, yet again, that despite himself he really did like Billy, "And, where are these *successfully* turned subjects at the moment?" The question caused Billy to shift uncomfortably in his seat before clearing his throat.

"Billy, the subjects?" Guiseppi demanded.

The old gunslinger cleared his throat again before looking Guiseppi in the eyes, saying flatly, "Dead."

Guiseppi Della Rocca's eyes glowed; and, instantly, he was on his feet. He was a blur that moved faster than Billy could follow. That is, until Della Rocca's hands snapped around his throat. Suddenly, William H. Boney a.k.a Billy the Kid a.k.a Billy Blackshanks, was hovering off his feet as a gigantic, claw-tipped paw began squeezing him about the neck, strangling him.

"What do you mean, *dead?*" Guiseppi growled as he slammed Billy's head into – and through – the custom, walnut-paneled wall of his study. He brought Billy's face close to his, slobbering drool over the smaller man's face while Billy bled green from the trauma racking his neck.

"We...were...attacked," Billy gasped, though only just, as the bands of his windpipe screamed under the pressure.

"Attacked," growled the old wolf, "by whom?"

"SKUL." Billy, though immortal, found himself panicking as he struggled for air in the grip of the Eldrich wolf.

Hearing this, Della Rocca released his grip on the young True Wolf and forced himself to calm. "SKUL you say?"

Billy was still doubled over, gagging from the trauma, but managed, "No doubt. Almost didn't make it out myself, and lost several of my crew in the process."

"And, your mule? Did he make the next drop with the vial intact?"

Billy nodded and smirked a little - but only just a little, "Of course, what do I look like, an idiot. That was priority one."

"Good, boy," patronized Della Rocca even as Billy continued.

"Speaking of, he should have checked in by..." Billy stopped mid-sentence and began patting himself down. His face fell off the mountaintop of triumph and into the pits of despair.

Seeing the young wolf's reaction, Guiseppi demanded, "What's wrong, Billy?"

"Well," Billy gulped, unused to being the scared one in a conversation, "my man should have checked in before we were attacked, but he didn't. I didn't think too much about it, but now...I...well, I must have lost my cell phone when the house was stormed."

Della Rocca's face clouded as he sat back in his plush, leather chair. Quietly, he said, "So SKUL has a direct link to your transporter, a way to track you, and possibly even the vial itself." Della Rocca closed his eyes, again attempting to calm himself down.

"I'm on it, Guis..."

Della Rocca cut him off, pointing an angry finger at his chest while growling terribly, "Shut up! Get out of here now, Billy. If I see you before I want to, I'll kill you myself."

Billy stood and walked to the door. Over his shoulder he flippantly said, "Okay, but don't say I didn't try to warn you?"

It was not the old gunslinger's words that caught Guiseppi's attention but rather his Cheshire cat grin. "Billy…"

"I mean, it's not like someone like *you* could ever need anything from someone like *moi* is it?" Billy added emphasized smugness on all the little important words like *you* and *moi* which just happened to be more than Guiseppi could stand.

"Billy!" the old werewolf only barely forcing a blanket of calm over his anger, but it was a thin blanket. "Do not make me ask again."

Billy, knowing he was dangerously close to pressing his luck with the old wolf, pulled a small glass ampule from an inside pocket of his vest. He rolled it over in his hands before holding it before him. The green liquid swirled angrily in the study's low, warm light and upon seeing it the Eldrich wolf gasped. Guiseppi, knowing whose blood this belong too, looked upon the ampule with sheer wonderment etched across his face. Memories, long since forgotten, flooded his mind. Memories of wars and blood. Memories of being worshipped and damned in equal portions.

"I, ah," Billy stammered, unnerved by the feeling he had something extraordinary in his possession. Something that was capable of giving pause even to an ancient and powerful being such as Guiseppi Della Rocca. "I hung on to this…just in case." Billy smiled that devil-may-care smile of his then added, "Still friends, right?"

Della Rocca gazed at the vial desirously for a long while before finally saying, his voice but a whisper, "One hundred percent success rate you say?"

Billy nodded, "One hundred."

"And, how many can you turn with this sample?"

Billy shrugged, "I dunno…a whole bunch. Like I said, I'm not sure where this came from but this. Shit. Is. Potent."

Della Rocca closed his eyes tight, calming himself yet again before he commanded, "Then go. Do what you do best."

Billy, confused now more than ever, asked, "Which is?"

Guiseppi opened eyes which were now more or less cauldrons of fire and smiled. It was an evil smile, a wicked grin. It was the smile of a psychopath. A low growl, terrible and hungry, rolled across the room as the old werewolf spoke, "Chaos."

# 22)
## Side Job (part 3)

### Admiral's Quarters
### 2000

The Admiral addressed the knock at his door, "It's open, Con," before grabbing a second tumbler from a shelf.

"You wanted to see me, sir?" His second in command stood rigidly at attention just inside his doorway.

*Always the officer,* the Skipper thought with slight disdain though his tone was warm and cordial. "Yeah, son." He motioned to a stool at the small bar which was the centerpiece of his eloquent stateroom. "Come in and have a seat...drink?"

"Thank you, sir."

The Admiral poured a healthy glass – bourbon and ice – and slid it across the mahogany countertop. "Con, I'm wondering what you hoped to gain with the direction you took *Nightshade*'s debrief?"

Taggert was in the middle of raising his glass to his lips, and the Admiral's question caused him to stop the glass halfway along its journey. He thought about the question for a moment, took a healthy mouthful from his drink, and then held the Skipper's gaze. "Debriefs always get heated, sir. That's why the men call them *hot washes.* I am unaware of any changes in our operational procedures or that anyone deserves any special treatment."

"You're exactly right, Con. We haven't changed anything; and no one deserves any kind of special treatment; yet, you've certainly treated Stackwell differently than any other TL we have. You're letting your grudge against him affect your ability as a Commander."

Taggert dropped the glass on the bar a little more forcibly than intended, "I'm sorry you feel that way, sir; but with all due respect, I fail to see how pointing out mistakes made – mistakes which could have negatively affected the outcome of the operation – constitutes grudge holding. It's my job to ask those questions."

"Fair point," the Admiral conceded, "but, I'm more concerned with the way you cut off both Stackwell and Meadows – two team leaders – as they stepped in to assist their men. In times such as these, we need men who'll stand by their subordinates through the good times and the bad. That's not only being a good teammate…that's being a good leader, Con."

"Understood, sir. Won't happen again."

"Do you understand?" asked the Admiral as he stepped away from the bar and crossed his arms. He searched Conroy Taggert's face for a moment then continued, "As you know, Iroquois team is tracking an unknown, yet high priority, object. I want you to link up with them and take command of that side of the operation."

Taggert became rigid and his voice was wooden, "You're shipping me out over how I handled today's debrief?"

"No, son. I'm sending you out to command a very important mission. I would go myself if I could, but we both know I can't. With the way these savages seem to be multiplying, I need English here to lead the bulk of Kilo." The Admiral searched Taggert's face and knew he had failed

282

to placate the officer. "This'll give you a chance to get off the ship and away from the pressure and scrutiny that comes from being SKUL's second. You'll finally get the chance to develop your own command philosophy without my fingerprints all over everything. Con, the fact of the matter is I won't be around forever, and I need to know that when my time comes, you'll be able to answer the call and keep SKUL moving forward.

"So, it's a *test?*" Taggert snapped, cutting the Admiral's words off like a hangnail. "After all these years, I'm still being *tested?*" Though his words and anger were bad enough, it was his fractured tone that worried the Skipper the most.

"Yes, son," the Admiral said through a heavy sigh, "that's exactly what this is. We're all tested every single day, and you're no different. Whether you're the analyst scrounging for actionable intel and praying it's on the money, a member of the alert team that will be inserted into what amounts to a four-fire-alarm shit storm, or the commander giving the green light, we're all tested daily to be the best we can possibly be. Hell, son, the simple act of getting out of bed each morning – given what we know of the *real* world – and are able to function normally is a test ninety-nine percent of the populace is incapable of."

Taggert sat a little taller now, and the Admiral knew he had said what needed to be said. So, he let his words linger. He let Taggert feel as though he was part of the decision even though, in truth, he was not.

"I'll do my best, sir," Taggert stated confidently.

"I know you will, son," the Admiral agreed, and that was the truth. "Take a full tactical load out with you...might be good to kick a door or two down. And, Taggert, keep me up to speed. You're my eyes here, son."

Taggert smiled, "Yes, sir."

The Skipper looked his younger protégé over one last time, smiled, then said, "Your helo is off the deck at 0600 tomorrow; so, get out of here. I've had two drinks which means I'll have to take a piss forty-eleven times tonight; so, I might as well get started."

"Yes, sir," Taggert held out his hand, and the men shook. "I won't let you down, sir," he said, turning and walking out of the stateroom, smiling. Though an unplanned circumstance, he certainly could not imagine a better situation he could have been placed in.

The Admiral's voice trailed after him, "Take care of yourself, Con...but, after you take care of your men."

## 23)
## Would You Like Fries With That Foot?

**Ops Center**
**Silver Moon**
**1600**

Two platoons – Whiskey, the alert platoon and its support element, Kilo – were present in full while Foxtrot's platoon leader, Stan Woods, and a smattering of operatives from various Foxtrot teams joined the briefing. Foxtrot, fresh from a recent combat deployment along with serving as Whiskey platoon's cadre at SEE-S, was the *standby* platoon, in case the shit hit the fan. Many of Foxtrot's operators were taking advantage of the downtime by reconnecting with family – if they had any – or by attending any of SKUL's dozens of training blocks. Even though most of Foxtrot was off-ship, Dane knew that the guys could be stepping off a helo and onto the deck of the Silver Moon with nary a moment's notice.

Seeing familiar faces that had been so involved with Whiskey platoon's recent training comforted Dane in a way that was difficult to understand. Seeing them back, ready for action so soon after their own combat trials also said a lot about the men that called SKUL home.

What was a roomful of shooters bantering boisterously – and on a noticeably obscene level – silenced immediately upon the Skipper's entrance. Now all sat listening and attentively taking notes as they were updated with the latest intel.

"As guessed initially, none of the savages show any evidence of being bitten. Granted, we have to consider they've developed some modicum of the unnatural healing rates we've come to expect from the werewolves. Still though, given how recently the individuals in question had been turned, it's safe to assume they have developed another way of inducing the transformation...a more successful method."

The presenter, Dr. Hyram, SKUL's chief pathologist and foremost expert on the biological nuances of werewolves, allowed the murmurs that stirred throughout the room to settle down before continuing. "As frustrating a process as this has been, we have identified a single commonality shared by each subject. Each has traces of cocaine in their blood stream," reported the doctor succinctly. "Keep in mind, this is only a preliminary report, but I feel confident in my findings thus far."

"Thank you doctor," said the Skipper. "I'd appreciate an update the minute you have any further news."

"I'll deliver them personally. When I know, you'll know, Skipper," Dr. Hyram assured. "Now, if you'll excuse me, I'll get back to work."

Once the door closed on the doctor, Admiral Briggs continued, "Mrs. Steele?"

Sam Steele stood at the opposite side of the large table sitting in the middle of the Ops Center's stage. She was dressed in tan cargo shorts and a white linen shirt. Her sleeves were rolled up and served to highlight her dark tan skin, hair, and almond eyes. Wearing what could be but a hint of makeup – if any at all – Dane could not help thinking the intelligence officer had the unique gift of looking incredible without trying. In fact, she looked purely radiant as she grabbed the clicker and addressed the audience. "Thank you, Admiral Briggs."

Without thinking, Dane's eyes locked on Sam's perfectly proportioned curves until, finally, he became conscious of the fact. He was so lost in her beauty he physically had to shake his head thinking, *stop it you idiot.* After that, he managed to listen to her part of the briefing, but it was hard – the listening, that is. Due to his exhausted state – he and the rest of his team had been going strong for nearly thirty-six hours – his mind wandered periodically back to…well, Sam.

"Thanks to the intelligence Mr. Brusseiux was able to supply, our analysts and SI-2s were able to locate Barney Stansberry a.k.a Three-Nips. Once pinning down his location, a quick reaction force of Kilo operatives was sent to apprehend the man and take him in for questioning." Sam clicked the remote in her hand and the CCTV revealed a gruesome scene. "This is all they found of him and the rest of the membership of his club. Intermingled among the bodies are their wives, girlfriends, and…" Sam's voice broke off. Dane could tell she was swallowing a heavy dose of emotion. She cleared her throat, "…there were even some children among the dead."

Composed again, Sam clicked through several slides, stopping on each for several long seconds, before moving to the next. Each revealed severed appendages, spilt viscera, and beaten and mauled facial features. In truth, the photos depicted nothing more than wholesale slaughter.

The room fell starkly silent when Sam clicked to the slide with the photo of Three-Nips. It was a gruesome, nightmarish scene that left what was once a man looking like mere hamburger meat left out in the sun for too long.

Dane raised his hand.

"Yes, Commander?"

"Not to sound like an ass ma'am, but how do we know this is actually Three-Nips? I mean, it looks more like a hundred and eighty pounds of spilt fuck." The rumble of shocked, choked-off snorts of laughter rolled across the room. The men fought to keep it professional – some doing better than others – while Dane sunk in his seat a little. He could feel the heat rising into his cheeks as he silently cursed his stupid internal filter that never worked properly. "What I mean, Sam, is…"

Sam threw her hands in the air, shot him a look of frustration, and cut off anything else he had to say, "I get it, I get it!" She clicked the remote quickly to produce a slide that revealed an arrest record affixed with a photo on the upper right hand corner and two sets of fingerprints. The man indicated on the record was Barney Stansberry. "Luckily, several fingers were found intact which helped ID Mr. Stansberry." Sam clicked the remote again to reveal a document filled with letters, numbers, and signatures. "DNA analysis has subsequently confirmed Mr. Stansberry's identity."

"Roger that," Dane replied, scratching a quick note before attempting to recover from his blatant violation of professional behavior. "Apologies for the *fuck*, Sam."

The snorts picked back up in earnest and were now bordering on outright laughter. Someone behind Dane finally lost it and struggled to say as quietly as possible, "Oh dear Lord!" – which is to say, not very quietly at all. Dane looked around the room, unsure what the big deal was, until it hit him. His face flushed crimson and he felt hot. Quickly, he realized he should have just kept his mouth shut; but, to his great surprise, Sam chuckled softly and shook her head. Mercifully, she steered the room back to other, less explicit topics.

As she spoke, Jed leaned into Dane's ear. He spit a wad of tobacco-laced saliva into a water bottle half full of the same before whispering, "Speaking of *fuck*, Boss. For your own sake, would you please shut the fuck up?"

Dane sunk further in his seat, face-palming himself, and just nodded his head by way of reply. The rest of the briefing went as well as could be expected, considering. Fortunately for both he and Sam, Dane managed to keep his mouth shut the entire time. Upon dismissal, teams Saber and Titan were told they were to stand down for the next forty-eight hours. This would allow the guys to get some rest and recover from any bumps and bruises incurred during *Operation Nightshade*.

\*\*\*

After the briefing was adjourned, Dane quickly ducked out without speaking to anyone. He really, really did not want to discuss his most recent bout of oral dysentery and so, he headed to his stateroom alone. He had not written Henry in a while, Abbey either for that matter; though, he imagined that little factoid was just as well to her liking. After the last day or so, he just needed to talk to his son; regardless of the fact that it was only a one way conversation with only his thoughts to spill out on the paper.

He missed Henry; so much so, he ached on a higher plane than a meaningless, metaphorical pain. He physically hurt. The letters helped but were understandably a poor substitute for time spent with his son. He wanted to toss a ball with his boy, to go to his ballgames, and even attend his son's PTA meetings. He wanted the normalcy of most modern families; and, though Abbey would never believe him, he wanted his little family under one roof. Dane placed his head in his hand and massaged his temples. There was gray hairs cropping up in his blond beard and hair that had not been there before. His body was older than its years. The stress and abuse forced upon it by what felt like a lifetime of war was only beginning to take its toll, and for the millionth time since saying goodbye to his son – again – Dane wondered just how much *soldiering* he had in him.

*Dear Henry,*

*How's it going, bud? I hope you and your mom are doing well. I'm doing pretty good, I guess. I just miss you guys and wish I was there with you. I hope school's going well, and you're getting settled in. Try to remember that in order to have friends you have to be a friend. I know it's hard being in a new place and not knowing anyone, but the kindness of people will surprise you if you give them a chance.*

*Anyway, I just wanted to write you and tell you I love you. Tell your mom I miss her, too.*

*Talk soon,*

*Dad*

*P.S. You remember all those times your*
*mom and I got on to you about talking back to*
*grownups, and how your mouth was always two*
*seconds ahead of your brain? Think about what*
*you're going to say before you say it, Henry. Trust*
*me.*

\*\*\*

"Hey Millie," Dane called to the Admiral's assistant just as she was closing the office door for the night.

"Oh, hey Dane," the pretty, older lady called. "I was just about to head to my quarters."

"No worries," he replied genially, "I'll check back in tomorrow."

"Nonsense," she waved as he approached, "what can I do for you?"

Dane produced the letter from his pocket, "Just wanted to get this to the Skipper is all."

Millie took the letter, knowing full well what it was and to whom it was meant for. She smiled warmly and, with a wink, said, "I know where that old coot is. I'll make sure this gets in his hands tonight."

"Thanks, Millie," Dane said, but as he turned to head back down the hall, Millie called to him from behind.

"Dane?"

"Yes, ma'am?" he said, turning back to Millie.

"Women, specifically ladies, tend to respond a bit better to a little less vulgarity."

Dane's shoulders slumped, and his head fell as he mumbled, "Yes, ma'am. Sorry ma'am."

Millie smiled, shaking her head as he fled quickly down the hall. While locking the door to her office, she chuckled quietly, "Men."

## 24)
## Drinks With…Friends?

After handing the letter off to Millie, Dane headed to the Silver Moon's workout center where he hoped a hard workout would calm his nerves. Fighting savages was one thing; but now, it seemed that every time he opened his mouth, he was saying something ridiculously stupid. Military officers in general, not to mention officers of special missions units such as SKUL, should comport themselves in a much more professional manner than he had recently. He knew that, and the more he thought about it, the angrier he became. The problem was he had only himself to blame. Sure, the overwhelming denominator was dealing with Sam Steele; but, that was no excuse, and he knew it. If he could not trust his actions around her, how could his men trust him in battle?

Were the two situations linked?

*Could* they be?

He was still mulling over these troublesome thoughts as he rounded a corner and made his way to the sliding glass doors of the workout center. SKUL's ship-bound workout center was larger and better equipped than most college athletic facilities. Nearly the size of a football field, the center was equipped with a monstrous free weight area full of benches, bars, dumb bells, and enough cast iron plates to compliment the needs of a small army.

Basically, that summed up SKUL - a small army of elite warriors.

Another section of the cavernous room contained several pull-up bars and thick ropes – even a series of caving ladders – that hung from the ceiling high above. There was even a huge tractor tire weighing close to two hundred pounds decorating one side of the workout center. The operators enhanced their leg and shoulder strength by flipping the tire end over end for nearly one hundred feet. Those that either preferred low impact exercises or their rehabilitation regimen required such could choose from one of the many treadmills, elliptical machines, or stair climbers lining the walls. But that was not all, a second floor held a four lane running track that circled the outer wall of the center and offered views down into the weights area.

With that in mind, Dane bypassed the lower level weight room for the time being and instead, lumbered up the stairs to the upper level track. There, he set his watch timer for thirty-five minutes and his mind on five miles. This pace, he hoped, would get him warmed up for a workout and melt the ill-feelings and embarrassment from his mind. Placing buds in his ears, he cranked up the volume on his iPod and took off. The first song was one of his favorites – *Where the Devil Don't Stay* by Drive By Truckers – which he took as a good sign. Within the first half mile, he was lost in the rhythm of the music and his own footfalls. In that wonderful place where one finds their mind free from constraint, Dane allowed his to wander. Thirty-five minutes later and with absolutely no memory of any step taken, he came to a lumbering stop. His body was slick with sweat and only then did he realize he had traveled over five and a half miles in the time allotted. A faster pace than he had intended, but pushing himself always made him feel more relaxed with a clearer train of thought.

Today was no exception.

Mentally in a better place, he went back down the stairs and through the glass doors to the main room of the center. Upon entering – and as if drawn by some unnatural force, Dane's eyes fell on Samantha Steele; or some of the better parts of her, in any case. Like Dane had just done, she was busy killing herself on a stair-steppers located on the far wall. Not willing to press matters any further than he had already done, Dane gave a brief wave in her direction. Not returning his wave, he realized she was either still pissed at him or was so focused on her workout she failed to notice his overly friendly greeting. Silently, he hoped it was the latter and not the former.

Either way, he kept moving to the bench press area, tossed several forty-five pound plates on either side, and began his workout.

He had just dropped the bar back on the rack, completing a third set, when he noticed a new message from Tweeker on his SICS. The message, sent nearly a half hour ago, was a simple one:

*High Tide, thirty minutes, drinks*

Dane groaned. He was exhausted and wanted nothing more than to get a shower and hit the rack. Moreover, he would rather spend the free time having a few drinks in Shamus' pub, where the unspoken but heavily guarded rule was *shooters only*. The *Hide Tide*, located on the top deck next to the pool, was the watering hole where one could find most of the intelligence operatives, computer analysts, and other support staff. Tweeker's choice of venues was puzzling, and he would be sure to ask about. As he was pondering this, another message came across:

*Dude, you coming or what?*

Dane sighed, then replied with an equally simple message:

*Working out, need a shower, be there in twenty*

Ten minutes later he was out of the shower. He dressed comfortably in khaki cargo shorts and a *Gov't Mule* concert tee that hugged his muscular frame. Stepping from the men's locker room, he nearly walked right into Sam.

"Commander," she said genially enough. Dane held out his hand for her to go through the glass doors first.

"It's Dane, Sam. What's up?"

"Meeting a friend for a drink," she said simply and pressed the elevators' *up* button. Despite what had occurred only hours ago, she was not speaking in an unkind manner. Rather, it was just the matter-of-fact tone one gives another when they do not know each other well.

"Cool. Me too, actually." Dane hoped the inflection of his voice did not give away the fact he really, really did not want to be seen in the *High Tide*.

She arched a perfectly groomed eyebrow, "Hmph, I figured you and your boys would be rebel-rousing down at Shamus' tonight."

*Me too,* he thought before responding as brightly and hoping he sounded more mature than normal, "Nah. The guys might be, but I need to hit the rack soon."

*Ding.*

As the elevator door opened, Dane decided to take a chance and attempt – *again* – to explain what he meant earlier, "Sam, about today…"

"Commander," Sam raised a hand, "don't. Just don't." She chuckled, just a little – *it sounded cute* – and Dane was struck again with how attractive she was. "It's cool, okay? And, I know what you meant. Let's just drop it before you say something equally as ridiculous."

She was smiling now, warm and…what?

*Inviting* maybe?

*Damn she's cute,* he thought as his mind turned to oatmeal. *She's real, real cute but…*

Dane drew himself up, eager to do and say the right thing. Something maybe she would respect to hear from him. Something, hell, anything that made him look more responsible than he had earlier. "Look, Sam, I get it, I do…but, I'm married."

Her smile fell, and her eyes turned to slits as the elevator doors closed though those standing nearby heard her first salvo, "Dammit, Dane Stackwell, do you really think just because…" Her voice rose with the elevator and was loud enough to be heard by those walking the hallway below. Curious as to the receiver of the ass-chewing, many stopped to listen. Her voice faded and finally disappeared into the floors above altogether.

*Ding.*

The elevator opened just as she finished letting him have it.

"And, don't you ever make the mistake of thinking that just because you do what you do, and I do what I do, that I'm supposed to just fall out of my panties when you come around!"

Dane tried to sink into the far corner of the elevator and find a hole to crawl in. It was only when the elevator door opened and she stormed from it that he was able to escape. Several sets of wide eyes were staring at him accusingly, causing his temper to flare.

"Gotta problem?" he growled and stormed through the crowd of gawkers causing them to disperse like they were running from a flaming paper bag full of turds.

*Just keeping the streak going aren't you, you jackass,* he was thought to himself. He rounded the corner in time to see Sam stamp her foot fiercely on the deck. Looking over her shoulder, he followed her gaze and realized the focal point of Sam's ire. The friend she was apparently meeting, Dr. Monica Taylor, was already there. Ansil was seated with a drink in hand, as well.

The problem was that they were sitting together, already engaged in a playful conversation.

To his side Sam hissed, "Well this should be an interesting evening," before stomping through the crowd to their friends' table.

Dane put his face in his palms – a move he was growing accustomed to – and silently agreed with her opinion.

# 25)

## Outbreak

**Five days later**
**Ops Center**
**0800**

Whiskey and Kilo platoons were gathered in full strength for the 0800 briefing. Foxtrot had been alerted and, as each hour ticked by, more and more of the platoon's operators were back on board the Silver Moon. They were filtering in from all points on the globe; so, it would take time for Foxtrot to be at full platoon strength.

The operational tempo since *Nightshade* had been frenzied. The teams were in a constant state of combat. Unlike the horror stories of their youth, SKUL shooters and analysts knew the truth concerning werewolves; their madness was *not* necessarily dictated by the moon. From the moment they were bitten, they slid rapidly into the madness. Those newly turned needed a full moon to complete the process, and they were their strongest and most psychotic on the nights of a full moon; but, the longer a werewolf lived, the more control he had over the transformation. In short, daylight held no sanctuary for man or beast; in fact, it meant very little in the grand scheme of things. When the intel was solid and the situational environment allowed, SKUL was just as likely to visit doom and damnation on the savage horde at midday as it was at midnight.

The element of surprise SKUL held during these missions was welcomed; but, the mission pace was already taking its toll.

As Dane scanned the gathered operators, several using those few sweet moments of inaction to grab a few winks, he knew it would only get worse.

*It always does,* he thought sardonically.

Suddenly, the door to the Ops Center flew open, ripping those shooters nodding off from their slumber and tearing others – Dane included – from their tormented thoughts.

Admiral Briggs stalked to the stage with Wild Bill Kipling, English Whitherton, and Stan Woods – PLs of Whiskey, Kilo, and Foxtrot platoons, respectively – in flanking positions. The Skipper took control even as the men were still rising to attention.

"Seats people," he growled sternly. By eschewing formal military protocol, the Skipper caused the room to take on the appearance of a cresting and falling wave. The men rose quickly, but not quite to their full height, before falling in accordance with the Admiral's command. Briggs stepped to the stage and turned, taking every man and woman in his gaze simultaneously. Unlike the SKUL shooters, most of the analysts never looked up, never so much as stopped pounding on their keyboards. Whoever was not working at a keyboard seemed to be glued to a large CCTV screen showing a map of the city littered with a handful of glowing dots. Every few seconds, the screen refreshed itself to reveal more hotspots.

"Ladies and gentlemen, we have reached critical mass." At that, the room held its collective breath, forcing the Admiral to wade headlong through the sea of shock and horror alone. "The screen before you shows a map of New

Orleans. The dots are the locations of suspected recent savage activity. Less than twenty-four hours ago, we had fewer than five hotspots." He nodded to Elbert who had slipped in unnoticed and was now at his side. Stratham dropped a ruggedized laptop onto a table and began working over the keyboard. "This is a real-time, no B.S. assessment of our current situation." On cue, the screen changed and revealed as many as three times the number of hotspots.

Astonishingly, and to the terror of all present, the number of hotspots was growing. The growth was slow and insidious but apparent all the same.

The room fell silent and still as no one could tear their eyes away from the screen. "What you see began at nightfall with a slow yet steady increase in activity since. Elbert and his colleagues are monitoring internet activity along with cell phone communications trying to get a bead on the source. Unfortunately, at this time, we have no clue what's truly going on, just guesswork."

A discordant grumble rolled across the room, and the Admiral, with no other recourse, waited for it to die.

"I know you guys must have a lot of questions. That's understandable; so, I'll turn this briefing over to one of our lead intel officers. Sam?"

By now the room was breathing again, though everyone remained silent.

Noticing a raised hand, Sam looked up from the computer readout she was monitoring, "Yes, Major Meadows?"

She was referring to Titan's team leader, Tim Meadows, who had been a Major in the United States Army's

301

elite 1st Special Forces Operational Detachment – Delta before coming on board with SKUL.

"Have there been any confirmed savage sightings, from non-SKUL personnel?  Civilians maybe?"

Sam shook her head, "Negative, nothing confirmed.  It can only be a matter of time before those reports start rolling in, though."

Tim nodded before asking another question, one many had on their minds, "Do we have any idea how so many people are being turned so quickly?  I've never seen activity like this and doubt anyone else has either."

The more experienced operators silently nodded their agreement with Tim.

"Good question," Sam acknowledged while referring to her notes.  "About the same time we started noting the increase in activity, agents throughout the city caught wind of a hot new drug hitting the streets.  It's being called *God's Milk,* though no one knows who's slinging it.  Current intelligence leads us to believe it's a green solution with a cocaine base.  This certainly gives teeth to Dr. Hyram's original theory.  Considering the full picture of what was found in the aftermath of *Operation Nightshade,* along with Brussieux's testimony and from what we've been able to put together from the intel gathered during our on-going operation, *Side Job,* I'd say it's a better than average guess that this drug is the vehicle for what we're seeing.  If there is any good news in all this, it's that none of the suspected savages have exhibited the ability to use any of the gifts one would expect of a True Wolf.  The obvious downside is that they are still throbbing masses of sheer inhuman strength, speed, and hunger."

Dane cleared his throat before asking, "Sam?"

"Yes, Commander?"

"Given the lack of civilian sightings and the fact these are very *young* werewolves, is it safe to assume they may not be able to invoke the *change* at all?"

"No," Sam shook her head incessantly. "Intel is so sketchy at this point that it's safer to assume nothing."

Dane nodded and scratched a brief note in his wheel book.

"Ma'am," came Jed's slow, Texas drawl, "I know we're all just slinging spitballs here, but this is the most activity I've ever seen yet there have been no sightings. To my knowledge, there have been no murders yet, either."

He waited long enough to register a shake of the Admiral's head, along with vocal confirmation. "No murders...yet."

"In that case, isn't it entirely possible the intel is bad? Maybe our guys have been duped with a load of crap hoping we'll shut down the team that's hounding the cargo they seem to think is so precious. Hell, maybe it's a glitch in our system...it's happened before." Jed was being respectful but frank, and his reputation demanded the same from Sam.

She nodded, understanding the old warrior's trepidations. A click of the remote revealed another image, this one a close up via FVS technology. "The image you're seeing was taken from one of our Pegasus drones." This image burned much hotter than a human's would. She clicked the remote several more times, and each photo was the same as the last. They were all definitely werewolves. "We've analyzed dozens of suspected individuals under FVS scopes…they're all the same, just entering various stages of madness. As Admiral Briggs stated, it's only a matter of time. Bill?"

She pointed to Whiskey's platoon leader, who was seated on the front row between Woodrow and English.

"Isn't it entirely possible these savages could develop *gifts* over time? I mean, we're dealing with an awful lot of unknowns here."

This was the question she had been dreading but, in the essence of full disclosure, honesty was not only the best policy, it was the *only* policy. "It's certainly a possibility."

"What about the other savage strongholds – Seattle, Chicago, Denver, and Boston? Are we seeing increased activity in these cities?" this from T-Rex Carston, Titan's ATL.

The Admiral stepped forward, "Negative. Whatever the savages are doing, it seems they've elected to focus on New Orleans at the present time. Though, again, for how long that continues is anyone's guess."

"What's the deal with those clusters?"

The question came from Hammer, the only other new guy training with Whiskey during C-school. Hammer acquitted himself well during their training and while in combat, becoming a well-liked and respected member of Copperhead, another of Whiskey's fire teams. He was referring to the growing number of hot spots that were moving toward each other, clumping together. What appeared to be totally random movements at first glance slowly began to take on a strangely organized appearance. Order out of chaos, and the truly frightening thing about it was the fact it was occurring right before their very eyes...in *real* time.

Sam shuffled her papers, obviously shaken with what she was about to say, "We believe the werewolves are exhibiting some form of pack behavior. They seem to be drawn to others of their kind. Eventually, a pecking order is established before moving on to the next group, and the process is repeated. It's theorized they will keep doing this until..." She paused long enough to master her fears and compartmentalize her emotions, "...well, until we have a lot bigger problem on our hands than we do right now."

The air in the Ops Center became practically electric with tension as operator and analysts alike watched their greatest fears play out before their eyes.

Tweeker leaned into Dane's ear and with a whisper summed up the horrifying images forming in nearly every operator's mind with his thoughts, "Jesus, Boss, are you looking at what I am? They're not forming packs; they're creating an army."

Dane simply nodded.

Turning his attention to Stan Woods, whom everyone called Woodrow, Foxtrot's PL, Briggs asked, "Woodrow, you guys look to be at about eighty percent, correct?"

"Yes, sir. The last two teams are inbound. Both should be on the deck by noon."

The Admiral nodded then tilted his chin to Wild Bill Kipling, "Bill, you have anything to add?"

"Most of what I have to say I'll save for each team's mission briefing, but I do think one fact should not go unsaid." He looked to the operators gathered through eyes burning with an intensity not of this Earth. "You people need to understand the savages you are about to target were humans only days ago. Some may have been turned only hours or minutes before, and there's a strong possibility these people did not ask for this. The tensile strength of every moral fiber you possess will likely be tested over the next forty-eight hours. It's a job no one in this room should relish and certainly one no one wants to undertake, but humanity is depending on you to see these missions through with resolute certitude. Gentlemen, there can be absolutely no fuckups. Understood?"

Everyone in the room gave a resounding affirmation. Everyone knew full well exactly the razor thin room for error they would be operating within.

"Good," said Briggs taking the briefing back over. He checked the digital clock on the wall, "It's 0900 now. I want the team leaders gathered back here at twelve hundred hours for a follow-on briefing. That gives you guys a few hours to gear up. Individual team briefings will begin thereafter. Bill and I will be present for all mission briefings; so, they'll be staggered throughout the day. Millie will upload the schedule to your SICS devices and tablets ASAP; so, keep them on you. Anything else?" The Skipper looked around the room matching the intensity exhibited by Bill only moments before by a power of ten. Seeing none, the Admiral absently scratched at the scar jutting from the empty socket his eye patch hid, then dismissed the men.

As the operators rose – the intel and computer geeks never so much as looking up – Toad squeezed his eyes shut and said, "Ain't this just some shit?"

"Yeah, no kiddin'," remarked Twitch with a smirk. "It's damned near nine o'clock, and I haven't had breakfast yet."

Jed held a hand up pointing his index finger skyward, "For the first time ever, you and I are in total agreement."

"*Seven*," Tweeker pounced on the movie quote like a kitten on a fresh ball of yarn. "Not bad…for an old dude."

Jed winked, "Yeah, well, you want to hop back in the ring with my old ass?"

Tweeker started to say something but, remembering the beat down he had taken at the hands of Jed during SEE-S, bit off the retort. "What I thought," said Jed through a smile. Somehow the man managed to pull off the perfect mix of friendly joviality laced with venom. Once again, Dane and the others were reminded of just how dangerous Jed Blackmoor was.

Toad shook his head in aggravation and forced the conversation back to a more serious topic, "No, I mean all this. Savages coming out of the woodwork, and we know nothing. *Why are so many turning?* We don't know. *What's causing it?* No damn clue. *Are they just super strong or can the mofos shoot lasers out of their eyes?* Your guess is as good as mine. See what I mean?"

He looked to Jed then Twitch. Both shrugged. "No," they answered in unison.

Toad laughed. Despite everything, he could not help himself, "C'mon, I'm buying."

As they walked from the Ops Center, Jed added some levity back to the conversation. "Marcus, can I ask you something?"

"Sure."

"If you really don't want to do all this stuff, why put yourself through it? Why not just get out? Go be an accountant or something."

"What, and miss the chance die every second of the day?"

"Cut the bullshit, I'm serious."

Dane and Tweeker, following close behind, heard Toad explain in an equally serious tone, "I dunno, man. I guess I just like hanging out with people that like to do this crap too much to leave."

At that, Jed had to laugh. It sounded strange, like a rusty wheel unused and left out in the weather for too long.

"Now that, I understand." Jed looked around to his teammates and with a wink said, "Change of plans. Twitch, you're buying."

***

**Ops Center**
**Team Leaders' Briefing**
**1230**

"Okay, men, questions?"

Wild Bill had just finished his follow-on briefing with his team leaders. During that time, he outlined the night's operations from, as he called it, *go to whoa*. From this point on, mission development would be in the hands of each individual team. Concerning its operations, SKUL had but one rule; and, it was the law of the land, iron-clad in every respect. That rule was simple and born of common sense – those conducting the mission *planned* the mission. Having men, no matter how well-intentioned they were, direct the movements and planning of missions while being removed from the heat of the battle seemed less than intelligent. Fortunately for all, SKUL and its leadership sought to avoid *stupid* at all costs. Sure there was oversight, but it was more about senior officers with years of experience combatting savages offering advice laden with a heavy smattering of guidance versus any real, tangible oversight.

"What type of security are we talking, Bill?" The question came from Tim Meadows standing akimbo around the table on the stage.

"Agents from our intelligence division, both SI-1s and SI-2s, have been inserted and will be providing minute by minute intel updates. Kilo platoon will provide QRF and blocking forces for each mission. After insertion, the Little Birds and Blackhawks will be on standby with rotors spinning at a nearby Black Site. They'll provide overhead cover in the event the shit hits the fan, but gentlemen, that will not happen."

Meadows scribbled a quick note then tilted his head in a slight nod, comfortable with the information.

"What about the local LEOs, sir?" Dane, his mood serious and mind racing, stood with his arms wrapped across his chest. The older Section 8 crest tattooed on his right forearm was stacked on top of and over the newer tattoo on his left, the SKUL shield.

"NOPD, along with other departments working the area, has been advised that a joint task force of special operation forces will be undergoing an extensive urban workup. Our cover story is that we are prepping for direct actions against numerous *high value targets* in various and similar urban environments. Obviously, upon hearing this, they readily agreed and pledged their support. All pertinent departments have been informed the training operations will start tonight, and that they will be notified once the training cycle is complete. This cover story has been continuously leaked to local news outlets for the last twenty-four hours and backstopped by several strategically placed SI-2s within local and federal law enforcement agencies and media outlets. Further, Elbert and his crew of computer techs in concert with Mrs. Steele and her agents are working to curtail any inadvertent LEO action on scene. Hopefully, this will help us to avoid any loss of operational integrity by a well-meaning but ill-timed visit from *Officer Friendly*. I predict it to be very much a nonissue but understand, in the event you are confronted, explain that you are part of the training op, explain no more than that, and for the love of all that's good and pure, under no circumstances are you to confront them if they push their point. No exceptions. They are doing their job, same as you, only they are completely in the dark about the *real* world. I'll have it taken care of before the black and white is cranked." Bill looked to the Admiral for confirmation. The Skipper nodded, and Wild Bill turned back to the team leaders with an intense look, "Am I understood?"

Most everyone in the room nodded. Dane figured those that did not thought their understanding was a given.

"Make no mistake about it, ladies and gentlemen. From this point forward, you are smack dab in the middle of a war zone, Indian country in the truest of sense, and it's on U.S. soil fighting an immortal enemy." Wild Bill again looked every man, woman and would have looked a child in the eyes had they been present, all in the beat of a heart, "The protocol here is *Hunter-Killer.* Anything short of that is unacceptable. I need savages dead and lots of them, understood?"

This time the room erupted in vocalized agreement.

"Good. Anyone have any further questions?"

"Sir," said Sonny Hamm - call sign, Hawg. Hawg was a former Army Captain in the 2nd Battalion, 75th Ranger Regiment. He was from Hot Springs, Arkansas, and got his call sign honestly. Yes, *Hamm* was his last name which made things easy, but the real reason for Hawg's particular call sign was the fact he was the biggest talking, most ultra-obnoxious Arkansas Razorback fans on the planet…and, considering their fan base, that was saying something. Jed once described Hawg as *the most unbearable fan of college anything this side of those burnt orange pissing, Texas Longhorn loving faggots down in Austin.*

And, he meant it.

"What's on your mind, Hawg?" asked Kipling.

"Any word from Iroquois?"

Wild Bill cleared his throat, "It's an extraordinarily fluid situation, but they're working through it."

Another malignant rumble of discontent rolled across the Ops Center causing Wild Bill to hold up his hand, "I understand your concerns, but that is the best I can do at this time. Anything else?"

This time, no one spoke. This was probably because they were sated on bad news for the next lifetime.

*It's only gonna get worse,* Dane thought yet again.

"Okay, bring your guys up to speed. Team briefing times will be uploaded to your SICS devices ASAP. Bill looked each man over carefully one last time and smiled, "Dismissed."

# 26)
## Operation Zookeeper

**Helipad**
**Silver Moon**
**2345**

Dane and his team spent most of the day working up their mission profile. Sam, Elbert, and the rest of Saber team's support staff were there as well, chipping in with updated intelligence from the agents on the street. Considering they were operating on domestic soil, in the heart of not only a major US metropolitan area but a high priority port city to boot, the team had given the highest level of care in designing a mission plan that would not only be successful but maintain the unit's anonymity.

Suffice it to say, it had been an excruciatingly long day; but now, it was *go time*.

Now, the only thing that mattered was the completion of a successful mission with all of his men making it home safe. As Dane stood on the helipad smelling the salt-tinged air of the Gulf of Mexico intermixed with the sickly stench of hydraulics, he said quietly to himself, "Nothing to it but to do it."

The engines of seven Blackhawks' began to whine as they began spinning up. The crews of each bird were going through identical routines, all in final preparations for the flight to their respective landing *LZ's* – or landing zones. Dane, KtacS helmet in hand, watched as first Toad then Twitch, Jed, and finally, Tweeker boarded and waited for him to join them. All along the Silver Moon's gigantic helipad,

313

men from the other teams hustled to board their respective choppers.

Meadows leaned into Dane's ear and yelled over the spinning blades, "Keep it tight, bro!"

Dane nodded and, remembering Shamus' words to him a few days prior, grinned, "Don't get bit."

With one last smile to each other, the two bumped fists then ran to join their men. Seconds later, they were up and over the ship, disappearing into the deep dark of the night. The septuplet's steady beat of rotors faded eerily into the inky blackness over the Gulf of Mexico. Their flight would be a squirrelly affair, low to the deck, mere meters above the surface of the waters of the Gulf of Mexico. The Blackhawks would come overland southwest of the city. From there, the squadron of helos would land in a field on a secluded piece of farmland that happened to be a SKUL black site. Each team would then hop aboard *MH-6 Little Birds* for the final leg of the flight. The Little Birds were sterile with no serial numbers or other identifying markings and disguised with paint patterns designed to mimic civilian craft. They were, however, retrofitted with exterior benches on each side. This is where the shooters would sit for their trip to their target sites. Few things on Earth are more exhilarating than a fast moving flight with nothing but air under your feet. Dane, enjoying the rush of wind assaulting him as they flew, watched the shifting blotches of differing shades of blackness. Finally, after what felt like an eternity, he could see a bloom of light off in the distance.

*New Orleans.*

Dane checked his gear one last time. His ritualistic need for everything to be perfectly in place was born during BUD/S and nurtured over a lifetime of combat.

Tonight, they would confront nightmares buried deep within the primal subconscious of every man, woman, and child. Tonight, those nightmares would manifest into the physical. These were nightmares capable of snuffing out the lives of an entire neighborhood, an entire city, in an instant.

The simple truth was there was not a man in SKUL that didn't recognize that the next mission could be the last. They neither made it a focus of anxiety nor did they carry any delusions of grandeur that it could never be so; they simply accepted the inherent occupational costs and were prepared to pay the price.

In full.

Taking a breath, he looked to his ATL, Jed Blackmoor. Jed, a slab of granite against unyielding storms, exuded a *come-what-may* countenance that served to relax everyone on the team, Dane included.

Over the intra-squad comm link came the pilot's voice, "Three minutes."

In answer, the men of Saber began engaging their helmets. The futuristic helmets with the alien-like lenses began to whine as they came online. Shifting their eyes they toggled through their helmet's visual spectrum to get to the FVS – or fused visual system – mode. Instantly, what had been a dark, featureless world exploded into view in varying shades of gray. It was like looking out upon a landscape locked in a perpetual state of twilight. Faded and bleached out color intermingled benignly with the wild oranges and yellows of warm blooded animals along with inanimate objects that carry thermal signatures. Old heat burned dirty orange; humans, bright yellow; and, werewolves appeared so white they literally hurt to look at too long.

It was like looking at the sun, if the sun was hungry for flesh and bent on dominating all life on Earth.

"Eyes on target," updated the pilot. "One minute."

Dane, sitting just behind Twitch on the bench, confirmed with their pilot they were *good to go*.

Forty-five seconds after that, the Little Bird touched down softly on the wild, flat expanse of multiple soccer fields. This was a recreational area in New Orleans known as the *Fly*. In accordance with their seating arrangement and order of patrol, Twitch and Jed hit the ground and moved roughly ten meters ahead of the chopper at nine o' clock and three o' clock angles, respectively. Each man trained their weapons over their individual sectors while Dane and Tweeker did the same on the backside of the helicopter.

Toad, on board the Little Bird, moved to a position on an outer bench. He would be dropped off in an overwatch position last.

The entire movement took less than thirty seconds from rails down, to boots on the ground, and the bird lifting back skyward. Unlike the men overseas, mired in the shit-shows of Afghanistan, Iraq, and various other corners of hell we continually ask our best to venture into, SKUL shooters typically did not drop into a hot LZ; in the conventional sense, in any case. On a typical insertion, there were no bullets or RPGs to worry with; much less, SAMs that the enemy does not have, but really *does* have, only we pretend they do not.

Who needs guns anyway when you are immortal and can tear a man's arms off with a flippant flick of a claw? It was entirely possible for a savage to bring a helo down with nothing more than its raw strength and power. So, in essence, the insertions and extractions were still one of the most vulnerable points of any mission.

Once the rotor wash and storm of flying debris abated, Twitch rose.

"Moving to target," he reported then loped off into the night. The others quickly fell in behind him according to their preordained patrol order and moved unflinchingly toward death. Twitch was just crossing the railroad tracks on the south side of the zoo, its tall chain link fence looming in the distance, when the rhythm of the chopper's blades, having faded momentarily, became louder one last time.

Toad was delivered to his sniper hide.

From the roof of the main entrance tower, he – along with his suppressed .300 Win Mag – would provide overwatch for the fire team. His choice of stations was perfect. The tower, due to its height and location, offered a nearly unfettered view of three quarters of the zoo. His position meant he would also serve as a mini blocking force for any savages snuffed out by Saber.

A very effective, *very* deadly, mini blocking force.

With silent, deliberate steps, Twitch led the team down a short gravel drive where eventually, they came to a heavy metal doorway. A thick chain and heavy lock secured the door. "Simple enough," he reported to Dane.

317

"Get it done, bro."

After his graduation from C-school, Twitch had an axe of solid silver custom made. It was much larger than the standard issue tomahawk and could open almost any door he needed to breach. On this mission, however, he bypassed the loud *thuwack* of the axe for the silence of his lock breaking tools. It took him longer to pull out the kit than it did for him to pick the lock.

With a gentle push, the doors fell open on rusty hinges. The creak of the two doors shattered the night air; and, in its wake, the team flowed through silently, primed for come-what-may.

And that *may* certainly include a battle with immortal werewolves.

The first oddity that struck them was the zoo animals. At this hour, all but the most hardcore of nocturnal predators should have been asleep. Instead, there was not a cage that was not going crazy. Monkeys squawked, jaguars screamed, and birds raised a mighty ruckus.

In the near distance, a lion roared.

Craziest of all was the wolf howl that ripped the night air asunder. It did not seem lonely or forlorn; rather, it felt angry...unnaturally so. The howl sent chills up the shooters' spines.

Outside the walls of the zoo, the city's canine population was feverish. Bawling howls mixed with incessant barks that drowned out the normal city sounds.

These weren't normal sounds. These animals were livid, wild, crazy.

318

Something had spooked them, and men stalking the grounds knew exactly what that *something* was.

Savages…newly turned.

Quietly, though there was no reason for it given the nature of their helmets, Dane spoke, "Darkside, this is Saber-one-one, over."

"Saber-one-one, this is Darkside, overwatch secure."

"Roger that, hang tight." Dane checked his team. Each man was in position and training their weapon out from their tight semicircle perimeter. Dane flicked his eyes and moved the cursor its proper place, changing radio channels to call up SKUL's higher leadership.

The Ops Center was a beehive of activity as the large support element coordinated with intelligence agents on or near the each target location. Standing in the middle of this controlled chaos was Rear Admiral Bartavious Briggs along with Wild Bill, English, and Woodrow. The four men were rotating their attention between multiple video feeds at once. These screens showed overhead Pegasus drone and satellite feeds as well as live, on-the-ground feeds from the operators' helmet cams. The teams were beginning to check in.

"Saber-one-one to Nest. How copy?"

"Reading you lima-charlie, Saber-one-one," Sam responded in a blatantly neutral and utterly professional voice.

"All boots on the ground and in position."

"A-firm Saber-one-one. All boots on the ground and in position. Be advised, LEO radio traffic clear, op is a *go*."

"Roger that Nest, executing assault now."

# 27)
## Into the Madness

As one, they moved out.

Their standard patrol order ruled the day. Twitch walked point and was followed by Dane, Jed, and lastly, Tweeker. The team moved silently down a manmade path utilizing a five meter pacing between each teammate. That separation ensured the team was far enough apart to prevent an instantaneous annihilation of their entire team; yet, each man was close enough to engage savage coming down on their mates. Within a few short minutes, Twitch led the team to the zoo's aviary.

Silently, Twitch tested the door.

"Unlocked," he reported. A second later, he gave it a shove. The men stacked up behind him moved almost in unison. Dane shot through the door, taking the heavy side of the aviary, by going right and following the wall all the way to the opposite corner of the screened room. Jed mimicked his TL's movements only to the left, stopping at the nearest corner while Tweeker entered right of center, Twitch to his left. The angles of fire meant that the entire room was dominated by the SKUL shooters within seconds. It also meant there must be total trust among the teammates as bullets would be snapping mere centimeters from each other's faces. Dane's HK 416 clapped twice, sending two controlled silver slugs into the savage encountered. Jed, registering the intense heat bloom in his FVS, pushed forward and put two more silver rounds into its chest.

All four confirmed, "Clear," and Dane, Jed, and Twitch continued moving, clearing the large, screened in expanse sector by sector. Tweeker remained with the dead savage, covering his teammates' *six* until they returned. As he moved past Tweeker and the dead savage, Dane shot a look over his left shoulder to the body. The savage was male, mid-forties, and had two growing green dots billowing from its forehead and another two from its sternum. It held a headless parakeet in one hand, and a clump of feathers from the same bird decorated its chin. Nearby, a zoo employee lay sprawled across the floor. Her neck, obviously snapped, was twisted at an odd angle. As Tweeker and Twitch checked her for bite marks, Dane looked to Jed. The look on his face was apparent even as he shook his head, "Thing acted confused, Boss. Like it had no clue what was going on. Weird."

"Probably didn't, Jed."

Behind their backs, Twitch's SCAR barked twice, putting two into the woman's head. Dane turned back to the men. In his ear, Tweeker confirmed, "She was bitten, Boss."

Dane nodded, knowing the risk she might come back was too great, then nudged his rifle barrel forward, "Keep moving."

Outside, Toad's voice came over the comms and announced, "Savage ID'd, Boss. Coming from the sea lion pool. Female. Thermals and heart rate are off the charts..." Toad's voice caught in his throat, "Dane, she's dragging a kid in one hand...a little girl. She's crying one second and laughing hysterically the next." Toad then added almost perfunctorily, "Kid's dead, Boss."

"Fuck!" Dane hissed over the comms but really just to himself. "This is beyond messy."

Twitch stopped and trained his rifle straight ahead with the others taking covering positions as well. Silently, they waited while Dane directed another part of the mission. This was the moral fiber test Bill spoke about during their briefing. There was no bluffing in this card game of souls, no calling for more cards. No, in this game, there was only decisive and violent action or unquestionable death. In this game, you played the hand you were dealt.

*Period.*

"Take her out, Toad."

He could, and would, hate himself later…if he lived to see *later.*

Seconds later, "Savage down, Boss. Body temp trend confirms."

"Eyes tight." He squeezed Twitch's shoulder gently, "We're moving."

"Roger that, Boss."

Slowly, the team made their way to a fork in the path where Dane halted the team. Using his eyes to engage the helmet's RRT, he pulled up a map of the zoo. It was nothing more than a cartoonish visitor map, but considering it was just as accurate as anything they had, Elbert had it uploaded to their SICS. Dane and the others knew going right took them south through the *South American Pampas* and *Louisiana Swamp* exhibits. Left meant clearing the *Primates* area and the *Asian Domain* along with several small, enclosed exhibits and cafes.

On any other night, due to the unmitigated spacial enormity of the zoo grounds, this mission would involve several direct fire teams. But, on this night – as thin as SKUL was stretched – it was just Saber team on site.

"Jed," Dane said over the comms, "you and Tweeker head right, Twitch and I will take the left hand path. Lock it down as tight as you can but don't take any chances. Lots of area for a savage to hole up."

"Roger that," the men said simultaneously and moved off into the darkness.

"Boss, you hear that?" The question had come from Twitch.

"No, what?" Dane said, a little perturbed they were not moving yet; then, he too heard what Twitch was referring to.

"Dogs," answered Twitch. His voice a stormy mix of awe and confusion. "Must be every dog in the city barking, yapping, and howling right now."

Dane listened for a second and briefly allowed a trickle of fear to penetrate his innate, self-sustained armor, before commanding, "Let's move, Twitch. We can worry about that later."

Twitch obeyed, and the two men began working the open areas and clearing the little buildings serving that served as exhibit houses. They worked quickly, fluidly, yet cautiously. Strangely, they encountered no savages along the way.

Jed's voice came over the squad net, "Two savages neutralized. Human form but thermals and heart rate confirm."

"Not to mention they were gorging themselves on a freakin' jaguar," Tweeker's voice broke in. "A jaguar," he repeated somewhat absently.

This mission was messing with their minds a bit, and Dane could feel it.

"Copy that," Dane acknowledged choosing to skip past his friends' remarks. "So far, this is a dry side."

Not confronting savages would normally be a welcome sign; but, as they moved further into the zoo, Twitch and Dane knew that was not the case. All around the two dripped, oozed, and hung what could only be described as sheer carnage. Here and there, the path was littered with the bodies – *pieces* of bodies, really – of after-hour workers and veterinarian staff.

None of them were left among the living. In fact, they were ripped to such an extent that there was no reason to add silver to the equation. Most would not be coming back; though, if either had any doubts, they popped two into the head or heart and kept moving.

Though the volume of blood, viscera, and death definitely maxed out Dane's *what-the-fuck-o-meter,* they had a job to do; so, they pushed on. Up ahead, the primate area loomed. Moving closer, they began to hear a *squelching* noise. It sounded like sopping wet socks padding across an equally saturated tile floor. The sound was coming from the outcropping of rocks encircling the gorilla's home.

Twitch stopped and knelt in the shadows. Dane could tell his point man was watching something by the way his head tilted to one side.

"Twitch? What is it?"

325

When the point man did not respond immediately, Dane asked excitedly, "Dammit, Twitch, what is it?"

Over the comm unit, Jed, on the other side of the zoo and heavily involved in his own part of the operation, spoke. His voice was strangely gentle, like a father speaking to his frightened son, "Kris, what is it?"

Twitch, still as a stone, answered after a long pause. His response came by way of a *clap* from his suppressed SCAR, followed a millisecond later by another one. The rate of fire was very fast but evenly controlled. Instantly, he was moving, and again, Dane followed. As he rounded the corner, training his weapon down into the gorilla area, his FVS revealed the scene. There, with her head buried in the chest of a gigantic silverback gorilla, lay a woman. Her heat signature began to dissipate along with the immortal life forced upon her. Judging from her clothes, she was one of the veterinarian staff meant to care for the animals. She was small, maybe one hundred and ten pounds soaking wet; yet, she had ripped the chest of a gorilla wide open.

Apparently, when Twitch first saw her, she was eating the gorilla's insides like it was her last meal.

That was the squelching noise they had heard.

Twitch, still training his weapon down on the lady-turned-savage, had yet to say a word.

"Twitch?"

No response.

"Twitch!"

"Huh?" he stammered. His voice sounded far away.

Twitch shivered.

"She looked up at me, Boss, and smiled. She looked just like anyone else…except for the intestine hanging out of her mouth."

He shivered again.

Cold fear brought on by the way Twitch was shaken forced Dane to grab him by the shoulders and shout, "Dude, you cool? We can take a minute if you need it."

"Nah…yeah. Fuck, I mean, I'm cool…I'm cool." His voice sounded stronger, more *Twitch-like*. The irony that Dane was actually comforted by Twitch's stoned-sounding voice was not lost on him, not even in the heat of the operation.

"Then, we need to move."

Twitch shook his head, again, and began moving along the cement walkway. Here and there, they passed more dead workers until finally they linked up with Tweeker and Jed at the upper end of the zoo.

"It's a blood bath, but our side is as clear as it's going to get," Jed reported while training his weapon on the nearby reptile house. That particular den of death had not been cleared and stood waiting for them, ominous in the deep dark of the shadows.

"Yeah, no better on our side," agreed Dane. "We'll need the boys from Kilo to help sweep the place. That's the only way I think we can lock this down tight."

Jed nodded his agreement, "Like I said…as good as it's going to get."

Suddenly, Sam's voice came over the comms, "Saber-one-one, this is Nest, how copy?"

327

"Solid, go ahead, Nest," said Dane while training his weapon over his sector.

"NOPD just received a complaint concerning the animal noises coming from the zoo. They are sending a black and white to cruise the area. ETA two minutes."

"Roger that, Nest. Can our SI-2s not handle it?"

"Negative. Intervention at this point would risk exposure. You're on your own. Hold movement until further notice."

To his men, Dane ordered, "Company's coming...find some cover."

Silently, operators disappeared into the shadows of the zoo's shrubbery to wait. "Saber-one-one to Darkside, over."

Toad's voice was emotionless, completely professional, "I heard, Boss. No movement as far as I can tell."

"Roger that. Hang tight and keep your head down."

Across the zoo, many of the animals had fallen silent. This was most likely because they were dead, while others – the carnivores, namely those of canine origin – continued to shatter the night with angry, hungry howls. The shooters could not smell it, but the coppery tang of blood hung heavy on the humid air.

"Saber-one-one, an SI-2 has eyes on the black and white. Cruising past now...he's slowing." Sam was talking to multiple people at once. Finally she said, "Vehicle has stopped. Main entrance."

Several minutes past until finally Sam's voice sounded in his helmet, "Saber-one-one, LEO is out of the car and approaching front gate."

Just then, the beam of a powerful flashlight played across the immediate area and, eventually, bathed their hide in white light. Their FVS adjusted to the new light source nearly as quickly as the human eye. For a nerve-rackingly long heartbeat, the light held on their position before moving away slowly. Just when the team was ready to begin breathing again, the door to the reptile house flew open with a bang that echoed across the grounds. From the depths of the inside darkness, a large, newly turned savage leaped forward. The thing landed mere feet from the men hidden in the azaleas and roses. The savage stood so close to the men that when it shook, sticky, fresh blood sprayed the prone operators. It looked like a nuclear explosion in their FVS lenses. Dane, shifting to the noise, trained the muzzle of his rifle on the newly turned savage's face. He felt, more than saw, the flashlight whip back around now trained, yet again, on their position. Obviously, the cop had heard the noise and was trying to discover the source of the racket. Luckily, the high, locked front gate prevented him from getting the beam directly on the savage. The team's world froze as they watched the savage follow the beam of light back to its source. There was a certain level of amusement on its face; but then, there werewolf forgot the beam and tilted its face skyward. Its chest expanded further with a deep inhalation.

The posture was reserved for an animal on the hunt. Feral and wild and utterly frightening; yet, carved on a human's face. It was truly one of the strangest sights Dane had ever had the displeasure of beholding…and, considering his life in total, that was really, really saying something. The intermingling of converging realities on the beast's face and body was sickening.

Slowly, the flashlight's beam began to recede again.

*He smells us,* Dane thought. *He doesn't know how or why, but he does.*

In his ear, Sam reported, "Saber-one-one, LEO moving back to vehicle. Radio transmissions state *all clear.*" Seconds later she began to report, "LEO in vehic…"

Dane didn't bother waiting.

*Clap.*

The bullet entered the savage's forehead making a dime-sized hole before exiting and taking the back half of its head with it. Dane rushed from the shrubs and put two more rounds in its chest. The *thing,* because that's all Dane could rationalize it as, had a half-eaten anaconda in its hands.

"Jeeeesus." It was Tweeker. His voice held something that was normally not found on the big Nordic's tongue.

*Fear.*

"Pretty sure Jesus has left the building, Tweeker," was Jed's matter-of-fact response.

Tweeker glared at the team's ATL through the lifeless lenses of his helmet. Silently, Dane agreed with Jed.

"Darkside, status report."

"Nothing in my line of sight, Boss. That last one caught me totally off guard; so, there could be more holed up somewhere on the grounds."

"Roger that. Hold your position until the area is secured. Once the *Cleaners* arrive, make your way to us."

The Cleaners were SKUL's answer for the bodies.

Once an area was deemed secure, they came on the scene and literally "cleaned" it of evidence. They were part forensic team, part body baggers and taggers, and part *ichor removal engineers*. The cleaners were not members of SKUL, likely did not even know exactly who they were working for; even more likely, they did not care. Rather, they were a contracted private company paid exuberant amounts of money to carry out the dirty jobs SKUL required post-mission. The company's official name was *International Cleaning Specialists*, but this was nothing more than a cover to appease the IRS. *ICS* had offices in every major city in the United States along with dozens of the smaller municipalities that were near historical hotbeds of werewolf activity. They also had an immense presence in both Canada and Central and South America. Keeping the company separated from SKUL kept things nice and compartmentalized. The cutouts, backstops, and front companies required to breach ICS's security kept the company working within an impenetrable veil of secrecy. Consequently, both entities enjoyed a very amicable relationship.

"Saber-one-one this is Alpha-Kilo," came the voice of a Kilo TL unfamiliar to Dane. "We understand you need a little assistance sweeping out the trash?"

"A-firm, Alpha-Kilo," Dane replied. "We've got a shit ton of dirt down here and don't have a broom big enough to do the job. Would request a helping hand, ASAP."

"Roger that, Saber-one-one. Have a team toting big brooms inbound, ETA five mikes."

"Thanks, Saber out." Dane turned to his guys, "You heard him. Set security and prepare to assist Kilo once they are on scene. Twitch?" The former snowboarder who was looking off into the night turned his way slowly. "Front gate, you and Jed. Lock it down."

Twitch snapped a nod and loped off in the direction of the gate. Saber's ATL followed.

"Tweeker?"

"Yeah, Boss?"

Dane, working fast, used his SICS docked on his forearm and called up the map on his helmet screen, again. He began overlaying the pathways with lines of varying color. The map was simultaneously displayed on his team's head-up display as well as the incoming Kilo team's display. His orders were also being relayed to all. "I'll take two of Kilo's guys and clear this area." Dane double-tapped the screen on his forearm and highlighted the area known as the *Louisiana Swamp* in blue. This was the area Jed and Tweeker cleared hastily earlier. "Each squad's call sign is the color corresponding with your sector. My unit is *Blue*. You, Jed and Twitch take a Kilo shooter each and clear your indicated sector. You're yellow, Jed is green, and Twitch, you take the red path."

"Roger that," they responded together.

"Toad?"

"Yeah?"

"Maintain overwatch."

332

"Always the bridesmaid, never the bride," replied the sniper in a mockingly whiney voice.

Dane guffawed, "You'll meet the right man someday, honey."

\*\*\*

It took another thirty minutes for the two teams to lock down the zoo. During that time, two more savages were neutralized. Finally, after what seemed like an eternity, Dane was able to report, "Objective is secure," and subsequently add, "send in the Cleaners."

\*\*\*

The iron gate's hinges creaked as they were pushed open. During the day, with hundreds of people milling about, the sound would have been inaudible; though, now it pierced the night with a shrillness that caused tooth fillings to ache. A count of *one-Mississippi, two-Mississippi* occurred when all of a sudden a dozen nondescript men stepped through the darkness and loitered around the front landing of the zoo's entrance. The leader came to stand silently before Dane. He was a pale, bookish man with round rimmed spectacles seated across a beaklike nose. A wreath of salt and pepper hair hugged the sides of his head giving him a *Friar Tuckian* appearance. The little, gravitationally challenged man rocked on his feet from toes to heels in anticipation. Though he never said a word, his eyes held an intensity that seemed ill-fit for such a diminutive figure.

*He enjoys this,* Dane said to himself. His arms became pocked with goose bumps as he realized just how weirded-out the thought made him feel. "Tweeker, Jed, show these guys where the bodies are, okay?"

"Shit, Boss, you can't toss a starved maggot without it hitting a piece of meat for it to gnaw on."

Dane's glare said what he refused – in mixed company – to allow his mouth to pleasure of verbalizing.

"Well, ah…okay…there's one," Tweeker said, taking Dane's hint of a slow death, as he pointed to the obviously dead savage with the headless anaconda still in his hand. "Don't ask me what the fuck he's doing eating a snake, though. The rest of them are kinda all over the place; so, if you guys will follow me, I'll give you the dime tour."

The leader snapped his fingers, and a group of four cleaners set to work. Jed and Tweeker then led more of the strange, silent men along with their leader through the zoo. As they moved deeper into the zoo, they pointed one way, then the next, and each time, more of the cleaning crew broke off from the group and set to the macabre work.

Dane turned back to Twitch, who had not exactly been right since he offed the woman feeding on the gorilla innards, "Dude, you cool?"

Twitch shrugged noncommittally, "Bro, shootin' savages is one thing, but these," he motioned to the dead snake eater, "these ain't savages, man. You see that last one? He smelled *us*, man; but, did you see that look in his eyes? It was like he knew he was different now and hated himself for it. The mom Toad took out still had her kid in her hand. Her dead kid *she* killed and even then, she was unable to decide whether to laugh or cry. I mean what the fuck? And, that gorilla-eating chick? She ripped that overgrown monkey's chest wide open with what? Her fingers? Teeth? Who fuckin' knows, bro? And, the bird muncher didn't even put up a fight. Hell, Dane, none of them did, if you think about it. It was like they didn't even *know* what they were or why."

Twitch, his helmet off hanging at his side, turned his head away. The action spoke of shame in the work. "She smiled at me, bro. As she chewed on that monkey's guts, she smiled like it was Christmas morning."

Dane knew where his friend was coming from. The whole thing had been an amalgamation of the surreal and the violent.

"Twitch, dying right here tonight was the best thing that could have happened to these people. Newly turned or not, they are savages, bro. Tonight was just the beginning. What if we'd left them alone? What if we'd let them live? How many others would have died tomorrow night or the next or next week, because we fucked around and didn't do our jobs? Christ, man, look at what they did...what they are already capable of. You say they aren't savages. Well brother, they damned sure ain't human."

Now, it was Dane's turn to look off into the night. His mind, focusing on the only sane thing in his life, wandered to his son for a brief moment. He added in a soft, sad voice, "The Skipper's right, Twitch. It's only gonna get worse from here."

"So, you're cool with this, Boss?"

Dane shook his head but could not meet his friend's eyes, "No man. I hate this shit, but we're in the right, bro. No doubt about that."

Twitch nodded as Jed, Tweeker, and Toad came running up. They were followed by the ever-silent lead cleaner. He was sweating and breathing hard from the exertion of the run.

"Boss," Jed said quietly, "we gotta problem."

Dane grimaced knowing that if there was anything more problematic than the obvious they had a real goat-roping on their hands.

"What?" he groaned.

"Bodies, bro," Toad informed him. "There's a ton of 'em, way more than we first thought. And…" a series mad howls shattered what had become normal city sounds again. The canines in the surrounding neighborhoods had become crazed again. The group listened as did everyone within eyesight. "…some of them are waking up."

Dane and Twitch said *Oh shit!* in uniform fashion.

"It's cool, though," Tweeker added, "We ended the threat before it started…I think."

Dane cursed through gritted teeth. This was something he should have been working out in his head instead of playing *sidewalk confessional* with Twitch. The men waited in silence for a subjective eternity until they were sure the zoo was completely safe. Finally, Dane shared a weird, mischievous smirk with the group, "Bag up that gorilla along with the savages and anyone with a bullet hole in them. Leave the others."

\*\*\*

## Strapped to a Blackhawk
## 0300

It had been one helluva night, even by SKUL standards. Initial reports were just rolling in, and by all accounts, Saber team was the low team on the totem pole as far as contact was concerned. They were also one of the few to escape unscathed.

By physical definition, at least.

The team that had seen the most action was Copperhead, Hammer's home squad. Things got so hot that Copperhead had to call in their QRF Kilo team to pull them out of the fray. According to Hammer, their buddy from SEE-S, they were "that close to being overrun."

He emphasized the *that close* part.

At the end of the night, Copperhead neutralized twenty-two savages; though, one of their guys, former 2nd Battalion Ranger whose call sign was *Stank*, would need a few days – maybe a week – to heal. Stank received several claw wounds to his thighs. He was *Winchester* on ammo and faced the savage with only his silver 'hawk.

His freaking tomahawk.

By any sane person's definition, the world had definitely gone to shit.

Before allowing himself a moment's peace, Dane confirmed that Hammer had, in fact, made it through the night on the right side of the dirt. After a bit of radio assisted verbal fist-bumps between the two, Dane thumbed his iPod on and rested his head on the wall of the helo's fuselage.

Tweeker leaned into his ear and asked in a loud voice, "Whatcha listenin' to, Boss?"

"What?" asked Dane, half asleep and having trouble hearing him over the noise of the helicopter.

Tweeker grabbed a headset, pulled it over his ears, and adjusted the mic. He then tossed a second set to Dane and pointed at his ears. He still had to speak loudly and enunciate every word, "I said, whatcha listenin' to?"

"Oh," Dane yelled loudly into his mic, "*Heavy and Hanging.*"

Tweeker's face split into a bright a smile. He leaned back against his own piece of sheet metal, laughing as he said, "So's my Johnson!"

In spite of himself, Dane laughed, "It's a Patterson Hood song, you ass!"

"Sure it is, Boss!" Tweeker said between laughs. "Sure it is!"

# 28)
## Aftermath

**Whiskey Platoon Area**
**0500**

Joe Jefferson, *Dogger* to his teammates, was Rhino team's ATL. Rhino was one of Whiskey platoon's finest, most experienced teams. He was old school Marine Force Recon who visited innumerable shitholes worldwide, seeing combat in each and every one, before being recruited to SKUL. A born-again-hard Marine, Dogger was a squared-jawed, taut-muscled black man whose one snub at the organization he so loved was his Mohawk. His *do* gave his solid, six foot frame another three inches. Along with knowing dozens of ways to kill an individual – werewolves included, Dogger walks the earth with a quick, biting sense of humor and a booming, foghorn laugh that drew his teammates to him and gave them a rock to lash their vessels to. Dogger's wit is self-deprecating by habit, disallowing him to fully recognize the value of his ten years of hard service within SKUL or the other eight as a Marine.

He simply *is*, and he's comfortable with it.

Dogger, fussing over the cup of coffee he was putting through a French press, related the story of Rhino's raid on a nursing home in the suburb of Metairie. They had taken down eight newly turned savages, all of them in their *seventies*. The geriatrics had made a total mess of the other patients there, literally decorating the upholstery with viscera.

"My question for the congregation," Dogger said in a voice that commanded attention, "is this: What in the name of all that's good and pure are a bunch of retirees doing hitting up on some drug like cocaine? Nevermind savage blood being mixed up in that shit."

"Children of the sixties, maybe?" Came a muted, uncertain reply from the somewhere around wall of the platoon area.

Jed, one of the oldest active operators in SKUL – certainly within Whiskey platoon, corrected, "People smoked weed, burned bras and flags, and watched Andy Griffith in the sixties, man. Coke is a product of our pissant generation...the eighties."

"Hell, man," said another shooter, drawing from his cup of coffee, "maybe an orderly doped 'em up just to see what would happen?"

Dogger turned from the press and gazed quizzically in the postulator's direction, "Dude, that's fucked up."

Dane and the other TL's heard every word.

Were they worried? It was nothing more than adrenaline being bled off after a successful night, and it was successful on all fronts. Well over three dozen savages were eliminated with only a few minor injuries to report.

But, the banter around the room was absent something. Something inherent to every operator gathered.

*Confidence.*

The Admiral's words hit Dane like a ball-peen hammer to the cranium – *This is just the beginning.*

Dane felt cold just thinking about what was coming their way.

There was a palsy in the crowd, a sickness, as the guys peeled one layer of the riddle away only to find another in its

place.  Instead of fist bumps, high fives, and shoulder slaps;
the operators nestled in their chairs and lost themselves to
darkness.  A heavy feeling of worry hung over the group like
a wet blanket, and no one was truly comfortable with the job
they had just completed.

The reality of the whole thing was the job wasn't
*completed,* and they knew it.

This was a test, nothing more.  The savages were just
feeling them out.

Every man gathered felt the savages had an ace in the
hole.  Something unexpected and unforeseen; yet, regardless
of it, these men – these warriors – thrummed with an ever
louder spirit while in the company of their brothers,
pontificating over the unknown.

This was true for every man in the crowd, save one.
*Twitch.*

Jed stood to the side and sipped from a fresh cup of
coffee.  He tugged at the ends of his long, handlebar
mustache, quietly watching the young, undeniably deadly son
of his old friend and TL, Kyle Metcalf.

Kyle – call sign *Rash* – was the team leader of Jed's
first SKUL team.  Kyle and his son, Kris', history would
make for a best-selling novel; that is, if SKUL's non-
disclosure statements would allow for anything other than a
maximum security prison and a consistent rotation at shower
time if anyone ever spoke a word about its existence.

Needless to say, Kris and his dad did not have the
most understanding and loving of relationships, but Jed made
a promise to his old mentor long ago.  A promise he would
die keeping.  The day after SKUL rescued the MARSOC

CSO – Kris Metcalf or Twitch, Kyle's son – the elder Metcalf looked Jed square in the eyes and said, "Promise me you'll protect him. Keep him safe."

That night, Jed's gaze was steady as he sold his soul, "With my life, Kyle," Blackmoor said firmly, "with my life."

Now, he saw that Twitch was displaying all of the signs of someone wrestling with the kind of thoughts that would eventually erode the indelible armor surrounding a warrior's soul. After studying the situation and giving it some thought, he quietly beckoned Tommy Granderson, Rhino's team leader, to his side.

As the story goes, Jed, then a Master Sergeant in the Unit, and Tommy, a young Unit member as well, had been loaned out to the CIA – *sheep dipping*, the practice is called. Together, Blackmoor and Granderson were the tip of the spear for dozens of hunter/killer operations carried out against known or even suspected *HV* – high value – Al Qaeda targets operating in and around Iraq. It was Baghdad, 2004; and, only months prior, the U.S. had claimed victory in that particular piss-pot of a war. Even so, the two found themselves fighting an insurgency that would only get worse. The two were good, real good, and began taking out terrorists before they could strap explosives to their bodies. During that time, they continually revisited the inner sanctums of Hell both day and night. There, they repeatedly experienced the worst in humankind. During those days of blood and misery, a bond between the older Sergeant and his younger protégé spawned. There, in the piss and shit, that bond became like iron, forged in the battle fires burning along dusty streets and downtrodden, bullet-ridden homes of

*Everytown, Iraq.* It was that bond, that total and complete trust in one another, that allowed them to weather the storm, to endure the worst man had to offer…to thrive in a dry sea of death.

Something in Jed told him he was coming full circle. Something nudged him forward when normally he would keep his distance. Seeing yet another young operator at a crossroads, Jed knew Twitch needed to hear a story. No, he had earned the right to hear *the* story – now, more than ever.

Jed and Tommy's conversation was quick and imperceptible to anyone who may have been watching. In fact, no words were passed as the older operator caught Granderson's attention and tilted his head toward Twitch. Tommy nodded and quietly, so as not to draw anyone's attention, he pulled up a chair beside the young, seemingly troubled warrior.

"S'up, Twitch," said Granderson, a wiry Oklahoman with close cropped brown hair and a handlebar mustache. Tommy-Gun – not so much a call sign as just a name many used when referring to him – had a quick wit and easy manner that drew others to him like the proverbial moth to the flame. An educated soldier, he held a degree in biology from the University of Oklahoma. There, he was a star on the wrestling team, but he was much more than that. Tommy could just as easily talk straight line politics with a U.S. congressman as he could talk his next victim out of her panties. Unflappable in battle and undeniably loved by the men in his charge, Granderson permeated an aura of quiet confidence in every facet of his life.

343

"Hey, Tommy." Twitch said despondently as he swirled the contents of his coffee mug.

"You cool, bro?" Rhino's team leader tried some *Twitch-speak* in the hopes of gaining a reaction.

Twitch only shrugged in response.

Undeterred, Granderson took a more direct approach, "Shit's fucked up, huh?"

For the first time Twitch looked away from his mug and into Tommy's eyes, "Way past that, man."

"Yeah, I heard," Granderson admitted. With those simple words, he tore through the pretense of his visit to Twitch's little patch of world. "She would have killed you had you not pulled the trigger first. It's what they do, what they live for."

Twitch looked back to the lip of his mug, "Maybe." The young operator shivered before adding, "I guess."

Granderson leaned back in his chair and crossed his muscular arms over his chest. By doing so, he's revealed tribal tattoo's surrounding the word RELENTLESS in block lettering on his right forearm. More tribal tattoo's surrounded SKUL's shield on the other. He thought about what he was about to say, choosing each word as wisely as he could, until finally, "Twitch, you ever hear why Jed and I are so close?"

"Nah, rumors mostly." Twitch took in Tommy's stare with his own, "I do know you guys were dick deep in some heavy shit, but that's about all, man. They called you guys the *ashbah* – ghosts...if you believe the stories."

"Yeah, we were...in some heavy shit, that is. We were inserted into Baghdad shortly after our declaration of *victory.*" Tommy-Gun Granderson spat the word *victory* to emphasize just how ridiculous it had all been. How do you defeat a fifteen hundred year old ideology, anyway? "We were part of a task force meant to stem the tide of the insurgency and were pretty much left to our own devices. No command to speak of, no real oversight, either. It was all a matter of perspective, but depending on the end of the barrel you were on, it was a pretty cool gig." With the ease of adding mustard to a sandwich, Tommy verbally grabbed Twitch and held him close, his attention on every word; and, more importantly, his mind off his own troubled thoughts. "Baghdad was already Indian country in the strictest sense. Murders, rapes, kidnappings, you name the most vile acts one human can do to another, and it was a daily occurrence. Every-godforsaken inch of that shithole seemed to give birth to death, destruction, and sorrow at a moment's notice; and, me and ol' Jed waded through the very center of that particular expanse of hell. In the early moments, we managed to hit 'em so fast we took out dozens of terrorists before they were able to get their shit together. Eventually, they got it together and, oh man, did they throw the kitchen sink at us. We had bounties placed on our heads, car bombs, snipers, IEDs…you name it. They wanted us sent straight to Satan's doorstep. We were the walking dead, going day and night, sending in intel from one op only to have intel bounce-back and lead to another. We were two *Alices* traveling down an endless rabbit hole; but, we were prepared to see it through."

Tommy spit a wad of tobacco spit into a Styrofoam cup and leaned back into a relaxed position. He looked like somebody's crazy uncle recounting an old home story; which, in truth, was exactly what he was doing. "And then, one day, one of our CIA contacts passed some intel concerning a high value meet on the outskirts of the city. Intel was solid, vetted, and we got the word from *higher* to move on it with an order to kill. Not capture, kill. Given that those assholes didn't work on our timetable, we had to hit the house at a bastardly hour – middle of the day, with a thousand eyes on us. For whatever reason, I remember being so damned scared when we hit the target. Maybe it was because it was just Jed and I and the stress was getting to me, I dunno. What I do know is that from jump, the op didn't feel right. It was *off*...somehow. Worse than that – and this is what really, really petrified me – was that I could tell Jed wasn't just thrilled as shit to be hitting that hole, either. Anyway, it was a hard entry with Jed in the lead. He took a corner, disappearing, and began to immediately shout, "I'm putting my weapon down," before I could flow through behind him. Instead, I squatted behind that corner, sweating and breathing like you haven't ever seen. It felt like a damned eternity that I sat there, and all the while, Jed talked, giving out hints to the target's location and what weaponry they had. Turns out it was a suicide vest filled with C-4 and lots of it. Little shit was strapped with enough to take down the three of us, the house, and most likely, the entire city block. Finally, I could tell by Jed's voice he had moved. It was slight, but he gave me just enough room to round the corner and take the shot. God bless his wicked soul, Jed was still talking to whoever was in the room; and, I knew it was then, or we'd all die. I rounded the corner with my gun shouldered, acquired the target...and slapped the trigger twice. *Clap clap* – the rounds shattered the brain stem instantly and kept the fingers from pushing the button. Jed cleared the room and the rest of the building, for that matter. The whole time I just stared into the dead eyes of a little Iraqi girl not much older than my own daughter. The HVT's we were there for were nowhere to be found; though, they left us little care packages…"

Tommy became very still and his eyes glazed at the memory. He shivered, then continued, "As you know, women – even little girls – are fodder to those people, nothing more. So, in the suit she went. She had tears in her eyes when Jed rounded that corner, but she never dropped that damned phone. Jed could see what I couldn't. She was going to do her *duty*."

Twitch noted how Tommy spat the word like a king cobra might sling venom at its victims. Completely enthralled by the story, Twitch said nothing while the team leader lamented sadly and in a voice that was but a whisper, "All she had to do was *drop* the goddamned cellphone from her little hands, and it would have been over…but, she didn't."

Granderson felt Twitch shift as he continued, "Fucked me up, seriously, for a long time. Every time I shut my eyes, I saw that little girl. Couldn't sleep for weeks until one day Jed saved my life. There was this little boy set to push the button on a remote IED near my position. Jed took him out without blinking an eye. That night I broke every rule in combat and asked him about it. Wanna guess how he replied?"

Twitch stared blankly, enraptured by the story, daring not to say a word.

"He said, *Dude, that boy would have killed us both if he could have. That girl that's mind-fuckin' you would have, too. It's just war, man. It sucks and it's unfair; but, in the end, you do what you got to do to survive.*" Tommy looked to Twitch intensely, his eyes red-rimmed and puffy. It was as if the memory was still too much to bear, "Kris, you understand what I'm getting at?"

"Yeah, Tommy." Twitch's words said one thing, but his voice said something completely different. His voice hinted that he was still struggling to come to terms with what he had done.

"No you don't, Twitch," came Tommy's flat, gravelly voice.

He spit into his cup again.

"You don't get shit, because you're young and stupid. You're trying to rationalize with the irrational." Tommy shoved his index finger repeatedly into his temple, "And you're getting in here, man. Don't. This place is a black box. Columbians, Iranians, Libyans, North Koreans, even those godforsaken half-turned savages from tonight – it don't matter, bro. They all want you dead. You better get with that if you want to survive; because, I have this awful feeling this shit's gonna make the Black Plague look like a spring sinus infection before it's over."

For some reason, Tommy-Gun's dark outlook mixed with Twitch's perverted sense of humor forced a smile out of the younger shooter. He held up his mug which Granderson tapped with his own, "Thanks, Tommy."

Rhino's TL smiled, "No problem; but, just in case, I've been asked to tell you to stay the hell away from the explosives for the next few days."

Twitch shot his eyes over to where Jed stood. He smiled, winking to Twitch.

"Dammit, Jed...it was one damned time."

Granderson pulled Twitch to his feet, "Glad you're back on Earth man. Let's get something to eat."

They hadn't made it far when Elbert ducked his head into the platoon area and yelled, "Ops Center, five minutes!" Smelling the fresh coffee, he added, "Admiral says one of you guys had better be bringing his coffee."

***

The guys filing into the Ops Center were greeted with "*SSSSHHHH!*" from Tim Meadows, Titan's team leader. One of the monstrous flat screen TVs, tuned to a New Orleans station, flashed:

*BREAKING NEWS!!!*

...scrolled across the screen just before revealing an attractive blond anchorwoman:

*Tragedy has struck the Audubon Nature Institute. In the early morning hours, it has been discovered that Ed, the zoo's giant silverback gorilla, escaped from his sanctuary, killing multiple nighttime employees before disappearing into the New Orleans' night. As of this announcement, the police have no leads concerning the ape's whereabouts but urge citizens to walk in groups whenever possible. They are also imploring citizens to not approach the animal. If confronted, do not make any rapid movements. The police are coordinating with zoo personnel who have set up a hotline for reporting any possible sightings...*

The anchorwoman continued her morning monologue, promising an interview with one of the world's foremost authorities at noon. The Ops Center erupted. Tim and Tommy, standing closest to Dane, slapped him on the shoulder admiringly.

"Dude, that's solid work," chuckled Tim with Tommy adding, "Never in my life would I have thought about doing that."

Dane grinned sheepishly and shrugged, "You should have seen that weird little head cleaner's face when I told him what I had in mind. First time he spoke, he tripped over every word. He was like *whadammygonnadowithagorilla.* His accent was so thick, and he was so confused and excited, I could barely understand him."

"Dude seriously creeps me out," admitted Tommy, who jerked his eyes to Dane. "He spoke? I ain't ever heard him utter a word."

"Yep," Dane confirmed. "Did you guys know that dude was German?"

Around the three, the room had degraded into the comical. All kinds of jokes bounced off the walls. Some were ridiculous, others bordered on the obscene. Special operators, not unlike any other facet of expected to work under extreme pressures, tended to mock the dire circumstances in which they were often found. For example, one need not look any further than to the nearest operating room and listen in on the filth that pours from the surgeon's mouth.

SKUL or any other unit under fire was no different nor should it be.

The banter died with the next news segment. This time, the story was delivered by a man sporting a fake tan, an overly deep and pompous voice, and a face caked with makeup. He looked like the sort of pansy that drank bottled water from a glass and prided himself on his ability to parse out the area of France the wine he was sipping came from. He began his diatribe with:

> *The skies of New Orleans were busy last night, but not from the normal traffic of Louis Armstrong International Airport...*

His smile was so greasy it looked like it would drip off his face at any moment. It was fake in every since of the word. The pompous ass continued:

> *Last night the sky was full of military helicopters, Blackhawks and smaller craft colloquially called Little Birds, mostly, but there have been unconfirmed sightings of an Apache attack helicopter. Why were these hovering over our fair city is anyone's guess, and government officials are offering little in the way of response. One military official who spoke on the terms of anonymity stated this was part of an on-going urban training exercise.*
>
> *Stay tuned for updates as they come in. Now, back to Andy with the weather...*

The room collectively cringed. Going into the city via the helos always carried a risk, but to make the news?

Not good.

Looking around, Dane noticed Sam and Elbert with Hammer and some of his boys from Copperhead. They were talking with a smattering of guys from Renegade and

351

Mustang. He was just about to slide over and see how Hammer was doing – he would be lying if he said he was not interested in having a pressure free conversation with Sam – when a hand of iron grabbed his shoulder, spinning him in place.

It was the Admiral. He had a grave look in his good eye while the scar growing from the underside of his patch twitched.

"Son," he said in his gravelly voice, "can I have a word with you?"

Dane immediately bristled, "Are they okay?"

He was referring to his wife and son. They had been living under SKUL's protection since Dane's recruitment. He did not know where they were, or what they were doing. This was by design. The families of SKUL operators lived in a constant state of danger – Twitch and his family was a prime example. Because of this, SKUL now sought to ensure their protection fervently. Most were placed under a passive protection detail while others were taken off the grid. Those families disappeared, became memories, and were forever *gone*.

Dane's wife and son fell into the second group.

Seeing one of his own, a man who had proven to be one of his finest leaders in very short order, so dangerously close to a high speed come-apart, he added quickly and almost apologetically, "They're fine, Dane."

"They're fine."

Dane immediately relaxed. He had literally just seen his life pass before his eyes, a phenomenon he did not believe in…now, he did.

"But we still need to talk."

# 29)

## The Fork in the Road

### Admiral's quarters
### 0700

While Dane read, the Admiral poured a drink. Then, thinking better of it, he poured a second one.

This one a double.

Yes, it was early. Yes, he was breaking a personal rule. But, he figured they would be need a drink after this was all over.

The Skipper walked back to his desk, careful not to disturb the younger officer. He noted Stackwell was shaking as he read what the letter had to say. It was hard to tell if the shakes were born from rage or a broken heart; though, Briggs did not think it really mattered. He slid the double shot of whiskey across the desk, took a sip from his own, then said quietly, "If you need some time, take it. No one will look down on you. God knows you've got good enough reason."

Dane slid back from the table and stood without taking a sip of the proffered drink. He had to wipe at the corners of his eyes, "Thank you, sir; but, that won't be necessary."

The Admiral lit one of his legendarily huge, illegal Cuban stogies and took a long puff while regarding Dane. After a second, he asked, "You're sure?"

"Yes, sir. It's probably better for everyone this way."

The Admiral sighed, "I doubt that son, but...okay. Just understand, I'll pull your ass off your team the second I

355

think your mind isn't where it needs to be. Too many lives are at stake, am I clear?"

"Crystal, sir."

After wrestling with his thoughts and beating his anger down, he asked, "What about their security detail, sir?"

"I'm sorry?" asked the Skipper. He truly did not understand his young officer's question nor his apparent concern.

"Well, sir, with this situation I was just wondering if their protection would be taken away. I understand if it is, but i will have to…"

"SKUL doesn't abandon its people, Commander Stackwell," snapped the Admiral, his anger obvious if only just below the surface. "Never has, never will…not on my watch, in any case."

Dane could see by the look in the Briggs' one good eye that he meant every word. He could also tell his doubt concerned the Skipper.

"Thank you, sir. I'm sorry, sir."

The Admiral's demeanor softened. "Think nothing of it. I'd worry if you didn't ask those questions, honestly." He cleared his throat uncomfortably, then continued, "I'll have our attorneys work out the details. They've already spoken with Abbey and assured me she wants nothing more than an amicable separation and what's best for Henry. They'll work out the details and make sure this is as painless for everyone as possible, considering the circumstances. In the meantime, it might be best not to contact Henry…at least until we get this squared away."

Dane's shoulders slump. He was defeated inside and out, and only managed to say softly, "If you say so, sir." Dane turned for the door.

"Dane?"

"Sir?"

"You need to sign it." The Skipper nodded toward the small stack of papers on his desk.

"Yeah," Dane said, moving back to the desk. "I guess I do."

***

Dane leaned out over the railing of the top deck of the Silver Moon. The warm, salt-tinged air wrapped around him in a warm embrace. He was hurting, and no amount of *it's better this way* could ever possibly take that hurt away. Dane walked across an earth in which failure was never an option; yet, the one thing that should have been most important of all, he had managed to fail.

His marriage.

Dane had known Abbey since she walked into his grade school class. It was a warm, late spring day. She, being a recent transplant to his little Mississippi town, stood nervously before his class. He still remembered her curly blond hair and angelic features as Mrs. Tripp introduced her. They lived a storybook existence. He was the star athlete; she was the captain of the cheerleading squad. As expected, they dated off and on through high school and college. He actually told Abbey that he had applied for and been selected to attend the Navy Officer Candidate School before telling his parents. Neither Abbey nor his parents were overly thrilled about the idea; and, even less so when he shared his ultimate goal of serving as an officer in the Navy SEALs.

The ring Dane gave Abbey changed her tune and against both parents' wishes, they were married just before Dane reported to Naval Station Newport in Rhode Island. Eventually, she followed Dane to Coronado, California, where he attended BUD/S. She was pregnant with Henry at the time, managing well enough, until Dane began post-BUD/S training called SEAL Tactical Training or *STT*. When STT – later renamed SQT – rolled around, Henry was only a few months old. This was Abbey's first taste of what Dane's life – and by default, hers as well – was going to be like. That bitter pill of reality settled in the pit of her stomach and, like acid, began eroding her and Dane's relationship. They both tried to keep it together, more for Henry than themselves, but this last assignment with SKUL had obviously been too much. It was not Abbey's fault, Dane always said she was the strangest woman he had ever met...and, he meant it. He certainly held no ill will toward his now estranged wife, but that certainly did not keep the anger away. Outwardly, the people he passed on the deck – many, fellow operators and friends – where none-the-wiser but that anger, dangerous though it be, simmered just below the surface.

Strangely enough, it was only out of his love for Abbey that he signed the divorce papers. She deserved a better life than she had with him. That was exactly why it hurt so badly. He felt numb all over as read the letter for what seemed to be the thousandth time.
*Dane,*

*Before you read anything else, please understand this was the hardest thing I've ever done. I just can't take it anymore. You're never here, and I never know if the next knock on the door is someone coming to tell me you've been killed.*

*Our lives were at a fork in the road this last time; but, instead of choosing the path that included me and Henry, you once again chose to leave and fight another war. I can't do it again; I'm not strong enough for this anymore. And, you know it's not fair for Henry, either. He needs a dad, Dane; someone who's there to help him figure out life. I know you could be that person, but not while you're still fighting your wars. I just hope you realize you've done your duty and let someone else do the fighting before something happens to you.*

*I don't think Henry could handle that.*

*He adores you, Dane. He practically worships the ground you walk on, even though he barely knows you. He tells everyone he wants to be just like his dad, but when they ask what you do, he can't answer. I won't keep you from him. I swear I won't, but Dane, it's not fair for you to pop in and out of his life when it suits you. Look at where that left us. Please Dane, give him time to figure this out. When he's ready for you to be a part of his life; and, you're actually ready to be around, we'll figure the rest out.*

*Please be safe, Abbey*
P.S. *Please sign the papers, Dane, and make this easy*

Dane's head fell between his outstretched arms. He held his hand open, and allowed the letter to float on the wind and out to sea. He was intently studying it flit with the currents of the wind when someone jogging on the deck called out between breaths, "Hi, Commander."

She gave a wave as she passed.

359

Dane was so focused on the complete and thorough shit-show that had suddenly become his life, he barely acknowledge the person who had spoken. His only response was to grunt. It was all he had in him. Unused to inattention, the jogger stopped short and came back around to Dane's side.

"Hey, what are you doing up here, anyway? Shouldn't you be off spitting tobacco juice everywhere or cleaning your gun for the hundredth time today?"

She was needling him, for reasons only she knew. Unfortunately, she wasn't aware of the viper pit she was about to step off in. Had she known, she would have just kept jogging.

But, she didn't.

"Hey, I know. Maybe you could put together one of your world class mission briefings and impress me with your command of the English language."

"I came up here for some peace and quiet," he snarled, but the woman did not back down. Either she could not recognize unadulterated rage just itching to boil over into wrath, or she simply did not care.

"What, no snappy comeback? No arm around my waist and hand on my ass?" She batted her perfectly long eyelashes and pantomimed fanning herself, "Why, I do declare, I'm just plum bothered by the lack of attention." And she was, truth be known. "Isn't that something those rednecks you dated would have said?"

*Camel's back, meet straw.*

She chuckled lightly, thoroughly pleased with herself.

360

"Look, I get it! You don't like me! Well, you know what? Take a damned number and get in the back of the line! My job is to ask questions, regardless of how they may sound, in order to keep my men alive. If that means interrupting what I'm sure is a brilliant, if not completely memorized, presentation then so-damned-be-it!"

He was raging, and it felt good. Unfortunately, his mouth was moving about a day ahead of his brain. Had he stopped to reign it in, he could have prevented what he said next.

"Look, let's get this straight. You're intel. You take some photos, cut and paste some data onto a bunch of PowerPoint slides, and deliver it to men who step out the door and put themselves into harm's way on a minute by minute schedule. After that, you get to take a shower and have a beer. Me and my men? We get to take that intel – *your* intel – and pretend to ourselves that it's right on the money. But, it never really is, is it *Mrs. Steele?*" He drug out her name using profound Southern drawl taking any doubt - if there was any left - that he could get down and just as redneck as anyone, "Remember *Mexico?*"

He would later admit that he should have tabbed out long before saying any of that; but, he was nowhere near being through. No, no. Why show a little self-control and ruin a perfectly good opportunity to make a complete ass of yourself?

She stared, jaw agape, as he flung the Molotov cocktails of coup de grâce while walking away as if she didn't exist, "Anyhow, if you want to be helpful, why don't you be a good little woman and go check on the boys. I'm sure they have some clothes that need washing and folding or a sandwich they'd like made."

Behind him the air got very, very still.

The simple fact of the matter is that women – each and every last, solitary one – have a line you never, under any circumstances, cross.

Dane did not just cross it. He ran over it, backed up, ran over it again, then barked his tires, and left the line somewhere in the next area code.

The heat that radiated from Sam could have boiled water.

Had Dane been looking, he would have seen the emotion of anger manifest itself in the physical. Her words came out as merely a hiss. A long, frigid, dangerous hiss.

"You ASSHOLE!"

Dane never looked back, he just tossed his hands up in dismissal and bellowed over his shoulders, "Whatever!"

He stalked off one way, she the other.

Both borderline homicidal with rage.

\*\*\*

### Saber team's weapons locker
### 0800

By the time Dane managed to cool off and make his way to Whiskeys' weapons locker, the guys had stripped and cleaned their weapons, replaced the batteries in their weapons' sights, swapped out damaged KtacS suits for unblemished models, and stowed their kit back in their respective lockers. Dane would never admit it, but he was an emotional wreck. His family was in shambles which was, admittedly, largely his fault. He had also been asked by his

362

soon-to-be ex-wife to cease and desist any and all contact with their son for the foreseeable future – again, the fault laid squarely on his shoulders. Admiral Briggs had advised much the same. To top it off, he had acted like a complete ass – again – to Samantha Steele. Forget the fact that she was as attractive as a Greek goddess; she was his team's lead intelligence agent. She and her agents kept his team safe, and he had seriously crossed over the line and into the territory of unprofessional behavior.

In short, he felt like shit; so, it was with no small amount of appreciation and affection that he realized the guys – his men...his friends – had already taken care of his equipment's needs, as well. Everything was laid out on the table, pristine in its condition. The only thing left for him to do was double-check their work and place it in his locker the way he preferred.

Toad, busy tidying up the area, gave him a reassuring pat on the shoulder as he worked. It was a simple gesture, one made without words – none were needed – but a gesture that told Dane he was there for him.

Jed, brewing another pot of coffee in the corner, nodded in his direction like a grandfather would a child. That was pretty much the most emotion Jed Blackmoor ever showed...to anyone.

Knowing Jed the way he had come to know him, Dane felt himself extraordinarily grateful for the gesture.

Twitch held a dust pan like a Roman Centurion might have held a spear. He was trying to look busy, look normal; but, realizing he just looked stupid, he tossed it on the table. The pan missed the table and hit the floor with a loud *clang*.

If being clumsy was a superpower, Twitch would have been a high-ranking member of the Justice League. *Capt'n Clumsy* cringed at the noise but, undaunted, drew himself up to his full height and walked over to Dane's locker.

"Boss, if you need anyone to talk to, I'm here. I've got a lot of experience dealing with fucked up family situations."

He was also a world class communicator that would have made President Reagan jealous.

"Ah, thanks, Twitch. I think."

"What I mean is my dad was never around either..."

Twitch was also a card-carrying, shade tree psychiatrist.

Dane's eyes turned to slits, and his face flushed.

"Jesus, Boss, I suck at this, okay." Twitch looked around the room. No one was too terribly willing to jump into the fray. "Damn, guys...thanks."

Dane laughed. Given the last couple of hours, the release of pressure felt both strange and exhilarating at the same time. He knew what Twitch was trying to say. He was just Twitch and was bound to screw it up. "Yeah, dude, you suck at this; but, thanks."

Twitch nodded then went to help Toad sweep up the dirt off the floor. It took less than five seconds for Toad to throw the broom angrily at him. "Dude, you have got to be shitting me!"

Twitch looked down. He had walked through the pile of dirt and tracked it all over the once clean floor. "Soooory. Sheez."

Last to acknowledge Dane was Tweeker. He stalked over and stood nose to nose with Saber's TL, staring intensely into his eyes for a long time. The two special operators had known each other for over a decade. A little known fact outside of Section 8 was that Tweeker was one of the first men Dane recruited to the new unit. So, there was not much the one didn't know about the other. Another, universally known fact was that Tweeker was huge. Saber's medic had arms that looked like tree trunks and his legs, slabs of granite. With his long, blond hair and stark, blue eyes, he was every bit the image of the Norse god, Thor. And, now, he towered over a seated Dane with his thick arms crossed about his chest. The two had matching tattoos, one on each forearm. Section 8's unofficial crest of a dragon perched on a Templar's cross on one, SKUL's shield, the other. Tweeker's chest would give a fifty-five gallon drum a run for its money. It rose and fell with every breath the big Nordic took.

He looked pissed. Dane did not care.

"Heard you went full retard on Sam a little while ago."

"Word travels fast around here," replied Dane, matching Tweeker's intensity with his own. His voice was dry, flat even, yet somehow filled with venomous undertones.

"Yeah," Tweeker immediately softened and put a little more air between the two. "Look, Boss, I know I may have overstepped my bounds here, but I explained to Monica what you were dealing with. I told her to talk to Sam. She may never speak to you again – can't say I'd blame her, honestly – but at least she knows you're not a complete woman-hating asshat."

"Thanks, man," he said across a sheepish smile.

Tweeker held out a closed fist which Dane bumped with his own, "No worries, bro."

"Seeing that we're all hugs and bumping dicks again, how 'bout some PT?" asked Jed gruffly. "I want you pissants suited, booted, and in a full combat load in fifteen."

Collectively, the room grumbled, but no one argued.

## 30)
## Killing the Thing You Love

**Rue Bourbon**
**Old Absinthe House**

"Sir, you have a phone call," said Della Rocca's bodyguard quietly into his ear.

"I'm certain I said *no interruptions,*" he growled dangerously in response. Unconsciously, the people crowding the surrounding booths and tables found something to else to focus on, something located in the opposite direction from where Guiseppi Della Rocca and his guest sat. It was an unnatural desire to look away, metaphysically forceful, unearthly, and utterly alien to the human subconscious. Those in the bar had no choice but to obey, for they had not the strength to fight it. The feeling they were experiencing was the same a lesser dog might feel when confronted by the alpha male of a pack - unworthy and pathetic in its mere existence. That feeling of domination, that supernaturally powerful force scratching and clawing at their minds, was emanating from Della Rocca and his guest.

Two of the most unwholesome yet powerful beings on Earth.

The man sitting opposite of Della Rocca wore heavy boots, blue jeans, and a Satan's Bastards cut. To the crowd, he was Billy Blackshanks, president of the New Orleans chapter of the Satan's Bastards Motorcycle Club. The immortal world, however, knew him by a different name. They knew him in formal fashion as William H. Boney, colloquially as Billy the Kid.

A century's worth of history and tall tales preferred the latter to the former.

"Sir," his bodyguard said nervously, "the caller states he's an acquaintance of your Washington friend."

"And?" snapped Della Rocca.

Billy, wearing a wicked grin split unevenly across his face, watched the exchange curiously. A short, hyena-like chuckle escaped his throat and rolled across the restaurant. That was purposeful on Billy's part. He loved to strike fear in the hearts of men. Always had. For a brief second, the other patrons stopped what they were doing, frozen by a feeling of dread as invisible yet undeniable as a current of electricity. They did not look toward the two werewolves; their minds would not let them. Most silently debated whether or not they should just run for their lives.

The bodyguard cleared his throat.

The sharp dressed man – and that's all he was…a *man* – was petrified and seriously regretting the interruption. Unfortunately for him, the caller made mention of a certain package he was protecting – very, very important package – so interrupting his employer was not an option. It was a must. "Sir, the caller says he's the individual assuring your package makes it to its final destination."

Della Rocca cut his eyes – now tinged yellow around the edges – to Billy, "I need to take this."

Billy thrummed his knuckles across the table, eyeballing an attractive blonde at the bar, "No problem. I needed a bit to eat anyway."

Della Rocca smiled, noting the focus of the younger werewolf's attention. The lady really was attractive.

Once Billy was at the bar and assaulting the blond with his interpretation of charm, the ancient Eldrich spoke into the phone, "This is Della Rocca, what can I do for you?"

"Mr. Della Rocca," began the unfamiliar voice, "you can start by listening. My situation is such that I cannot repeat myself."

"Consider my attention yours and yours alone, Mr..."

"No names!" snapped the caller.

"I was going to say *Mr. X,* but as you wish. I'm listening until directed otherwise."

"How would you like to hamstring your little paramilitary problem currently hounding your efforts?"

His words were met with silence.

"Della Rocca, are you still there?"

"I am."

"Did you hear my question?"

"I did."

"And?" unmistakable frustration leaked into the mysterious caller's voice.

"And, I'm waiting. My brothers and I have been battling SKUL for decades with little to no headway. If anything, we have come up short more times than not. So, let's just say that anyone who promises SKUL's instantaneous demise is either dumb or delusional."

"You know who I am...what I've done?"

"I have been informed, yes."

"Then, you should know I'm neither," said the caller in an affronted voice. "I assure you, I can make it happen."

"Then, I'd like to hear what you have in mind." Della Rocca got Billy's attention with a wave, summoning the gunslinger back to the booth. Something told him he was about to need the muscle Billy had at his disposal.

"The first thing you need to do is round up all of those recently turned savages left walking the streets. Get them out of town, in one spot, and keep them there a few days…a week, tops. Those that won't go, kill them."

"Shouldn't be too difficult. There aren't many left after the raids conducted by SKUL, but I'm left to wonder as to what end would find me wasting valuable resources on mere animals?"

"SKUL is an enterprise of action. Starve them for it. They get edgy when there's nothing to shoot. After a few days, start kidnapping people off the streets; the more, the merrier. Hell, make a party out of it, shouldn't be too hard for those things you command. You need something that will get a lot of attention, quickly. Then, get the word out on the street where they are being held and by whom. SKUL *will* hit the target. That's what they do. Be there waiting."

The ancient wolf chuckled. It sounded ominous, like faraway thunder rolling closer. "I fail to see the fresh, innovative genius promised with this plan," Della Rocca incredulously stated.

"I never promised anything new or genius, Mr. Della Rocca," said the caller snidely. "I only promised results. That's the problem with werewolves…"

"Let me tell you something, you insigni…"

The caller cut off Della Rocca's rant midstream and momentarily, the Eldrich was knocked off-balanced by the brazen nature of the caller.

"Oh, shut up and let me finish. The problem with werewolves is that you have thousands upon thousands of years of knowledge at your fingertips; yet, you consistently miss the point."

"Oh," growled Guiseppi dangerously. "What point is it that we're missing?"

"You'll never stop them, ever. These men hunting you, they aren't like anything you've come across. They don't fight for themselves, not for even their countrymen. They don't fight for anything so obtuse as that...they fight for the man to their left and their right. You cannot stop them. They'll keep coming to their last; so, you need to hurt them. Hurt them bad. Use their strengths against them - secrecy, speed, and violence of action. Hurt them. Make them watch their brethren bleed. Make them crazy with death, then *destroy* them utterly."

The cell phone rudely went dead, leaving Della Rocca to momentarily stare at it in anger.

Finally, after several minutes, he looked to Billy. The younger werewolf was staring at the blond who was leaving with someone else. "Billy, we've got work to do."

Saber team's next operational rotation

Action Room 4

Dane stopped short of the door and took a deep breath. It had taken several days of nervous preparation to get to this point.

"Might as well get this over with," he said to himself before stepping through the door into AR-four. He was tense, his muscles taut, as he threaded his way through his team mates before coming to a stop behind Elbert and Sam.

371

The two of them were sitting at a computer putting the finishing touches on their briefing slides.

He cleared his throat, loudly, causing them to turn, "Hey, E, mind giving us a sec?"

Elbert, bug-eyed from sleep deprivation and surprise, looked from Dane to Sam then back to Dane. His eyebrows knitted together in confusion for a millisecond before he realized Dane was talking to him. He also realized the big, blond behemoth expected him to vacate the immediate area RFN – *right fucking now.*

"Oh, yeah, sure Dane. I'm just finishing up here, anyway," he closed his laptop so fast he managed to slam his fingers between the two halves of the reinforced computer. Agony flashed across his face as he gingerly pulled his fingers free and ducked out of the room. Dane smirked then turned back to Sam. The look on her face nearly made him lose his nerve. Her cheeks were splotched crimson from the heat of embarrassment, and her eyes burned like little cauldrons of fire.

He took a deep breath.

"You could have waited until there were fewer people around, you know?" Her voice was cold, like a fresh tray of ice cubes cold. "I mean, it's not like we're not living on the same ship or anything."

Dane started to compliment her on the sarcastic remark – sarcastically, of course – but, thinking better of it, said quietly so as not to draw any attention, "Just hear me out. Please."

While the attempt at privacy was certainly a noble gesture, it was completely useless in execution. *Everyone* still in AR-4 had turned to watch the exchange. To be blunt, the two had developed quite the reputation for heated arguments, and this one promised to be epic. Sam crossed her lean, tanned arms over her chest. The defiant action caused some of her better physical attributes to press ever so tighter against the fabric of her shirt.

*Don't look, you asshole,* Dane thought quickly, hoping she couldn't read his thoughts. *Concentrate, and get this over with, but don't you dare look.*

Completely involuntarily, against everything his mind was commanding, his eyes darted southward. Just for an instant. Sam, noting his downturned pupils, huffed in frustration, dropped her arms to her sides, and stamped her foot angrily. Her eyes flared and her faced scrunched up as if to say *Seriously!*

Mentally, Dane admitted even that was cute on her.

*Damn,* he chastised himself in silence, *you weak-minded sonavabitch.*

He cleared his throat and, eyes back in their proper orientation, began his rehearsed apology. "Look, Sam, about the other day. I wasn't really in my right mind, okay? I've got some stuff going on with my son…"

"You mean you've got some stuff going on with your wife, right?" She interrupted, totally throwing a monkey wrench into his plan. He knew she was not going to let this be easy – who could blame her after what he said; but, he had hoped she would not make it unbearably difficult, either.

"Yeah, right. Her too." Dane admitted, only just now realizing he had never really talked about Abbey to another female before. For whatever reason, it felt really,

really strange. "Anyway, she's filed for divorce." He felt hot – unbearably so – and his face flushed a brilliant red.

Sam's features softened somewhat. She could tell this big man, by all accounts, a killer in every regard, was very uncomfortable talking about his outside life.

"Anyway, you pretty much came up on me just after I had signed the papers. Doesn't make what I said right, and I'm not making excuses for myself; but, I did want you to know I'm sorry, okay?"

Sam wanted to hate the man, but she simply could not. Admittedly, there had been times when she had wanted to throw him off the ship while it was underway, but she also realized that Dane was like any other special operations' warrior she had worked with over the years. His bravado was rooted in a personal ethos that drove him to be the best at everything he did. Suddenly, she realized how hard failing at his marriage must have been for him. Seeing the stone cold killer humbled forced her to look past the outer shell of machismo and see the man beyond.

Hell, half the time Dane's machismo and bravado was enduring…and *that* she hated more than anything else.

"Look, Commander Stackwell…"

"Call me Dane, Sam."

"Okay," she fidgeted uncomfortably with some paperwork, "Look…Dane, it's no biggie, okay? Call it bad timing or whatever. I'm just as much to blame as you are. I should have kept my mouth shut, but I've always been a button pusher." Sam then flashed a smile. It was such a wickedly beautiful smile that the heat in it made his breath catch somewhere deep in his lungs. "Besides, I was the one

374

that called you a...well, I shouldn't have said that. Let's just move on, okay?"

"I'd like that, Sam."

She nodded, grabbed her papers, then trailed off after Elbert. Dane watched her go. Drawn by forces not of this Earth, his eyes were forced to focus on her perfect hips as they swung back and forth like the pendulum of a fine grandfather clock.

He shook his head and thought, *Dude...savages. Focus on them not her ass.*

# 31)
## Side Job (part 4)

"Supper's almost ready, boys," proclaimed Connie Dickerson. Connie was Maxwell T. Dickerson I's wife. *Maxie* – his old SKUL call sign – was a legend in the unit. He was a graduate of the first training class SKUL put together following that first, fateful operation in '75. Maxie, a former Marine who worked EOD for a Recon unit in Vietnam, was recognized by those in leadership positions as having a savant-like a gift for building explosive ordinance. He was also looked upon as a modern-day Van Gogh when it came to designing, building, and maintaining small arms. Seeing the potential and learning of Maxie's near death experience at the hand of a small-town werewolf with large scale desires, Shamus himself began recruiting Maxie. It took several months, but finally, the gritty soldier accepted Shamus' offer and began his training. This was long before the unit had formalized any set training schedule; so, Maxie's training - along with the other recruits of the day – was based off of a hand's on approach. There was no graduation, only survival, and survive Maxie had. In fact, he did more than survive, he excelled; and, today, a SKUL shooter would be hard pressed to look upon the walls of Shamus' pub and not see Maxie staring back with his patent devil-may-care smile.

For SKUL and its members – both present and former, Maxie Dickerson was *straight up O.G.* and went down in history as one of its original death-dealers. He was not a legend because he was one of the first to be recruited to SKUL; rather, Maxie was a legend because he was one of the first to survive. He, along with many others, paved the way for men like ChiTown and his team. To ChiTown, an old Marine himself, the Dickerson name was right up there with Zeus and Apollo.

According to Shamus, the man lived for the hunt…and the kill.

Nowadays, Maxie and his wife ran a dog training facility a few miles west of Annapolis, Maryland. The two specialized in training Labrador and Chesapeake Bay retrievers and were not only active but very successful on the regional field trial circuit. At night, Maxie tinkered with the guns and other weapons he continually collected, built, and rebuilt. He still held a federal firearms' permit which legitimized many of the weapons he owned; though, admittedly, there were several pieces that were not so much on the up and up. *Many*, definitely not *all*. There were also the thousands upon thousands of stockpiled silver ammo rounds, but to the guys of Iroquois, this was normal.

They had a son, Maxwell T. Dickerson II, who everyone called *Deuce*. Following in his dad's footsteps, Deuce enlisted in the Marines out of high school, excelled there, and eventually ended up a MARSOC CSO. It was while working with the ANA in northern Afghanistan as a special operations liaison that Deuce was confronted with his nightmares. It was there that he saw his first werewolf. The fact he survived said a lot about his character. The fact that he refused to deny what he saw, what he saw that werewolf do to a dozen of his ANA counterparts, put him on SKUL's list.

Considering who his father was, it was a smooth recruitment process and Deuce Dickerson was slated for SEE-S next training evolution which would be conducted by Whiskey, the current alert platoon.

The team and Maxie's family had hit it off right from the second the Skipper had made the call and asked Maxie for assistance. The guys had been in a massive gunfight, with an untold number of savages, in the badlands of Washington, D.C's inner-city. The guys from intel had pinned the package's location, and it was supposedly protected by only a small contingent of guards. Once confirmed, Commander Taggert gave ChiTown the *go,* and the TL ordered his team to execute the mission. From the moment of entry, it was like hell had opened its great, black maw and spat out dozens of savages.

They fought their way valiantly through the warehouse where the package was supposedly held, ending the werewolf threat after a nearly hour long fight. The team sustained only a few minor injuries in the process, but the package was nowhere to be found. Lacking the ability to contain the situation quietly, ChiTown ordered the warehouse be rigged with explosives and vaporized.

*That* made every local news outlet.

He then radioed Taggert, explained the situation, and they both agreed the team needed to be taken off the streets and given time regroup.

That's where Maxie and his family came in, and without blinking, they accepted the beleaguered team with open arms. Over a handshake, ChiTown stated that his team would be more than comfortable racking out in the barn. At this, Maxie pulled the big, black man close and stated firmly, "My family don't sleep with the dogs, and you're SKUL; so, you're family." He then stepped back and smiled, "Besides, maybe you can fill Deuce in on what to expect...been a while since I've shaken the tiger's tail."

That had been a day and a half ago. In that time, fresh KtacS suits and ammo had been airdropped into one of Maxie's fields and, thanks to Mrs. Connie's cooking, everyone managed to gain at least five pounds.

The woman was simply an artist in the kitchen.

Deuce tossed the KtacS helmet back to Diggs, "That thing's gonna take some getting used to." As a Marine, Deuce was used to being very proficient at everything he did, but the helmet continually flummoxed him.

"Don't worry, man," Pat Vorhees, an SF 18D qualified medic known as *Nightmare* said understandingly. "It takes a lot of practice. No one is ready for it the first few times they use them."

"Besides, you hick cracker," quipped Dimetric Cortez, a towering black man and former Recon Marine. His call sign was *Poncho*. "You'll have a long time to figure it out." Poncho was from South Central Los Angeles; so, to him, everyone was *dawg, cracker,* or *es'e.* It just depended on the nationality he was dealing with and his mood at the time.

"Yeah, Deuce," Clarke Todd – a former SF sniper everyone called, Shakes – added encouragingly. "By the time you graduate, you'll be a pro; or, Jed Blackmoor will beat the information into your brain. Either way, you'll be locked down tight."

"Dude, that guy is freakin' scary," said Nightmare in a voice that bordered on reverent. "I once saw him…"

As the guys bandied about old Jed Blackmoor stories, ChiTown pulled Taggert aside. The two had managed to maintain an amicable enough relationship, but their leadership styles were vastly different. ChiTown was a former Marine. He was wired for action and, more specifically, destruction. He and his team were used to violence of action and decimating everything in their path. Taggert's was a more conservative approach. Taggert preferred to let the intel work and the situation develop. There was no denying the wisdom in the philosophy, but it just was not Iroquois' style. In particular, it was not ChiTown's style. "Commander, we've got to keep moving."

"Where do you want to go, Chi?" ChiTown's name was often shortened to just *Chi*. "We have no intelligence, no leads, and no damned idea where they are heading with the package next."

"Understood, sir," pleaded ChiTown as he pulled Taggert deeper into the house. He whispered hoarsely, "We can't stay here, Con. We've put a bull's-eye on Maxie and his family. Hangin' out here…this is wrong, man."

Taggert held his hands up in placation, "I get it. I really do. But, we have to stick for now." Before Iroquois' TL could argue further, Taggert added, "Look, let's give it tonight. If we don't come up with anything before sundown tomorrow, we bail, hit up some roadside roach motel, and start running our assets up and down the coasts. Fair enough?"

"No," ChiTown muttered, "but, it's as good as I can ask for, I guess."

"Good," Conroy Taggert said over a wide smile, "can we eat now?"

***

By the time dinner was over, it was getting late. Those lounging in the den were starting to feel their beds calling. The intel support staffers, along with the guys on the team, were scanning local news stations, blogs, and various other news outlets inherent to the area. They hoped to find some clue concerning the direction they needed to head to next – disappearances, unexplained murders…stuff like that.

While those guys did their thing, Taggert and ChiTown picked Maxie's brain. They hoped the older local might see something they may be missing. Earlier that day, Taggert put out feelers to every SI-2 working the area; but, so far, they were coming up empty.

The rain was coming down in sheets, and every few seconds, lightning tore the night asunder. Those streaks of madness were followed closely by deep, ominous thunder that rolled across the countryside. The thunder seemed all-encompassing, like Gabriel's rapturous horn. It was a bad storm, getting worse with each minute, and the news outlets gave no indication it was going to let up anytime soon. In between the lightning strikes and thunder, the dogs down in Maxie's kennels could be heard howling and barking.

The weather was affecting them too.

"Dad, did you leave the barn door open again?"

Maxie stopped his conversation with Taggert and ChiTown and thought about the question. "I don't know, son. Maybe."

Deuce smiled and shrugged on a waterproof slicker suit, "I'll go check and make sure the dogs are okay."

"Thanks," was all he said.

Deuce grabbed the AR-15 propped beside the door. It was one of several equipped with night vision optics. Deuce pulled his collar tight against his neck and dove into the storm without a sound.

"Good kid, Maxie," commented ChiTown.

"Yeah, he'll do," Maxie said with a smile. "Why don't ya'll show me again where you guys have been? Maybe there's a pattern we're missing."

Taggert and ChiTown marked the map: New Orleans, Hattiesburg, MS, and then up to Shiloh National Military Park. From there, they tracked the savages northeast to Washington, where they disappeared after the failed raid. While Maxie engrossed himself in the map, ChiTown worked the updates from his intelligence officers and fed them into his operators' SICS devices.

Taggert checked in with the Silver Moon.

Deuce had been gone about ten minutes or, roughly one hundred thunderclaps, when Maxie suddenly jumped out of his seat. With the fluidity of practiced motion, he grabbed a rifle and shot out the front door. ChiTown, Taggert, and the others met him on the porch.

Lightning slashed the night like a razor sharp knife through silk.

It was so bright that, when it struck, the countryside took on the pale glow of dawn. Compounding upon that, were the rain and thunder. They created such a raucous cacophony that the men nearly had to yell to be heard.

"What's up, Maxie?" said ChiTown loudly.

Maxie pointed to his barn. It was an old structure that he had renovated and modernized on the inside to suits his needs. The ten dogs under his charge lived the life of luxury with indoor/outdoor kennels. This kept fresh air moving yet allowed them to get inside and out of the weather. Weather just like this.

"Every dog is outside and still going crazy."

Chi noticed his voice. It was shaky and sounded small - very much unlike the Maxie he had come to know. Lightning lit up the sky, and the men could plainly see the dogs down in their kennels. Many were on their hind legs with their front paws high on the fence while others were pawing at the concrete flooring where it met the chain-link fence. Regardless of the method, one thing was clear. They were trying to get away.

Lightning struck again.

This time, a figure could be seen standing in the dogs' airing yard beside the barn. The thing was big, really big, and covered in hair. It held something in its paws that looked like a bowling ball at a distance. The werewolf tossed whatever it was toward the house. The object, thrown with the nonchalance one might use when tossing a piece of crumbled paper into the garbage, sailed the full two hundred yards and landed with a muddied splat at the foot of the porch stairs.

Through the gore, blood, and mud, Deuce Dickerson's dead eyes stared up at his father.

Maxie's scream of "Oh my God!" was so tremendously heart wrenching it overwhelmed the boom of thunder.

As ChiTown drug Maxie back into the house, the retired SKUL operator emptied a thirty round magazine. Iroquois' TL immediately began shouting orders; though, there was no need. His men were already taking defensive positions and calling out movements. Luckily, he and his team, including all three intelligence agents, were still dressed in their KtacS. This was a common practice while deployed with an active team. It definitely kept the dirty laundry concerns down. All they had to do was strap on their helmets, wait the requisite second or two for the helmet to engage and come online, and they were ready to rock.

Only Maxie and his wife would be completely vulnerable.

"Maxwell," screamed Connie Dickerson as she flew down the staircase dressed only in slippers and a bathrobe. Maxie tossed her an AR and a couple of magazines which she caught with surprising ease considering her age. More surprisingly still was the speed in which she rocked a magazine into the well and charged the weapon. It was obvious to ChiTown that Connie Dickerson knew her way around a firearm. That should not have been surprising, considering who her husband was.

"If anything comes into this house, sweetheart, shoot them," Maxie ordered without further explanation.

"Any*thing?* What do you mean?" Suddenly her eyes widened with panic. She knew what he meant. "Maxwell Dickerson, what's going on? Where's my son...my baby?"

The tears stung Maxie's eyes; but, not nearly as bad as his next words stung his heart, "He's gone, baby."

"Nooooooooo!" Connie's legs went weak, and it was only because Maxie held his wife tightly that she did not crumple to the ground. "Nooooooo!" she sobbed into her husband's chest.

Lightning again shattered the night, illuminating the yard in an eerie glow. ChiTown watched as the previously lone werewolf down was joined by at least a dozen more werewolves. All of them were big and hairy with glowing, yellow eyes that ChiTown could easily see from his position a couple hundred yards away.

"Dammit, we've got a dozen down by the barn!" He yelled before strapping his helmet down. After a split second wait, his helmet engaged, and he ordered, "Diggs, check our backside!"

A moment later, his ATL reported ominously, "Got another handful loping across the field, Chi!" Those words were followed by the controlled *clap clap* of his M4.

"Taggert, you and Poncho go help Diggs," ordered ChiTown over comms. "Nightmare, you're on me. Shakes, I want you on the second floor. Hell, get on the roof if you can! See if you can't reach out and touch a few of these assholes. Make 'em think twice about taking this house!"

"On it!" yelled Shakes as he took the stairs two at a time.

"Maxie, you and Connie need to get into a central room and barricade the door as best you can." Through the filters and respirators, Chi's voice was tinny, metallic, and absent any emotion. That was a good thing because, frankly, ChiTown doubted any of them were going to see another sunrise.

Maxie looked defiantly to the team leader, his eyes red slits of pain, and for a split second, ChiTown thought the old SKUL operator was going to pull his weapon on him. The two held each other's gaze for a subjective eternity. The air between them was as electric as the sky above. Finally, Maxie nodded before grabbing his wife's hand and pulling her away from the den. "We've got a panic room on this floor. Should be safe."

ChiTown shattered the glass out of a window and raked his rifle along the seal to clean off the jagged shards. He fired a handful of rounds downrange before turning back as Maxie's comment sunk in. *A panic room?* The thought was random, and he found it strange to have even entered his mind at such a strange time. A split second later, because that's all the time he had to waste on such extemporaneous details, a moment of clarity washed over him. *Of course Maxie has a panic room. Old man's probably been preparing for this day since he left SKUL.* "Outstanding, Maxie!" ChiTown turned, "You!" He pointed to one of the intel agents whose name was Jasper, "Go with them, and keep them safe! I want you to send out a Serial 6 to the Moon and let them know what the hell's going on! Make damned sure they understand we have civilian casualty…no! Belay that. You tell them we

387

have a SKUL operator down and that we need some air support on station, ASAP!"

The guy snapped an awkward nod, obviously unused to the bulk of the helmet, and took off to follow Maxie and his wife. Lightning cracked overhead, casting a brilliant light over the lawn and surrounding area. The dogs down in the kennels were crazed with fear. They wanted out, wanted away from the terror visiting them. ChiTown could not blame them one bit.

"You," ChiTown turned to one of the other two intel guys, "I want you to help out the guys covering the back of the house." The man bolted off in the direction of the gunfire coming from the rear. "You," he pointed to the remaining intelligence staffer, "you're with us. Nightmare…" His words were cut off as the front wall exploded inward, pelting everything in wood, brick, insulation, and plaster. The werewolf causing the destruction speared ChiTown and took him down in a shower of sparks from the KtacS suit.

# 32)
## Side Job (part 5)

Shelby Richardson had had a long day. A real long day, but such was the life of a UAV – *unmanned aerial vehicle* – pilot. She had held her Pegasus drone on a twelve hour loiter, leaving her mentally drained. Her head had just hit the pillow when her SICS vibrated on her nightstand. She snapped it up quickly and read the message:

> *Action: IMMEDIATE RECALL*
> *Location: UAV TOC*
> *Re: IROQUOIS IN CONTACT*
> *REQUESTING AIR SUPPORT*

Not believing her blurry eyes, she reread the message. She had not been dreaming, but this was definitely a nightmare. She threw the covers off in a panic and yelled to her empty stateroom, "Holy crap! They were going to bed!"

\*\*\*

"Get in there with her!" ordered Maxie.

"Sir, I was told to stay with you and your wife!" countered Jasper.

Maxie pushed the younger intel officer with enough ferocity he nearly knocked the much younger man over. "This is my house! I don't take orders from you or anyone else. Now, get your ass in there; and, if anything happens to her, I'll shoot you myself, understood?"

Jasper shrunk in the face of Maxie's unbidden wrath.

"Maxwell, don't go! I've already lost my baby, I can't lose you, too!"

"You won't! I swear it, sweetheart, but I've got to go…I've got to make sure these sonsabitches pay for what they did to Deuce!" He held his wife close for a second, then pushed her away. Quickly, he passed both of them a few more magazines. "I'll call you over the intercom when it's clear, and you can let yourself out, okay?" Connie started to argue, but Maxie cut off his beloved, "Sweetheart, don't argue with me. There's no time. When this is over, I promise you can scream at me all you want." He smiled at his wife. It was full of love but definitely dimmer than it had been prior to the attack. Just then, a loud crash sounded from out front. Their house was being torn apart. He pushed his wife inside. Just before he shut the door, he reminded her and Jasper, "If anything comes through this door, *anything*, you shoot them, and you don't stop shooting them until they stop coming."

The door slid shut silently, and Maxie did not move until he heard the locking system engage. When he was sure his wife was safe – or, as safe as she could possibly be – he turned away. Maxie dropped his mag from the well and checked to make sure it was at full capacity. It was; so, he slammed it back home, pulled the charging handle, and rocked a round into the chamber. He sprinted back through the house screaming, "You've picked on the wrong sonavabitch this time!" He rounded several corners before entering the destruction the den – his den – had become. Immediately, he began firing. His maniacal screams corresponded with each trigger pull, "The. Wrong. Mother. Fucker. This. Time!"

***

Maxie took the savage tearing into ChiTown out first, only because it was the first he saw. He hit him in the throat, twice, then spun and engaged the werewolf straddling Nightmare. That savage was doing his dead level best to punch through the KtacS. Maxie hit the beast with one in the shoulder which spun him. The next two rounds caught the savage in the forehead. Both holes could have fit inside the diameter of a quarter.

It was violent, yet surgical.

Maxie never stopped moving, clearing every corner of the room, before a groan caught his attention. Part of his front wall had fallen flat and whatever was in pain was under it. The section of sheetrock and two-by-fours began to wobble as someone grunted, "Help."

Against his better judgment, Maxie helped lift it off only to find the intel agent under the mess. Maxie pulled him to his feet then began patting him down with his gun aimed at the agent's vitals.

Satisfied he had not been bitten, Maxie said, "Son, maybe I should take you back to the panic room."

The agent's voice was digitized but firm, "I'm fine. They hit us at the same time is all."

Maxie nodded and handed him back his weapon, a suppressed MP7, "Well, shoot where they're heading, not where they are."

By this time, ChiTown and Nightmare had pushed themselves out from under the savages lying on top of them. Lightning and gunfire melted together to form one, long-assed battle hymn.

Maxie drew down on the two operators and began screaming, "Down Down Down!"

Both complied. They knew what concerned Maxie and knew the score. If they were bitten, Maxie would end them. He poked at Nightmare's suit, ran his fingers along the claw marks, and assessed the overall damage. He moved to ChiTown without a word and searched the team leader's body. After a minute's worth of analyzing, he stepped away from the men and back into the house. ChiTown pointed frantically to a window for Nightmare to cover and he took another. Together, they had most of the front of the house covered.

Most of it.

ChiTown fired then over his shoulder, asked "We cool?" His voice, digitized though it was, carried well enough; or, it did until Taggert, Poncho, and Diggs opened up in the rear of the house again.

"Yeah," Maxie stated simply. "Both of you have gashes down to the second layer, but you're cool…for now. You get bit in those areas one more time, and you're done, though." The shooters in the den heard a *ping* that sounded strangely like an elevator arriving and a hiss of air. "Can you boys keep those savages' heads down for a minute while I change into something more comfortable?"

ChiTown looked over his shoulder thinking the old man had lost it, but a howl out in the yard brought him back to their sad reality. The thing landed on the front porch and was so heavy it crashed through the wood. ChiTown and Nightmare cut him down as he struggled to get out of the hole he had created. They had no time for anything but firing

392

into the onrushing werewolves coming up on them quickly. "Maxie, we need you up here, now!"

The retired operator popped his head out from a corner room, "Yeah, I know. I'm coming." He snapped his AR to his shoulder and popped off a single round that passed dangerously close to ChiTown's shoulder. The round struck the nearest savage in the sternum and the thing fell in a heap. The others that had been running with it dove for cover. From the room Maxie was working in, something mechanical whined to life. The sound was vaguely familiar, and ChiTown recognized it as the sound of a finely tuned machine doing what it was meant to do. That was followed quickly a sounded similar to a heavy chain being drug across a metallic surface. Following that was a ratcheting sound that clanked smoothly to a stop. Maxie stepped back into the living area as Taggert and the guys continued to lay down suppression fire from the rear of the house. He was in full battle dress: black Nomex flight suit with knee pads, a black, lightweight ballistic helmet with flip-down, two-tubed NV goggles, and one helluva piece of weaponry.

The thing looked like an amalgamation of every wet dream a soldier could ever possibly have regarding small arms.

It was practically *Frankensteinian* in appearance.

The barrels – all eight of them – where short yet looked to be wide enough a freight train could crawl up in them and take a nap. A belt of linked twelve gauge shells fed from the weapon itself and disappeared into the bottom of a hardened ruck. Judging by Maxie's facial expression as he shifted the straps on his shoulders, it was not the lightest implement in his arsenal. The thing, because that's all that ChiTown and Nightmare could think to call it, looked like a Gatling gun. Only this thing looked like it was supposed to be shoulder fired, and it definitely handled loads a tad bit more impressive – if that was even possible.

Simply put, it was a bastardized version of the world's most terrific and most terrifying shotgun ever created.

"Dude..." ChiTown gasped.

"What. The. Fuck!" Nightmare finished eloquently.

"What?" asked Maxie as he looked over both shoulders. Turning back he chuckled, "Oh, you mean *Anthrax* here?"

The two operators just nodded in silent reverence. Meanwhile, the rest of their team was locked in a fight for their lives.

"Ol' Anthrax here was a project me and Deu..." His eyes glassed over for a second. "...Deuce worked on." He cleared his throat and choked back the tears, "Took us nearly five years of off and on work, but she's a pretty solid piece. On full auto, she can eat one hundred rounds of twelve gauge shells a minute and spit out slugs of pure silver just as fast. She won't jam, but I'll be damned if I can handle punishment. On semi-auto she's a dream, though."

"Dude," repeated ChiTown in pure awe.

"Yeah," Maxie said with a smile, "I like her t..."

A third wall exploded as a werewolf crashed into the den. Maxie, unperturbed, simply shouldered Anthrax, spun, flipped off the safety, and fired. The slugs – all ten of them – stitched the savage from his forehead to his groin. The

394

devastation was so brutal the werewolf was nearly torn in two…long ways.

"Dude," repeated ChiTown a third time. A gun nut himself, he found himself lusting over Maxie's creative genius.

Over the intra-squad comm link, Taggert reported, "Three more down on the backside. At least one still unaccounted for."

The retired SKUL shooter gestured with a hand to ChiTown and Nightmare, "You punks gonna help or just sit there?" Maxie ran to the front door with the others in his wake. This was a good thing as three more savages had just mounted the front porch. All three operators opened up on them. The first two never had a chance, but the third moved quicker than lightning which, incidentally, continued to crackle overhead. With one lithe bound, it disappeared through the thick sheet of rain. Undoubtedly, it was hiding among the trees dotted the yard.

"Clear!" reported ChiTown and Nightmare.

"For now," yelled Maxie. He and ChiTown scanned the front of the house. Other than the howling North wind, rain, and forbidding thunder; the yard had fallen strangely quiet. Beyond the property, in the deep dark that lay beyond the houselights, plumes of heat appeared then disappeared as the werewolves moved among the shadows and behind the trees.

Lots and lots of heat signatures moved and suddenly, the men were hit with the grim reality was the chance they would soon be overrun was very real.

"We need to get to the barn," Maxie said in a tone so low as ChiTown almost missed it.

"I'm sorry, Maxie, but what did you say?"

"The barn...we need to get there," the older man said a little louder and surer.

"Maxie," began ChiTown, "that's a two hundred yard run across open ground oozing with savages. We stay in this house...at least it's some cover."

A shot rang out overhead.

"Savage down, ChiTown," reported Shakes. "There are more out there, Chi, but I can't pinpoint them. They keep ducking behind the trees."

"Roger that, Shakes. Anything out there is a savage at this point so let that big rifle of yours eat."

Seconds later...*clap clap clap*

"On it, Chi," Shakes' voice was filled with mirth.

Maxie grabbed ChiTown's arm and squeezed. The look in his eyes was frightening. "We need to get to the barn, now!"

"Maxie..."

"Two people," Maxie interrupted. "The rest of your people can stay here, but I need a shooter while I drive."

"Drive?" asked ChiTown. "Drive what?"

Maxie just smiled, "You'll see. Let's go." The old dude loped off into the darkness without a backward glance.

"Oh, fuck me!" ChiTown looked to Nightmare who shrugged noncommittally. "Well damn, dude, at least lay down some fire."

With that, he strode off in Maxie's wake.

# 33)
## Side Job (part 6)

They made it to a small copse of trees with little issue and no signs of the werewolves they were hunting. Or, maybe it was the werewolves were hunting them. Frankly, it was hard to tell. What they did know was that there were multiple savages out there with them. At any time, they could be taken. Maxie and ChiTown leaned against a heavy-trunked oak tree and scanned the area. A tractor, backhoe, and bulldozer lay about seventy-five yards away, just between them and the barn.

The expensive heavy machinery forced ChiTown to comment, "SKUL must have a helluva retirement program, Maxie." Through the respirators, Chi's voice sounded tinny.

"It does," Maxie confirmed while training his weapon over the grounds. "If you live long enough."

Rifle blasts again poured from the house, every third round a tracer that angrily cut through the rain. It looked like some strange, demonic fireworks display. Thunder boomed and behind it came the unmistakable sound of wood and brick being torn apart. More shots followed; only this time, they never seemed to stop. The battle for the house had just turned into the battle *in* the house.

Over comms, his men screamed out battle movements and where the next threat was coming from. It was the closest of close quarter battles, and the guys from Iroquois were at a distinct disadvantage. Instinctively, ChiTown moved away from the tree and toward the house.

Maxie grabbed him by the arm firmly, "The barn...we've got to get to the barn."

Just then, something hot, heavy, and more viscous than the rain falling dripped on Maxie's outstretched arm. It slurped off the man's arm like molasses and hit the ground with an audible splat. It took them both a second to realize what had just happened; and, by then, it was too late. A massive paw swung down from the limb above, striking both men across the across the chest so quickly it happened all but at the same time. The blow sent them both flying across the yard, though in slightly different directions. Though he landed twenty feet away in a shower of sparks ChiTown's suit managed to protect him from the worst of the blow. The claws of the savage did manage to cut through the suit down to the last layer, causing the surrounding area to harden. As large as the momentarily immobile area was, it made it hard for ChiTown to move normally.

Maxie had not been so lucky.

His suit, an older model with standard ceramic plating, was only coated in a thin layer of silver. The savage's claws easily cleaved through the plate armor and ripped through his skin. The sheer force of the blow threw him against the large, front wheel of a nearby tractor. A cloud of red mist followed, chased away seconds later by the torrential downpour. He hung against the tire for a split second, bent at an awkward angle and then slid to the ground.

He made no move to get up.

"Maxie!" screamed ChiTown as a huge foot stomped down on him in the small of his back. The air rushed from his lungs as the crushing pressure slowly increased.

His legs tingled, and his toes became numb knobs of flesh.

The thing reached down and grabbed him from the back of the neck, lifting him off the ground both violently and literally. Chitown's feet dangled several inches off the ground, a feat in and of itself considering the man was well over six feet tall. The werewolf pulled him close and sniffed. The influx was so powerful it felt as if it was scouring ChiTown's body of its cells. The savage's eyes bloomed with heat in his FVS and swirled with yellow hate. He felt like his own stench served to stoke the werewolf's internal fire. The savage squeezed, and the cartilage in his throat began to snap and pop. With that, came the blackness that slowly bled into the corners of Chi's eyes. Again the werewolf ratcheted its powerful grip, finally cutting off any chance for air. Still, ChiTown struggled against his inevitable death, pounding on the werewolf's face, shoulders, and arms – anywhere he could – with massive hammer strokes.

It was like hitting a steel beam with an old, dry-rotted fly swatter.

In his head, he heard, "The thing I've never understood about you mortals is your inability to face facts. You *are* going to die, every last one of you." He pulled ChiTown away from the tree, then slammed him back against it.

"We hold the power of the gods at our fingertips, yet you fight."

He pulled him back again, only to slam him violently against the tree trunk, yet again. Leaves fell, but not from the wind and rain, from the sheer force of the blows.

"What don't you understand about your place in the pack?"

*Pull…slam.*

"Why fight it? We *are* getting the blood out of this country and into Canada."

*Pull…slam. Pull…slam.*

The wolf spoke in his head, but its long snout never moved. He was projecting his thoughts into ChiTown's mind. That thought alone stopped ChiTown's heart cold, but he managed to hold on to what the thing had just said…*Canada.* The savage's arrogance at his prey's death had just overwhelmed its small amount of common sense. Now, all ChiTown had to do was stay alive.

It picked Chi up even higher off the ground, pulled him away from the tree, and then throat slammed him into the mud. Again, ChiTown's breath was stolen from him.

The thing palmed ChiTown's helmet and, in a massive display of power and shower of sparks, ripped it from his head. How his cranium was still attached was anyone's guess. ChiTown could not guess, however. He was too busy bleeding.

The werewolf opened its wide maw and began to howl triumphantly, only it was cut off. A gasp of air left the werewolf one last time before it fell, dead, to the side.

A solid silver tomahawk was buried deep into the back of its skull.

Two strong hands pulled ChiTown and said with a wet, wheezy voice, "You cool, Chi?"

"Yeah," the TL said while attempting to shake the fog in his mind away. He could still hear that damned wolf in his head. "Helmet's fucked, so I don't have any thermals, but I'm good. You?"

"Back's a mess, and I'm pretty sure I've got a couple of broken ribs, but other than that, I'm having the time of my life."

The two laughed, and Maxie doubled over in pain. It was dark humor that was keeping them sane; so, it was worth it. They hid behind the tractor and attempted to cover all angles.

"Thanks, Maxie."

"No need, Chi," the man looked to Iroquois' TL hard, "damned things always want to play with their food...remember that. Now, I'll cover you while you find your rifle..."

Gunfire poured out of the house again, although, it sounded like the guys had handled their previous situation and were just keeping heads down. How many heads they were keeping down was anyone's guess. How many of his men – his friends, his brothers – were left among the living was a question neither wanted an answer to at the moment.

It would probably hurt too much, anyway.

"...we still gotta get to the barn."

***

They made it to the barn with no further issue and, right away, Maxie let the dogs out of their kennels. They scattered to the four points of the compass within seconds.

"Can't blame them," said Maxie quietly. "The scent of so many alphas is just too much for them to handle." He was quiet for a second, then mumbled, "Hope they'll be okay."

He became rigid, like he had just remembered what he was in the barn for.

"Help me with this tarp," ordered Maxie. As they brought it off, ChiTown's eyes got even wider than they had when Maxie revealed Anthrax.

"Dude..." This was evidently Chi's favorite word, and the level of reverence he held apparently coincided with the quietness and amount of time the word was drawn out. In this case, he said it super low and drug the word out an exceptionally long time. "A *DPV*?"

"Yeah," chuckled Maxie, "I knew this old dune buggy would come in handy one day. Me and..." He paused long enough to swallow thickly, "...Deuce worked this thing over after his last deployment. That's a .50 cal M2HB..."

"A MaDeuce," Chi interrupted. "Jesus, man."

"Yeah, like I said...we needed to get to the barn."

"What's under that tarp?" asked Iroquois' TL as he pointed to another area of the expansive barn. With all the weaponry around, he had almost forgotten about the werewolves basically at their doorstep.

"Old Ford," Maxie replied simply. Seeing the look of disappointment in the TL's eyes, he added with a twinkle, "Old Ford with a Mk19 40mm cannon bolted to its bed."

"Fuckin' awesome," ChiTown said admiringly.

"Yeah, but it's no good in the muck. Turning radius is too wide, and it's so heavy. It'll only bog down. The buggy's the ticket." He brought Chi's attention back to the rig and ticked off some needed knowledge. "I modified it from what they've been using over in the sandbox and built a raised turret. That joystick you see controls a three hundred degree turn radius. That screen there is tied to the thermal array that surrounds the buggy. But, there's no need to even worry about that…if it's not one of your men or my wife, shoot first, ask questions later. The coverage you won't have is directly behind, but that's what this is for." He dropped Anthrax onto a rear pivot and clamped it in. Between the turret and the pivot, he placed his ruck containing the belt of death. Lastly, he tossed ChiTown a helmet. "Get in! You shoot, I'll drive. We don't know how many more are out there, so be conservative with the ammo. Won't be any reloading this puppy. We run out too soon, we die."

*** 

To ChiTown, the idling buggy sounded just like a growling hellhound at the gates of Hades might sound. It was deep, foreboding, and all encompassing. They roared out of the barn on two wheels. ChiTown held on for dear life as Maxie negotiated a wicked ninety degree turn while refusing to let off the gas. The knobby treads on the DPV from hell ripped up sod and mud and spit the sludge twenty feet behind the buggy. After the initial shock and fear of being in the DPV's elevated crow's nest, ChiTown settled in and began firing conservatively as opportunities presented themselves. Maxie's battle cry of, "You picked on the wrong sonavabitch this time!" drowned out the DPV's engine noise and the gunfire. He was crazed with his hatred of the savages he now destroyed with clinical psychosis coupled with the loss of his son. To Maxie, the situation had become the dictionary definition of *personal*. When nothing was dying or they were chasing down the next victim, Maxie just screamed incoherently. With Maxie's relentless driving and knowledge of the land, they managed to run down and kill nearly two dozen savages by the time it was over. The last savage fell as the fifty went black. There was a certain level of reluctance and apprehension in each man as the last *clink* fell free of the mammoth weapon. It was really a moot point, though, as nearly five hundred rounds per minute had poured down the barrel and created so much heat it has become swollen, warped, and virtually unusable. The fact the last savage was even hit was astonishing. The fact he had his head taken off by the .50 BMG round fired from a warped barrel was nothing short of a miracle.

Unfortunately, several escaped into the darkness well beyond the house. But it was no matter, and honestly, the very few that managed to escape were no real threat to the collected group of SKUL operators.

The wild adventure ended much the way it began – on two wheels – as they slid to a stop at the porch. The behemoth buggy with the bad attitude purred like a demon cat. Maxie did not wait on ChiTown to get down. He sprung from the buggy and darted into the house, side-stepping and jumping dead bodies as he went. ChiTown heard the old man shakily say, "Connie, this is Maxwell."

"Safe word?" she demanded over the intercom.

"Jesus," he muttered to himself. It sounded like he forgot the safe word for a moment until he sputtered, "Mustard. Safe word is mustard, Connie." There was a gasp on the other end of the intercom. It sounded like a relief valve giving way under an incredible amount of pressure. ChiTown remained outside, scanning the area. Something just did not feel right. From inside the nearly destroyed house, came a series of big, wet kisses and several *I love you's.* After another few moments of silence, Chi vacated the post and moved indoors. Slowly and methodically, he moved deeper into the house and met the rest of his team – along with Taggert – in the first hallway.

Taggert tipped his head as if to say, "We're good," but to Chi's eyes, he was clearly not. His KtacS was in shreds, and he was bleeding from a dozen different spots. Poncho, Diggs, and Nightmare appeared from different areas of the house. They looked just as beat up as Taggert, but they were alive.

"Commander, you weren't bitten, were you?" Chi's hand drifted to the .45 strapped to his thigh. He did not want to be forced to pull his weapon on his commanding officer and SKUL's 2IC, but he certainly was not averse to ending the ACO's life if need be.

Nightmare, the team's 18D combat medic, saved Taggert from having to defend himself. "He's cool, Chi. Just beat to hell...we all are. Checked out everyone myself."

"And, I checked Nightmare over," added Diggs, the former Air Force JTAC and his ATL. Diggs raised his M4 threateningly, "Speaking of, Chi, why don't *you* drop your weapon and let Nightmare check you out."

Anger streaked the team leader's face, but only briefly. No chances could be taken; it was just too dangerous to do so. He pulled his sidearm – the only weapon he had left other than his tomahawk – slowly from its holster and gave it to Nightmare as he approached.

"Shakes?" asked Chi quietly as the medic poured over his KtacS with a fine-toothed comb.

The sniper called down, "Here, ChiTown! Dude, that freakin' dune buggy is a bad boy!"

ChiTown smiled and leaned against the wall. The next time he opened his eyes was the first time he noticed the bodies of two of his intel staff. They were torn apart when the werewolves laid siege on the house.

"Chi," Taggert said with obvious difficulty, "we did all we could."

He nodded stiffly. His voice was wooden and inflectionless as he asked, "They bit?"

"Yeah," confirmed SKUL's ACO. "I was going to let you and your guys handle it how you felt best."

Jasper, released from the bowels of the panic room, stepped forward. "They're my guys, I'll do it."

ChiTown started to argue, then seeing the determination in the man's eyes, he stepped aside. Jasper stepped forward and, without hesitation, put two silver rounds in each man's skull.

The lonely intel officer stalked from the room without another word.

Suddenly, Shakes voice sounded from above just as he fired two, three, then four rounds downrange, "Folks, we've got a problem!" He fired another two rounds, then added, "A big fuckin' problem!"

"Where?" screamed ChiTown as he reached instinctively for his rifle which he had lost along the way. He had to settle for his pistol which Nightmare tossed back to him quickly.

"Front," was all Shakes said as he fired his rifle again and again and again.

Everyone ran to the front windows and saw their doom.

Nearly fifty werewolves were stacked up at the tree line just beyond the barn. Their angry growls could be heard over the storm. They were hungry; they were mad; and they were coming.

"My God," gasped Diggs. "Where in world are all these things coming from?"

"Hell," replied Maxie concisely. He grabbed his wife's hand and squeezed. The others looked down the line, took each man's gaze in their own, and nodded. They grabbed a weapon if they were near one, or had one, and fanned out along the porch. Helmets, along with other damaged and otherwise useless gear, were tossed aside. No one hid, and no one sought cover. They would meet their death like they lived their lives, alongside their teammates, their brothers, and fight to the last.

This was the last stand…their Alamo.

The gathered savages were mutinous in their madness, fighting among themselves for a place in the vanguard. One particularly crazed werewolf plainly ripped the head off the savage to his right. The blood spilled there caused their cravings for the same to increase; yet, they remained in place to allow their force to grow to its fullest potential.

ChiTown, sensing the moment had arrived, looked to his men, including Taggert, and said, "I'm not much for words, but it's been an honor." Everyone agreed though with head nods only.

Suddenly, Diggs, former Air Force JTAC, jerked his still viable helmet off and threw it at Chi. "Sir...listen."

ChiTown complied and heard the most wonderful words a soldier in harm's way can hear – the call sign of your air support coming on station. "Snake charmer-two-five to Iroquois-six, I have positive thermal readout on a..." The voice paused, searching for the correct adjective to use. Finally she settled for the obvious, "...*shitload* of savages, but there's so many of them, I can't distinquish you in my scopes. You boys still down there or what?"

ChiTown smiled so wide and bright it looked like a white picket fence. To those on the porch, he ordered, "If you have any strobes, toss them. I want this area painted with everything we have."

Into the helmet, he said excitedly, "Snake charmer, this is Iroquois...was wondering when you'd get around to making the party..."

"My invitation must have gotten lost, sir, but I'm here now."

"Roger that," ChiTown said as he and the others tossed infrared strobes about thirty feet away from the house. "Snake charmer-two-five, target is sparkled, how copy?"

"Good copy, Iroquois-six. I have visual. Will be firing *danger close*, suggest you find some cover."

"Roger that, Snake charmer-two-five, you are cleared hot. Iroquois-six, out."

"Snake charmer-two-five copies all. Good luck, Iroquois."

High above, in the blackness of the sky, ChiTown heard a high pitched, whistling sound.

"Ya'll may want to step back in to the panic room for a moment."

***

At first light, reinforcements arrived in the form of two teams of SKUL operators from Lima platoon. They were joined by a small force of ICS cleaners from their D.C. office. The shooters immediately began securing the perimeter while their team leaders and one of their medics ran to the house. ChiTown and the other survivors, not trusting the battle was over, lay hunkered down in a defensive positions throughout the house.

One of the Lima team leaders, Bostick, approached cautiously. "Chi? You guys okay?"

"No, Bostick, not really." He looked his team, who had now joined him on the porch, then turned back to the newcomers, "Commander Taggert needs medical attention, ASAP. He's lost a good bit of blood."

Seeing their concerned looks, ChiTown added, "No one's been bitten. We've also got two dead SI-2s back in the house. The rest of us are pretty beat up, but nothing's critical." ChiTown stepped close to the TL and spoke quietly so as not to upset the parents of Deuce Dickerson, "Maxie's son was murdered, as well. A Marine. He was slated to begin C-school soon."

Bostick stepped back, not believing his ears. Seeing the fire in his colleagues' eyes, he knew he was telling the truth. Bostick nodded sadly, "He'll be given a SKUL burial." He looked down the porch where the SKUL legend sat holding and rocking his wife softly. They were speaking quietly to themselves. Every few seconds, they would either smile or begin sobbing again. It was obvious they were sharing stories of their son. Bostick shook his head again and mumbled, "Legend like Maxie deserves better."

ChiTown agreed but said nothing. Taking the hint, Bostick and the other TL left to see to their teams, and the medic began administering aid. Chi quietly sat down on the porch and stared across the yard at nothing in particular. After several minutes, Maxie joined him.

ChiTown turned to the retired SKUL shooter, "Maxie, words don't do justice to how sorry I am we brought this down on you and your family."

Maxie chuckled softy and then grimaced in pain. He had several cracked ribs. "It's a part of the gig. I don't guess you ever really leave SKUL."

"Yeah," ChiTown said heavily, "that's what I hear. So, what'll you do now?"

"Oh, I don't know. Connie and I have been talking about coming back on board with SKUL." His voice sounded far away, like it was coming from a time long ago, a better time. "Did you know we met while I was still an active shooter?"

"No, I have never heard that," ChiTown admitted.

"Yeah, you probably wouldn't. She was intelligence, and we both tried to keep it pretty quiet. She was just about the prettiest little thing I'd ever laid eyes on. Anyhow, Bart's been on us for years about coming back, and with Deuce's recruitment, we started giving it some serious thought. Our initial thoughts were on developing a training cycle that married shooting with some of the blacker aspects of

410

intelligence. That was Connie's specialty as strange as that sounds. Now, with Deuce's death..."

His voice trailed off, and a lone tear ran down his face.

"There would be no better way to honor your son than to come back to SKUL, Maxie. You're an artist, man, and once you guys are up and running, my team will be first in line to attend. Hell, I'd love to just sit around and talk gun theory some time."

"Ha!" Maxie snorted as he grabbed his side. "Theory, that's a good way to describe it. What about you guys? Where to next?"

ChiTown recalled the words of the werewolf that beat on him so furiously. The same one Maxie saved him from. "The werewolf that ambushed us confirmed it was blood and said it was headed to Canada. I don't have a clue where, though. It's a pretty big country."

"Hmm," Maxie said in a tone of deep contemplation. "Probably safe to assume the Eastern side of Canada, most likely. It'll be secluded, fortified, but easily accessible." He was quiet for a while, and ChiTown allowed the former operator time to think. Finally, Maxie said, "An island. That package is heading to the Canadian Maritimes, I'd bet my farm on it."

"Why, Canada? Why that area in particular? There are millions of islands dotting the Eastern seaboard."

"Yeah, but SKUL ain't in Canada. It's a sovereign country and staunch ally. Operating there, without approval, and getting caught would be considered an act of war in the eyes of the world."

"The Maritimes, huh?"

"Damned right. I'd bet the farm on it."

ChiTown thought about it for a minute then said feloniously, "We'll need to take them down before they leave U.S. soil if we can."

"I was thinking the same thing. They'll take a boat from Maine if I had to guess. Airport security will be too risky, as will customs. They'll take a boat, either a ferry they can pay off or a private boat. You guys need to focus on the coastline of Maine." After a second, he added, "Might be a good idea to go ahead and get Briggs to get approval for you guys to head into Canada, too."

What Maxie said made all the sense in the world once ChiTown stepped back and thought about it. Across the yard, he yelled, "Diggs, get the Skipper on the horn! He's gonna have to call in some favors!"

## 34)
## Highway to Hell

**10 miles west of Columbia, MS**
**Highway 98, westbound**
**2200**

The motorcycles roared down the highway under the cover of darkness, a dozen solid black bikes riding two-by-two. The red tail lights of the rear bus shone brightly less than a half mile away. The leader of the gang held out his left hand and waved a van forward.

It too was solid black. Just like the motorcycles eating away at the asphalt, the van was a blacked-out abomination driven by a member of the New Orleans Chapter of the Satan's Bastards MC. The driver punched the gas and sped around the group of bikers and, eventually, the three buses before disappearing over the horizon. The bikers, every last one of them werewolves, howled defiantly at the moon and forced their motorcycles on faster.

\*\*\*

*Best Promises'* tour had been extraordinarily successful up to this point. Who could have ever predicted their movie adapted musical score would have garnished the fame it had given today's political and religious climate? But, as Marquissa Clements, the choir's director, felt screeching air brakes grind the bus to an angry halt, she knew something really bad was about to occur. She could feel it deep in her soul. They had been stopped in the middle of a four lane highway and as Marquissa craned her neck to see out the front window, she could see a black van. It was parked running perpendicular to their direction of travel.

*BOOM BOOM BOOM*

Heavy fists pounded on the bus' door. Their driver, Leadfoot Larry, stood and looked back to his passengers nervously, "Stay seated, folks." Larry pulled the handle to open the door, "We'll be back on our way shor..."

A hairy, grotesque hand grabbed Leadfoot around the neck and pulled him out the door. A wet crunch cut off his screams for help just before another figure stepped onto the bus. He was short with a slight frame and dark hair that framed a thin smile and crazed eyes. He wore blue jeans and heavy boots, and though the passengers had no clue about the vest he wore, they knew enough to be frightened.

"Evening, folks," the newcomer said. "I'm afraid there's been a change of plans."

Maquissa was out of her seat instantly. She was a portly black woman with a no-nonsense attitude, "Like heck we do! What did you do with Larry?"

The biker's eyes swirled strangely in his sockets, "Ate him...well, I didn't, but he was made into a meal all the same." Laughter filled the inside of the bus. It sounded animal in existence, feral, like a hyena hovering over an antelope's carcass. "Has anyone ever told you that you look just like Aunt Ester?"

Marquissa, nauseous at the thought of poor Larry being eaten - though she did not believe for one moment he was telling the truth, was having trouble making sense of anything the biker was saying. It was like something was in her head, scrambling her mind and tainting her thoughts.

*Are his eyes yellow?* she thought shakily.

The biker continued unabated, "You know, *fish-eyed fool, I'm comin' to join ya, Liz'beth, Fred G. Sanford...the G stands for genius.*" A second went by without a reaction, "No? Seriously?" He turned to the others, "Surely you people have heard of *Sanford and Son?*"

Marquissa's eyes stared back at him blankly for a second before she finally shook the cobwebs loose.

"Like I said, there's been change of plans," the biker stated flatly before the inflection in his voice took on the tenor of exuberance. "You're the guests of honor at a party...a very, very special party."

"Like heck we are!" repeated Marquissa in an unfamiliarly high-pitched voice. "Now, you let Larry back in here so we can be on our way!"

There was more of the same sickening laughter.

Purely out of self-preservation and panic, she swung, connecting with the biker's cheek with her open hand. It felt like she had just slapped marble.

"You don't know me, do you?" asked the biker as he shrugged his way out of this vest. Instantly, he *changed*. The eye sockets burned with yellow hate as bones snapped in two, bent, then reformed. Hair, bristly and black, grew heavy, and his face seemed to shatter, elongate, then snap back together. The resultant features were much longer than a human's should have been. The snout was also filled with more sharp, overly long teeth than should have been possible for a human.

Only, this was not a human; this was a werewolf...death incarnate.

415

The bus erupted in wild, animalistic screams of panic.
The men and women in the bus began banging on the
windows, trying to shatter them, trying to escape. Only
Marquissa held her ground, though she knew not why. She
knew she was as good as dead. "I was known in other more
civilized times as Billy the Kid."

The hyena-like laughter drowned out the raucous
screams for help to the rear.

Marquissa stood mesmerized as the one calling
himself Billy the Kid's great maw opened. In her head she
still heard his voice, "Let me show you the fate of poor
Larry."

Like that, Marquissa Clements was no more.

***

## Saber's team room
## 0530

Dane finished pouring his first cup of coffee when
the wall-mounted flat screen TV blasted:

*BREAKING NEWS!*

This was followed by music meant to entice the
viewer to continue watching; but, really, it was the pretty
blonde newscaster that sealed the deal for most.

*Emmy award winning gospel choir,* Best Promise, *is missing...*

Jed walked in saying, "Mornin', Boss," around a cheek
full of tobacco. Dressed for a workout in Ranger panties,
tennis shoes, and a gray T-shirt with *Army* in big, block
lettering, he poured a cup of coffee and took a heavy swig.
Dane turned from the TV and responded in kind before the
blonde's voice brought his attention back to the newscast:

416

*Last known location of the choir is this gas station outside of Columbia, Mississippi, along U.S Highway 98.*

Jed recognized the deep look of concern on his friend's face, "Something wrong?"

"Grew up near there," glued to the TV, Dane mumbled, almost to himself, without turning. "Know the area." Snapping to, he turned back to Jed as the newscast continued with its hypothesis and conjecture. Some were plausible, some came from way, way out in left field. "Maybe it's the job, but I can't help but think that's not a random situation. I mean three busloads of singers and equipment do not just vanish into thin air."

"Yeah, I know what you mean. It's getting' kinda spooky 'round here, ain't it? I just got the scoop from Tim on their last little piece of hell's half acre." Jed spit tobacco juice into the team's big, brass spittoon, "Man, talk about a mind-fuck. It's beginning to feel like we're the zit that showed up teeny-bopper's forehead before prom. It's not *if* but *when* you're going to get the shit pinched out of you."

Dane knew how Titan's last op went down, and it was a truly fucked up masterpiece. Titan entered a home off St. Charles Avenue only to find a blood-covered man at his kitchen sink, sweating profusely. His eyes burned yellow; and, in their thermals, he registered a body temp nearing the two hundred degree mark and rising. Suddenly, his body convulsed uncontrollably with such force it threatened to tear him in pieces. Lying at his feet were the bodies of his family. They were his wife and two children, and he had just reduced them to nothing more than pulps of meat in an apparent fit of rage. Gouges of flesh had been ripped from their bodies,

417

and their faces were frozen masks of confusion, pain, and terror. Per Tim, the man looked to the team through helpless, tear-filled eyes just before laughing hysterically and lunging at the nearest operator. The team's training kicked in, and their silver bullets nearly cut him in half before he hit the ground.

Jed took a sip of coffee then spit tobacco juice into the team's big, brass spittoon. He genuinely looked indifferent at his most recent observance.

"How, Jed? How have you done it all these years?" Dane asked between sips of his own coffee. "Rangers, Delta, and now, this; Christ, I can't imagine." Dane was no spring chicken, in years or experience; and, in truth, Jed wasn't that much older than he was. Still though, that did not keep Jed from being something of an anomaly. The man walked through life behind a shield of indifference that seemed unhealthy; because, no one could just not care about dying.

No one.

Saber's ATL took a sip of coffee as he considered the question. He spit into the spittoon again before answering, "Sure you can imagine what my life's been like, Dane. SEALs, Section 8...now *this.*"

*Spit...sip*

"Everyone here has lived my life or one a thousand times more dangerous. It's what we do."

*Sip...spit*

'It's just a job, man. Before this, when we were *just* part of the special operations community, we went out and hit a target that some higher up officer looking to punch his ticket said we were going to hit. Good intel or bad...didn't matter. We were hitting that target and expected to make split second decisions on life or death, the gallows or the flex-cuffs. Shit dude, compared to that, this is easy. There ain't any decision to make. The savages make it for you before you ever show up. Here, you hit the target and shoot the savage; and, you keep shooting until you're certain it ain't getting up again." He saw Dane scrunch his face in incredulity and uncharacteristically felt the need to pontificate further, "Look, before you ask, I'm not some axe murderer or anything like that. Like I said, it's just a job, no more, no less. My point is that these things, these savages, they're not human. They are a force of nature, and analyzing it any further than that is going to get your ass killed."

Dane stood and smiled, "Yeah, yeah, so I won't be adding you as a benefactor to my life insurance policy anytime soon." He poured another cup of coffee and strode to the door, "I'm going to Ops just to see if anything's spinning up. You ever find time to schedule the team's PT?"

Dane knew he had. As Saber's ATL, it was Jed's job. Plus, the older operator loved the competition their PT sessions always turned into.

"Roger that, 0700."

Dane smiled as the door closed. Jed was all business, all the time.

***

## Ops Center
## 0600

Dane took the stairs down to Elbert's station two at a time. In passing, he gave Tim Meadows a friendly nod. Tim was conferring with Titan's lead intel agent, most likely

419

concerning their next rotation on alert scheduled to begin at 0800 tomorrow. Saber, along with Mustang and Roughneck, were the active teams tonight. Saber was the primary fire team of record.

"What's up, E?" he asked his computer analysts genially. "Got anything for us?"

"Yeah," replied Elbert without looking up from his screen. "Sam got a call about an hour ago. One of our SI-2s took down a newly turned savage with a wolfsbane dart."

"Holy shit, are you serious?" Dane demanded as he sat beside Stratham.

"Very," his friend said while typing furiously. "She hitched a ride on a helo five minutes after the call. That's all I know right now, but she's due to arrive at the black site the savage is being held soon. Should have more for you then."

"Cool, E. Keep me in the loop."

"Will do," Elbert confirmed then added, "Dane, Sam wanted you to make sure you and the guys got some rest today. She said she had a feeling it may be the last you'll get for a while. I've never seen her so excited."

Dane, already typing out that very message into his SICS, failed to notice Tim listening in.

"Damn bro, she got you making her sandwiches, too?"

Dane's fingers froze, and he turned slowly in his friend's direction. Elbert's fingers conspicuously ceased their rapid-fire assault on his keyboard, as well.

Seeing the fire that had settled in his friend's eyes, Tim immediately threw his hands in the air, "Joking, Dane, only joking."

"It ain't like that, man," growled Dane.

Tim laughed, "Whatever, dude. Like I said, I was just joking."

# 35)
## Tortured Soul

**SKUL Black Site**
**0800**

Sam pulled the armored SUV she drove up to a nondescript warehouse just south of the city situated along the river. A worker in a hardhat came running over to the driver side window, "Can I help you ma'am?" Though his smile was polite to the point of being disarming, Sam knew there was a concealed missile system trained on her position. All she had to do was make a wrong move, speak a wrong phrase, and she and the vehicle would be turned to nothing but paste.

"I'm here for the job interview." She said lightly as if out for a morning run, but this was deadly serious business. She had just verbalized the entry phrase forcing a thousand things to happen simultaneously behind the scenes.

The worker nodded, "The boss is running late today, ma'am."

The *challenge* phrase.

"Is there anywhere I can wait, then?" she asked in just as bubbly a tone as before.

"Yes, ma'am, just through those doors," he said while motioning in the direction of two gigantic bay doors that were slowly sliding open. Without another word or backward glance, Sam put her vehicle into drive and entered one of several SKUL Black Sites that clandestinely blanketed the country. Completely secure and off the grid, these sites provided SKUL's intelligence agents with a *tactical operations center* – TOC – as well as a safe place for interrogations. They also allowed for the more aggressive methods of obtaining needed intelligence they were sometimes forced to employ.

Like say…*torture*.

Sam pulled into the darkness of the warehouse and stopped while the doors behind her closed with an ominous *boom*. For an instant, Sam was thrown into absolute darkness until a single spotlight flicked on. The pale glow of the light revealed a retinal scanner in the center of the warehouse. Slowly, she pulled the SUV up to the scanner, and rested her chin on its small platform. For a subjectively long time, there was no indication she would be admitted into the ultra-secret facility. Objectively, it was only a few seconds later that the floor below the car began lowering slowly and soundlessly. Using the gigantic elevator was always an exhilarating though unnerving experience for her. After lowering the car several hundred feet below the crust of the Earth, it came to a halt. As Sam exited the vehicle, lights flicked on one by one. They revealed a long hallway with a door at the end. For whatever reason, the way the lights sounded when they came on – a low click followed by another and another until the hall was lit – always caused goose bumps on her arms. It felt like she was inside a B-rated horror flick. Hurriedly, Sam made her way down the hall; and, as she passed, the lights clicked off one by one in her wake. At the end of the hall, she entered her SKUL serial number – SS-18532-SI-1 – on the punch pad. An airlock hissed, and the door slid open. The room she stepped into was as busy as a beehive. Dozens of people were working the phones or tapping at computer keys. Others conferred with one another while working a white board. These were the men and women that silently supported ongoing SKUL operations across the globe. Had Sam not been in the middle of one of the most secure facilities on the planet, she would have guessed she was standing in one of the thousands of offices within New Orleans' city limits. She crossed the room, nodding to those she knew, and stepped into another elevator. This one built solely for humans.

She pressed the only button on the console, forcing the elevator deeper into the Earth. This was where the interrogation rooms were located. Even though she had been on this elevator a thousand times before, the speed at which the floor fell from under her feet always managed to take her stomach. Several stories and hundreds of feet of dirt and rock later, the elevator came smoothly to a rest. She stepped from the elevator and walked down a darkened hallway she knew was lined with two feet of slick, cold cement. Backing that, only centimeters thick, was a silver meshwork that was the first and most subtle of the site's defense systems. The rest could be best described as very, very painful implementations for any werewolf attempting to escape.

That happened to be the most succinct method of explanation as well.

She took a deep breath to calm her nerves. Sam knew what had to be done and how things would inevitably end, but that didn't make any of it easier on the palate.

Or, the soul.

"C'mon Sam, you can do this," she whispered to herself before stepping through the door.

For a long moment, she stood stone still in the dark room and watched the bank of TV's on the far wall. Each screen gave a different angle of the same shackled being. She used terms like beasts or beings, even the operators favored *savage*, instead of calling them *humans* or anything else along those lines. This helped her compartmentalize humanity from immortal. It shielded her from what would come next, from what she would have to do to get the answers she needed. Regardless of any wasted effort in devising some extemporaneous justification for it all, she was absolutely right. The beast in the next room was not human, not anymore. As a drug dealer, a pimp, and a murderer, he had given his soul up long ago; though, it was only recently that he truly sealed the deal. Apparently, he had taken a taste of his own product – God's Milk – the latest hot shit drug to hit the streets.

Most who had experienced the pleasure of the drug died within the first twenty-four hours. They were the truly lucky ones. The others, those that survived to see the sun rise, generally had minds so fractured they focused only with feeding their need for human flesh and blood.

Sam knew the relative few of those they had exterminated were just the tip of the iceberg.

A very, very big iceberg.

These were the easy ones forming the low-hanging fruit that SKUL operators spent their nights and days picking from. They were simple fruits of pure evil spreading from something much larger, something much, much worse. Incapable of empathy compassion, or any other human emotion, these beasts were want for only one thing.

*Human flesh.*

And, to Sam's great discontent, a prime example turned his head to the lens situated directly in front of his dirty face. His eyes burned yellow and drool dripped from the corners of his mouth. He sat like that for several seconds until...

...he *smiled*.

***

Not only was the werewolf videoed from a half dozen different aspects, he was analyzed via an array of FVS and biometric sensors. He bloomed under the FVS like a radiological disaster, and his heart rate was off the charts – like, two hundred sixty-eight beats per minute off the charts. The savage's breath came in short, shallow, and ragged parts not unlike a dog that had run a long distance.

"Mike!" Sam exclaimed affectionately, delighted to see her former protégé. "Congrats on the promo, man! Ark/La/Miss Duty Chief in under a year? That's got to be some sort of record."

Mike Fornet blushed crimson, "I owe it all to you, mon chéri."

Fornet first came in contact with werewolves as a boy on his dad's cattle farm outside of Bogalusa, Louisiana. Following that event, a battery of psychiatrists played with his mind; yet, Mike Fornet's story never changed. Approached by SKUL only months after the incident, Fornet was faced with the horrifying truth that werewolves were real, and he was damned lucky to be alive. Eager to make more of a difference than he ever thought possible, Fornet accepted the assignment as a Tier 2 asset of SKUL intelligence – called an SI-2 – on the spot.

As it happened, Mike Fornet was the youngest SI-2 in SKUL's history.

A gifted child, Fornet took to the training and excelled in every phase. In turn, SKUL's higher command pulled the right strings and pushed the right buttons in order to ensure he was imbedded exactly where they needed to him the most – the NOPD. After surviving a particularly horrifying call at a prestigious New Orleans nursing home, Fornet was promoted to New Orleans Station Chief. Upon the promotion, he was told to recruit his own people and make his own way. Again, everything he touched and every decision he made turned to gold. Because he was a proven leader with the respect of his subordinates and an unblemished record in the field, in just the short side of a year, Fornet was given command of every SI-2 duty station in Arkansas, Louisiana, and Mississippi; but, Mike knew what very few outside of his inner circle knew. He knew the striking woman standing in front of him now was more responsible for his success than any other thing. Samantha Steele was the only woman to screen for and complete the United States Naval Special Warfare Development Group's assessment program – Green Team. That same woman trained him, molded him really, into what he was today.

"Bullshit," Sam snorted, "You made your own way. I was just there for guidance. Now, what do you have?"

"Sonny Duchaine," Fornet announced flatly. "Long time coke dealer, small time pimp, and most recently, suspected of murder." He looked back to the screens, "I guess being nothing more than a complete shithead wasn't good enough."

"Who took him down?"

"I did, Sam."

Recognizing the voice of an old friend, Sam looked past Mike to see a small, somewhat emaciated man with a scruffy beard step into the room. Seconds later, a greasy fog of body odor hit her nostrils. The man obviously had not bathed in a while.

"Jesus, Jerry, you need a bath." She smiled warmly to the older intelligence officer though made no move toward him.

"Good to see you too, Samantha," said the old operative who had once been her mentor. The inflection in his tone spoke of hurt feelings. "No need to thank me, just doing my job. All in a day's work."

"Shut up, you old coot," Sam said throwing her hands up and moving away. "I know it's all part of the job, but damn, I never thought you'd take it that serious."

Jerry Tinksdale had once been a case officer with the CIA. He eventually came on board with SKUL after an incident in which his cover was blown by what he could only truthfully describe as a werewolf. This was the mid-80's, in an insignificant country along the Black Sea, and he had just lost an informant with vital information concerning Mother Russia. There was no internet in those days so it took nearly a year for SKUL's higher command to get wind of the story and another to locate Tinksdale. Since then, he had been with SKUL, and Sam had been his most prized pupil.

She smiled again and shook his hand, "Good work you stinky, old fart. If you weren't so dirty, I'd give you a kiss."

"I thought you liked dirty old men, Sam?"

"Dirty I can deal with," Sam said with a wink and a smile, "but I don't do *old*, Jerry."

The smile she flashed to her old mentor could have melted a cake. True to form, her playfulness only lasted a minute before she was all business again. Sam stuck a small earbud in her ear and turned for the door. Before exiting, she had a thought and turned back.

"Wolfsbane?"

Jerry nodded.

Sam shook her head. Standing in the room was a literal family tree of intelligence officers. The immutable works performed by Jerry, herself, and now, Mike were certainly humbling. The fact they were all alive spoke volumes. "Jesus, that's amazing work." To Mike Fornet, she added, "Stay in touch, Mike."

And then, she shut the door.

***

She nodded to the two SKUL operators from Wraith platoon guarding the cell. While she would never know their names, much less their faces, she knew these men must have been some true badasses in their day; otherwise, they would have never drawn this assignment. As aged warriors opting for SKUL's AAP program, they made a conscious effort to remain active within the community. Without a word passed among them, the right hand operator punched a series of buttons on a keypad while the one on the left moved to a

430

position behind her. Sam entered the holding cell, and the Wraith operators took a position in each the rear corners of the room.

The werewolf was propped at an angle against a sheet of stainless steel. It was held in place around its neck, wrists, and ankles by a rope of solid silver encapsulated in a highly friable polymer. Any movement, at any speed and power, within a very finite distance would result in the cleaving of its hands...and feet...and head.

*Simultaneously.*

And, Sonny Duchaine knew it.

To the fore of the beast sat the only other piece of furniture the room had to offer – a steel table. Sam, still behind the animal and out of sight of his yellow eyes, put her hand to her mouth, closed her eyes, and exhaled. How many more times would she have to do this? This werewolf was a human being when?

A day ago?

A week ago?

Did it really matter?

She knew the true answer to that question, but that certainly made the job no less difficult. Collecting her wits, Sam stepped around Duschaine to the table and silently began unloading the contents of the pockets of her cargo shorts. She forced herself to return the werewolf's gaze; and as she did so, if only briefly, the savage's smirk faded.

"You ain't got the stones to hurt me, bitch," the newly turned werewolf snarled before screaming - though he was awfully careful not to move, "Jiggy, you backstabbing

431

motherfucker! I swear I'm going to rip your head off and wipe my ass with your fuckin' brains!"

Jerry's cover was that of a homeless vagrant called *Jiggy* who spent most of his time in the shadows under the bridges of I-10. At the werewolf's words, Sam stopped what she was doing and looked up, flashing a savagely cold smile.

Her pretty yet incredibly flat affect unnerved the young werewolf. Her eyes played over him with the clinical detachment a pathologist has regarding a week old corpse. Duschaine's eyes grew wide as Sam slowly began laying several objects out on the table.

Screwdrivers, knives, and bullets, and he could sense their elemental makeup. It was like smelling rain just over the horizon.

They were *silver*.

Nearly as frightening was the strange little tubular device she placed beside the silver items. Nervously, he began to fidget though he remained careful not to break the covers of his bindings. Lastly, she placed a pistol on the table which added tenfold to his nervousness. That nervousness grew as she slowly loaded the pistol's magazine, never taking her startling eyes from his. That same nervousness nearly boiled over as she screwed on the weapon's suppressor.

Finally, she spoke, "I know who you are and what you do. What I don't know is when you were turned. I also don't know if it was a natural turning or whether you were you turned by the drug? Both of these things I would like to know, and both of these things you will tell me."

"I ain't tellin' you shit, whore."

A look, baleful and menacing, flashed across Sam's face, yet she said nothing. Instead, she held one of the blades before her appraising eyes. She turned it into and out of the light, marveling silently at its edge.

"Sonny? May I call you Sonny?" she asked still eyeballing the razor edge. "At present, you are my pet. You are nothing more than a dog, collared and useless." She drew the silver blade across Sonny Duchaine's inner thigh, and the werewolf gasped from the white hot pain.

The next time she looked to Duchaine, it was through dead eyes, "This...is by design."

Anger and blood lust combined to form a terrible, otherworldly power, and as Sonny screamed, the concrete infrastructure vibrated.

Slowly, she lowered the blade to his nether regions which caused Sonny's eyes to bulge. Sam smiled, "Two buses carrying a touring gospel choir went missing last night. A third bus, the one with your fingerprints and massive claw marks on the seats and roof was also found." Sam paused and then added, "Wanna tell me where they are?"

Despite the pain he was in, Duchaine leaned as close as he dared and growled, "I don't know; but, why don't you bend over, and I'll look for them?"

Sam's smile was still apparent, but it had turned wooden, "That's funny." She placed the knife back on the table and picked up one of the strange, tubular devices. The werewolf could sense no silver in its construction, but the fact the woman was smiling so malevolently curdled Duschaine's blood.

"You've heard of water boarding, no?" Sam phrased the words in the form of a question, but they really were not. "Having been in those rooms and seen the blood thirsty animals we held shit and piss themselves due to the unmitigated terror of it…well, let's just say the process is highly effective. But, Sonny, I'm going to fill you in on a little secret. It's all mental." She tapped the side of her head with the device, "You have to believe you're going to survive before you can actually expect you will."

She let that linger on the sterile air for a moment.

"You know how many terrorists I witnessed make it out of those rooms unbroken?"

Sonny shook his head cautiously.

"None."

Again, she allowed the silence to play with Duschaine's mind. The savage's eyes darted from one side of the room to the other, expecting, at any moment, to face his end. Sam continued to smile as she held the tube right in front of his face and said, "Consider this your water boarding," before pushing a button on the head of the tube.

Sonny Duschaine roared with hate, rage, and pain at the tiny WIPP device racked his brain with ultra-sonic pulses for higher than anything Sam could ever hope to hear.

"I swear to all that's good and pure, I'll eat your soul, you motherfucker!" he roared as Sam grabbed a second WIPP.

She moved back to the table and sat, allowing the werewolf digest what she had asked. Sam noticed a tiny trickle of green ichor drip from the savage's right ear. Finally, she said, "Sonny." The werewolf only managed a whimper so

434

repeated more forcibly, "Sonny!" Strictly for effect, she tapped the WIPP on the steel table.

The savage turned to her voice.

"Good. Now, Sonny, I can make this painless; or, I can make this very, *very* painful for you, understand?"

The savage nodded, fighting back the fear and doubt attacking its mind.

"Good. Give me the truth, and this'll all end quickly, okay?"

The sulking werewolf nodded again.

"Was your turning natural by way of bite or was it this drug called God's Milk?"

"What do you think? I'm a drug dealer. I hit that shit. It's kinda a perk of the job," the werewolf said through clenched teeth. "Just before the last full moon. Sat around waiting on that goddamned moon for three days...thought I was going crazy, which I guess I was." He laughed despite his predicament. "Then that moon rose..." Duschaine's voice trailed off, but Sam had what she needed. It was as they expected, at least in part. They need the power of a full moon to complete the change.

Sam nodded and jotted a note down, "Now, we're getting somewhere. Where is this drug coming from?"

At first, the werewolf looked back at her with defiance in his eyes refusing to speak. That was, until Sam reminded him of the WIPP in her hand. The savage had come to truly fear that little tube.

"Okay okay. A member of Satan's Bastards MC gets me the shit...I dunno where he gets it from, though. I swear."

In her ear Mike Fornet confirms, "Vitals say he's telling the truth on all counts, Sam."

Sam made no acknowledgement of Mike's information, "I believe you." From a drawer in the table she pulled a photo of Billy the Kid. He was sitting on a motorcycle, wearing the vest of the Bastards. In his hands were two semi-auto pistols, "Is this who you get the drug from?"

Sonny looked at the photo seemingly eager to help, now. After reviewing it a second, he shook his head.

"Do you know who that is?" Again, Sonny shook his head. A second later, Mike again confirmed that, according to the biometrics, the savage was speaking the truth. Sam placed the photo on the table and continued, "Who gets you the drug then? I need a name, Sonny."

"Low level member...goes by *Skinny*. Whoeverthefuck called that fat ass Skinny has a warped sense of humor, though. Bastard's huge, and he sweats...constantly."

Sam looked on without emotion but knew the savage in question. In fact, they had a dossier six inches thick on Johnny Parks a.k.a Skinny.

"Why's the drug so special?"

The werewolf looked at her stupidly.

"It's *not* the fucking cocaine that made you change, Sonny!" The venom hitching a ride on her voice slapped him in the face. "What is it?"

Duschaine cringed and withered under her glare. This was a subject the savage really did not want to broach. Sam, her patience spent, activated a second WIPP. Sonny's face contorted in pain and, unable to keep his body from spasms, a foot fell free of its body. The silver cord sliced through Duschaine's right leg like a hot knife through butter. The silver binding was smoking, and the whole room smelled like burnt hair and flesh. The vessels were instantly cauterized; therefore, the stump bled very little. The pain was there, though, and it was absolute in experience. Savages could do a lot of unholy things, but regeneration of a limb was not one of them. Sonny was sweating, panting, and nauseous. His brain, refusing to accept that the immortal could be made mortal, screamed for both relief and retribution.

"What's it made of?" Sam growled.

"Blood," Sonny spat through the pain. "Werewolf blood...Eldrich blood...that's all I know, I swear it."

"Okay," she continued even while thinking, *Blood from an Eldrich. That's new and completely horrifying*, "I've already asked this but; this time, you *are* going to answer." Sam looked to the werewolf; he looked back to her. His face said he was eager to help, but she reinforced her view by adding, "Quick and easy or slow and painful? It's up to you."

Sonny nodded profusely.

"Where are they Sonny?" Sam demanded with an edgy tone. "I know you know."

Sonny remained quiet, unable to comprehend the futility of his existence. Sam activated a third WIPP. The concrete walls again shook under the might of Duschaine's howl. His body bucked against the incapacitating noise beating his eardrums senseless. A hand fell to the floor like a plucked petal from a dead flower. Sonny roared, "You merciless bitch!  I'll tear you limb from limb!  I swear I will!  I am a god to someone like you, and I will make you pay!"

"You aren't a god," Sam said icily.  "You are a blight, a cancer, and I won't be running out of ways to hurt you anytime soon."  Sam leaned close and made sure he could see the WIPP she held, "I'll ask you again and remember, easy or hard?  Fast or slow?  It's your choice.  Now, where are they?"

Duschaine's chest heaved, but he had nowhere to go and no way of escaping.  He was missing a foot and a hand, and he could barely hear anything anymore.  He was done, and he knew it.  Done before his life – his *real* life – ever got started.  Defeated, Sonny caved.  He told her everything.  Location, numbers of savages – dozens, and that was if no others had been turned – even a description of the warehouse where they were being held.

She had done it.  She had broken a savage.  It took her a long moment to get past that realization.  Finally, she spoke to the room, "Jerry?"

Over the intercom system Duschaine heard the voice of the one who captured him – Jiggy, "What do you need me to do, Sam?"

"Patch Elbert in, Jerry.  Send all the material we have to him now...*everything*.  Alert teams are Saber, Roughneck, and Mustang.  QRF and standby teams per protocol."

She vaguely heard Jerry say, "On it, Sam."

She was smiling again.  It was beautiful yet ugly in equal measure; and, it froze Duschaine's blood.  This was the worst part of the process.  The part she hated more than anything.  The part that put her on the same level as the savages she hunted.  It was also the most necessary part.

438

Sam racked the pistol's slide.

"You said if I told you the truth you'd let me go!" Sonny screamed. One of his arms came loose – really loose – and hit the floor with a heavy thud, cleaved from his body by the bindings. Again he screamed in agony.

Sam was no longer smiling.

"No," she nodded to the men and simultaneously three weapons – the two MP7's and Sam's Sig Sauer 9mm – jerked from the kick of the weapons. "I said it would be quick and easy you decrepit sonavabitch. Be glad you didn't live to see slow and painful."

Sonny Duchaine was dead, and as green ichor dripped from his body onto the floor, Sam was left to wonder if some part of her own humanity was dying as well. She forced a deep breath, turned, and left the room at a run.

## 36)
## Insubordination

**Silver Moon**
**Helo flight deck**
**1930**

"Sir," Tim Meadows said as he fell in to step, "are you sure you want to go down this road?"

"Yeah, Bill, the Admiral might just view this as gross insubordination," noted Tommy-Gun Granderson. "Will definitely depend on which side of the bed he wakes up on."

Wild Bill Kipling spun on them. His voice was low but held an air of mutiny about it, "Did we not all agree that something does not feel right here?"

"We did," both admitted. And, truth be known, the operation and the ease at which the intel came did feel weird. All three had admitted as much earlier in the platoon's common area. No sooner had Tommy and Tim voiced their opinions than Bill had his men suiting back up. Bill's order came right on the heels of the Admiral himself standing down the four teams – Titan, Rhino, Renegade, and Copperhead – in order to maintain continuity of the overall operation. Those teams had been on alert for nearly seventy-two hours, gathering intel, sitting in on briefings, and hitting targets. They were bloodied and ragged and needed rest; but, the Skipper knew they would not just sit around while their brothers dove headlong into such a hairy operation. So, he ordered them to sit around. They were good soldiers, and the Admiral knew they would do as told.

Admiral Bartavious Briggs was wrong.

"So, why am I having to defend myself to you two now?" demanded Wild Bill.

"Bill, you aren't having to defend yourself here, but dammit man, we're looking at a heavy stint in the brig after this is all over." Tommy-Gun had known Kipling a long time and Tim was content to let the two talk this out.

"No, you aren't, Tommy," said Bill flatly. "Failing to get your ass on that chopper this very goddamned minute will constitute an *Article 92* violation – dereliction of duty – by you and every other man standing on this pad."

Granderson's eyebrows knitted together; and his face fell in on itself in disbelief for a split second; and, then, it broke into a wide grin, "So, my commanding officer has just ordered the men of his platoon to board that helo there," Granderson pointed to the Chinook spinning up. The last of Foxtrot's men were loading up at that very moment. "And, that same commanding officer has threatened all with dereliction of duty for failure to follow said orders?"

"About covers it, yes," Bill said, much more relaxed now.

Tommy thought about it for another moment or two then held out his hand, "You're going to do hard time for this, sir." The two shook hands, "But, it's because of this that we will follow you through the depths of hell."

Bill smiled and over the whine of the rotors, had to yell, "You're going there tonight…make sure you all come back!"

While Bill and Tommy spoke, Tim led the other men toward the helo getting ready to lift off the deck. Their heads were down, and they moved with speed toward the Chinook, but that did not stop a lean, swarthy looking character from blocking their way. He wore a green flight suit and a bright, yellow jersey.

"What the fuck is your problem, and why are you shitstains decorating my deck?" screamed the man over the rotors. "If you aren't a part of the flight crew, you can see your sorry ass off this deck immediately!"

Tim cringed. He knew who was addressing him. His name was *Charlie...something,* but that did not really matter. What mattered was he was the *air boss,* and he was in charge of, and ruled with an iron fist, everything that happened on the flight deck...*his* deck. Tim shook his head. Why the air boss was down on the deck instead of up in his tower at this particular time was anyone's guess.

"We need to board that helo, sir," Tim said calmly and with as few of words as possible. Men as busy as *Charlie-something* could get completely bogged down in the confusion of too many words thrown at them all at once.

"Negative, *sir.*" The asshole slurred the word *sir,* sarcastically, like he was spoiling for a fight. Once it was all over with, Tim would use the air boss' tone to justify what happened next. It really did not cover it, but to the people who actually heard the story, it was enough. "Your people aren't on the flight manifest; so, you can put your dick in your hands and fuck what you *need,* sir. I got a deck to run here!"

The asshole turned his back on the men to discuss whatever it is the air boss needed to discuss with whoever it was he needed to discuss it with. A vague sound, strangely familiar but on the edge of his memory, caused him to spin back to Tim. He was greeted with the barrels of over fifty assault rifles pointed directly at him. The sound that roused him was that of safeties being switched to *fire* positions, charging handles being pulled, and rifles being shouldered.

He gulped.

The man he had been a purposeful ass to smiled.

"I wasn't requesting to board, *sir*. I was telling you we were boarding, *sir*." Tim stepped close enough to violate everything from international waterways to personal space. Nose to nose, he glared at the air boss and snarled, "Don't make me do something I'll regret and you won't survive...step aside."

For the first time in his professional career, the air boss allowed others to take over his deck...for the moment, in any case.

***

## South Louisiana swamps
## 2200

"Hold one, Boss, hold one," exclaimed Toad over the intra-squad comm link. Toad was one of three snipers – one from each fire team – taking up overwatch positions around the target. Their job was to take out any guards, provide cover fire for the teams, and eliminate any squirters attempting to escape once the assault had been initiated. Toad's frantic voice halted the tri-pronged assault momentarily. "I have a lone savage that's just stepped from *Penthouse*."

*Penthouse* was the codename given to the main structure of the mill. The other two teams would hit targets codenamed *Roadhouse* and *Outhouse*.

The other overwatch positions reported the same thing.

The map said the target – a sugar cane mill – was situated deep within the swamps and fields of South Louisiana. That was all fine and good and sounded simple enough, but the assaulters waiting to initiate their mission were pragmatic men. They could sum up the location of the target far more succinctly. Simply put, this sugar mill was located smack dab between the middle-of-nowhere and the ass end of Bumfuck, Egypt.

From the start, the shooters felt weird about the target. The intel came a little too easily – though Sonny Duschaine would certainly disagree; and, the hostages – an Emmy award winning gospel choir whose disappearance had garnered national attention – were too rich a target. Add that to the fact there was no evidence to persuade SKUL's intelligence officers to believe the savages had attempted to disguise their involvement, and the pipe hitters SKUL was sending pretty much knew they were heading to an international goat-roping event. It was going to be like Wrestlemania, only, instead of fake injuries and blood packets, there was going to be the very, very real possibility of death...or worse.

The target site only lent itself to that line of thinking. The mill was a sprawling, cankerous mass of crumbling cinder blocks and rusty, corrugated metal spread out over nearly twenty acres. Between the three largest structures, a system of conveyor belts and railroad tracks wound around a half dozen boilers and smoke stacks. Dane estimated there were approximately four hundred eleven points of potential disaster and death.

*Conservatively.*

The size of the facility and, now, the appearance of the guards would definitely add a kink to the operation; but, it was not an unworkable situation. Saber had already taken out a savage walking the perimeter fence surrounding the mill; so, Dane and the shooters onsite just looked to the newcomers as a minor hazard...nothing more than par for the course.

"Coordinate with the other guys and handle it, Toad. We'll move on you."

"Roger that, Boss."

Toad's target was in the circle, as was the target in *Skunk's* sector. Skunk, otherwise known as Chad Sistrunk, was Roughneck's sniper. The same could not be said for Roger Keyes – call sign, *Skeeter* – Mustang's sniper. The savage in his sights had positioned himself behind a corner in the cinderblock wall of the mill. Skeeter reported being able to see the afterglow of body heat along with the tip of his cigarette but nothing more.

"Saber in position, requesting sitrep," Dane ordered tersely.

"Mustang's in position."

"Roughneck's in position."

"Saber copies all, move on the snipers."

"Roger," was the reply from both team leaders.

Dane and his guys crouched deep within the shadows of the wood line. Though they were only twenty meters from the savage, their KtacS suits masked both their scent and their heat signature. The suits served to confound the supremely evolved senses of werewolf, inherently making them all but invisible. Their largest problem was the twenty meter sprint over open ground they had to make. Twenty meters, in the open, against beings possessing the strength and power of a werewolf, was a recipe for disaster.

But, Dane and the others knew they did not get to choose the time and place they battled the savages. Over the comm system, they listened in to the ongoing exchange between the snipers.

"Roughneck green, Mustang red…"

Green meant the sniper in question had a clear shot; red meant they did not. Once someone reported being in the red, the process started over.

"Roughneck red…"

And so it went like that until finally, "Mustang green, Roughneck green…" Only Toad failed to update his status. His silence served as fertilizer for an already growing pit of unease in everyone that was listening in.

"Status, Toad?" sounded Dane's stressed interrogative over the comm unit.

\*\*\*

The savage in Toad's sector stood before the main entrance to the mill. The target was just under a hundred meters away with little to no wind to deal with.

A chip shot for someone with Toad's skill.

Saber's sniper, nestled in the thick, lush undergrowth of the surrounding swamp, held the crosshairs on his target's face. His updates generally acknowledged he was green; yet, each time, one or both of his colleagues would call *red*. Suddenly, the savage in his scope ducked inside a recessed

447

area and out of sight. He knew Dane and the others had seen the movement and adjusted accordingly. He also trusted his team leader enough to know that if anything untoward was going on, Dane would have already ordered to execute the mission.

Instead, all was quiet except for, "Roughneck red…" Seconds later, the savage before Toad reappeared, the glowing tip of a fresh cigarette hanging from its mouth. He tightened his favored .300 Winchester Magnum against his shoulder and looked through the proprietary sniper optics all SKUL snipers utilized. With his crosshairs again on the target, Toad was settling into the rhythm of his breathing when he felt a gentle pressure build over his extended, left forearm. Taking his eyes off the target, he froze as a cottonmouth water moccasin slithered over his left arm and rifle barrel before coming to a rest with its ugly, diamond-shaped head lying on top of his scope. Its vertical pupils stared unblinkingly into the lenses of Toad's KtacS helmet. In his ears came the voices of the other snipers; only now, they sounded like they were calling from the next area code.

He hated snakes with a passion. Clowns too, truth be known; though, even he doubted one of those infernal horrors was likely to emerge from the woods and torment his soul like this snake was currently doing.

If one did, however, he would be calling it a night.

His vision tunneled and a trickle of sweat rolled down his forehead as he watched the reptile that was watching him. Unconsciously, he held his breath to the point he could feel the rapid *lubdub-lubdub-lubdub* of his heartbeat and was all but positive the pressure was going to rip his eardrums to shreds.

There was a moment when the two silent killers locked eyes, separated only by the state of the art goggles integrated into Toad's helmet. As the dead, evil-looking eyes bore through Toad's skull, he began to believe his KtacS suit, body armor developed to withstand assaults from both werewolf and conventional small arms fire, was about to be tested by the bite of a poisonous snake.

Dane's terse voice tore him from his current nightmare, "Dammit, Toad, respond!"

"Sorry, Boss," the sniper said quietly into the comm system while praying the snake couldn't hear his voice. "Snake."

"What?" demanded Dane. "Say again."

Toad bypassed further explanation and began the sequence again, "Saber green..."

\*\*\*

"...Mustang green, Roughneck green."

A split second later the three snipers pulled the triggers of their rifles simultaneously. The savage's head shimmered green in Marcus' FVS and instantly turned to an ichorous mist.

And then, the snake struck – twice – and Toad missed the initial assault on the compound.

\*\*\*

The savage was pinned against the cinder block wall with the shot. The thing stayed on its feet for a two-count then slid silently to the ground. Blood, bone, and brain dripped from the wall and pooled around the dead werewolf. Twitch reacted instantly, running full tilt for the doorway. The others followed, staggered at a prearranged five meter pacing. The team knew from the blueprints, the main building - their target responsibility, codenamed *Penthouse* - was an immense, multistoried structure of concrete and steel. The size and depth of the compound rendered a loud, violent breach useless in the best of times and, quite possibly, deadly in the worst. Twitch put two more silver slugs through the downed savage's chest before inspecting the door's lock. While he was doing this, the others stacked up on either side of the entrance and waited for his assessment.

"That's weird," said Twitch rocking back on his heels.

"What?" demanded Dane.

"It's unlocked."

Quickly Dane reviewed the last few seconds, remembering the sudden appearance of the three guards just outside the warehouse.

Jed voiced what the others had already suspected, "They're expecting us."

Tweeker agreed, "Yeah, gotta be."

"Well," Dane said and had the helmet not completely covered his head they would have seen a broad grin, "let's not disappoint them."

Using his eyes, Dane engaged his helmet's RRT and changed his radio channel to the open net. This allowed all teams onsite, the QRF elements, and the command back on the Silver Moon to hear.

"Saber-one-one to all units. Be advised we are in position at target *Penthouse*. Suspect they know we're here. How copy?"

"Good copy, Saber-one-one, Roughneck in position to take *Roadhouse.*"

"Mustang in position at *Outhouse*. Awaiting orders."

"Saber-one-one copies all...*Execute!*"

He reached above Twitch and pushed the door open. The team flowed into the dark waiting area beyond like water, commanding every square inch of their tight battle space in seconds.

***

Toad watched his team's silent entry through a stream of venom that dripped down his goggles like rain splatter. His nerves – normally made of steel and ice – were shot. Knowing he had a moment to spare, Marcus buried his helmeted head in his arms and spent some quality time collecting his wits.

Beside his right arm laid the writhing body of the snake. Its head he had only just separated from its thick body by the keen edge of his silver tomahawk. On one side of the gleaming silver weapon was the SKUL shield; on the other was the name of one of the unit's fallen – John Calloway. Calloway succumbed to injuries sustained while on an operation in '91.

After a few moments of deep breathing, Toad was ready to rejoin the fight. He pulled his rifle back to his shoulder and searched for savages. The snake's ugly, hateful mouth repeatedly opened and closed as its nerve endings continued to fire.

# 37)
## Out of the Frying Pan...

The Admiral, along with everyone else, watched Toad's feed with a combined measure of fear and awe. On a separate screen, the overhead feed showed the teams' coordinated assault.

"What's the status on our QRF?" demanded the Admiral.

Sam, lead intelligence officer and facilitator of the mission, spoke. Her tone was businesslike and clipped, "Kilo is on standby, sir."

"Position from target and assets?" asked the Admiral.

"Twenty mikes from the target, sir," Sam reported, even while receiving and logging updates from both the teams on the ground and their support elements. "Kilo's Chinook is supported by four Apache gunships, Skipper."

The Admiral looked to English Whitherton, Kilo's platoon leader.

"My guys are locked, cocked, and ready to rock, Skipper."

Briggs nodded then turned to Foxtrot's PL, Stan Woods, "What's the status of your boys, Woodrow?"

"Lifted off the Moon two hours ago," Woods confirmed. "They are due at Kilo's position any minute."

The Admiral nodded then looked again to the overhead footage. Unease had taken root in his mind and had been growing. Something was not right here. Intel had as many as fifty hostages on the scene with a heavy, werewolf presence; yet, there had been very little resistance.

453

This was *wrong*.

The Skipper spun in place, fear causing his scar to twitch crazily under his eye patch, "Get Kilo off the ground and moving to target, now. Something's not right here. I want them hanging five klicks out to await further orders. Hopefully, the end of the world will not have begun by the time they get there."

On any other day of any other week, that comment would have seen ludicrous to any number of people; but not tonight, and not to these people.

He spun to Foxtrot's PL, who was already typing a message into his SICS, "Woodrow, redirect your guys and have them hookup with Kilo en route."

Woods pressed send and looked to the Admiral, "Done." He pushed past the Skipper to get with the air support staffers working furiously at the consoles and computers at the front of the Ops Center. He needed to help his guys and the crew of their Chinook coordinate with Kilo platoon.

***

Twitch flowed into the room following the left hand wall until he stood in the far corner aiming back across the room. Tweeker mimicked his movements on the right hand wall, though he stopped at the first corner, training his weapon across his sector. Dane and Jed flowed into the waiting area a heartbeat behind the first two shooters, Dane stepping to the left, Jed to the right. The only noise betraying their entry came from the dull *thump* of their booted footsteps on the concrete floor. Though outwardly soundless, the guys were in constant communication via their closed comm link.

454

"Clear right!" Tweeker bellowed into the intra-squad comm link.

"Clear left!" acknowledged Twitch

"Clear," came both Dane and Jed's voices.

They were in the mill's small, reception area. The room's decor was spartan with only a small desk in the center. The room, completely dark, was portrayed in shades of gray in their FV system; though, the light bulbs overhead, having recently been turned off, appeared violet through their goggles. The body heat a werewolf generates is so massive, and their FVS so sensitive, the team could see the path walked by the savage Toad had killed only moments before. The savage had obviously come from somewhere deeper within the mill.

On each side of the hall were two doors. Dane remembered from the blueprints that each opened into four small offices at the front of the warehouse.

"Tweeker, Jed, you guys take the rooms on the right. Twitch and I will handle the left."

Twitch pushed the door open, and Dane moved into the office silently with his partner right behind him.

"Clear," acknowledged Saber's team leader.

"Clear," repeated Twitch, and each man heard an identical report from Jed and Tweeker.

"Moving," they called, and the men moved out of the nearest room. The two stacked to either side of the next door and repeated the process.

Dane was again the first to enter and promptly made contact with a newly turned savage. The thing was busy feeding on the soft belly and sickly smelling innards of one the hostages.  It wore clothes that appeared to have once been a blue business suit, though now hung from its body in tattered shreds.

All of this Dane recognized instantly.

Dane, moving quickly, slipped on the office's tile floor as it had become slick with blood.  Taking advantage of the momentary confusion, the savage lunged, snapping its massive jaws shut around Dane's right thigh.  This caused a shower of sparks to spew from the areas of contact as the suit absorbed and repelled both the blow and the savage.  The werewolf's howls of pain were cut off instantly.

*Thump.*

The muffled report of Twitch's SCAR sounded over Dane's shoulder, and the back of the savage's head exploded.  The far wall was coated in the green, ichorous sludge that was the savage's life blood.  Twitch stepped forward with his rifle trained on the downed on the werwolf.

*Thump thump thump.*

He put three more 7.62mm rounds into the savage's chest before moving to the hostage.

*Thump.*

He put a round into the hostage's head to ensure it would not be coming back to haunt them later.

Twitch turned to Dane, "Boss, you okay?"  He held his rifle on his TL.

Dane was already checking his leg over in a state of panic, "I'm cool," yet he kept looking over his thigh.  "No no, I'm cool, bro.  I'm cool."

Per protocol, Twitch bent and assessed the damage before calling out over the comm link, "We have one hostage and one savage dead. Saber-one-one's suit is compromised but functioning."

"Roger that," came Jed's terse reply. "Our side is secure, moving back into the hallway."

Both elements of the team regrouped before moving further into the infinite darkness of the corridor.

"That savage was newly turned," reported Dane to the others.

Twitch agreed, "Still had on a business suit, but the fucker was fast."

Dane could tell from their downturned lenses, the others were looking at his leg with concern.

"Guys, I'm cool. Twitch checked it out thoroughly, okay?" The nods were slow in coming and seeing no good could come from belaboring the point, he ordered, "Move out!"

Twitch led the way further down the hall until they came to a right hand turn in the hall. With the fluid movements of a predator, he stepped around the corner.

*Thump*

Dane followed, then Tweeker, and finally, Jed. Twitch had downed another savage. This one was still in human form, but its thermal signature left little doubt. Saber's point man pumped two more silver rounds into its chest and kept moving.

This section of hallway was much longer, void of offshoot hallways or offices, and ran perpendicular to the main work area Dane knew they were fast approaching. Up ahead, the end of a hallway was bathed in the glow of harsh, halogen lights. The lights illuminated what they understood to be the main work area. Silently, they moved toward the light.

"You know, they make horror movies every day that start just like this," Tweeker observed as nonchalantly as humanly possible.

"Yeah," agreed Twitch, "remember that Nightmare on Elm Street that started in the hospital with the light at the end of the hall...Freddy was being born or something?"

"Knock it off," Jed ordered. "Judas-Titty-Twisting-Priest, we're in a damned horror movie, a real one; so, shut up and stay sharp."

"They're right, though," countered Dane with a slight chuckle.

"Don't you start."

Seconds later, the team knelt just on the other side of the corner formed by the change in the hallway's direction.

Silence reigned once again, though the shooters could feel their hearts beating in their chests.

"Saber-one-one to Mustang-actual. Need a sitrep. How copy?"

"Reading you lima-charlie, Saber-one-one," came the team leader's response. "Two savages down. Outhouse is secure. Zero hostages present. Falling on your position and will help with security."

"Roger that, Mustang-actual. Roughneck-two-one, status?"

"Roadhouse secure, zero contact," reported Jack Yarborough, the former Green Beret captain serving as Roughneck's TL. "Commencing security check of the perimeter."

*Strange,* Dane thought before forcing the ill-feelings from his mind. Those thoughts were not going to help him, and that which could not be of help could get him killed. "Roger that," Dane replied from a position just off Twitch's hip. He hazarded a glance over his shoulder to the others. Each shooter nodded, and Dane turned back, placing a gloved hand on Twitch's shoulder.

Twitch's nod was quick yet firm.

He was ready.

Dane squeezed his shoulder, and Twitch rounded the corner swiftly. This time, Twitch took taking the right wall, while the others went through the necessary paces in order to secure their sectors.

The site that met their eyes would haunt the men the rest of their days.

***

Toad froze upon hearing a twig snap. The woods had gone quiet minutes before, so quiet that the noiseless night was deafening in its nothingness. He had known something was wrong but had no clue what was coming.

No one did.

Suddenly, they were all around him, burning with radiological intensity. Unconsciously, Tolar attempted to make himself smaller as the first wave of *hot bodies* passed by his position.

From the sounds of it, many, many more were to come.

***

The Skipper's jaw went slack as the first throbbing; nuclear-like plume appeared on the screen. It was followed a second later by another then another until dozens of the

459

white hot outlines appeared and began moving toward the mill. Everyone in the Ops Center was asking the same question.

*Where had all these savages come from so quickly?*

No one seemed to have any logical answer until it hit the Admiral like a ton of bricks. He had seen this very thing before in Vietnam. The VC would appear in the jungle like night wraiths and wreak havoc on an unsuspecting patrol, only to disappear just as quickly. The savages, like the Vietcong before them, had been lying in wait in the only place that would allow them to get in close to the SKUL operators unseen.

They had been hiding in an underground tunnel system.

Realizing – too late – the implications on the screen, the Admiral bellowed, "Get Kilo and Foxtrot moving to target!"

***

In the center of the mill, an impromptu stage had been built. A spotlight – the light they had seen from the hall – shone down on the *Best Promise Gospel Choir.* Shackled to the stage in leg irons, they were dressed in their choir robes.

No one moved.

Hostages tended to be either overjoyed at the thought of being rescued or frightened to the point they would recoil and fight against their saviors. Either way, you generally had to control the hostages just as you would the bad guys. These people had done neither, though. It was as if they had not even noticed the men spilling into the cavernous room.

Taking a closer look, a cold feeling of fear gripped Dane's spine.

The hostages had not noticed their entrance, because their eyelids had been sewn shut. The same could be said about their mouths.

Over the comm link, someone whispered in shocked awe, "Jeeezus Kerrrist..."

Dane knew the voice, but his mind was too occupied with the horror his eyes were drawn to in order to place it. He was still processing the scene when one of the members of the choir stumbled off the stage blindly. The person, a female, had not been shackled as the others had. Her movement amid such stark stillness and silence shocked the team. She hit the floor face first with a sickening smack, causing her choir robe to fall open and reveal the belt of explosives strapped across her chest.

Before Dane could react, Tweeker shoved him to the ground and draped his massive body protectively over his team leader.

As the weight of Tweeker took him down, he saw Jed and Twitch diving away from the woman. He barely registered Tweeker's scream of, "Bomb!" before the concussion and heat of the blast engulfed every inch of the mill.

***

Admiral Briggs' breath caught in his throat, and he had to fight back a wave of nausea when the overhead footage of the warehouse went nuclear. The pressure of the blast was directed outward, and it disintegrated windows and tore apart concrete walls in equal measure. After the initial shock and outrage of what had occurred only seconds prior, the Ops Center became quiet. Everyone stared at the burning and wrecked mill unsure of what to do or say next. Eyes never wavering from the footage, Briggs gasped, "Bill..."

"They left with Woodrow's guys, sir," the platoon leader admitted. "The guys were seething at being ordered to stand down. Christ, Skipper, those men strewn somewhere in that rubble are their brothers. When Foxtrot was cut loose, I ordered my guys to hitch a ride and do so with force if they needed to." Bill's look was apologetic yet uncompromising, "This is on me and me alone. I'm willing to accept the consequences for what's been done, sir."

Briggs tensed causing the scars on his face to pucker which lent an inhuman quality to his features. Unconsciously, he adjusted the eye patch covering his dead, useless eye. Finally, he said in his trademark gravelly voice, "Bill...shut up. We've got a fight to win." As an afterthought, he added, "We'll discuss your court martial after this is over..."

"Yes, sir," Kipling replied with the inflection on his voice a piece of oak might have.

The room watched, helpless and impotent, as scores of savages poured out of the surrounding woods and into the burning wreckage that had once been a sugar cane mill.

*** 

The blast had knocked him out; Dane knew that immediately, but for how long was anyone's guess. Dane forced his eyes to clear. When he was finally able to focus again, he silently wished his vision was still blurry. Flames licked at him from all sides, and behind those flames roared the chaos of battle. Amid the crackling fires, he could hear

462

muted *claps* of suppressed gunfire which would intermittently be drowned out by the feverish howling of the savages. Even though his mind was thick and moving slow, Dane knew there were only two things that could force that level of intensely inhumane rage from werewolves. One was the WIPP grenades every SKUL operator carried. The other was freshly spilt blood.

He imagined both to be in large quantities right about then.

His eyes caught movement coming through the flames, and everything around him seemed to bleed away. There were no flames, no gunfire, and no stench of burning flesh. There was only the savage moving toward him.

He recognized the yellow, baleful eyes at once. He had seen them during their most recent briefing. They belonged to the savage known as Johnny Parks. Parks was called *Skinny* by those wearing the Satan's Bastards cut. He moved through the flames with the slow grace of a night predator on the hunt. Under normal conditions, the movement would have been eye-catching; but, considering Parks was walking through a wall of fire, it was practically miraculous.

Like *Shadrach, Meshach, and Abednego* – type miraculous.

From Skinny's demonic face and monstrous body hung its smoking, charred skin; while, other parts of his body held skin that was still bubbling like boiling oil.

Dane tried to crawl away, but every cell in his body screamed in agony. Somehow, he realized he was badly concussed and probably burned in other places worse than that.

A furry, claw-tipped foot, easily twice the size of a large, human male's, slammed beside his head with cement-shattering force. Dane groaned as he again tried to pull himself away.

With no effort whatsoever, Skinny grabbed Dane around the neck and pulled him up to face level. Dane's helmet had been ripped apart by the explosion; so, he was forced to look directly into Parks' eyes which swirled with yellow hate. The savage was so tall Dane's feet dangled over a foot off the ground, and he felt his eyes bulge in their sockets as the werewolf tightened its grip around his neck. Drool dripped slowly down the werewolf's overlong fangs before falling to the rubble-strewn floor.

Its breath stank of death.

With its free hand, Skinny ran a long, razor sharp claw over the now useless helmet of Dane's KtacS suit. The silver-lined ballistic helmet peeled away from his face like a dried corn husk. In its wake, a long, thin sliver of red began to grow. His face burned like someone had cut it open and packed the wound with hot coals.

"Death is a foregone conclusion for you, mijo," Skinny said as he slammed Dane into what was left of a cinderblock wall. The force of the blow was so violent that the concrete cracked. Dane's spine screamed in pain, and the blackness of death began to creep into his vision. "The only question now is how quickly you will die." The savage pulled Dane close to its snout, then slammed him against the wall again. Dane's brain turned to mush, and he slumped against

464

the beast, defenseless against the massive force of the werewolf. The savage tilted its head skyward and sniffed the air, taking in the smells of death filling the destroyed mill. It was sickening the way it savored the thick, musty smells before slamming Dane yet again into the concrete wall. Skinny looked upon the beaten man, the man sent to kill him, and a chuckle began to rumble from deep inside the beast's chest.

Unable to lift his head, unable to focus on anything, Dane slid his fingers along the outline of his thigh, searching for his pistol. He had lost his rifle in the explosion.

*It's over,* Dane thought as his fingers finally fell onto the empty holster, *I'm done.*

The words and – worse still – the defeatist attitude, were a bitter pill for someone like Dane. It was like being force fed an energy drink of brimstone. Refusing to give in to the immortal bent on ending him, he forced his head back up.

The savage smiled in the face of Dane's defiance. "I can't wait to suck the marrow from your bones." Skinny slammed him against the wall with such force it finally collapsed in a plume of dust. The savage's maw opened to reveal row upon row of serrated teeth, the largest of which where its canines.

They had to have been over six inches long.

Vaguely, just before the darkness finally took him, he registered another running through the flames and destruction the mill had devolved into.

# 38)
## ...and, Into the Fire

When Dane came to panic flooded his mind. A werewolf had just beaten him to a pulp.

He should be dead; yet, his head bounced off the backside of whoever – or whatever – was carrying him. He took a second to wipe away the blood from his eyes. In doing so, his fingers raked over the fresh, screaming wounds of his face. His vision cleared just in time to see a hulking savage with a blood stained snout leap from the smoke and fire of one of the warehouses on the grounds. Its skin and fur reformed instantly from charred, burnt meat into the picture of the perfect killing machine. He leaped on top of a pile of rubble nearly ten feet tall and howled. The sound was not one of triumph; but, rather, it was born was the very pits of hell. Dane tried to scream in an attempt to warn whoever was carrying him; but, the only thing that bubbled up from his throat was a searing heat followed by murderous pain. Only then did he remember the savage's grip around his throat. He remembered how it had tightened around his neck like a vise powered by hydraulics, and he wondered if he would ever be able to speak again.

No time to think further on the subject, he did the only thing that came to his mind. He began slapping the back of whoever was hauling him. It was a weak move, one befitting a child, but it was all he had left in him. Feeling the slaps on his back, the runner whirled to a stop and dropped Dane from his shoulder to the relative safety of a section of wall still standing. He then shouldered his assault rifle.

*Jed Blackmoor.*

The savage leaped through the air with a snarl and came straight for Dane with inhuman speed. The thing did not make it very far before the side of its head exploded in a fine, green mist. The beast had been moving with such speed and force its momentum carried it into the base of the wall Dane had been tossed behind. The wall groaned, wobbled, then just as he realized what was happening, it toppled over. He tried to move, but his mind and feet were not functioning in concert. At the last second, he put his hands over his head and did everything he could to protect himself from the inevitable.

The blocks of broken concrete were being tossed aside even before the mess had fully settled.

"Dane!" screamed a familiar voice as block after block was pulled off. Finally, after a few seconds of work, a hand grabbed him and pulled him free. "Dane!" The man repeated his name a second time while a hand slapped his face. This pretty much put to bed any doubts he may have had concerning whether or not the night had well and truly gone to hell, "You alive?"

*Pretty shitty,* he would later complain to his ATL, *hitting a man whose hands were held down by who knows how much concrete...repeatedly.*

With tremendous effort, Dane opened the eyeball that was NOT swollen shut. He tried to speak; but, to him, it sounded like dried parchment paper being crumbled. Finally, he managed, "I am, but I won't be if you keep hitting me, Jed." His hot breath felt like lava was being poured over his raw throat and vocal cords. He grimaced and groaned as he

468

tried to swallow which was impossible as dry as his mouth was. Recognizing this, Jed passed him the tube from the water bladder integrated into his KtacS suit. Dane drank greedily while Jed covered their position. Once he had his fill, he passed it back. In a raspy voice, he said simply, "Thanks, bro." Jed grabbed it, took a few swigs of water, and then quickly shouldered his rifle and fired a controlled burst of silver that dropped a savage with each trigger pull. Only then did Dane notice that Jed was in just about as bad a shape as he was.

Possibly worse.

Jed's helmet was gone, and his KtacS suit hung in shreds from his body. He either took the explosion head on or had been in one hell of a fight. Probably both, Dane imagined.

He pulled Dane to his feet and croaked over parched vocal chords, "Can you walk?"

"Think so," he said, though it came out as *hink ho*.

Jed got the meaning, but seeing movement in the shadows, Dane jerked at the holster molded within the suit on Jed's right leg. He ripped Jed's HK .45 pistol free and fired. Damned near at their feet, the savage fell from the darkness, dead, with a bullet hole in the center of its face just above its snout.

Seeing Dane had no weapons of his own, Jed said, "Keep it." Jed spun in place, attempting to get his bearings. Finally, he pointed over Dane's shoulder, "If you can walk, you can run. Hundred meters, straight ahead, through the green smoke."

Dane nodded and attempted to run only Jed held him back. In his ear, the older operator screamed, "No matter what happens, you keep running until you're through that smoke, you hear me?"

Dane nodded again, and together they left the fires of the building and staggered through the night. Dane became curiously aware of several things all at once. The first being that overhead several helos were positioning themselves for strafing runs. Secondly, he knew that the green smoke denoted friendly positions. Lastly, it occurred to him that he and Jed were on the wrong side of said green smoke. Dane gritted his teeth through the pain and forced his legs to pump faster. Both he and Jed were so focused on making it through the field of smoke and linking up with their comrades, neither noticed the two gigantic Chinooks and their Apache gunships thunder by overhead, tree top high, and bank.

***

"Dear God!" yelled Meadows over the roar inside the helo.

"Gettin' pretty damned salty down there," agreed Granderson. He turned to Dax Nguyen, a TL from Foxtrot, "How you want to work this, Dax?"

"We need to get out of this floating tin can, ASAP! From the looks of it, the boys on the ground are about to be overrun. My guys on one rope. You and your guys on the other."

The three then joined everyone else in engaging their helmets. Once online, Dax received last minute adjustments from the pilot.

"Okay, guys, listen up," Nguyen ordered, and every helmet turned his way. "We're having to land this can in a tiny hole about three hundred meters out. There's not enough room for both helos; so, we'll rope in first with Kilo and the Apaches providing top cover. Once down, we're pulling security for Kilo as they rope in, understand?"

The men aboard the Chinook acknowledged their understanding by moving into position at the loading ramp. Hammer, the former Air Force JTAC who went through SEE-S with Dane, Tweeker, and Toad fought his way to the front. Those were his friends down there, and he would be damned if he was going to hang back and let them be killed by a bunch of soulless savages.

As the Chinook banked and began its descent, Tommy Granderson – the most senior man on the helo – came over the comm link, "Since 1975, SKUL has led the vanguard against an immortal horde of savage. These savages, they don't want your homes or land, they want your very soul; and, down there, in that congealed mass of shit and blood are our brothers fighting to the very last. Well, IT...STOPS...HERE! Tonight, we take the fight to our enemies on open ground! Tonight, we follow each other into the breach once more! Tonight, we give our last full measure. Not to a simple flag or declaration. Not even to SKUL and its shield, but to our brothers to the left and the right! *Per tenebras venimus tamquam lux*, gentlemen; and, you can bet your sweet-ass that tonight we will pour forth from the darkness and come as light!"

With those words, Hammer leapt from the helo and slid down the rope. His next stop, some three hundred meters away, was nothing short of his worst nightmare.

***

Finally, after their exhaustive sprint, Dane and Jed managed to stagger through the smoke and fall at Toad's feet. He and handful of other guys had set up a defensive position and were providing suppression fire for those still in the building fighting their way out.

Jed screamed out to Toad while pointing to Dane's face, "He's got a bad wound to the face, took several blows to the head, legs and back are burned to shit, and damned near had his throat ripped out."

Toad fired several rounds downrange then screamed, "Jesus, Jed…he still breathing?"

"Yeah," Jed answered simply even while he engaged another target. They were coming from everywhere.

Toad looked back and down at Dane and then shook his head, "Oughta call you *Lucky* instead of *Boss.*"

While continuing to update Saber's sniper on the situation at hand, Jed ripped open a pocket on Dane's right arm and removed his blowout kit. Before he could do anything more, Jed had to drop the kit and draw down on another savage that had broken through whatever battle lines SKUL still maintained. He fired twice, and the savage fell dead only feet away. Jed screamed, "Dammit, Toad, keep these things off of us!"

"I'm…"

*Clap…Clap*

"…trying!"

472

There were others there with them; but, given the chaotic circumstances, there was no way to know who they were or how many still stood. The immediate area clear, Jed dropped his sidearm and grabbed Dane's blowout kit again. From it, he grabbed a tube of gel. Dane's eyes were glassed over; and, instead of sweating in the South Louisiana humidity, he was shivering.

*Shock,* Jed thought desperately.

He pulled Dane's face close and ran the gel along the length of the cut on Dane's face, smearing it over the wound. A work of bonafide medical genius, the gel immediately began to react with the blood to form an artificial clot. The thrombin gel would also deliver a dose of broad spectrum antibiotics to the wound and potentially help stave off infection. From one of his pockets, Jed pulled a small flashlight, shining it in Dane's eyes, before announcing, "Pretty sure he's going into shock, Toad! He needs medical attention, ASAP."

Toad fired three quick rounds downrange. Jed could not see what he was firing at, and truthfully, he probably did not want to know. In one seamless motion, too quick for the untrained eye, Toad performed a battlefield reload, dropping his rifle's empty magazine and slamming another one home. He then fired several more shots into the darkness.

Dane pushed Jed away and struggled to his knees. He aimed the sidearm Jed had given him shakily and fired. Looking to Toad on his right and Jed on his left, Dane's heart flooded with both endless love and infinite sadness. Love because these were his brothers and they were not only willing to die *for* him but *with* him; and, sadness because

473

neither man was still firing their personal rifles. This meant that there were SKUL operators dead out there…somewhere. Toad noted the pain and sadness on Dane's face, fired at a half dozen savages, hit a couple, and dropped the spent mag. The problem was that he had no more to replace it with. Toad cursed and flung the weapon aside only to unsheathe his silver tomahawk. Over his shoulder, he asked, "You alright, Boss?"

Dane saved his voice, or what was left of it, and tried to stand, only to wobble on weak knees. Jed grabbed his shoulders to steady him and led him to the ground gently. Dane's eyes began to swim again, and that damnable darkness crept into the corners of his vision. He fought to focus, "Twitch?" he rasped. After a second, he forced his eyes open one last time and into those of the elder soldier as he repeated, "Twitch and Tweeker…where are they, Jed?"

Helplessness flooded Jed's eyes as he looked back to the building. He could only shake his head in reply. Resignation seeped into Jed's eyes as he stood and passed Toad his rifle and arsenal of Puffers and WIPPs. He put a finger to Toad's chest, and even in Dane's stupor, he could tell Marcus was putting up one helluva protest. Jed then drew two dangerous-looking, solid silver tomahawks from their sheaths. Sabers' ATL turned to Dane, gave him a thumbs-up, then turned and ran back into the wreckage and flames of the mill.

Dane fired his pistol from his haunches, but his hands were shaking so badly, the bullets were virtually useless. He struggled to focus his thoughts and barely understood the significance when Toad screamed to the others at their position, "Cover left!" followed milliseconds later with, "Cover right!"

The werewolves had finally flanked their position.

They were about to be overrun.

Dane looked forward, always forward, and saw Jed disappear into the flames of the burning mill just as the structure fell in upon itself. Heartbroken, Dane jabbed his hands frantically into the dirt for anything that he might use as a weapon.

He found none.

Suddenly, Toad disappeared from his side in a miasmic blur of KtacS, fur, and sparks.

They were no longer *being* overrun. They *were* overrun.

His mind was thick, like molasses on a cold morning; so, Dane's reactions were all but nonexistent. Dane was slammed onto his back causing his mind to turn from thick soup to chunky chowder. He saw the werewolf standing on his throat pull its jowls back in a snarl. Dane lifted Jed's sidearm, put it right on the savage's face, put it right between the savage's yellow, terror-inspiring eyes, and pulled the trigger.

*Click...*

The mag was empty.

The gun fell from Dane's hands as he welcomed death.

## 39)
## Out of Body Experience

When Dane's eyes opened, he was high above the battle. Internally, he knew the wind was blowing, but he felt nothing. He was neither hot nor cold. He just *was*. Down below, he watched as three platoons of SKUL shooters ran pell-mell into the fray. Even from a great height, Dane noticed his old friend, Hammer, at the head of SKUL's vanguard. His smile evaporated; and, in its place, a tumorous lump of dread grew as he became aware that the battlefield was littered with fallen SKUL operators. Among them, he saw his own body – badly beaten – though that did not bother him nearly as much as his dead friends. He had long ago come to terms with the high likelihood that he would die in battle.

Dane suddenly became acutely aware that there were *others* around him. He felt them more than he could actually see them. When he turned toward them, they were simply gone. It was like looking at wisps of smoke.

Terror, unearthly and unwholesome, began to claw at his brain. He was certain the feelings he was experiencing were coming from the dark shadows his eyes could not pinpoint.

"Am I dead?" he asked with a scream only his voice sounded muffled, like he was trying to talk inside of a bucket.

"No," boomed the ethereal voice. Unlike Dane's, this voice carried across the night with clarion strength. "Not yet, though the Reaper is near."

477

"Yeah, I've heard that a time or two lately. You and Jed must be reading from the same playbook for pump'em-up speeches."

Laughter rolled across the night's sky, but there was nothing human about it. The darkness bled away and revealed the haunting, cloaked figure of the one who had spoken. The silhouette revealed little save for a human form that held a strangely animalistic quality. The shroud made it impossible to see the face hidden in its depths.

"Who are you?" Dane asked in an utterly frightened voice. For some time, the figure remained silent, content to watch the on-going battle far below. Finally, the being turned its head to reveal eyes that burned blood red. He could feel strange, alien-like claws picking over his mind and thumbing through his thoughts and memories like one might flip the cards of a rolodex.

"We are the greatest of our kind, Dane Stackwell, the Vampire Lords thought lost to antiquity." Other figures surrounded him, but they chose to remain hidden within the darkness.

*Vampire Lords?* The words tore through Dane's senses with the power of a throat punch.

The vampires began receding, and though he no longer felt their presence, he heard the thing's words in his mind, "It is not your time, Dane Stackwell."

With those words, the world below became black; and, for Dane, time stood still.

***

Though he dared not open his eyes, not yet in any case, he recognized the sterile chill that could only belong to a medical facility. It was not cold, per say; rather, it felt clean, crisp, and fresh. Heaven had been described in similar fashion, but not believing he would be finding out the truth to *that* anytime soon, Dane laid odds that he was in a hospital.

*Regardless*, he thought, *I really don't want to wake up, even if it is on the right side of the dirt.*

After some debate, he risked opening his eyes; or, more appropriately, his eye – singular – as the right one was swollen shut.

*Yep*, he smiled through cracked, screaming lips, *hospital.*

He was naked with only a white sheet to cover him. The room itself was white with a mirror and sink, a small closet, a couch that looked comfortable only when comparing it to the matching chair, and a door Dane assumed led to the bathroom. Instinctively, he tried to wiggle his toes and became overjoyed when they moved in accordance with his thoughts. The pain he felt, and there was much of that to be sure, felt muted and blunt like it was trying to attack him from some distant place. His eye fell on the I.V. pole beside his bed. It held two bags, one much larger than the other. One, the larger of the two, was a bag of lactated ringers. The smaller one, he assumed, held an antibiotic, given the name:

*Cefa...cefa...cefa-somethingorother.* He said in his mind. *Doesn't matter, anyway.*

His eye followed another IV line. This one came from a box attached to the IV pole. It was there that he found what was muting his pain.

*Morphine, gloooorious morphine.*

He could not help but laugh. Or, did he just giggle?

479

*Surely not,* he thought and laughed again. *No, that was definitely a giggle.*

His thoughts were coming randomly now, all manner of lucidity gone.

*Moooorphine.* He pictured Chewbacca, the Wookie from Star Wars, saying morphine. He giggled some more and then conjured this hugely, deep voice in his head, *gooood.*

"Bout damned time you woke up," said a voice that was harsh but kind, with an Irish wisp about it.

Dane turned his head and found Shamus Mactavish kicked back in a chair chewing tobacco.

*Where in the world did he come from?* he asked himself then giggled again.

Shamus' smile beamed across the room, though he never took his eyes off Dane. He brought a can to his lips and spit a mouthful of brown-stained saliva.

Dane smiled and groaned at the same time, "Shit's gonna kill you man." He then fell back into his pillows, being shown a whole new meaning to the word *pain.* He took several deep breaths before Shamus grabbed something with a button on it.

He pushed it for Dane who immediately felt relief.

"Yeah, I know," stated Shamus as he reached into the back pocket of his pants and produced a bag of Levi Garrett. "Want a pull?"

Dane shook his head, "Thanks, but no." The two sat quietly for a minute or two until Dane asked, "How long have I been out?"

"A few days. You had some swelling around the brain; so, the docs put you in a medically induced coma until

480

it subsided. You looked like you had been thrown into a wood chipper when you were brought in. Hell, you all did." Mac's voice was softer than usual, like a father talking his child through a bad situation. The two again fell into companionable silence as Dane fought with his thoughts and his pain. Strangely, they found themselves on equal footing, as Shamus was struggling with the same. Shamus spit again before rising, "I'll go tell everyone you're awake and get your nurse. She's a pretty little thing. I personally made sure she hit all the high spots when she gave you your sponge bath this morning." He chuckled and walked quietly across the room, "Thank me later."

Just as he opened the door, Dane called to him, "How many, Mac?" Shamus glanced to the bed expecting – hoping – to confront a man on the edge of unconsciousness. Instead, Dane's glare was piercingly intense, "How many did we lose?"

The sadness in Shamus' eyes answered the question even when his voice refused to, "Get some rest, Dane. There'll be time for all that later."

As the door shut, Dane found himself fighting to keep the tears in his eyes and off his face.

***

Several hours later, a tap on the door caused Dane to peek open his usable eye.

"Come in," he said in a raspy voice still ragged from his near strangulation and the tube that the medical staff had shoved down his throat. He felt like he was talking around a cotton ball laced with shards of glass.

Admiral Briggs stuck his head in the door, "Got a minute, son?"

Using his elbows, Dane pushed himself up in bed, "Yes, sir. Not planning on going anywhere anytime soon."

Dane tried to smile…the Skipper did not.

Briggs walked in and sat without another word, resigned to the silence that pervaded the room. He looked tired and exhausted, like a trash bag stretched to its physical limits and on the brink of ripping apart. The scars on his face seemed deeper, almost otherworldly, and lent a certain weariness to his half destroyed face. Unable to stand it any longer, Dane asked the question he had first asked of Shamus. He dreaded the answer but needed to know all the same, "How bad is it, Skipper? No one will tell me anything."

Briggs flinched as if he had been struck, and a thick veil of sadness fell over his face, "Bad, but better than it should have been. Had Bill not disobeyed my order to stand Whiskey down, things could have gone a lot differently. As it stands, we needed every man to quell the surge. Initial intelligence in the aftermath shows that we ended the majority of the threat; though, certainly there were those that slipped away in the confusion." He shook his head still not believing what he had witnessed, "Jesus, you guys fought like Spartans."

Dane knew this to be true, but he still felt as if his heart was being ripped from his chest in slippery little pieces.

The Skipper continued regurgitating the information as flatly as one might inspect a slab of meat. It was like someone hit the *play* button in his brain, and he was on autopilot, "Mustang and Roughneck lost two men apiece including Mustang's sniper, Roger Keyes. He was bitten. The savages surrounded his hide; and even when he went black on ammo, he continued to fight using his tomahawk." Briggs' voice caught in his throat, and he had to force the last bit out, "He was still alive when they found him. Keyes begged for someone – *anyone* – to end his life before he had a chance to turn. They say his eyes were already beginning to turn yellow, and his body was convulsing so forcibly they thought it was going to tear itself apart. Damn a full moon, damn them!" Dane stared at the admiral in horrified silence, not believing what he was hearing, and afraid to ask the question that hung in the air. Thankfully, he did not have to as Briggs just kept talking, "No one could do it, Dane, *no one*. Jesus, who'd want that job? In the end, Keyes was given a sidearm and…" Briggs wrung his hands in frustration, "Goddammit, Dane, what happened out there?"

Dane initially found the answer impossible to come by. A long while later, he was able to gather himself enough to answer, "They knew we were coming, Skipper. It was calculated, no doubt, and it stinks of inside knowledge. It all makes sense if you look at it. The evidence at the crime scene…they knew we'd pick up on that. And, that savage, Duschaine? You don't just capture werewolves with the kind of knowledge he just so happened to possess. None of that is even taking into account the fact we hit that shithole on a full moon, when werewolves are at their strongest. That wasn't some random trap; they dictated our mission not only down to the place but damned near to the second we would make our hit. It's just too easy, too convenient. I can't prove it, it's just a feeling in my gut; but they knew we were coming for them, sir." Dane looked down to his hands, "We were lucky, Skipper, not Spartans. None of us should have survived that."

Briggs' voice was but a whisper as he said, "I've spoken with Jed and a few of the others – namely, Granderson and Meadows – and they feel similarly. I just can't believe..." It was the Admiral's turn to look away, "...I just can't believe one of our own could do something like this."

"Maybe I'm wrong, Skipper. Like I said, it's just a feeling I have, but if Jed, Tommy-Gun, and Tim feel the same way..." Dane didn't finish the thought; rather, he left it lingering and unsaid.

The admiral cogitated on the implications and then rose, "Yeah, I know. We've got a problem." Briggs grabbed the door knob and paused, "Dane, keep our suspicions inside these walls, okay? Morale's in the shitter as it is. Last thing we need is to be looking over our shoulders instead of focusing on the mission, understand?"

"Yes, sir." Before the Admiral could step out, Dane said, "Skipper, when I was out I had..." Dane struggled with the concept of his vision. "...well, I guess you would call it an out-of-body experience..."

The Admiral snapped his finger to his lips in a *be quiet* gesture. "I know what you saw, son. Trust me, we'll talk about that when the time is right, but now's not your time."

The vampire said something very similar, and for a second, Dane just stared at Briggs. "How? How do you know?"

Briggs smiled crookedly.  It was a mischievous, *I-know-something-you-don't-know* smile.  "You talk in your sleep. Get yourself well, son.  Kilo and Foxtrot will rotate in to handle any missions that crop up until you and the other guys get patched up."

"Sir?"

"Yeah, Dane?"

"We can't beat them, can we?"

The question hit the Admiral like a punch to the gut, and it forced the air from his lungs.  The Skipper thought about how to answer for several seconds.  "Dane, it's not the KtacS suits and silver that make you guys so good at what you do.  It's your spirit, and that's something a savage can't take from you.  You ask me if we can beat them, and I tell you we *have to*."

# AFTER ACTION

Dane was dressed and pacing his room for hours before his discharge from the medical wing finally came down the pipeline. Jed greeted him when he stepped from the room.

"You look good, Boss."

"Thanks, but I feel like a pile of shit that's been in the sun too long." The swelling had come down around his eye, and the bruise had begun healing. Now, instead of a huge blotch of black and purple covering most of his face, he had a huge blotch of sickly, yellowish green covering most of his face. He felt like a huge, walking bruise, and he moved gingerly as the burns over much of his legs and lower back had begun to scab over and tighten. Luckily, if you can call it that, the facial laceration, compliments of the savage, Skinny, was largely superficial.

"Well, there's that, too," said Saber's ATL with a grin. "They wheeled Tweeker back to the ICU a little while ago."

"How's he doing?" asked Saber's TL. "Everyone's been pretty vague."

Jed shrugged, "You know how it is. Everyone says he'll be okay; and at the same time, the man's just lost his leg. That's gonna fuck with anyone, but with someone possessing an ego the size of Tweeker's? We both know that's going to be a tough pill for him to swallow."

Jed spoke the truth. He and Dane had known too many men who'd left parts of their bodies – and minds – in shitholes like Iraq and Afghanistan; most never truly recovered. Tweeker, a mountain of a man and the next best thing to a Norse god, had much of what defined him ripped away. With the exception of his soon-to-be ex-wife, Dane had known Ansil Lattimore as long as he had known anyone in his life, and the implications hit him hard. Tweeker had saved his life so many times over the years that Dane had quit counting; and now, he found himself helpless to so much as help his friend. He could not speak much less acknowledge what Jed was saying.

"Look, I'm sure he's gonna be okay," Jed stated. "Dude's too big of an asshole to die, anyway. Whether he's ever operational again is anyone's guess. It's the doc I'm worried about. She hasn't left the waiting area since he was flown here, and I don't think she's slept in days."

"The doc?" asked Dane. He could not imagine a licensed medical professional working for a unit such as SKUL being troubled over a wounded soldier. They see it on a daily basis.

"Yeah," Jed said before spitting into an old water bottle that now served as his spittoon. "Doctor Monica Taylor, the KtacS creator. I guess her and Tweeker have gotten a little closer than he lets on."

"Oh, right, her," Dane said, only now putting two and two together. He knew Tweeker had been spending a lot of time with her when they were on stand down status. At Tweeker's insistence, he had tagged along on a few occasions. It always seemed that Sam was there, too. Tweeker insisted it was coincidence, but Dane got the idea there was more to it than that.

"Anyhow, I put Twitch on the case. Figured he can talk anyone to sleep. Pretty sure her ears are bleeding from the bludgeoning; but, unfortunately, I haven't seen her so much as nod off for a few minutes." Dane smiled but said nothing, and Jed changed the subject, "Along those same lines, I've got another nugget of information for you. We're headed back to Tortuga."

"For what?" Dane exclaimed in exasperation.

"Dane, we're down a man. Roughneck and Mustang are down two apiece." Jed paused and almost, *almost,* looked apologetic, "The rock has to keep rolling, bro."

Dane was infuriated, "Piss on that shit!"

"Yeah," Jed agreed, "I don't like it any more than you do, but we can either whine like two petulant children or get it over with."

Dane spun on his ATL and friend like a pissed off rattlesnake, "Fuck that shit and fuck you for saying some dirty-assed shit like that!"

Jed instinctively slid to Dane's weak side – the one with the eye swollen shut. Not only was Jed a practitioner of multiple forms of martial art, he was a disciple of each discipline. Considering, there were very few men he truly wanted to avoid tangling with.

Dane was in that small group.

"You know that's horse shit, Jed, and if you ever say anything like that again, I swear to all that's good and pure, I'll walk a mud hole in your ass and walk that sumbitch dry!" Dane's raised voice caused many of the passerby's to stop and gawk. He did not give a shit. Most were computer geeks anyway, and nearly all of them had witnessed him making an ass of himself in some way, shape, or form over the last year or so. Even so, those words and the threat they implied hung heavy in the air as the two - juxtaposed though their mindset was - glared at each other like two alpha males sizing the other up for a fight.

Finally, Jed lunged.

The movement was almost feline in execution as he grabbed the back of Dane's head and jerked Saber's TL inside his defenses just long enough for Jed to plant a big, wet kiss on Dane's forehead.

"I'd kill you, Boss," was all Jed said, all he needed to say, and Dane knew it to be true. Dane had only seen one other creature move faster - werewolves.

Jed continued as if nothing had happened. "Gotta name and former unit," the older SKUL shooter said. "Charlie Macgrath, goes by *Maddawg*. He's Army SF from 3rd Special Forces Group, medical sergeant – 18D. There's several more to choose from, including a few SEALs," Jed spat the word in mocking disdain.

"Army, huh?" Dane considered Jed's thoughts as they walked.

Blackmoor, to his credit, caught the sideways glance from Dane, "Look, man, we've already got three of you dick bumpers on board; which, if any of these other assholes had one ounce of imagination, would be more than enough material to turn this whole *Saber* team deal into a real clusterfuck for all of us. We're down a man, a *medic*. So excuse me if I lean toward a hard-chargin' yet well-versed Army pissant versus another SEAL shooter that enjoys the community showers a little too much."

490

At that, Dane died out laughing, and it was several seconds before he was able to collect himself. He needed the comic relief Jed was supplying as things had just been way too tense for way too long. "You made any calls?"

"Not yet," Jed admitted, "wanted to talk to you first and see how you wanted to roll."

"Make 'em," Dane said. "Not sayin' I will agree with it, but I want to know if he's a shit stain or a shooter."

"Roger that," Jed said, then spit again.

"When are we slated to leave?"

"Soon as you're deemed medically fit for flight."

"Well, get packed then," Dane said as the two leaders of Saber team stepped through the doors and into the intensive care waiting area.

***

"Coffee?" Dane asked the bookish yet very pretty woman sitting in one of the few chairs found in the spartan waiting area.

"Yes, please, thanks," replied Dr. Taylor before taking the Styrofoam cup from his outstretched hand.

An ICU nurse poked her head out, "Just wanted you guys to know, we're cleaning Chief Lattimore up, but it should only take a few more minutes. Visiting hours aren't until noon, but we'll sneak two of you back if you'd like to step in for a few minutes."

"Thank you," said Dr. Taylor in a voice of genuine affection.

"You bet."

The tension in the room increased tenfold as the nurse disappeared back into the unit. It was the unknown that bothered the men and women gathered. Tweeker had lost a massive amount of blood, and even now, while on fluids and vasopressors, his blood pressure was running low while his heart raced. They had tried to save his leg, but in the end, the savage's blow had crushed his lower right leg beyond repair.

Samantha Steele, who was sitting beside her friend, got up, "Dane, can I talk to you for a second?"

"Sure."

The two stepped back out of the waiting area for a little more privacy. The guys stayed behind, nervously talking with the Admiral who had come down from *Ops* to personally check on the big Nordic.

Once the glass doors slid shut, Sam turned, "I'm worried about her, Dane. She won't eat, won't sleep, won't do anything but sit in that room and wait for news."

"Jed said pretty much the same thing," he admitted. "I'm sure things will get better once Tweeker is in a regular room."

"Maybe," Sam allowed, though her eyes and body language told him she was not so sure. "They're serious, you know? Every second they aren't working, they are together."

"I knew they were getting close, but I had no idea just how close." Dane thought about the implications before adding, "If that's the case, though, she better get used to this."

Sam crossed her arms and stamped her foot, "Only you could say something so ridiculously stupid."

"Sorry, Sam," Dane said a little softer, a little less sure of his convictions. "It's just the way it is. We go out on these operations, and sometimes, we don't come back."

Sam's eyes fell to the floor, and she muttered, "That's a pretty dark way to look at life, Dane." She brought her eyes back to his, and he was dumbstruck yet again with her beauty, "I know you're right. I just don't want…"

At that second a scream of pure, unadulterated anguish pierced the air. It was coming from the waiting area, and both of them bolted back through the doors. Monica Taylor was being helped back into her chair by Jed and Twitch. Sam flew to her side. On the other side of the room, away from the distraught doctor, the Admiral and Toad talked to one of Tweeker's surgeons. Dane saw the look on Toad's face and found his feet would no longer move. He tried to hear what was being said, but it was like trying to hear underwater. The doctor listened to what the Admiral had to say and nodded quickly before ducking back behind the ICU's door.

The Admiral noticed Dane several feet away. Saber's team leader stood, frozen in place, with a mouth that opened and closed like a fish out of water. SKUL's commander looked older somehow, and the scar ruining the right side of his face twitched. Dane knew this happened when the Admiral's stress level was high. When he spoke, his gravelly voice was choked, "There have been complications…"

Dane didn't hear the rest of what the Skipper had to say.

***

## River Walk
**0800**

Billy materialized seemingly from thin air, unnoticed by the old man's security detail, and stepped to the bench. His presence had been so sudden, even the old, Eldrich wolf was momentarily taken by surprise.

"You're getting stronger," Della Rocca acknowledged in a slightly begrudged tone. "Impressive, especially in one so young."

"I'm over a hundred and fifty years old; it was bound to happen at some point. What do you want now?" The words were spoken nonchalantly enough but underneath lay a threat. Billy was tiring of the old wolf's constant demands of his time, not to mention he had lost several members of his Bastards over the last few months. SKUL had definitely gouged through his ranks; and, even though he currently owns the Southeast, he felt weaker than he ever thought he could. Worst of all was what went down just a few days ago. The debacle at the sugar cane mill had cost him dearly.

The older man looked at the Rolex on his wrist, "Too bad your growing strength hasn't improved your punctuality." He patted the bench, beckoning the younger werewolf to sit, "Billy, what do you know of our past?" It was such a simple question; though one a thousand years would not adequately cover.

Billy knew Guiseppi was referring to the extreme, distant past and the *Great Wars* between the Werewolves and Vampires. "Not much, to be honest. Feelings, mostly; from when Red Moon turned me. I know there were a series of wars between our kind and the vampires, wars that would make the World Wars look like a fight between two schoolyard bullies. I also know that suddenly they stopped, a cease fire agreed upon."

The old, Eldrich wolf snorted, "*Agreed upon*, indeed. More like, forced upon both sides and administered by powers greater than all others."

"Point is," interrupted Billy, "it stopped. The rest is just semantics."

Guiseppi sighed, "My young friend, you'd do well to keep your mouth shut and not interrupt me again."

An overwhelming feeling of domination washed over the younger werewolf in thunderous waves. He could not bear to look into the Eldrich wolf's eyes, and the air in his lungs became heavy with fear. It was a crippling fear – almost physical in its presence – that nearly drove him mad until, just as suddenly as it had overtaken him, it dissipated. While Billy gulped for air like a fish out of water, Della Rocca continued as if nothing untoward had occurred, "That cease fire, as you call it, came in the form of what is known of as simply the *Accords*. The Accords outline the terms of the truce between the vampires and our kind. We lost our native lands while the vampires were cursed to roam only the night. Each side had their absolute immortality stripped from them. Silver, an element it is said was formed from the tears of the gods and until then, not of this world, became the object of our mortality. Our vampire brethren would find death through massive blood loss. Though humans have distilled that down into such trivialities as a stake through the heart, the spirit of their superstitions is sound. Only two were spared the worst of it, Fenrir, our king and his brother, whose

495

name is of a language you've neither heard nor could comprehend. A beast history came to know as Attila."

He had learned more about werewolves in these last five minutes than in his entire lifetime; and, for the first time in nearly one hundred years, Billy the Kid was interested in something other than his own preservation. Like a child enraptured by a campfire ghost story Billy blurted the first questions that came to mind, "Who demanded the cease fire? Which gods?"

"That," Guiseppi said in a dangerously low voice, "is of no concern to you."

"But, they're real?" Billy broke in again, "The gods, I mean."

"Real?" Guiseppi asked, astounded by his young counterpart's lack of understanding. "In a manner of speaking, yes. Many of the gods you know from legend are *real*; though, just as many are not."

"Well, that's helpful," Billy said sarcastically, drawing a hint of laughter from the old wolf to his right.

"Not even I know everything, my young friend," replied Della Rocca with a notable hint of disdain on his voice.

"So, the terms held in the Accords...what were they?"

"Simple ground rules designed to keep the two warring factions from tearing each other apart. Without getting too deep into its pages, we were granted rule over the lands that became known as North and South America. The vampires hold Africa along with parts of Asia and the Middle East. Europe, native land to werewolf and vampire alike, was

496

stripped from both parties and made neutral, effectively making the continent off limits."

"All of this was done just to protect humans?" asked Billy skeptically. "That makes no sense."

"It does, when you think about it," Guiseppi began. "You see, the gods could care less about the murder, rape, and overall suffering, inflicted upon mortals by either the wolves or vampires; and, rest assured, Attila's *kind* inflicted its share of each. They don't care, because they need it. The fear we sow leads to the kind of devotion and worship the gods feed off of, the kind that makes them stronger; that makes them immortal. Without our kind or the vampires, not to mention the myriad of other beings that make up demon-kind, there would be no fear; and thus, no devout worship of the gods. No prayers for mercy. No bending of the knee in solemn servitude. That fear is pathological, virtually cellular in its existence; and, without it, there is only apathy. Apathy toward life – and more specifically, death – would cripple the gods on a catastrophic level. They would be weakened to a state that, by all accounts, would render them nearly mortal. By separating the warring factions, the gods accomplished two very significant things. First off, they ensured that fear was spread to all parts of the globe which drove people to seek out beings of higher power in order to beg for their protection. Secondly, by banishing us from our homeland, they ensured we would forever seek a way back. This, of course, keeps our vampire brethren on a constant vigil thus perpetuating the cycle. So, in a manner of speaking, we are both slave to and agents of chaos, bound to the gods through blood."

"Well, that's cool and all; but, I'm not sure anyone could predict the mortals would band together and hunt us down so efficiently."

Billy made a fair point, even the Eldrich wolf had to admit.

"I'm assuming you're referring to that little paramilitary group that keeps popping up at the most inopportune of times?"

"I am," replied Billy flatly.

"I can see where this would be a concern to someone of your youth," began Della Rocca. "I assure you, SKUL, as they are currently known, is not a new phenomenon. The problem is, the humans are hindered by the same circumstances that prevented us from defeating the vampires so many thousands of years ago...that being, simple math. In a given lifetime, a human may only produce a very finite number of offspring. Of those offspring, only a fraction have the fortitude to hunt us. Fewer still are actually successful in their endeavors. Similarly, only a fraction of our victims survive our bite. Those that do often those have minds that are too fractured to be of use. The same cannot be said for the vampire. They can produce legions in a relatively short length of time. It has always been their numbers, not their strength and cunning, that have held our kind in check."

"So, what's the point then?" asked Billy, now frustrated on a level had not ventured to since the early nineteen hundreds.

All became silent, even the wind along the river stilled. Billy could tell Guiseppi was thinking very hard on something. Several minutes passed before the Eldrich wolf finally spoke, "Billy, what would you say if I told you we were very close to evening the odds?"

Billy looked to the old man, "I'd say, *cool, bring it on.*"

"Would you? Could you?" Della Rocca was now leaning forward and holding his gaze. "Could you take life, en masse?" He flourished his arms outward taking a morning jogger in their path, "Could you take her, beautiful and at peace, and destroy her soul? Could you damn her to a life of eternal hunger? Then, could you do it over and over again, thousands of times?"

Billy thought on what was being asked for several minutes before slowly nodding his head, "Yeah. Yeah, I can, but I still don't understand how that will tip the scales in our direction. So, an army of werewolves large enough to challenge the vampires is created, so what? From what you have said, all that means is that the gods will step in and bring their wrath to our doorstep. I've read enough mythology to know I don't want to be invited to that party."

"No?" asked the Eldrich wolf with a crooked eyebrow. "Think about it. An army of humans turned immortal werewolves, no longer fearful of death, and capable of utterly destroying the blood drinkers."

"At which point, the gods step in and stomp a mud hole in our asses."

Guiseppi flashed his characteristically wicked smile causing Billy to pause and think. Finally, a little light went off in his head, "Damnations, you *want* a confrontation with the gods. That's what this is all about, the end game."

"Now, Billy, you understand," said Guiseppi Della Rocca around an even brighter, more soulless smile. A low chuckle, stuck somewhere between laughter and a growl, rumbled across the river front.

# Why this book?

Writing a book will test you in ways very few endeavors can. Don't believe me? Try writing one. This is my third novel, and I can tell you, there are very few things on this planet as frustrating – and rewarding – as writing.

I remember the night all of this started very vividly. My oldest child, Lila, waddled into the den and said, "Daddy, read me a book." You see, I'm a reader. I mean, I'M A READER. I'm reading something every night, hell, every chance I get. So, we read – *Pinkalicious*. While I was reading to her, I kept having this thought – *why don't you write Lila a bedtime story?* And so, *Stonecypher* was born. The main character's name is Alil Stonecypher (Lila flipped backwards). That initial *bedtime* story turned into thirty plus chapters of what could be described as a *horse and sword fantasy* complete with a hand drawn map of the land of Tarkraik. Book two of the Stonecypher Saga commenced immediately after the first was completed. When I finished the second book, my mind was fried. I still enjoyed writing, but I was burnt out; so, I took some much needed time off.

That's when the idea of SKUL began to take shape. In no time flat, I was back to creating this special missions unit and the men making up its ranks. Since its inception, there have been tons of late nights where I found myself in some dark recess of my subconscious, staring at a blinking cursor, and wondering if the words would ever come to me. Half a dozen times, conservatively, I quit writing this book; but, something always made me come back to it. The question *why am I writing this book* continually pounded my mind like a jackhammer and delivered blunt force trauma to my confidence over and over and over again.

I guess, at the end of the day, I have to say this book is extremely personal to me. No, I never spent one second in the military; and, honestly, that's one of the few regrets I have. I wanted to. Hell, I wanted the life I've given to Dane, Jed, Twitch, Tweeker, and Toad. I wanted to live the life of a special operations shooter. I wanted it so much I dreamed about it. I wanted it so intensely I could taste it.

There was just one problem – I'm color blind. In every unit I researched – remember, this is the mid-nineties – I found this as an absolute disqualification from even getting the chance to screen for the SEALS, the Green Berets, and the Ranger Regiment.

Heartbroken is too strong a word, as is devastated, but I will say rather emphatically that I still have those dreams I did as a kid. SKUL is not only a tribute to my childhood dreams but an avenue to show my appreciation to our military veterans at large. Given today's climate, I think we all need to stop and take a second to tell our veterans THANK YOU.

SKUL's admittedly not the perfect military novel nor is it the perfect fantasy novel, but I enjoyed bringing it life. I hope you enjoy it too. Thank you for checking it out.

# Bibliography

Below is a small list – certainly not an exhaustive one – of the books I used to help develop both the individual traits of the characters and the overall organizational structure of SKUL. The characters within SKUL – while none taken directly from any one source – are amalgamations of the traits I feel are exemplified in the books below. Hopefully, they are both believable and representative. Either way, the production of SKUL would not have been possible without the following:

*Inside Delta Force: The Story of America's Elite Counterterrorist Unit,* by Eric L. Haney. This book granted an inside look into the training of a Delta Force operator, along with the mindset it takes to plan and execute high priority missions. For a military enthusiast – particularly concerning the special operations community – this book is a must read.

*The Mission, the Men, and Me: Lessons from a Former Delta Force Commander,* by Pete Blaber. If you are looking for a book that transcends quality military leadership to bleed over into real-world application, this book is one you need to read. I borrowed dozens of nuggets from this one book to mold and form my ideals for a quality leader when penning SKUL's command structure and leadership hierarchy.

*The Finishing School: Earning the Navy Seal Trident,* by Dick Couch. Without a doubt, the finest, most complete account of post BUD/S training of the modern day SEAL. While writing the SEE-S portion of SKUL, I extensively researched Mr. Couch's book for the ideology of the training program and the mindset it takes to survive. If you read only one book regarding actual tactical training, read this one. Of note, Mr. Couch has written a number of books covering the breadth and width of the training within the Special Operations community. Each one has received stellar reviews; though, I've only just read his latest – *Always Faithful, Always Forward: the Forging of a Special Operations Marine*. Regrettably, SKUL had been completed by the time this book was released to the public, but I imagine it will come in handy in future SKUL installments, particularly when it comes to Twitch.

Other non-fiction works to which I owe a great deal of debt:

*Delta Force: a Memoir by the Founder of the Military's Most Secretive Special-Operations Unit,* by Col. Charlie A Beckwith (Ret.) and Donald Knox

*Navy SEAL Sniper: an Ultimate Look at the Sniper of the 21st Century,* by Navy SEALs Glen Doherty and Brandon Webb

*Kill Bin Laden,* by Dalton Fury

*Lest We Forget: a Ranger Medic's Story,* by Leo Jenkins

*American Sniper: the Autobiography of the Most Lethal Sniper in U.S. Military History,* by Navy SEAL Chris Kyle with Scott McEwen and Jim DeFelice

*Lone Survivor,* by Marcus Luttrell and Patrick Robinson

*No Easy Day: the Firsthand Account of the Mission That Killed Osama Bin Laden,* by Mark Owen with Kevin Maurer

*The Red Circle: My Life in the Navy SEAL Sniper Corps and How I Trained America's Deadliest Marksmen,* by Brandon Webb with John David Mann

*Special Operations Forces Situation Report,* found at www.sofrep.com – there is a ton of knowledge found within the articles SOFREP has produced over the years. Of note, there is at least one phrase found in SKUL taken directly from the "Shit Navy SEALs Say" series.

Fictional works that provided both entertainment and inspiration on literally a daily basis:

*Arisen,* books 1-6 (and going) by Glynn James and Michael Stephen Fuchs. If you're into special operations, larger-than-life door-kicking badasses, and zombies…this is a veritable wet dream of a book series!

*D-Boys* and *Counter Assault,* by Michael Stephen Fuchs. All the intensity Fuchs helped create in the *Arisen* series minus the flesh-eating undead. Outstanding writing.

*The Activity (vol 1 and 2)*, by Nathan Edmondson and Mitch Gerads. An absolutely kick-ass graphic novel series that highlights the ultra-secret Intelligence Support Activity.

Made in the USA
Lexington, KY
03 April 2015